Outside
a novel

Sean McCammon

VANCOUVER
NEW STAR BOOKS
2021

 NEW STAR BOOKS LTD

#107–3477 Commercial St, Vancouver, BC V5N 4E8 CANADA

1574 Gulf Road, #1517 Point Roberts, WA 98281 USA

newstarbooks.com ·

info@newstarbooks.com

Scripture quotations are from The ESV® Bible (The Holy Bible, English Standard Version®), copyright © 2001 by Crossway, a publishing ministry of Good News Publishers. Used by permission. All rights reserved.

The publisher acknowledges the financial support of the Canada Council for the Arts and the British Columbia Arts Council.

Cataloguing information for this book is available from Library and Archives Canada, www.collectionscanada.gc.ca.

Cover design by Oliver McPartlin

Typeset by New Star Books

Printed and bound in Canada by Imprimerie Gauvin, Gatineau, QC

First printing March 2021

For my mom. Always my biggest fan.

ONE

THE PHARMACEUTICAL EVIDENCE OF DAVID'S anguish was spread out on the table. The Japanese customs officer examined the pill bottles one at time. David wasn't sure if the woman spoke English, so when she picked up his sleeping pills, he said, "For sleep," and feigned sleeping. When she scrutinized his migraine medication, he said, "That's for headaches," and rubbed his temples.

The woman now turned to look at David. The expression on her face made David think she was waiting for an answer to a question. He looked at her helplessly, wondering if his poorly planned escape from Canada would end in this white room.

It was then that David realized the woman was wiggling a package of laxatives between her thumb and forefinger. Apparently she was looking forward to his next exercise in charades.

The suggestion of humour allowed David to relax, and the officer began repacking his suitcase more neatly than she had found it.

As she zipped up the bag, she asked, "Why have you come to Japan?"

The tone of her voice suggested that this was not an official question. It sounded like she was making friendly conversation, and David considered confessing everything to her.

Finally he said, "I just had to get away from home for a while."

"Of course." The woman smiled. "Like all the rest."

DAVID'S JOURNEY TO TOKYO HAD been precipitated by a series of events that began with a pact made in a rowboat almost two years earlier.

The night of David's graduation from teachers' college, he and his

1

girlfriend, Joanna, had walked down to a dock behind the Windermere Manor Hotel.

"We're graduates," said Joanna, jumping into an aluminum fishing boat beside the dock.

"Feels good," said David.

"Feels scary."

Joanna lay back in the boat, the fabric of her dress sticking to the dew on the wood. She said, "I hear they're looking for vets up north."

"North? Like the Arctic?"

"No. Sudbury. North Bay."

David sat on the dock and unclipped the rope that moored the boat.

"Would you go to North Bay?" Joanna asked.

"Would you go if I didn't?"

"We have to start somewhere. Unless your plan is to set me adrift."

"I'd go to North Bay," said David.

"We need money," said Joanna. "Wherever one of us gets a job, that's where we'll go." She sat up. "Deal?"

David jumped into the boat, and Joanna grabbed his suit-jacket to keep him from falling over the side. They floated around, looking at stars. Music from the party drifted in and out with the breeze.

"Well?" said Joanna. "Is it a deal?"

"I guess so," said David. "We're in the same boat."

TWO

DAVID TOOK THE TRAIN FROM Narita Airport into Tokyo. He had reservations for two nights at a *ryokan*, a small family-run inn near the Ikebukuro district. David had been expecting a hotel, but his friend Mitchell had made the arrangements for him.

The *ryokan* was in a quiet residential area, nestled among neatly manicured cedar trees. David's room was large and bright, and featured a traditional *tatami*-mat floor and rice-paper doors. Most travellers would have found the *ryokan* to be a peaceful oasis, but David was unnerved by family members entering his room unexpectedly to serve tea or leave towels. He could not figure out how to change the channel on the television and spent much of the first night watching a sumo wrestling tournament.

Breakfast was a communal affair, served around a long table, with guests seated on the floor. David was forced to wedge his legs awkwardly under the table. During one repositioning he lifted the entire table, causing the other travellers to lunge for their sloshing cups and bowls.

The shower stall in David's bathroom had a wooden stool in it, with a nozzle halfway up the wall. David's interpretation of the set-up was that he was expected to sit on the stool while washing. But there was no way he could sit on the tiny seat, so he ended up lying on his back with his feet up on the wall. He held the stool upside down on his belly, the warm water running over it: a lost astronaut in a leaky porcelain rocket.

ONLY ONE MONTH INTO HIS job search, David had landed a teaching position at an elementary school in Dumford Mills, forty minutes south of Ottawa. The offer to teach at Emily Carr Public School was a total fluke, a happy turn of events that David attributed to his rural upbringing. At his interview, he and the principal had talked as much about farm practices as teaching practices.

That summer, David and Joanna found a farmhouse for rent outside Dumford Mills. It was old and drafty but possessed enough rural charm to make them feel at home. The farmland around the house was rented out to a neighbouring farmer who planted corn. The owners of the farm had retired to Ottawa, and they encouraged David and Joanna to spruce things up wherever they were inspired.

During their first few weeks of country living, Joanna went on a baking spree, making muffins and pies for the neighbours, hoping to ease any suspicions about the strangers from southwestern Ontario. David sprayed insulating foam into the cracks of the house, his coveralls and mask making him look like a mad exterminator.

One night Joanna was on the phone, complaining to her mother about mice and raccoons and leaky sheds.

"Oh dear, Joanna," her mother said. "Are you happy out there?"

"Mom, you have to visit. The house needs a lot of work, and I complain, but there are so many stars and an old well, and a dinner bell. A dinner bell! Mom, really, it's perfect."

THREE

THE TIME CHANGE FROM CANADA to Japan meant that David was sleeping most of the day and watching TV through the night. Mitchell had reserved two nights for David at the *ryokan* so he could recuperate from his flight and prepare for the second leg of the trip to Kyoto.

Mitchell had taught English in Tokyo the year before. He had told David, "Tokyo is no place for a farm boy. That town will eat you up."

Despite the warning, on David's second night in Tokyo he wandered out into the street. The air smelled like car exhaust and burned sesame oil. David looked down the narrow road, trying to memorize the way back to his lodgings. A miniature flatbed truck drove slowly down the road, an announcement playing from a loudspeaker. The driver leaned out the window and casually asked David a question in Japanese.

From the way he spoke, David thought he might be saying, "Nice night, isn't it?" so David said, "Yes."

The driver stopped the truck and hopped out of his seat. He opened what looked like a cast-iron barbecue on the back of the truck. Smoke poured out. With a pair of tongs, the man grabbed something wrapped in tinfoil and put it in a cardboard cone. He handed the cone to David and awaited payment.

David pulled a handful of Japanese coins from his pocket and held them out. The man took what he needed and drove away.

David found a bench and unwrapped his accidental purchase. The Tokyo night was cool and damp. In the nine-hundred-year-old city, home to thirty-five million people, David Woods sat under a statue of Buddha and ate a baked potato.

DAVID PULLED AN IRON GRILL out of the farmhouse woodstove and leaned it against the wall. Joanna stood in the living room doorway, waiting for David to make eye contact. David dumped a shovel full of ashes out of the woodstove into a tin bucket. A cloud of dust rose from the bucket.

"I got the job."

"Which place?" asked David.

"Moreland Large Animal Veterinary."

"You don't seem happy."

"It's only two mornings a week."

David used the sleeve of his shirt to wipe ashes off the hardwood floor. "It's a start. It's a foot in the door."

"Don Moreland claims he's a large-animal vet, but the place is full of cats and dogs. I don't know if it's my thing."

Joanna had ridden horses most of her life and had specialized in farm animal care at veterinary school. Growing up, her family had welcomed an assortment of animals into their home, and Joanna had declared her intention to be a vet at a very early age. Her mother enjoyed telling a story of six-year-old Joanna bandaging a cat that had no particular ailment.

"There's hundreds of farms around here," said David. "If it doesn't work out, a vet somewhere is going to need help."

"It's easy for you to be optimistic when a great job just fell in your lap."

Indeed, David's first day at Emily Carr Public School had been full of handshakes and warm wishes. One of the students, Carrie Connelly, gave David a Mason jar full of wine gums. Anna Metz gave David a tin of homemade oatmeal cookies.

On David's second day of teaching there was an assembly, and David was introduced to the school. One of his students, Jesse Young, announced into a microphone, "Presenting Mr. Woods, the only teacher who can look down on Mr. Kressler!"

Jeff Kressler turned out to be the gym teacher, who was also tall.

Emily Carr was a small school with a population evenly split between rural students and students from a large new housing development on the north side of Dumford Mills. The new subdivision was full of professionals commuting to Ottawa. David's initial impression was that both student groups — rural and suburban — would be easier to teach than the inner-city students in London, where he had done his practice-teaching placements.

David's fourth-grade class consisted of fourteen girls and ten boys. David organized the class into six groups of four and tried to implement many of the collaborative learning techniques he had been taught at teachers' college.

The classroom tables were organized into a semi-circle. Whether it was because of the seating arrangement or the multicultural dynamic of the class, David began introducing lessons by declaring, "This session of the United Nations will now come to order!"

FOUR

WHEN HE LEFT THE TOKYO *ryokan*, the innkeeper's wife gave David a five-yen piece on a key chain.

"Lucky, lucky," she said. David bent over to hug her, but she turned away, giggling.

David left for Kyoto during morning rush hour. Tokyo Station was a madhouse. If that morning's swirl of humanity were indicative of life in Tokyo, David felt he would not have lasted long there.

The bullet train from Tokyo to Kyoto went through rice fields and small towns. When David went to the washroom, he found a urinal embedded in the floor. Unsure of how to use it, David removed his pants and got down on his knees to straddle the porcelain trough. When he emerged from the washroom, he noticed there was a sign which indicated "Japanese toilet" one way and "Western toilet" the other.

When the train pulled into Kyoto Station, David followed the other travellers out to the street. The air was much clearer than in Tokyo, and David could see mountains poking above the edge of the city. It was early April, and pink buds were beginning to show along the dark branches of cherry trees.

David felt buoyed by the beauty of this city of arbitrary choosing. He went back into the station and stashed his suitcase in a locker. It was a warm spring day, and David spent the rest of the afternoon strolling through neighbourhoods of shops and houses.

Mitchell had given him a list of *gaijin* houses — boarding houses for foreigners — to call when he got to Kyoto. David was content to wander, but with evening looming he made his way back to Kyoto Station to find a phone.

The first *gaijin* house on the list was called Apple House. David dialled the number, and a man with an Australian accent gave him a different number to call. David didn't have a pen and could not remember the number. The next residence on the list was The Monterrey House.

A woman answered. "*Moshi-moshi.*"

"Hello?"

The woman said, "Tyler?"

"No, it's David. I'm looking for a place to stay."

"You need a home?" the woman asked.

Through a big plate-glass window, David looked at the sun going down over the mountains of Kyoto.

"Yes," he said. "Yes, please."

EMILY CARR PUBLIC SCHOOL WAS set back off the main road in Dumford Mills. The school had two soccer fields behind it that were bordered by a forest. One day after school, David went jogging across the soccer fields and along the edge of the treeline. At one point there was a path that entered the forest, and David followed it. The muddy path led to a wider stone-dust trail that followed a stream. Down the trail, a sturdy steel bridge crossed the stream. As he stood on the bridge, David could see a cloud of minnows darting around in the shadows of the water. He wondered if he might be able to catch a few small fish to keep in his classroom.

David always liked to keep busy, and Joanna felt that jogging was just a way for David to feel like he had been working. She wished that he could sit and play a game or watch a movie with her without feeling guilty.

On his next after-school jog, David brought a dollar-store net and a large Ziploc bag down to the stream. Catching minnows in the creek proved to be much more difficult than he had imagined. The fish darted out of reach as soon as they saw movement on the bank. He lunged and stabbed without success. However, David was rewarded when he turned over some of the larger rocks close to shore. He returned to school with two crayfish, one of which was as large as a deck of cards.

The class named the big crayfish Katrina and the smaller one Hugo, after two famous hurricanes. Martin Staedelbauer volunteered to research what crayfish ate and promised to supply the needed nutrition.

David had planned to teach the science unit on habitats in the spring, but when the crayfish became a daily topic of conversation in the class, he rearranged the order of his units so the crustaceans could be the focus of some formal lessons. David had the students sketch the crayfish and research what all the body parts were. For a language arts lesson, students wrote stories about life on the bottom of a stream.

The crayfish were kept in an aquarium lined with marbles and rocks. Pieces of spinach and cooked chicken floated about. After some debate, the students agreed that the aquarium did not look like authentic crayfish habitat, and David suggested they go to the stream to collect more natural components. This was the beginning of much excitement. Also much tragedy.

FIVE

THE PHONE CALL TO MONTERREY House had been answered by the Korean property manager, Kim. She did not live at the house but collected rent and arranged for small repairs.

Kim met David at Kyoto Station. She arrived on bicycle and motioned for David to follow her. David did not know how far the house was or whether he would be able to keep up with her as he pulled his suitcase behind him. The manager bicycled just slowly enough that he did not fall behind, but fast enough that he could not ask her any questions.

After turning off a main street into an alley lined with wooden walls, they stopped at a white stucco house. Embedded in the stucco was a plaque that said *Monterrey House*. Above the door was a white awning made of tin. A few bicycles leaned against the wall, and an Australian flag was tacked under a window. Kim slid the glass door open, and David followed her inside.

In the front hall, dress shoes, running shoes, and several pairs of slippers were scattered about. They removed their shoes, and Kim led David down a narrow hallway to a small kitchen. A guy and a girl sat at a table drinking wine. David waved at them, and the guy said, "*Omedeto*," which Kim translated as "Welcome."

Through the kitchen was a staircase that led up to the next level. There were four bedrooms on the second floor, each with two futons. Kim told David that he could share a room on that floor with another Canadian or have a smaller bedroom to himself on the third floor.

The third level was essentially an attic. It was divided into two small rooms, each with a slanted roof. Although the ceiling in the attic room would require that David duck most of the time, it had a writing desk and offered more privacy than the lower floors.

Settling on the attic, David handed Kim the first two months' rent in cash, and she showed him how to use the kerosene heater in the corner. When Kim left, David shut the bedroom door and pulled a futon out of the closet. He swallowed a couple of barrel-shaped anti-depressants and sprawled across the mattress with his feet hanging off the end.

"Goodnight, Joanna," he whispered.

THE PRINCIPAL OF EMILY CARR Public School was Roger Dixon. Roger was nearing retirement and was happy to finish out his career at a small-town school. Although the job of principal was one of constant crisis management, the Dumford Mills dramas were less politically motivated than those in urban schools, and most issues could be solved with common sense.

Roger's least-favourite part of his job was interviewing teaching candidates. The young teachers all came in with the same desperate eagerness, and Roger found it hard to evaluate them based on their carefully memorized responses. Picking the wrong candidate could make his job much harder, and what they said during an interview rarely matched their actions down the road.

However, when David Woods had walked into his office, he and Roger made an immediate connection. During David's interview, the woman from human resources assigned to monitor the proceedings had become exasperated when Roger deviated from the standard interview questions to ask about horses, or the difference between peaches and nectarines. Although four other applicants were to be interviewed after David, Roger had known immediately that David would be his new fourth-grade teacher in September.

Now when they met in the halls of the school, David called Roger "Mr. Dixon." The principal would say, "Please, call me Roger," but secretly he appreciated the token of respect.

Roger was also impressed by David's rapport with students. He didn't yell. He didn't get exasperated with student behaviour. Roger had never read any research to support his hypothesis, but he always felt that physically imposing teachers had an easier time controlling a class of students. This seemed to be the case with David Woods. When David started to speak, his class generally fell silent.

As a bonus for Roger, David had replaced Janice Flanagan, a miserable battle-axe of a teacher who had publicly challenged the principal on his leadership. Each time Roger met David in the hallway, it reminded him that Janice was gone, and so he greeted David with genuine giddiness. If David wanted to arrange his tables in a semi-circle, Roger's response was "Go for it!" If David wanted to keep crayfish in his classroom, "Why only two?"

One afternoon David asked Roger if he could take his students down to the stream to gather some stones for the classroom aquarium, and to catch some additional animals.

Roger explained that the forest behind the school was part of the Condie Creek Conservation Area. The main section of the park was a few kilometres away, but a corridor of protected land followed Condie Creek from the conservation area north to the Rideau River. A hiking trail followed the western side of the creek from the conservation area. Halfway to the river it crossed the steel bridge to the eastern side. Where Condie Creek emptied into the river, there was a spot with picnic tables and garbage cans. It was a popular fishing spot during the summer.

Roger said that many classes went to the main conservation area for outdoor lessons run by the conservation authority staff. However, if David asked the conservation authority for permission, got field trip forms, and arranged for a few parent volunteers, then, declared Roger, "Have an adventure!"

SIX

THE JAPANESE GOVERNMENT HAD AN agreement with Canada, Australia, and New Zealand, which allowed citizens of those countries to get Japanese work visas before finding a job. The Working Holiday Visa gave Canadians a great advantage over Americans when it came to getting teaching jobs in Japan.

However, lying on the futon in his bedroom, David had no motivation to get up. He was in the attic of a house in a Japanese city where no one knew his name. This was as physically and culturally distant as he could get from Dumford Mills. David had told his family he was going to teach English in Japan, but really, he felt no inclination to do so. Indeed, if he hadn't needed to urinate, David would have stayed in bed indefinitely.

The only washroom in the house was on the first floor, so David changed into a different set of wrinkled clothes, brushed his hair, and prepared for the possibility of social interaction. He was happy to find a Western toilet in the bathroom, but was dismayed to see the same stool-and-nozzle set-up in the shower that he had used in Tokyo.

In the kitchen, a young muscular guy with blond hair introduced himself as Tyler. Tyler was from Vancouver and had come to Japan to study karate. On weekends he tutored a few students in the neighbourhood. Tyler started most of his sentences with "dude."

"Dude, with a teaching degree and a Working Holiday Visa, you'll be golden. Hang out with other *gaijin*. People come and go every day. They'll let you know where the jobs are. It's not like the eighties and nineties, when there were big English-teaching companies interviewing every day, but there are jobs. Keep your ears open."

David dropped bread into a toaster. Even though he had no intention of teaching in Japan, presenting himself as an English teacher would allow him to fit in with the stream of other travellers.

David found some instant coffee and opened cupboards looking for a mug. He confessed to Tyler that although he had walked from Kyoto Station the night before, he really had no idea where he was.

"Dude," said Tyler, "I'll tell you where you are. You are in mother-fucking Japan, brother! Monterrey House. The Mother Ship. We'll get you set up. No worries. Listen, be down here tonight at seven. We've got a place we all go to." Tyler clapped his hands enthusiastically. "Orientation!"

David slathered peanut butter on his toast. The idea of going to a bar or restaurant with this crude housemate or any other people held no appeal to him, but he accepted the offer.

"Game on," said Tyler, adding, "Also, dude, stop eating all my fucking food."

FOR THE CREEK EXCURSION, DAVID bought a dozen dollar-store nets and a book entitled *Fish of Eastern Ontario*. Students brought their own buckets from home.

There were four volunteers along for the field trip: Anna Metz's mother, Holly; Lyndsay Armstrong's mother, Maureen; Robbie Dickenson's mother, Amanda; and Jesse Young's grandfather, George. George was a fly-fisherman and said that he might be able to identify some of the insect larvae they would catch. Holly Metz brought bologna sandwiches. The students were impressed when Mrs. Dickenson arrived wearing hip waders.

Roger met them in the front foyer. He whispered excitedly, "Quiet! Quiet! We can't have the whole school knowing you're skipping class today."

Some of the children shouted, "We're not skipping!"

Roger said, "Mr. Woods, I'm not sure why I ever allowed this outing. It had better be educational. You'll need to write a report of your discoveries and have it on my desk tomorrow morning." Principal Dixon was happy to banter with the non-Janice Flanagan.

As a first-year teacher, David spent a lot of time on his lesson plans. He mapped out each hour of the day and tried to keep things lively. However, nothing he had done in the classroom generated the same level of anticipation as going into the forest. The students were raucous.

It was a twenty-minute hike to the bridge where David planned to set up the stream study, but after an hour they had not yet made it to the creek. The group was sidetracked by beetles and woodpeckers, and then by a hole in a tree that seemed to have a furry brown animal sleeping in it. The hole was twenty feet up a smooth grey beech tree, and, unfortunately, David had not thought to bring binoculars.

Robbie Dickenson said, "Raccoons sleep all day. It's probably a raccoon."

"Raccoons are omnivores," said Jenny Lin.

"Porcupines are nocturnal too," said Anna Metz. "It could be a porcupine."

"But porcupines don't have fur," said Robbie.

"Actually," said George, "porcupines do have fur. It covers their quills. My brother has a stuffed one in his garage. I'll bring it to your classroom someday."

Amanda Dickenson told David, "It was a mistake to wear the hip waders. My feet are killing me."

"Do you need to go back to the school?"

"Nah," said Amanda. "This is too much fun."

SEVEN

WHEN THE DIGITAL CLOCK ON his desk said 6:55 p.m., David reluctantly got off his futon. He took some migraine medication and went down to the kitchen. Tyler was wearing a Hawaiian shirt and a pair of dark sunglasses. Another guy in a dress shirt was using a wooden spoon to poke a short-haired girl in the ribs.

Tyler said, "David, my large Canadian friend, this is Rochelle. She's a sweetheart. And this stud here is Guy. He looks like he's from Hollywood, but he's just another fucking Kiwi."

David shook hands with the two.

Tyler said, "I thought there'd be more of us going on Yakisoba Night, but you snooze, you lose."

Outside, the housemates wove through back streets until they reached a cobblestone avenue of restaurants and shops.

Rochelle told David, "The places with the red lanterns are bars and *izakayas.*"

One red-lanterned bar had a picture of the Golden Gate Bridge painted on a set of curtains that hung in the entranceway.

Tyler said, "I'm home," and ducked through the curtains. David followed.

Behind the bar a Japanese man of about sixty was feverishly frying a mix of chicken and cabbage on a flat grill. He yelled, "*Irasshaimase!*" as the group entered.

Tyler bowed exaggeratedly to the Japanese cook and said, "Master-*san,* it smells good, but go easy on the fucking cabbage."

The cook said, "Tyler-*san.* No drink tonight! Just food."

Tyler said, "*Gomen-nasai.* I am sorry for last time. But it's Thursday. Of course we will drink. *Sho-ga-nai.*"

Seating in the pub consisted of four booths, three tables, and five stools at the bar. Behind the bar was a collection of baseball memorabilia, mostly from San Francisco. Among the pennants and signed photographs was a wooden sign with the words *Rising Son* burned into it.

The other walls were covered in Polaroid photographs of bar patrons mugging for the camera. David looked at the pictures and found one of Tyler standing behind the bar wearing a chef's hat and flipping what looked like a pancake.

They sat at a booth and Tyler went to the bar to get drinks. David had suspected that Rochelle and Guy were a couple, but when David sat down, Rochelle sat beside him. Guy slouched across the table from them with an elbow on one knee.

Guy said, "All right, mate, what's your story?"

On the walk to the pub, David had considered what fabrication he should tell his new housemates. A simple narrative would be best, something based in the truth, with as few details to trip over as possible.

David said, "I graduated from teachers' college last year, but then my girlfriend and I split up. I wanted to find a teaching job, but I really didn't want to hang around that town anymore."

That seemed straightforward.

Rochelle said, "You've lost your love, and you're heading out to see the world. That's good. It will leave you open to experience." Rochelle had short spiky hair and wore black earrings in the shape of peace signs. She spoke with an accent David had never heard before.

Guy said, "I've still got a girlfriend, and yet, I am also open to experience." He winked at Rochelle.

Rochelle said, "But the heart, the heart controls the mind. When your heart is broken, you can lose an anchor on reality. Is your heart broken, David?"

David played with his chopsticks. He supposed that there was no need to lie.

"Yes."

GEORGE TURNED OUT TO BE AN experienced naturalist. Instead of using the nets to lunge at the fish as David had done, George showed the students how to stand in the stream with their nets open to the flow of water. He demonstrated how to turn over stones so the animals hiding among them would be caught in the current and drift into their nets.

Near the bridge the stream was shallow enough that students could wade around without water getting in their boots. At first George stayed with his grandson Jesse's group, and David circulated among the students. However, it was George who could identify the animals, so David stayed with Jesse's group, and old Mr. Young taught the students about aquatic life. David made a list of all the animals that were caught.

Crayfish
Bloodworm (also called a midge larva)
Mayfly nymph
Dragonfly nymph
Damselfly nymph
Caddisfly larva
Cranefly larva
Darter fish (Johnny Darter?)
Shiner
Stickleback fish
Leopard frog (caught on bank)
Dead leopard frog in water (stepped on?)
Pill clam
Mink! (seen, not caught)

David climbed up on the bridge to take pictures of the scene below. The students were loud and laughing, but they were focused on their buckets, talking about the animals. He thought of the students back at the school who were staring at computer screens and answering questions scrawled on the blackboard.

George Young looked up at David and said, "This is like my days as a Scout leader. My knees hurt, and I can't bend over as well as I used to, but this is what we did forty years ago. It was part of the kids' fishing badge."

David yelled at Robbie Dickenson to stay away from a deeper bend in the creek.

Robbie said, "There's a crayfish. It's swimming backwards."

"Your choice, Robbie. Stay in the shallow area or go back to school."

Robbie said, "This is way better than school."

EIGHT

TYLER CAME BACK TO THE table with two big cans of Sapporo beer and four small glasses. The housemates toasted cherry blossoms, Japan Air, and the Stanley Cup.

Rochelle announced to Tyler, "David has a broken heart."

Tyler said, "And you are just the babe to fix it for him. Maybe tonight. Dude." Tyler held his fist out for David to bump. "She's a soldier, dude. She'll subordinate you. Make you crawl in the mud."

Rochelle said to David, "I'm the opposite of a soldier. I'm a draft dodger. If I had stayed in Israel, I would have been drafted."

"Just show them your wooden leg," said Tyler.

"Piss off," said Rochelle.

"Yes, sir!" said Tyler, saluting.

Guy also saluted. Rochelle leaned across the table and jerked Guy's wrist down.

She said, "If I had done my military training, I could break that hand."

Guy said, "It's my luck that you're a graphic designer. However, if there are any holds that you'd like to practise, I graciously volunteer."

"I've become immune to your advances," said Rochelle.

"I'll wear you down, Sheila."

"You can't grind me down like one of your diamonds."

Rochelle explained to David that Guy was in Japan because he hadn't wanted to take over his father's jewellery store.

Guy's great-grandfather had started the business with a manila envelope full of diamonds smuggled out of South Africa. Kelliher's Fine Jewellery was a landmark store on the main street of Guy's hometown in New Zealand. It was a solid business and certainly could have provided Guy with employment and income. However, Guy had spent much of his childhood in the back of the store watching his father squint through a monocle, tinkering tediously with gem settings. The idea of fiddling on such a small scale didn't seem like much of a career. Guy wanted to craft a future that would make retreating to the store impossible. Even though he had no college diploma, in Japan he was an English teacher, a *sensei*, and that made his mother proud. Tonight, though, his main goal was to sleep with Rochelle.

Rochelle said, "The Monterrey House is full of people running away from home."

Guy said, "Tyler's not running away."

Tyler shrugged. "Last year I got into karate. My parents were just happy to see me interested in anything, so they're paying my way. Next week we're going to chop real bricks."

Guy said, "So we have a draft dodger, a broken-hearted teacher, a black belt wannabe, and a jewellery store refugee. Seems like a typical table at the Rising Son."

Rochelle raised her glass. "Here's to my dysfunctional gaijin family."

Tyler raised his glass. "Here's to busting some fucking bricks."

BEFORE THE CLASS LEFT CONDIE Creek there were serious decisions to be made. They had more than a hundred animals in the buckets, and they wouldn't be able to keep them all in one aquarium. The crayfish, Katrina and Hugo, were still alive back at school, so the new crayfish were released. Grandpa George thought that the fish might need cold water to survive, so all the fish were freed except for one darter, which would act as a test case for the others. The class kept two each of the large insect larvae, plus all of the bloodworms and blackfly larvae as food for the others. They also had a bucket full of wet sand, and another with stones to mimic the stream bottom. Each adult carried a bucket of water.

As they walked back to the school, the students ate leftover bologna sandwiches. David walked beside Amanda Dickenson, who was now limping along in her hip waders.

"Holy crap, David, this was a blast. Call me for the next outing. My husband, Dale, would take a day off work to do this. These are actually his hip waders."

David said, "Yeah, this was good. I'm already thinking about educational excuses to go back."

"Why do you need an excuse?"

Up ahead George yelled, "Woodcock!"

A pigeon-sized bird had exploded out of the grass and was flying over the trees. Some of the students pretended to shoot it. David thought about reprimanding them, but his father had hunted woodcocks on the farm, and David kind of liked the connection to his past life. Most of the day had been cloudy, but now the sun was poking through. A fine autumn day all around.

The class returned to the school like a sports team that had just won a big game. They stopped at the office and asked Principal Dixon to examine their treasures. Roger made a point of looking in every bucket and asking questions about the animals.

Anna Metz said, "The caddisfly makes a home out of pebbles and sand in the stream."

Roger made the students go back outside and pose for a picture under the school sign. The students held up their nets and their buckets. Robbie Dickenson held up a bologna sandwich. David stood behind the students with George and the other volunteers.

The students were happy. Parents were happy. Principal Dixon thought that he would put the photograph in the school's newsletter. Indeed, it was a picture that would one day be on the front page of the *Ottawa Citizen*.

NINE

IT WAS CLOSING TIME AT the Rising Son. David used chopsticks to pick at a bowl of popcorn. Tyler sat on the back of a booth playing "American Pie" on a classical guitar. Guy and Rochelle were slow dancing while tipsy patrons joined Tyler in singing the choruses.

Mr. Tanaka, the Polaroid-snapping cook, was also the bar owner. He admonished Tyler not to sit on the back of the booth, but not before he had taken a picture for the wall. Tyler usually did something each night that annoyed Mr. Tanaka, but Tyler had a lot of friends, and this was where he brought them. Tyler was good for business.

The Rising Son had not started out as a *gaijin* bar, but Mr. Tanaka spoke English well and had adorned the pub with American sports memorabilia. His reasonably priced food appealed to the budget-conscious travellers.

Hitashi Tanaka and his wife went to San Francisco for one week each autumn. They had started this tradition in 1984. Mr. Tanaka's favourite actor was Steve McQueen, and Mr. Tanaka had been drawn to San Francisco by the chase scene in the movie *Bullitt*. Their first trip was memorable, but the vastness of America scared the couple. So they visited America each year (very exciting), but never left San Francisco (safe). As the San Francisco pennants and postcards had slowly given the pub a theme over the years, so had the clientele shifted from Japanese to Western.

"David-*san*, picture." Mr. Tanaka was holding his Polaroid camera and motioning at David to sit up straight.

David wanted to be friendly, but he wasn't sure he wanted his picture on the wall. What if someone recognized him? What if he were found to be partying in Japan while people were still mourning back home? In the end, David pretended to be drunker than he was.

He scrunched up his face, hoping to hide his features, and gave a peace sign to the camera. The world-travelling exiles of the Rising Son united for a rousing final chorus, cheering the guitar player who brought the spontaneous choir together.

Tyler raised his arms in triumph.

"Goodnight, Asia!"

ONE FRIDAY NIGHT IN OCTOBER the Metz family came for dinner. Joanna had been exchanging recipes with Holly Metz, and Holly had expressed interest in a casserole Joanna was preparing. David wasn't sure how he felt about a student coming to his house, but Joanna said that if they were going to be part of a rural community, David would inevitably attend social events with his students' parents. Plus the Metzes only lived one concession road away. They were neighbours.

When they arrived, Holly handed Joanna a rhubarb pie.

Anna jumped up and down excitedly. "There's raisins in it. On purpose!"

Ron Metz pushed their son, Louis, forward to shake hands.

Louis was a year older than Anna. David had seen him rambling through the fields with two other neighbour boys. Usually his hair was tousled and his pants were stained. Tonight he was pressed and bathed for the outing.

Joanna had started bringing animals home from the veterinary practice: rabbits that needed eyedrops in the night, cats about to give birth. She asked Anna and Louis to feed some kittens whose mother had been hit by a car.

Ron wore a tie and had his hair combed from one side of his head straight over to the other.

"We could use some rain," said Ron.

"Yup," said David.

"Oh God," said Holly. "Nothing more entertaining than listening to two farmers talk to each other." The two women laughed like old friends, and Joanna pulled Holly into the kitchen.

David had grown up on a peach farm in the Niagara Region. He looked like a farm boy and spoke in straightforward farmer sentences. Ron and David talked easily about seeds and soil.

Ron asked David if he would ever consider farming again.

David said, "My brother Kyle is two years older than me. He studied agricultural business at Guelph and is back on the farm now."

David could not imagine himself working with Kyle. Kyle was smart but also bullheaded, like their father. David often worried that Kyle and his dad would come to blows.

"If I'd been older than Kyle, maybe I would have taken up farming. As it is, Joanna and I are living on a farm. I love my job. No regrets."

Over dinner Joanna said, "David and I met at Guelph. I was taking vet studies, and David's brother, Kyle, was taking farm administration. Kyle introduced us."

David rolled his eyes. "We were with a bunch of people. I don't remember anyone introducing us, really."

Joanna said, "My friend Lisa was dating Kyle's roommate. One night, me and Lisa and her boyfriend were going to the movies — to a James Bond flick — and we got a speeding ticket on the way. By the time we got to the theatre the movie was sold out, so we just went back to Kyle's place.

"When we got there, Kyle and David were getting ready to go see a band downtown. We were all jammed in the front hall, and David had on this tight green John Deere T-shirt. He was trying to tie his laces, but there was no room for him to bend over. Just the way we were standing, it was easier for me to tie his shoes, so I laced him up."

"Shouldn't walk around with loose laces," said David.

"I remember you said, 'Thank you, ma'am.' "

"That's so cute," said Holly.

Joanna said, "Oh, I was smitten right there. He was like a cowboy."

"He roped you in, did he?" said Ron.

"I'm not sure who roped who," said David.

"Anyway," said Joanna, "we all ended up going out together, and things kind of went from there. If we hadn't got that speeding ticket, David and I might never have met."

Holly Metz said, "Isn't it funny how timing in life is so important? The most unlikely chain of events can change your whole life."

TEN

MONTERREY HOUSE HAD UNDERGONE A large renovation a
month before David moved in. To increase revenue, while simulta-
neously putting an end to noisy parties, the landlord had turned the
common room on the first floor, which had been the social centre
of the house, into two bedrooms. During construction, more than
half of the tenants had moved out. The tenants who had moved in
after the renovation were made to feel as if they had missed out on
the good old days.

"It was like a big family," said Tyler.

With the living room gone, the kitchen could not accommodate
all twelve of the house's occupants, much less offer enough space to
make meals. However, if a person were looking for a conversation,
the kitchen was the place to go.

Jock from Boston had lived at Monterrey House the longest —
three years — and at thirty-one was also the oldest resident. Jock
worked as a deejay at a club called the Savannah.

One evening several of the Monterrey tenants went to the Savannah Club to see him spin his music. Jock sat with them and bought
them drinks, but another deejay played the music. After that night,
Tyler teased Jock for being a "deejay understudy."

Jock spent a lot of time mixing musical beats on a computer in
the kitchen. He often asked people what songs were popular in their
countries. He would then steal pieces of songs from around the
world. "It's just sampling," he told David.

Because David had recently arrived from Canada, Jock wanted to
know what music was hot in the clubs. David said that the last club
he had gone to was the Kemptville Legion. He remembered that the
Chicken Dance had been pretty popular.

David said, "Three years is a long time to live in Japan."

Jock laughed. "Three years is a long time to live in this nuthouse. Usually people who come to Japan to teach or whatever, they stay for six months or a year and go home, or they end up staying forever. There's not much in between."

"So you're here forever?"

Jock said, "Well, it's kind of sketchy for me each time I renew my visa. I have to prove that I am filling employment that a Japanese person can't do. Deejaying is the one profession in Japan where being black helps."

David didn't know what to say to that.

Jock said, "Who's gonna lay down urban American beats? Some J-boy? Gimme a break. I know I've got the goods, but, you know, it's hard to explain on a form."

David nodded.

"So far the club has smoothed things over, but that could all change someday. I couldn't get a teaching job. A black man just doesn't fit the Japanese picture of a teacher."

David tried to empathize. "I don't feel like I fit in here. I'm a foot taller than everyone else."

"Black, white, short, tall. In the end, we're all *gaijin*."

"Foreigners," said David.

"More than that," said Jock. "Not Japanese. Not 'one of us.' Never be 'one of us.'"

"YOU'RE A GOOD TEACHER, MR. WOODS," said Anna Metz over dessert. They were eating rhubarb pie and vanilla ice cream.

"You're better than Mrs. Flanagan," said Louis Metz. "I had her last year, and all she did was yell."

"Don't speak poorly of the departed," said Ron.

"She's not dead," said Louis. "Just retired."

"She did run a tight ship."

Louis said, "I got put in the time-out chair just for looking out the window. I wasn't talking or anything."

Holly said, "When Anna gets home each day, she can't stop talking about what she did in class. She's never been this engaged at school before. I know you've only been teaching for seven or eight weeks, but, David, what you've got going on in that classroom, I think it's special."

"Mrs. Flanagan never would've let us keep crayfish in the classroom," said Louis. "She would have totally freaked out."

Holly said, "On the weekend, Amanda Dickenson and I had coffee. We talked a lot about the trip down to the stream. It was really neat how the students were pointing things out to each other about the animals, and asking questions, and just figuring out how to do things for themselves."

"All that stuff we did," said David, "it's all in the curriculum. I have to teach adaptations, food chains, pollution, photosynthesis. It makes sense to show them the real thing."

Holly said, "It wasn't a warm day, standing in that creek, but none of the students complained."

David tried to pick up melted ice cream with his fork. He said, "I'd like to use that forest for more lessons. I'm thinking of basing the light and sound unit on how animals communicate with each other."

"I wish I'd failed grade four," said Louis. "Then I'd be in your class."

"Mrs. Martin is a nice teacher," said David.

"She doesn't yell or anything like Mrs. Flanagan did, but she doesn't take us into the forest. She doesn't invite us to her house for dinner."

"It was just good to get the students outside," said David. "Having the conservation area beside the school is great."

"That outdoor stuff would be good for Louis," said Ron.

Holly sent the kids off to play with the kittens. When they were out of earshot she said, "Anna does well in school, but Louis, he can't sit still for ten minutes."

"Well that's the thing," said David. "Sitting in a chair for five hours a day might not be the best way for everyone to learn. Boys especially."

"School wasn't my thing either," said Ron. "I learned more following Dad around the farm than I did in a classroom."

"Maybe our next field trip should be to your farm," said David.

Later that night, when David and Joanna were getting ready for bed, Joanna said, "You are very popular with the Metz family."

"Yeah. The whole teaching thing is going pretty well."

"The *whole teaching thing?*" said Joanna. "You make it sound like it's an experiment or something."

David said, "Honestly, even when I was taking geography at university, I always thought I'd end up back on the farm."

"And now you're a teacher."

"Until now I've felt like I was just a farmer muddling my way through in the classroom."

"And now?"

David pretended to adjust a bow tie. "Now I'm Mister Woods."

ELEVEN

FOR THE FIRST FEW DAYS at Monterrey House, David stayed in his room, sleeping or just lying in bed. Sleep was filled with nightmares. A recurring scene involved David running through a dark tunnel toward a pinprick of light. Sometimes his feet were bound. Sometimes there was a strong wind in his face. He scrambled and tripped his way forward, but the light never got closer. He wasn't being chased, but in the dream he felt he would suffocate if he couldn't make it to the light. Lying awake helped him avoid the dark dreams, but consciously replaying the events of Condie Creek was no less terrifying.

Typically, David would have dealt with stress by working with his hands. Stacking an enormous pile of wood or shovelling a long snowy driveway would have given him great comfort.

That was the problem. No amount of work, no physical action, could make things better. David was paralyzed by a feeling, by a memory. He was an imposing physical specimen, yet the muscle and sinew that could dig fields of earth and cut forests of wood were just a weight on his body, keeping him pinned to the futon each morning.

Adding to his dysfunction, David had not found the combination of medications that would enable him to sleep, yet also allow him to move around in the world as a normal human being. He took random groupings of antidepressants and sleeping pills, hoping to stumble upon an effective mix. David attributed various mental tics to his medications, though it was impossible to tell which effects were chemically induced and which were expected consequences of trauma.

The main benefit of the drugs was to scramble his thoughts so he could not string together a clear memory of Condie Creek. Images from the past year flashed in his brain like someone was flipping pages in a book.

To stay out of his own head, David began walking. He started by exploring the streets and alleys around Monterrey House. Unlike Tokyo, Kyoto was laid out in a grid. It was easier to move about, but there didn't seem to be any zoning distinctions within the city. Neighbourhoods were a jumble of houses, apartment buildings, and shops. The Japanese seemed to have no problem putting a car dealership beside a daycare, or a karaoke bar above a pharmacy. The chaotic creativity of Japanese urban planning made each ramble a unique experience.

Eventually David began experimenting with the train system. Fushimi Station and Tambabashi Station were almost the same distance from Monterrey House, and David never decided before he left the house which one he would go to. The stations were on two different train lines, but both could get him to Kyoto Station, and from there he could get anywhere in the city.

David started his exploration by taking trains to stations on the periphery of the city. He would simply exit the local train station and hike toward the nearest hill. David found that if he followed the roads that skirted the base of the mountains, there would often be walking paths leading up through the trees.

One day, while sitting in a graveyard, David took out a pad of paper and sketched a gravestone engraved with an image of clasped hands. David had never pursued any artistic activities, but the leather satchel he carried around contained most of the supplies that a student might take on the first day of school. He wasn't particularly talented, but the task kept his hands busy. It gave him purpose. A random activity on a random path in a random city.

Near Miyakehachiman Station, David sketched a bridge that crossed the Takano River. While sitting on the bank, he wondered how Japanese aquatic animals would compare with North American species. However, as he took a few steps toward the water, his knees began to shake. David imagined the placid river boiling and churning, and he hurried back up the slope in self-induced panic.

Most people in Monterrey House assumed David was job-hunting each day, and David didn't do anything to discourage their assumptions. He went out the door in the morning wearing a collared shirt and casual slacks, and carrying his satchel full of papers. Tyler, however, doubted David's teaching ambitions.

"He doesn't want a job. Dude doesn't have a computer, doesn't have a cellphone. Dude says he's a teacher, but teachers iron their fucking pants."

ON A SUNNY AFTERNOON IN late October, David took his students on their second field trip to the stream. The air was crisp, and the water in the creek was noticeably colder than it had been two weeks earlier. David had prepared worksheets for the students, and they wrote on clipboards, describing the habitat, measuring the depth of the water, and identifying animals. They also needed to catch some prey for their carnivorous classroom creatures. All the blackfly and midge larvae had been eaten after one day in the aquarium.

The dragonfly nymphs seemed to be the most voracious. When the students had put the animals together, one of the young dragonfly larvae had grabbed a red midge larva with a sudden stabbing motion. Research revealed that dragonfly nymphs have long lower lips on a hinged joint. When the hinge straightened, the lip would shoot forward, and small pincers on the end of the lip would grab prey. A YouTube video of this hunting technique went viral in the Dumford Mills community.

After catching animals in the stream, David called the class together and showed them the microphone he had brought to record bird calls for the light and sound unit.

"Everyone be quiet," said Anna.

The students were silent, but on this day there weren't many birds to be heard. The afternoon had turned windy, and any sounds they might have heard were lost on the breeze.

Robbie Dickenson suggested they try recording bird songs in the morning.

"More birds sing in the morning."

"It's usually not as windy in the morning," said George.

"Maybe that's why they sing then," said Anna. "Maybe they can hear each other better."

"We'll come back in the morning," said David, deciding on the spot. "We'll test that theory."

David had broad shoulders and long arms that never quite touched the sides of his body. He had played a lot of sports in school, but there was a heaviness to the way he moved. He lacked a fluidity in his motion that kept him from becoming a really successful athlete. One soccer coach had told him, "You don't run, David. You lumber."

However, a few times in his life his large frame and sturdy limbs had coordinated themselves with memorable results. During a senior-year high school basketball game, time running out and his team down by a point, David had grabbed a loose ball in the other team's end. Normally he would have passed to a shooter, but with the clock ticking down he took two long strides and jumped toward the basket. He was too far under the rim to make a proper layup, so he reached up and under the far side of the basket and let the ball flip off the ends of his fingertips. It was a purposeful, almost graceful movement that won the game.

On the walk back to Emily Carr Public School the children chattered, the parents laughed, and out in front of them strode David Woods, a young man coming into his own as a teacher. Despite his size, on this day his step was light and full of purpose, and perhaps even *graceful*.

TWELVE

DAVID LAY THE SKETCHES FROM his hikes on the floor of his attic room, along with a map of Kyoto. He thought it was important to write down where he had been at the time of each sketch. He might need to show them to some psychotherapist in the future. A therapist might have pointed out to David that his sketches were of solid things, walls and gates and tombstones. Sturdy things that stood the test of time. Things that couldn't die.

One day, on a walk from Demachiyanagi Station, David found the Ginkaku-ji temple. Inside the temple was a simple stone garden with pebbles immaculately raked around several boulders. The boulders were meant to suggest islands in a sea. The impeccable arrangement was mesmerizing. David had sketched a bell outside the temple, but in his room he felt as though he should have sketched the garden instead. He was thinking about trying to draw the garden from memory when there was a knock on his door. It was Guy.

"Telephone."

David cringed at the prospect of talking to someone who knew who he was. To his knowledge, only the local authorities knew where he lived. As part of his visa requirements, when David found a place to stay he was required to get a Japanese Residency Card. David speculated that he might be getting deported for trespassing in the mountains, or for having a work visa and not looking for a job.

The Monterrey House phone was on a landing halfway up the first flight of stairs. It looked like a pay phone attached to the wall. To use the phone, tenants were forced to sit on the stairs. David sat down and tried to say "Hello" like a non-trespasser.

"David!"

"Jesus Christ! Mitchell, how did you get this number?"

"I called the Canadian Embassy. I told them you were a missing person. Where are you?"

"A place called Monterrey House. It was on your list."

"You need to call your parents. You need to call Joanna."

"How's Toronto? How's law school?"

"It's okay. A lot of reading. Listen, everyone blames me for you going to Japan."

"They should."

"Yeah, but they think I'm your travel agent."

"You are."

"Your mom and Joanna are calling me to find out where you are, when you're coming home, *if* you're coming home. David, make contact."

"Tell them I'm fine. I have to be home for September. I don't know if I'll be back before then."

"I'm giving them this number."

"No!"

David's sharp reply scared Rochelle, who was slipping by him on the stairs.

"You can't. You can't. They'd call every day. No way."

"They call *me* every day," said Mitchell. "You have to do something. Make contact."

"I'll do something. I'll figure something out. Thank you, Mitchell. Kyoto is beautiful. The cherry blossoms were beautiful."

"I know. I told you. Please call Joanna. I can't lie to her."

"I will. She's probably worried that I won't be able to eat Japanese food."

"No. She's worried you're going to kill yourself."

IN THE SCHOOL OFFICE, DAVID tried to persuade his principal that taking his students into the conservation area was a good idea.

"The forest is right beside our school."

Roger shifted in his chair, worried he was about to get into an argument with his new favourite teacher.

"You can't leave school property without the off-campus form filled out. That requires field trip forms signed by parents. That requires a supervisory ratio of one adult for every eight students. If you want, you can stand on the soccer field and point your microphone into the forest. But you can't go into the forest. It's not school property."

"I don't want to get field trip forms filled out every day."

"You can't go into the forest every day."

David said, "We're studying habitats. Habitats are outside."

"I know," said Roger.

"We've got the rocks and minerals unit coming up. Rocks are outside."

"I know."

"The superintendent of the conservation area said I could use the property with students whenever I want."

Roger felt trapped in the conversation. As a teacher he agreed wholeheartedly with the content of what David was saying, but as an administrator of school board policy he could not sanction David's actions. He wished he had more time to craft his words properly.

"Listen, David. I agree with you. I like your idealism. But parents need to know where their children are during the day. I need to know. If a parent shows up to take Billy to the dentist, I can't say, 'I'm sorry, Mrs. Jones. Billy's not here right now. He's somewhere in the Condie Creek Conservation Area.'"

David grimaced. He also wished he had more time to choose the right words.

That night Joanna told David, "You should have told him to say, 'I'm sorry, Mrs. Jones, Billy's learning about habitats by making a beaver dam out of stupid plasticine.'"

THIRTEEN

Dear Mom,

I am fine. I am in Kyoto. Even though Japan is quite expensive, I have found a nice place to live. I am eating well, but not as much meat as at home. I haven't found a teaching job yet, but some people I met have given me advice. The weather is turning warmer. The Japanese spring is about a month ahead of ours. I hope you didn't get any spring frost.

Tell Dad I was sorry to hear about the Maple Leafs.

Here is a picture I drew.

Love, David.

Dear Joanna,

I made it to Japan okay. I am living in Kyoto. It's a big city, but it has many parks and natural areas. I'm starting to develop a taste for Japanese food.

I haven't started to look for a job yet. I'm walking in the mountains nearly every day. I like it. Everything is so different here. Everything smells strange. Yesterday, I was on a path in the mountains and there was a small zoo on the trail. I paid about three dollars to get in, and the only animals they had in the zoo were squirrels. Apparently there are no wild squirrels in Japan. Weird, eh?

Joanna, I'm fine. I couldn't live with my parents any longer. I should have told you what I was planning, but really, there was no planning. Mitchell put it together for me, and I didn't know if I would really go until the last minute. I feel sorry about leaving, but I am here now. I couldn't go back to Dumford Mills. I can never go back to Dumford Mills. You must know that. Do what you need to do.

Here is a picture of a bell I found at a shrine. It reminds me of the dinner bell.

David

JOANNA SHAYNE GREW UP IN Bright's Grove, Ontario — the home-town of professional golfer Mike Weir. Her mother was a hairdresser, and her father sold insurance. At the end of their suburban street was a bird rehabilitation centre. People brought in birds that had hit windows or power lines. Sometimes the birds had been shot. When Joanna was twelve, she would head to the centre after school to see what new birds had been admitted. The staff were friendly, and they would give Joanna small jobs until one of her parents picked her up on the way home from work.

Because she spent so much time between the bird clinic and the riding stable, Joanna's parents were not surprised by her desire to be a veterinarian. It did surprise them that Joanna clung so tenaciously to this commitment through her high school and university years. When they suggested that becoming a veterinary technician might be a shorter and less-expensive career path, Joanna had scoffed at the proposition. This stubbornness had allowed Joanna to overcome the financial and academic challenges that arose in the pursuit of a six-year professional degree.

Today Joanna had brought home an African grey parrot with an infected eye. The bird sat in a cage on the kitchen table and said, "Good kitty," every time a cat walked by. Joanna was worried that David was running out of patience with the menagerie of animals in the house. After work he had stomped out the back door with a chainsaw in his hands. His frenetic sawing was a signal to Joanna that either school had not gone well for him or the talking parrot was one animal too many.

During dinner they sat in silence eating pork chops and apple-sauce. When David had cleared his plate and was gnawing on a bone, Joanna said, "Tough day at the office?"

David held the pork bone under the table for a cat to lick. He didn't say anything for a while, but when Joanna kept staring at him he said, "I want to record some bird songs in the forest behind the school."

"Birds," said Joanna. "One of my specialties."

David said, "I can't take the students in the forest without field trip forms and volunteers and blah, blah, blah."

Joanna said, "There are some great birding websites. You can find hundreds of bird songs. Anything you want."

The cat jumped into David's lap and he pushed it away.

Joanna said, "Getting good recordings of bird songs is pretty difficult. November isn't really a good month either. You can get some call notes, but —"

"But that's the thing, right? That's what our education system has become. Someone else goes out and experiments and discovers things, and then we just tell the students how it is. 'Here's how it all works. Look at this website. Watch this video. Sit there and don't make a sound. We'll give you good marks just for being quiet.'"

Joanna tried to be supportive. "You've taken your students outside more often than all of the other teachers combined. Your class has fun. You make things interesting. Emily Carr is lucky to have you."

David said, "I had this professor at Western who always said, 'Find your groove.' Find a way to teach that gets you excited. She said, if you can find that groove, you'll be a great teacher."

"You can still find your groove."

David said, "We have a conservation area right beside the school. It has wetlands. It has a stream. It has a forest. Why would anyone teach the habitats unit in the classroom when we have the real thing right there?"

Joanna tried again. "You can find your groove in the classroom."

"It's not just the habitats unit. I mean, education is just learning how the world works, and, let's face it, most of the world is outside."

Joanna didn't know what to say. She started clearing dishes from the table. "I euthanized three cats today."

"Good kitty," said the parrot.

FOURTEEN

WHEN DAVID MAILED HIS LETTERS to Canada, the return address on the envelopes was for a post office box near Fushimi Station. He hoped that sending the letters would take pressure off Mitchell. Despite the shock of the phone call, it had been nice to talk to his friend.

David and Mitchell had not been friends during their undergraduate studies, but they had recognized each other at an orientation session for the teaching program. At the time, Mitchell was looking for a roommate, and the two ended up living together in a loft apartment in downtown London. Their personalities were very different, but after a year of eating and shopping and studying together, Mitchell was the only person, besides Joanna, who David felt comfortable opening up to. Mitchell was grateful to have an even-keeled friend who was at the same stage of life as he was.

After teachers' college, David had landed the job at Emily Carr, and Mitchell had bummed around for several months before going to Japan to teach English. He was now enrolled in law school at the University of Toronto. For David, the thought of Mitchell going to law school seemed as random as David going to Japan.

After the tragedy, David had spent a few weeks chopping wood like a crazed lumberjack. However, the public scrutiny and media attention were too much, and he had retreated to his parents' farm. He had tried to lose himself in physical labour, but living with his parents and taking direction from his brother was not a manageable long-term situation.

One day after Christmas, Mitchell had stopped in at the Woods' farm. David was trimming branches in an apple orchard.

David said, "Kyle thought he knew more about farming than Dad before he went to university. Now he thinks he's running the show. He treats me like crap."

Mitchell felt that Kyle treated everyone like crap.

"What about your mom?"

David shook his head. "She spends her whole day planning meals. Cooking food. Dad and Kyle can be screaming at each other, and she's marinating salmon or some stupid thing."

"Maybe it's a coping thing. You chop wood and she cooks."

David sat on the rung of a ladder that leaned against a tree. "I thought when I came here that maybe my situation might bring the family together in some way. But really, they don't know how to deal with this any better than I do. It's totally dysfunctional."

That's when Mitchell said, "You should go to Japan."

David said, "Yeah. I should."

And that was that.

EMILY CARR PUBLIC SCHOOL WAS not large enough to have a full-time principal, so Roger Dixon taught grade six half of the day. He tried to insulate his students from the din of the office and instructed the secretary, Ms. Richardson, not to interrupt his lessons except for emergencies. However, when the school bell rang at 3:25, the classroom door would open, and the concerns of the school would flow in. On this day, Roger cleaned his blackboards while David looked glumly out the window.

Roger suggested, "Send field trip forms home the first of every month. Save one Friday a month for the forest. Make it a regular thing."

"There's no more risk for students in the forest than on the play structure."

"It's not a philosophical argument you need to make. You're up against board policy."

David said, "Every month, teachers take students to the conservation area on buses. Why? We have the conservation area right here. Teachers could just take their students into the woods themselves."

Roger sprayed soapy water on the student desks. "Most teachers like the structure of the field trip. They get on the bus, and from that point everything is looked after for them. Conservation staff meet them at the nature centre. They get the bird program or insect program all nicely packaged up for them. The conservation area programs are great. The staff are great. They have washrooms there, David."

"I signed up for a pond study in May."

"There you go."

David said, "But it's only once. Once a year. Two hundred and fifty dollars for the program, and a hundred and forty for the bus."

"The school pays for it," said Roger.

"Why should we pay for something that we can all have for free? The superintendent of the conservation area said that teachers from this school were free to take their students into the forest anytime. He told me that a forest was the best educational resource a school could have."

"We have a great schoolyard. Lots of trees. We see deer all the time."

David sat down awkwardly at a student desk. "I've brought this up with a couple of teachers. I haven't gotten much support."

"I'm not surprised," said Roger. "For most teachers, the classroom is safe. They have set it up the way they want. They've made the rules. It's structured. Outside, things start to break down."

David extricated himself from the student desk and stood up again. "That's backwards. My students are so excited to go outside. They're keen to learn. The way I see it, out there is where things come together."

Roger wiped down chairs with a wet rag. "A lot of teachers just don't have the skill set to control students outside, nor do they have a knowledge base to teach kids about anything they find out there."

"I didn't know what we'd find in the stream. I learned everything from Jesse Young's grandfather."

Roger wasn't sure what to say. On one hand, he felt that a first-year teacher like David should probably develop a consistent classroom routine. On the other hand, Roger was frustrated with some of the teachers in the school. It exasperated him to see them photocopying the same worksheets year after year.

Roger said, "You've inspired me to get out of the classroom. I'm planning to go down to the creek in the spring for our biodiversity unit. I'd like you to show me what you did."

David continued to look out the window.

Roger said, "Where *do* your students go to the bathroom?"

FIFTEEN

SINCE JOCK DOBBS HAD LIVED in Monterrey House the longest, he had accumulated the most cupboard space. He always cooked from scratch, and his culinary creations smelled wonderful. However, their complexity left little room for anyone else who wanted to cook.

While he prepared meals, Jock liked to listen to the music he planned to play at the Savannah Club. He often danced around the kitchen, adding ingredients and mixing in time with the music. The lack of communal space, combined with Jock's dinnertime dominance of the kitchen, pushed the more social tenants of Monterrey House out the front door for dinner. The Rising Son benefited greatly from the situation.

"Come on," said Rochelle, poking her head into David's room. "It's Kare Raisu Night."

"What?"

"*Kare Raisu*. Curried rice."

"Okay," said David.

At the Rising Son there was no menu. Mr. Tanaka cooked one meal per night behind the bar. Each day of the week featured its own dish, and each Tuesday he served curried rice. Every Wednesday the patrons got tempura, every Thursday, yakisoba, et cetera. The lack of diversity might have hurt the bar in some ways, but for the young travellers the predictability of the menu was comforting.

As Rochelle poured beer for them, she asked David, "How is your heart?"

David shrugged.

Rochelle said, "Loving someone, even if you lose them, teaches you more about love. You can love better the next time. The capacity to love is not diminished by the loss of love."

Guy was sitting next to Rochelle. They were a couple now.

"Look at me," said Guy. "I love my New Zealand girlfriend, and I love Rochelle. Loving one helps me to love the other. My capacity for love is unlimited."

"I'm not sure what this is," said Rochelle, rotating her thumb back and forth between herself and Guy, "but love is the greatest teacher. Even when we lose it. It's like music. It shows us how good life can be, even for a short time. That's what gives us wisdom. Knowing how good life can be."

"I had a pretty good thing going for a while," said David, trying to pick up a piece of chicken with his chopsticks.

"Then you know," said Rochelle. "You have wisdom."

Guy watched David drop his chicken over and over. "Master-*san* has forks," he said.

Rochelle said, "You have to keep a picture in your head of what a good life is. That picture is like a lighthouse that guides you through the ups and downs."

Guy looked at Rochelle. "I keep a picture of you in my head that gets me through the day. It also involves some ups and downs."

Rochelle started to scold Guy, but the words got stuck in her mouth and she ended up laughing into his shoulder.

Guy said, "She's most beautiful when she doesn't know what to say."

David laughed awkwardly and tried to look at something besides the couple falling in love. He stuck his chopsticks straight up and down in his rice and swirled beer around in his glass.

Tyler had come with them to the pub but had ended up sitting with two Japanese girls at another table. He yelled at David from across the room.

"Dude, *tsukitate-bashi*."

David stared back, waiting for an explanation.

"Dude, don't stick your chopsticks into your food. It's bad luck. That's what the Japanese do at funerals."

RIGHT AFTER MORNING BELL, DAVID and his class went to the

edge of the forest and pointed a microphone at the trees. Yet again, no birds sang. There were a few peeps and chirps, but no extended songs. They did get a good recording of a flock of Canada geese honking overhead and a hidden red squirrel chattering at them from a cedar tree. When it seemed like the students would no longer be able to stay quiet, David started to pack up the iPad.

"Crows!" yelled Robbie Dickenson.

At first it sounded like only a few crows, but then the chattering turned into a cacophony of agitation. The crows were in the forest.

"Something's disturbing them," said David.

Jesse Young said, "There's probably an owl. Crows attack owls in the day so the owls don't eat them at night. Grandpa always says to follow the sound of crows to find something more interesting."

Vicki Asselstine said, "You go in the forest, Mr. Woods, and see what's there."

The students knew about the "no forest" restriction on this current outing.

Lyndsay Armstrong started a chant: "Go in the woods, Mister Woods. Go in the woods, Mister Woods."

The whole class took up the cheer, and David let the chanting run its course. He held up his hands. "No, we'll do a little research. If there is an owl living in our forest, he'll still be there. We'll come back on an official field trip."

"What if I ran into the forest," said Anna Metz, "and you had to follow me? What if you *had* to go in the forest to rescue me? You wouldn't get in trouble for that."

"No, Anna, it's too dangerous in there." David used a deep, authoritative voice. "With the grizzly bears, and the angry squirrels, and the falling acorns. No child should be put in such danger."

The children laughed. He hoped they didn't think he was pretending to be Principal Dixon.

SIXTEEN

"GET LAID," SAID GUY. "THAT will help put things behind you. It could be a new start, a rebirth. Go sit with those Japanese girls Tyler is with."

"They look like they're sixteen," said David.

"You can't tell in Japan," said Guy. "They could be thirty. Master-*san* is probably seventy-five, and he looks fifty."

Rochelle asked, "How old are you, David?"

"Twenty-six."

"That's perfect. When you're thirty you'll have a wife and a job and a mortgage. You'll argue about whose turn it is to walk the dog. But here, today, you should take advantage of this." She waved her hand at the room.

"You're like an astrologer," said David.

"I don't mean take advantage like he means 'take advantage,'" Rochelle said, pointing at Guy. "Meet people. Talk to people. Go places. Monterrey House has the whole world in it. It's terrible living conditions, but it's alive."

"I don't think I've met everyone in the house," said David.

"If you only stay in your room, you'll have wasted a great opportunity," said Rochelle.

"I just need some time," said David.

"Time is going to go by no matter what you're doing," said Rochelle. "Do something interesting. Engage with the world."

Guy jumped in. "I'm serious about the getting laid part. It's a spiritual thing too. It's the spiritual side of love. It's cleansing. It's — what's the word? *Cathartic.* You can use sex to wipe the slate clean. Some girl cheated on you? What are you going to do? Mope around thinking about the past? No. Start a new chapter. Start it with a bang.

It's glorious. I'm not sure where Rochelle's at, but we made love and, bang — I'm in love with her."

"There's not much small talk in Japan, is there?" said David.

"Just be here in the moment. You should allow yourself that freedom," said Rochelle.

"Hey," said Guy, "you're a good-looking bloke. You've got a faraway look in your eyes that chicks dig. What you should do is take all your shitty emotional baggage, all your woe-is-me, take it, load it up, and blow it out your wang."

AS DAVID WAS GETTING INTO his car at the end of the school day, he saw a group of teenagers jogging down the sidewalk in front of Emily Carr. They looked like a sports team from Sir John A. Macdonald Secondary School. He had seen the same group jogging the week before.

David was about to back out of his parking spot when metaphorical bells started ringing in his head. He stopped the car, jumped out, and ran across the front lawn, catching up to the line of students.

"Hey," said David, jogging beside a pair of boys.

"Hey," said one.

"Are you guys from Sir John A?"

"Yeah," said the boy.

"Football team?" asked David.

"Cross-country."

David said, "Thanks," and sprinted ahead. At the front of the line jogged a short, wiry man with curly hair.

David caught up to the man and said, "Hi, I'm David. David Woods. I teach grade four at Emily Carr."

"Nice to meet you. I'm Ted."

Ted kept jogging but stuck his right hand out to David. David grabbed it with his left hand and waved it around.

"You coach cross-country?" David asked.

"I'm a runner. There's not much to coach in this sport."

"Good team this year?"

"Well," said Ted, "there aren't really many meets until the spring, but I like to get a group together at the start of the year. See what I've got."

"Do you run around town every day?"

"We've got a town loop, a school loop, and a conservation area loop."

"You run in the forest?" asked David.

"It's cross-country, so that's best when the trail isn't too muddy."

"I run too," said David.

"In loafers?"

"Well, I just wanted to catch you today. Do you get need to get field trip forms every time you run?" David tensed in anticipation of the answer.

"No," said Ted. "When students sign up for cross-country, parents sign a form. 'Participation in the above sport will entail leaving school property,' et cetera."

"So the cross-country running team can leave school property anytime?"

"It's a blanket waiver. It's part of the deal. If you sign up for this, we're going to run places. Are you planning to start a team?"

"I'm planning to start something," said David.

SEVENTEEN

DAVID SAT ACROSS FROM THE two Japanese girls. On Rochelle's advice, he was engaging with the world.

"*Kanada-jin*," said Tyler, pointing at David. "*Sensei desu.*"

"Ohhhhh," said the girls, nodding.

"David, this is Kaori and Den. They're Master-*san*'s nieces," said Tyler. "I wouldn't get too frisky or anything."

"No, no," said David. "Nice to meet you."

"How do you like Japan?" asked Kaori.

"Kyoto is very beautiful," said David.

Den whispered to Kaori.

Kaori said, "Den wants to know your height. How tall?"

"Six foot four."

The sisters whispered.

Kaori said, "How many centimetres?"

"About a hundred and ninety," said David.

"Ehhhhhhh. *Sugoi*," said Kaori. "Amazing."

More whispering.

"Den says you must be a great teacher."

"Because I'm tall?"

"You are a tall Canadian teacher. Strong." Kaori flexed her muscles.

"There are good short teachers too," said David.

"Are you a good teacher?" asked Kaori.

"I'm not as good as I thought I was," said David.

Kaori seemed puzzled by the comment. She said, "Tyler teaches us English. On Sundays."

Tyler had left the table and was pretending to karate-chop some girls at another table.

"What are you learning in your English lessons?" asked David.

Very deliberately, Den said, "I want to rock and roll all night."

David looked at her quizzically.

"Kiss," said Kaori.

"Wanted, dead or alive." said Den.

"Sometimes we read song-words," said Kaori.

"Hmm," said David.

"Have you learned any Japanese?" asked Kaori.

"Not much," said David. "What does *sho-ga-nai* mean? I have heard a few people say it since I came to Japan."

"Yes," said Kaori, "it is a common Japanese expression. It means 'It cannot be helped.'"

"Can you use it in a sentence?" said David.

Kaori thought for a moment and said, "Everybody has problems." She shrugged. "*Sho-ga-nai.*"

"You can't always get what you want," said Den.

DAVID HELD A COCKER SPANIEL between his knees while Joanna gently pulled a porcupine quill from the dog's nose and dabbed antibacterial ointment on the wounds.

Joanna said, "You just ran after this teacher?"

"They were jogging by. Like a gift from the gods."

"He must have thought you were mad."

"They sign a waiver. Parents sign a waiver. If your child is on the cross-country running team, they may leave school property to practise. Anytime during the year. Now until June."

Joanna said, "But those students are in high school. The kids come and go from school on their own anyway. They go to the Donut Den at lunch, they go to the park to smoke. It's different. Let's do his other end. Almost done, Simon."

Simon the spaniel was whining. David rotated the dog around between his legs so Joanna could work on its backside.

David said, "The running club, though, it's school-sanctioned. It's organized by a teacher. This isn't students running around by themselves after school. The teacher, Ted, he isn't sending forms home every day. There's just one form signed at the beginning of the year."

"It might be different for primary students."

"We're juniors. Fourth grade is junior. And Ted, he doesn't have to tell all the parents where he's going. One day he might run around the school track. If it's nice out, he might take them through the conservation area. If you join the cross-country team, this is what they'll do. It's part of the deal."

Joanna sighed. "Hand me the pliers. There's a broken quill right near the tail. I can't imagine your principal is going to go for this."

"I just have to present it the right way."

"It's not like the old days when kids wandered everywhere on their own. Parents want to know where their children are all the time."

David said, "Louis Metz and his buddies, they're roaming the fields every day. Danny what's-his-name, he was carrying a gun through our yard last week. Their parents don't know where they are or what they're doing."

"The Conservation Meadows parents do." Conservation Meadows was the name of the new subdivision on the edge of town.

"Well," said David, "as part of our commitment to excellence, our pursuit of, uh, ministry standards, our fulfillment of curriculum objectives, every once in a while we might take an educational stroll into the conservation area."

Joanna grimaced. "Hold him tight. I can just see the tip of a quill. Oh, Simon, how did you get quills in your butt?"

The spaniel whimpered and trembled.

David continued, "If you are in Room Four, if you are a citizen of this classroom, as part of our journey of discovery there will be times when we close our books, turn off our computers, bust out of these walls, and see what's going on in the world."

Joanna held the quill up in the pliers. "I got it." David hugged the dog. "*Viva la revolución!* Good boy, Simon. Good boy!"

EIGHTEEN

MR. TANAKA TOOK HIS PICTURES with a Kodak Polaroid camera he had purchased in San Francisco fifteen years earlier. The Polaroid pictures were not great quality, but he liked the impact of taking a picture and immediately tacking it up on the wall. For the transitory clientele of the Rising Son, the message was subtle but moving: We are here now, having fun, and suddenly we are a part of the past. Another photo in a big collage.

Tyler had taken a bowler hat off a hook on the wall and cut a moustache out of a piece of dried seaweed. He was inviting the patrons of the Rising Son to wear the hat and moustache while he took pictures with Mr. Tanaka's camera. Guy was currently sporting the disguise.

"You look like a gambler," Rochelle said. "A mysterious gambler on a train in America."

"And you are my whore," said Guy. "You stand behind me while I flip over a royal flush."

"Yes," said Rochelle, "and scream and hold your head to my bosom after you've been shot."

Rochelle was the next to sport the disguise. Guy waved his developing Polaroid in the air.

"Look, I'm a man," said Rochelle.

"You look like a fifteen-year-old boy pretending to be a man," said Guy. "It's not really doing it for me."

"Charlie Chaplin!" suggested Mr. Tanaka's niece Den.

When it was David's turn, he stuck the papery moustache to his lip and stood up for effect. He was clowning, and it felt good.

Rochelle said, "You don't look like a teacher."

I'm not a teacher anymore, thought David. David the Farmer was also a distant memory.

"You look solemn," said Guy.

Tyler said, "Dude, you look like an undertaker."

DAVID WAS NERVOUS ABOUT TAKING the unlimited field trip proposal to his principal. The day before, David had waited in the school office while Roger talked on the phone with his wife. When Roger started getting animated about a car-repair bill, the secretary, Ms. Richardson, gave David a look that suggested he come back another time.

Now David was sitting in the principal's office while Roger finished an email.

"Okay," said Roger, turning from the computer. "Let's get down to it."

David rubbed his hands together. "On Monday I was talking to a cross-country running coach from Sir John A. Macdonald."

"You ran past my window," said Roger. "I had Ms. Richardson find out where you were going. I thought a student had been hit by a car or something."

"The teacher, Ted, he gets the parents to fill out permission forms at the start of the year."

"Yes."

"It allows students to leave school property for practice for the whole school year."

"Yes."

"Blanket coverage, so to speak."

"Yes," said Roger.

"So I was thinking that…"

"You have to take a cellphone," said Roger.

David raised his eyebrows.

Roger continued. "You have to take a first aid kit. You have to take a whistle. You need the proper supervisory ratio of one adult for every eight students. Every time. You need to get me a map of the area and show me where you're going every time."

David could feel a lump in his throat.

"You can't go more than one kilometre off school property. You can't go in the forest when winds exceed fifty kilometres an hour."

"You've been thinking about this," said David.

"And you have to get consent forms for every single student. You can't drop three students off with Mrs. Martin and take the rest out. It's all or nothing."

David started, "Mr. Dixon, I just want to say …"

"Call me Roger."

"Roger. Roger, I …"

"Forget it."

"No," said David. "This is important to me."

"I get it," said Roger. "Listen, when I started here sixteen years ago, most of the kids walked to school. Nearly all. Now we have to assign teachers to direct traffic in the parking lot. Kids used to educate themselves by catching bugs, by building tree forts, by setting fire to stuff. Now every activity is scheduled and supervised.

"Did you know our school board spent seventeen million dollars on computer upgrades last year, and nobody can show me any research that demonstrates these technological necessities contribute anything to student learning. We cut librarians, we cut special ed, we cut outdoor rinks. But sure as hell, we all got Windows 5000."

"Thank you for your support," said David, standing up. He wanted to invite Roger to dinner.

"No need to hug me or anything, David. Keep up the good work."

They shook hands, and Roger added, "Remember, though, all or nothing."

NINETEEN

DAVID HAD BEEN IMPRESSED BY the quality of the trails in the hills surrounding Kyoto. It turned out that much of the time he had been on something called the Kyoto Circuit Trail, a seventy-kilometre path that circled much of the city.

Outside Fushimi-Inari station, David had seen a sign that said *Point of Starting for Kyoto Trail*. The aimlessness of his hikes did not mesh with David's rural work ethic, and the thought of beginning something from a definite Point of Starting was appealing. Although the title on the sign was in English, the rest of the sign was in Japanese.

While he was trying to interpret the symbols on the sign, a woman of about seventy asked, *"Eigo-no mappu. Eigo wa irimasu ka?"*

Eigo meant "English." *Mappu* must be "map."

"Yes, English map," said David. *"Hai."*

The woman led David to a newsstand and bought a map in English. David tried to pay her, but she waved her hand back and forth.

"Gif-tu. Good walk. Nice for pictures."

"I am Canadian," said David. *"Kanada-jin."*

"Ah, Canada. I go Bam-fu."

"Bam-foo?" said David.

"Bam-fu. Rocky Mountains."

"Oh, Banff," said David.

"Hai, Bam-fu. Very beautiful. More beautiful than Japan."

"No," said David. "Japan is very beautiful. I like Japan."

"Why come to Japan?" she asked.

It didn't seem right to David for him to say "To teach English." Instead he smiled and said, "To walk. I came to Japan to walk."

The woman laughed at him. "To walk?"

He liked the sound of his new vocation. "I am a walker. A professional hiker." It felt good to joke with this old stranger.

The woman bowed to him. "Have a nice day," she said. "Have a nice walk."

IT WAS LUNCHTIME AT EMILY CARR, and Robbie Dickenson was dropping a piece of lunch meat into the aquarium of stream animals.

"Really, Robbie?" said David.

"Crayfish like to eat dead animals, and meat is just dead animal."

"I doubt they get much salami in the stream."

At his desk, David had a satellite map of the conservation area open on his computer. He was using a geometry compass to figure out how far he could go with the class and stay within the one-kilometre restriction. The bridge was only about four hundred metres from the southwest corner of the school property. If there were another bridge crossing the creek downstream, they could complete a pretty good loop in a morning or afternoon.

Anna Metz approached his desk and knocked on the side of it.

"Who is it?" said David.

"Mr. Woods, is it true that we're going to go outside every day?"

"Not every day, Anna. A lot of days, I hope."

"We should go in the rain," said Anna.

"We could go in the rain," agreed David.

"Everyone says, 'Ooh, it's raining. Run. Get inside.' I went camping in the rain one time. It was fun. It's just water."

"I will send permission forms home tomorrow. You can get them signed over the weekend."

"And then we'll go out on Monday?"

"It will probably take a few days for all the forms to be returned. You know how it is, Anna."

"I'll bring mine on Monday."

"You are very responsible."

Anna turned around and yelled at the class, "Everyone get your permission forms signed this weekend!"

At the back of the classroom a few girls started chanting. "Go in the woods, Mister Woods! Go in the woods, Mister Woods!"

TWENTY

DAVID SAID GOODBYE TO THE woman who had bought him the map of the Kyoto Trail, but as he walked away, she called to him.

"No, no. *Chigao*. This way."

She pointed to the map.

"*Ichi-ban*. Number One. *Ni-ban asoko. Fushimi Inari Jinju*. This way. Come."

The woman led David down the street to the Fushimi Inari shrine. There was a bright orange gateway in front of the shrine. It reminded David of the symbol for *pi*.

The shrine was much more ornate than other shrines he had seen in the city or on his hillside hikes. As they entered the grounds of the shrine, there was a fountain with water coming out of the mouth of a stone dragon. In front of the fountain were wooden ladles.

The woman used a ladle to pour water over her hands. Then she used her hand to bring some water to her mouth. David was surprised when she spat the water on the ground beside the fountain. She handed David the ladle, and he repeated the ritual. He held the water in his mouth and looked at the woman, who indicated that he too should spit. She took the ladle from him and rinsed the spittle off the stones.

They walked up to the entrance of the main shrine building, and the woman motioned that David should remove his shoes. In the shrine was a large pot filled with sand in a structure that looked like a wishing well. Sticks of burning incense were stuck in the sand. The woman dropped some coins in a box on the wall and took several sticks of incense from a ledge underneath the box. She lit the incense sticks with a long matchstick and gave David two of them. David copied her as she wafted handfuls of smoke over her head and body.

They placed the sticks in the sand, and the woman clapped her hands and bowed toward the interior of the shrine.

She said to David, "Clean. Clean hands. Clean spirit."

David was happy to participate in this Japanese ceremony, even though he didn't understand it.

With the more solemn part of their visit over, the woman led David to a pair of stone lanterns.

"*Omo-karu-ishi*," she said.

In front of them was a young Japanese couple. The girl lifted the top off one of the lanterns and said, "*Tadai-desu. Oh honto-ni.*" She replaced the lid. The boy patted her on the head.

David's companion opened his new Kyoto Circuit Trail map and pointed at it. "*Omo-karu-ishi.*"

On the map there was a description of the Fushimi Inari shrine. It read, *At the stone lanterns, make a wish and lift one of the stone tops. If you lift up stone and feel it light, your wish will come true.*

It was their turn. "Wish, wish," said the woman.

David wished for the only thing he could.

"Lif-tu, lif-tu."

David lifted the granite cap off one of the lanterns.

"Heavy?" she asked.

"Yes," he admitted. "It is heavy."

"*Kawai-so,*" said the woman. "It's a pity."

Beside the lanterns, a wooden beam was cemented in the ground. The woman squatted down and acted as if she were trying to pull the beam out of the ground. She strained and grunted with exaggerated effort. Finally she gave up. She walked over to a lantern, put her hand on top, and closed her eyes. After a few seconds she lifted the lid.

"Oh," she exclaimed, "so light."

DAVID AND JOANNA'S FARMHOUSE HAD baseboard heating, but it was not enough to keep the house warm on frosty nights. The wood-stove provided more than enough heat, but the wood was expensive. To save money, the couple had purchased an electric heater for their bedroom. Each night as the cold closed in, they escaped to the only warm room in the house.

As a rookie teacher, David was still committed to designing daily lesson plans. In bed he would map out the following day's plan on his laptop. However, on this night, Joanna had commandeered the computer and was researching the side effects of cyclosporine on cats.

"How often do you think you'll go in the forest?" she asked.

"Well, I was thinking that maybe we could do a daily loop through the woods with some stops along the way. But we have a purpose. For example, in math we need to collect data and make graphs. So maybe we identify an area and count the number of evergreen trees." David drummed his fingers on his chest. "But there are stops. I haven't thought about this enough, but maybe the first stop each day is where I present the problem to the class. Then we walk. Then the next stop, after they have thought about things, they suggest solutions. Then we test out things."

"In the forest," said Joanna.

"I think so, or some stuff could be in the schoolyard. But we are outside. That's the important part. Then we end up back at the classroom, and we have to write what we learned, or troubleshoot for the next day. Some stuff would need to be done in the classroom, but we could be getting outside to learn math, English, geography, just about everything. Maybe a half day outside, half day inside."

"This is so crazy," said Joanna. "The drug company website says something completely different from the veterinary site. I don't know how much of the stuff I should be giving. Can you get two volunteers every time you want to go outside?"

"I have George and five parents who say they can come somewhat regularly, and I have an EA who works in the classroom two mornings a week. I think I can swing a schedule."

"I need to get out of the office," said Joanna. "Don keeps saying I can come with him to do cows and horses, but then he gives me some menial job to do in the backroom, and off he goes."

"Don will figure out how good you are. You just need to put in the time."

Joanna handed David the laptop. "You're getting more excited about your job, and I'm getting more discouraged."

"I understand," said David. "You want to go outside too."

TWENTY-ONE

AT THE FUSHIMI INARI SHRINE, the old Japanese woman led David to a wooden post with the number 2 on it. She told David that these markers would guide him along the trail. Beside the shrine were dozens, perhaps hundreds, of small orange gateways, or *torii*, which formed a tunnel leading up a hill. It was a stunning arrangement of architecture, and David asked the woman if she would join him.

The woman grabbed her knees, grimacing. "*Itai*. Too old."

David was disappointed that the woman wasn't able to walk with him. "What is your name?" he asked.

"*Oba-san*," she said.

"Goodbye, Oba-san." David remembered how the innkeeper at the *ryokan* pulled away when he had tried to hug her. He stuck out both his hands palms up, and she clasped them and bowed toward David. David did a half bow back.

Jock from Boston had warned David how aloof the Japanese people could be, but so far David had found everyone to be very friendly. This old woman had seen him looking lost and had bought him a map. When he had trouble with the map, she walked with him.

The week before, he had been lost on a path in the mountains when he met a man in a business suit coming down the trail toward him. David asked for directions but could not understand the man's explanation. The man ended up leading David to his car and driving him to the train station.

After the tragedy in Dumford Mills, many people had offered David help. The school board and the teachers' union offered a raft of professional services. A chaplain from the military base in Petawawa had called because he thought David could be helped by joining a group of veterans suffering from post-traumatic stress disorder.

The truth — which Joanna didn't seem to understand — was that David didn't want help. He didn't want to feel better. David felt guilty for taking antidepressants.

But now, as this playful old woman walked away, he was overcome with gratitude for the assistance she had provided.

He yelled after her, "I'm David. My name is David. Thank you."

Dear Parents,

As you know, this fall the class of Room 4 has taken a few trips into the Condie Creek Conservation Area as part of our Habitats and Communities unit. The students have been learning about the adaptations of plants and animals, and how they interact with their environment and each other to survive. The stream aquarium was fun to design and has been a focus of study and fascination for us all. The conservation area itself is a tremendous resource for our students, and we are lucky to have it so close to us.

Future science units will focus on Rocks and Minerals, Light and Sound, and Pulleys and Gears. I believe that the conservation area could provide a wonderful learning opportunity for these units as well. Given the students' enthusiasm for outdoor education, I think that elements of the natural area could also provide a focus for math and language arts. For our upcoming math unit, I am designing lessons on probability that relate to the survival rates of different plants and animals.

This week we recorded the calls of birds and squirrels as part of our Light and Sound unit. We are investigating how animals communicate with each other using sounds, and how they use colours and patterns for survival. The students heard crows chasing something in the forest and suspect there is an owl living there.

The conservation area provides such a rich opportunity for learning that I would like to be able to take the students into it on a regular basis. Usually the protocol for leaving school property involves filling out field trip forms each time. However, to save having a constant stream of permission slips going home, I would like to send home one permission form that covers students going into the conservation area for the entire school year. In all other aspects, each visit to the conservation area will follow the same procedure as regular field trips. We will have at least two volunteers per visit, and we will take a first aid kit, cellphone, and water. I foresee that most of our visits will take us less than 750 metres from school property, and last less than two hours.

Please fill out the permission form below, indicating if you would be interested in volunteering. Thank you for helping to make Room 4 a vibrant community of passionate learners.

Sincerely,
David Woods

TWENTY-TWO

DAVID WALKED BENEATH THE ORANGE gates that led from the Fushimi Inari shrine up the side of the mountain. From the bottom it was difficult to see how far the path curved upward, but after twenty minutes of hiking, David figured there must have been several thousand *torii* framing this trail. The sunlight reflecting off the *torii* gave the path a pale yellow glow. Despite the heavenly effect of the light, the trail had an unnerving tunnel-like quality that reminded David of his nightmares.

The trail emerged at a small shrine halfway up the hill. The map called this place the "middle shrine." At the entrance to the shrine there was a stone carving of a wolf. David sat down on a bench to sketch it.

David's sketches were comparable to what his artistic fourth-grade students might have produced. There was no thought process to this activity. He didn't outline what he was drawing. He never erased anything. He never evaluated his sketches after they were finished. David, the southern-Ontario farm boy, was somewhat Zen in this manner.

Mitchell had thought Kyoto would be a good place for David to engage in some reflective contemplation, but David had found a routine that precluded reflection. He approached his hiking like a job. Wake up, shower (lying under the tap), shave, eat some toast, buy a can of hot coffee out of a vending machine, walk to the station (Fushimi or Tambabashi), take the train, and walk into the mountains. If tired, stop and sketch. No thinking, no reflection. No remembering. It was a routine that protected him from his darker thoughts.

FIFTEEN OUT OF TWENTY-FOUR PERMISSION forms for the open-ended field trip came back on Monday morning. On Tuesday, six students were absent with a stomach virus, and by Thursday, four permission forms were still outstanding. The class wouldn't be able to get into the conservation area until the next week.

At lunch, David made a map of the area he intended to use. He divided the area into coloured sections and numbered three different hikes that the class might take. The first hike would leave the school-yard, head south to the bridge that crossed Condie Creek, and take a short detour up to a wetland David had discovered on the western side of the stream. Beside the wetland was a clearing where students might be able to stop and write in their journals.

The second hike would head north along the main trail toward the Rideau River, but circle back behind a small subdivision beside the school. The third hike would take them south down the main trail, but would have them weave back north through the forest without following any particular path. David thought that hike number three would be the simplest and would allow for some exploration. He felt if he could get the class into a good routine for taking that hike, he could gradually expand the repertoire.

Because Hugo the crayfish had died during the week, David believed the aquarium needed fresh water. He wrote the names of the students with outstanding permission forms on the black-board.

Robbie Dickenson
Martha Emerson
Chunhua Wong
Martin Staedelbauer

Out of the four, Robbie Dickenson and Martin Staedelbauer were still absent with the stomach virus. Martha promised to bring her form the next day. Chunhua's parents did not speak much English, but Chunhua's mother picked her up at school each day. David would try to catch her after school. It was possible the permission form was hard for Chunhua's mother to understand.

When school was out, David got a phone call from Amanda Dickenson saying Robbie hadn't thrown up at all that day and would bring in his permission form the next day. While she railed against the absence of cursive writing in the curriculum, David could see students gathering in front of the school.

"I'm sorry, Mrs. Dickenson," said David, "I have a meeting with another parent. I'm going to have to let you go."

"Yeah," said Amanda, "no problem. Put me on your volunteer list."

David found Chunhua standing with a couple of other Asian students outside the front entrance. When Chunhua's mother pulled up in a minivan, David approached the passenger-side door. The window slid down.

"Hello, Mrs. Wong," said David.

"Yes, yes, Mister Woods."

"On Friday we sent home a permission form."

"For walking."

"That's right," said David. "For hiking in the forest. But Chunhua hasn't brought the permission form back to school yet."

"Oh, I'm sorry. It is in the mail. Mr. Wong mailed it to the school."

"Okay," said David. "That's fine. That's good. I'll ask Ms. Richardson to keep her eyes open for it. Thank you. You should volunteer. You should come on a hike."

"Yes," said Mrs. Wong, "It is good to walk. It is good for students."

TWENTY-THREE

IT WAS KATSU-UDON NIGHT AT the Rising Son. *Katsu-udon* consisted of a bowl of noodles with deep-fried pork and egg on top.

David sat at a table with Rochelle, Tyler, and Junichi, a Japanese friend of Tyler's who was also studying karate. Guy taught English at a school called the Blossom Academy and would be joining them after work.

David was not sure why the Monterrey House gang kept inviting him out. He rarely contributed anything to the conversation. He didn't argue politics. He didn't make jokes. He listened to the Monterrey gossip, the English-teaching complaints, and the romantic ambitions of his housemates, mostly in silence. He practised using chopsticks and slowly sank into a Sapporo-induced haze until Tyler produced Mr. Tanaka's classical guitar and, as he did each night, serenaded them home.

Despite David's lack of social engagement, when Rochelle invited him to join them that night, he felt a twinge of anticipation, a sensation absent in his life for nearly a year. Now David did his best to coax a pile of ginger-flavoured noodles into his mouth, while Tyler stood beside the table demonstrating a karate stance.

"*Kokotsu-dachi*," said Tyler, legs bent, one in front of the other, hands in fists. "This is when people know I mean business."

Junichi squinted at his friend.

"Now," said Tyler, "this is where I take it to the next level."

Tyler's hands started trembling. Soon his whole body was shaking, and his face was turning red. Everyone in the pub had turned to watch the demonstration. With a final grunt, Tyler relaxed. Junichi laughed.

"That's the power," said Tyler. "That's *ki*, pure *ki* coming out of me. Coming out of my cells, flooding my muscles. And God help the asshole who stands in my way."

Junichi said, "I am confused. Who is the asshole?"

"Are you dissing me?" asked Tyler. "Listen, dude, I'm ready to go ape-shit on you. I'll do the Full Monty, the Boston Crab, the Power Bomb. Just name the time and place." He wiped imaginary sweat from his forehead. "Pour me another beer and we'll discuss your ass-kicking."

"I apologize for the ugly American," said Rochelle.

"I'm Canadian," said Tyler, sitting back down.

Junichi looked at Rochelle and said, "He is an interesting man."

"I know, Ju-man," said Tyler, "you think you are like Mr. Miyagi or something. But in a dark alley I'd rather have Bill Bunyan here than some Buddha wannabe." Tyler was pointing at David.

David raised his eyebrows. "*Paul* Bunyan?"

"Yeah, the dude with the blue cow."

"Paul Bunyan," said David, letting a noodle slip through his chopsticks into his lap.

"Whoever," said Tyler. "Listen, David, dude, I can't watch you eat food like this. Get a fucking fork."

AT THE BLACKBOARD, DAVID ERASED the names of Robbie Dickenson and Chunhua Wong from the list of students with pending permission forms. The only delinquent students were Martin Staedelbauer, who was back at school after his bout with the flu, and Martha Emerson, who was usually very responsible.

David stood at the front of the class and pointed to a scroll of paper on the wall that said *Resolutions of Room 4*.

"Number seven," he said. " 'Help Each Other Achieve Success.' We would like to go to the conservation area next week. However, we cannot go as a group unless each person brings back his or her permission form. So, Martha and Martin, come through for us. If you can get permission forms signed for Monday, we can plan our first hike for Tuesday. I bought speakers for the iPad, and I downloaded the call of the great horned owl. If there is a great horned owl living in the forest, hopefully we can get it to call back."

David transitioned into his math lesson.

"Now, great horned owls have a territory of ten square kilometres. If we are in the territory of an owl, and our iPad speakers can project sound over an area of one square kilometre, what is the probability that the call will be heard by an owl?"

Anna Metz raised her hand. "Ten percent."

"That's right," said David. "We haven't learned about percent yet, but remember how the chance of flipping heads or tails on a coin was 'one in two'? What is the probability that we will have an owl hear our call? Jesse."

Jesse Young said, "One in ten. One in ten, but it'd be more if we move around. We should try different spots."

"Good thinking, Jesse. We should try different spots. That will increase the probability that we will hear an owl. Also, great horned owls are nocturnal. They come out at night. So the earlier in the morning we can do this, the higher the probability that an owl will still be awake to hear our call.

"But remember resolution number seven. Help each other achieve success. Get those forms in. If we don't have everybody's permission form, then the probability that we will find an owl is zero."

TWENTY-FOUR

ROCHELLE ASKED DAVID, "WHAT WAS your girlfriend's name?"

When the table had been cleared of dishes, Rochelle often started in with personal questions, though not always with David.

"Joanna."

"How long were you a couple?"

"Three and a half years."

"Were you engaged?"

"No. Not really."

Two Decembers back, Joanna's parents had come to the farm for a visit. One night, when Joanna was on the phone, Joanna's mother, Linda, took David aside and handed him a small box. Inside was the wedding ring of her mother — Joanna's grandmother. It had been made in Scotland and had thistles engraved around it.

Linda whispered to David, "Joanna was my mother's favourite. She would want her to have this. I see Joanna now, and she is so happy. You have jobs, you are living together. I don't know what the next step will be, but I didn't want to wait until it was too late."

Joanna's father, Doug, was easygoing and had always been friendly with David. Linda had been slower to warm to her daughter's boyfriend, unsettled by his imposing size, and disappointed that the relationship was taking Joanna far from the family home in Bright's Grove.

The deliberate way she handed the box to David made him believe that the ring was very special to her. He nodded his appreciation. "Thank you for your trust."

Linda said, "I shouldn't say this, but if for some reason things don't work out, please give it back to me."

That was seventeen months ago. For David, it could have been seventeen years.

Rochelle brought David back to the present with a staccato of questions.

"Did you have any children?"

"No."

"Did you live together?"

"Yes."

"Who ended it?"

"Me."

"Did she cheat on you?"

"No."

"How did you come away with a broken heart when you ended a relationship with a girl who was true to you?"

As much as he'd grown comfortable with the Rising Son gang, there was always a level of anxiety for David in these conversations. He didn't want to lie to Rochelle, but he didn't want to open up about his personal history either. The impossibility of reliving the past outweighed the smaller pain of inventing a lie.

He said, "It just didn't work out."

DAVID HAD A LARGE HUNK of a maple tree balanced on the frame of a wood splitter. David's father, Archie, pulled on a black knob that sent a hydraulic wedge creaking through the knotted grain. It was an exercise that required a lot of trust. If Archie pulled on the black knob before David was finished positioning a log, David's hand would be trapped between wood and steel. They communicated mostly through subtle nods.

Archie would not have driven six hours for a visit, but David had had ten cords of wood delivered the previous weekend. Crossing Ontario to help with a job was more within Archie's motivational orbit.

"That's good wood," said Archie.

"Sugar maple," said David, readjusting the slab for another run. "You should have brought Kyle."

"He was going to an equipment auction in Milton today. We need a new trailer."

"You don't give him a blank cheque for that, do you?"

"No, but you know Kyle. He likes to wheel and deal. He'd rather scheme to save a couple bucks than have to work for it."

David kicked at a piece of wood that was almost split.

"Flip it around," said Archie.

"Don't let Kyle manage the books," said David.

"No, no. Listen, he's doing okay. He got us a good contract with the processor in Blenheim. And we're experimenting with a couple of hybrids for next year."

David swung a sledgehammer at the stubborn log, and the big slab fell apart.

David repeated, "Don't let him run the books."

Archie pulled a glove off with his teeth. "Kyle will never be out there digging irrigation ditches or nothing, but he's got good business sense. He thinks about the future. We'll be all right."

"Just don't give him too much too soon."

Archie turned off the splitter and said, "Let's stack for a bit."

A tin overhang extended off the kitchen roof at the side of the house, and David had put down wooden pallets there to keep the logs off the ground. It took them half an hour to pile the wood they had split. The stacking proceeded mostly in silence.

When they were done, Archie retrieved his cold coffee out of the truck and leaned on the hood. "In my mind," he said, "the farm is still half yours. Not now, but when your mom and I are through. Fifty-fifty with Kyle."

"Oh, Dad, Jesus. How do you think that would work?"

"I know," said Archie. "You've got something different going on now, but some day you might need the place. And just because Kyle's in there now, that don't mean forever neither."

"Dad, I'm a teacher."

"Listen," said Archie, "for a couple of years there, I thought I'd be a welder."

David shook his head. "I don't know what you're saying. You want

Joanna and me to quit our jobs and move in with you and Mom and Kyle? We're a little far down the road for that."

"This ain't for now," said Archie. "For the future."

TWENTY-FIVE

AT THE RISING SON, TYLER had left David's table to join a crowd from the High Five House, a dormitory-style hostel two subway stops down the Keihan Line from Monterrey House. Tyler was replaced by Guy, arriving from his job at the Blossom Academy.

Rochelle was still trying to figure out what had precipitated David's heartbreak.

"She didn't cheat on you?"

"No."

"She didn't love you?"

"She did."

"Something happened."

David shifted around in his seat. He wondered if his face looked as red as it felt.

Guy jumped in to rescue him. "Listen, babe, there are lots of girls I could love but not live with. Being in love doesn't guarantee a happy ending."

"That's true," said Rochelle. "But that type of relationship slowly breaks down. David left his job. He left his home. He left his country. He can't even talk about it. Something happened."

Tyler's friend Junichi was still at the table. He was studying his hands clasped in front of him.

"Please forgive my new Israeli girlfriend," said Guy. "Please forgive *girlfriend number two*. She knows we have to split up eventually, so she protects herself from the hurt. She is fascinated by those who feel more deeply."

"He's right," said Rochelle. "Next year I will be stringing barbed wire in the IDF, and he'll be in Auckland cutting diamonds with the future Mrs. Kelliher. But that's why we're the perfect people to talk to.

We have no connection to you except right now. We are here now. On Katsu-udon Night in the Rising Son in Kyoto. It's a miracle we are here together at this moment."

"That is true," said Junichi.

"Listen," said Rochelle, putting her hand on David's arm, "I'm just going to ask you, and you can answer or not, but I have to ask you." Rochelle scrunched up her face. "David, did Joanna die?"

Suddenly the Japanese pub was too small for David. There was not enough room under the table for his legs. The lightshade above the table was too close to his head. Junichi, who was sitting beside him, could sense the panic and stood up. David scrambled out of the booth and through the Golden Gate Bridge curtain that separated the bar from the street.

It was late May, and the diesel-scented air was still warm. Across the street from the Rising Son was a park designed for young children.

A woman washing her dishes looked out the window of her third-storey apartment. What she saw was a very large man sitting on a small red dragon. The wooden dragon was connected to the ground by a thick metal spring. The man had his hands on the ear-shaped handles and was propelling himself back and forth with such force that the head and tail of the dragon were hitting the ground.

The probability that this man was suffering from emotional distress was one hundred percent.

KNOWING THAT DAVID AND HIS father would not take a break from stacking wood to eat lunch, Joanna had brought the men some buns with turkey and cheese.

When Joanna went back in the house, Archie said, "She's a good woman." He said it in the same way he had said, "That's good wood."

David thought his father probably meant, "She keeps a good house." Archie had grown up in a world where the men conducted business and the women kept the home fires burning. Archie would have felt at home in a Mennonite community.

Archie was also impressed by Joanna's way with animals. Archie owned a temperamental gelding named Hershey. He loved the horse and whenever possible would forgo the tractor and use Hershey to pull a wagon or sleigh around the property. Early in David and Joanna's relationship, Joanna had secured Archie's approval when she removed some locust thorns from Hershey's lips.

In his first year at university, David had dated a Filipina named Sampaguita. The only time Archie met Sam was outside the barn on their farm. Archie had formed a negative opinion of her based on her insecurity around Hershey.

"The girl's too skittish," he had declared.

Now, as Archie surveyed the field behind David's house, he made another assertion: "The ground's too rocky."

"It's fine for corn," said David.

"Yeah, well we've got three feet of topsoil at home."

"That's why your land is so valuable."

"It's your farm too."

"I'm a teacher, Dad."

"Well, teach at home then."

David was happy his dad wished they lived closer, but when David and Joanna visited, Archie would putter around in the barn or go to the racetrack without telling anyone.

Part of the problem was that Archie was uncomfortable with David living east of Toronto. Eastern Ontario was a different world for Archie, and he made a point of telling David so. The hardware store had a strange layout; the eggs at the local restaurant tasted funny; the soil in the field wasn't deep enough.

David said, "Joanna and I agreed: whoever got a job, wherever it was, that's where we would go. I thought she'd get a job first, but it was me, and it was here, so here we are."

Archie dropped a scrap of turkey to an orange cat that was weaving between his legs. He said, "One time your mother decided we'd take a trip by spinning a globe and sticking a finger on it."

"Where did it stop?"

"Finland."

"You've never been to Finland."

"Nope. Went to Boston instead."

David laughed. "How does that relate to us?"

"Well," said Archie, "fate — fate will take you anywhere if you let it. Sometimes you got to decide not to let it."

TWENTY-SIX

DAVID SAT ON A STAIRCASE that led to an apartment above the Rising Son. He'd been there for half an hour, wondering if he should go back into the bar and brave its intimate conversations. It would probably be better to tell his friends the truth than to skirt around their questions. He knew he would have to go through the whole story in excruciating detail when September came. He had been hoping to live in painless anonymity for his five months in Japan.

Mr. Tanaka came out of the bar with two crates of bottles stacked on top of each other. He could not see over the top of the boxes and would have walked into David if David had not said something.

"Let me help," said David.

Mr. Tanaka looked around the boxes. "Ah, David-*san*. So."

David took the top box, and Mr. Tanaka said, "*Asoko-de*," motioning up the staircase.

David followed him up the steps into the apartment above the Rising Son. Mr. Tanaka put his box down and turned on a light. They were in a small kitchen. Off the kitchen was a room, probably a bedroom by design, stacked to the ceiling with boxes. Mr. Tanaka took David's box and disappeared into the cardboard maze. He reappeared and announced, "Welcome to my home."

A woman in a bathrobe entered the kitchen through a curtain beside the refrigerator. The curtain had a picture of Mount Fuji on it. She smiled and bowed to David. David returned the gesture with an awkward bow-nod combination.

Mr. Tanaka said, "This is my wife, Atsuko." He said to his wife, "David-*san*."

Atsuko said, "Ah, so, so. *Kanada-jin, ne?*"

"Yes," said David. "I'm from Canada. Near Niagara Falls."

Mr. Tanaka said, "Atsuko guessed you from your height."

David said, "You've talked about me with your wife?"

"Yes. Yes, of course."

David looked around the tiny apartment and said, "This is your home?" He felt ashamed the moment he said it. He added, "I mean, I didn't know you lived above the restaurant."

"Yes," said Mr. Tanaka. "It is very small, *ne?*"

"I'm sorry," said David. "That was rude."

"No, it is tiny compared to American houses, compared to Canadian houses. In Japan we say, 'Rich Japan, poor Japanese.'"

Atsuko said something to her husband.

Mr. Tanaka said, "Atsuko says that you have not seen our living room, our bedroom, or our dining room."

David looked around. Mrs. Tanaka motioned toward the Mount Fuji curtain. David went forward uncertainly. He pulled back the curtain and saw a small room with *tatami* mats on the floor. There was a table in the middle with some books and teacups on it. A baseball game flickered on a black-and-white television with no sound.

"Same. Same," said Mrs. Tanaka.

Mr. Tanaka said, "Would you like to see the music room and reading room and entertainment centre?"

Mrs. Tanaka pointed to the curtain, laughing. "Same. Same."

AFTER PILING WOOD, ARCHIE AND David washed their hands in the kitchen. David's mother, Lillian, set the table. At dinner, Joanna served cabbage rolls with carrots and wild rice. She said, "I made my mother's cabbage roll recipe, with the Woods family's cinnamon twist."

"What's the twist?" asked David.

"Cinnamon," said Joanna.

"The key," said Lillian, "is that you add just enough cinnamon that you can't taste it."

Joanna laughed.

Archie said, "What's funny is she means it. We've been eating cabbage rolls for thirty years. Each time it's a different recipe. Ginger cabbage rolls. Maple cabbage rolls. I'm a good husband, so I always say, 'These are delicious,' but honestly, they all taste the same to me."

Lillian said, "Archibald, I could serve you pieces of cabbage wrapped around hotdogs and you'd say, 'These are delicious, dear.' I don't think you'd notice. But if I give him a light beer by mistake, he can tell the difference in one sip."

"Well, these cabbage rolls are delicious," said Archie. "And this beer is a delightful nineteen- twenty-five Chateau Molson."

Lillian said to Joanna, "Tell us about your job, dear."

Joanna said, "What would you like to hear about first, Mrs. Woods? The cleaning up of urine, the cleaning up of feces, or the cleaning up of vomit."

"Start with vomit," said Archie, plopping sour cream on a cabbage roll.

"It's terrible," said Joanna. "I feed the animals and clean cages and put down pets. It's not what I hoped for. It's not what I studied for."

"Are there other vets you could work for?" asked Lillian.

"There are, but it's all the same. You have one old vet that the place is named after — mine is Moreland Large Animal Veterinary, after Don Moreland. The old vet sees the animals, and the young people are stuck in the back doing all the dirty work."

"You just need to put in the time," said David. "In a few years you'll have the Shayne Veterinary Practice, and you'll have kids in the back doing your dirty work."

"He's probably right," said Archie.

Joanna said, "You didn't put in any time, David. You've been at Emily Carr a couple of months, and you're a rock star. Oh, Mrs. Woods, you should see it. We walk around town and everyone's waving at him. Kids are hugging him. It's like he's the mayor or something."

"Your time will come, dear," said Lillian. "Though maybe your clinic will be called *Woods* Veterinary Practice."

"Maybe it will be called Mrs. Woods' Shit-Cleaning Services," said Archie.

TWENTY-SEVEN

MR. TANAKA LED DAVID BACK down the stairs to the entrance of the Rising Son. As David stood outside, he could hear Tyler singing a Neil Young song.

He took a deep breath and entered the pub. Rochelle saw him first. She came over quickly and wrapped her arms around him.

"I'm sorry," she said. "Your personal life is none of our business. You don't need to tell us anything." She was talking too loudly. David suspected that Rochelle had downed several glasses of Sapporo since his breakdown.

Tyler was sitting on the bar, banging away on Mr. Tanaka's classical guitar. He winked at David as Rochelle dragged him back to the table.

Guy patted David on the back. "He has returned. Our circle is not complete without our lumberjack."

"I'm sorry," said Rochelle again.

David said, "Things are a little complicated."

"Don't worry," said Rochelle. "We're here now. The past is past. The past is wasted time and old girlfriends and failed expectations. This is it right here."

"She didn't die," said David.

"It doesn't matter," said Rochelle, close to yelling. "This is it right here." She reached out and grabbed David and Junichi's hands. Guy joined in and they held hands around the table.

Rochelle shook their arms. "This is it, right here. Sing it, Tyler."

"Keep on rockin' in the free world."

David leaned over and said to Guy, "She didn't die."

Guy yelled back over the singing, "Did you kill her?"

85

ON SUNDAY, DAVID WASHED BREAKFAST dishes with his mother. Archie announced he was going to town to put gas in the truck. Archie didn't go anywhere without a full tank.

"You have a very nice house," said Lillian.

David said, "It's falling apart. If Joanna can get full-time work, we could start thinking of buying our own place."

Lillian scrubbed at a pot that was already clean. "Your father still hopes you'll be part of the farm someday."

"Mom, that ship sailed the day Kyle enrolled in agriculture."

"We didn't know Kyle would come back to the farm."

David snorted. "What farm did you think he was studying to run?"

"Well, there's room for both of you, I think. There's the office part of the farm, there's the orchards, there's the fruit stand."

"You're right, Mom. There is enough physical space — enough acreage — for two people to exist comfortably."

"Kyle has mellowed. He's reading books."

"Machiavelli?"

"We miss you, David. We didn't know you'd end up so far away."

David took the pot out of his mother's hands. "Look, Mom, I miss you too, but Joanna and I have got a good thing going here. The town is great. The school is great. My class is fantastic. I mean, I love the farm, but I'm a teacher. I might be a good teacher."

Lillian started crying.

"Oh, Mom."

"I'm happy for you, David."

Joanna came into the kitchen carrying a kitten. When she saw Lillian crying, she turned to leave.

David said, "Don't go. Mom's happy."

Joanna put her hand on Lillian's shoulder.

Lillian said, "Take care of my baby."

TWENTY-EIGHT

Dear David,

Thank you for your letter. I have been worried about you. We heard on the news there was an earthquake in Japan. Did you feel it? Japan seems so far away (farther than Dumford Mills!). I looked at websites of Kyoto. It looks very pretty. I hope you are eating well. I hope you find a job you like. I miss you very much. Though summer will come and go faster than you know.

David, I am sorry about your time at home. I wish we could have been a more supportive family. We will never be able to understand what you are going through, but you never spent any time in the house. You never talked to us. Kyle said he invited you to hockey all the time.

Anyway, I don't want you to be going through your troubles alone. Please call me. I want to talk to you. I want to talk to my son.

I put your picture on the fridge, just like when you were in school.

Take care. Love, Mom.

Dear David,

It was good to hear from you. Just seeing your handwriting meant a lot to me.

It's nice that you're walking and drawing pictures and visiting squirrel zoos, but I wish you had more to say. "Do what you need to do"??? What does that mean?

When you left me to go back to your family, I thought that was a good idea. It was good for you to get out of Dumford Mills. But you were gone for eight months! The only thing that kept us going were my visits to the farm, and even then you were distant.

Then I get an email saying you're going to Japan. Japan? Why would you go to Japan? I don't understand why you're still running away. I feel *like you are running away from me. Are you punishing yourself? Is this your way of making things even with the world?*

My mother told me that you were going to propose to me. We were going to be husband and wife. The point of being married, David, is so that you can share things with another person, good and bad. These are shitty times, that's true, but you are stronger with me, and I am stronger with you.

I am trying to understand your behaviour, I am trying to be supportive, but I don't understand this Japan thing. It makes no sense to me. I want to be there for you, but it's impossible when you fly off to the other side of the world. And you can't even tell me. You let me know in an email! If this was Mitchell's plan, that makes more sense, because Mitchell is an idiot.

David, I am scared and angry and sad, and I don't know where I am in the world anymore. Maybe this will become clear to you in September but I have news for you. It wasn't your fault. The sooner you can get to that conclusion the better.

CONDIE CREEK WASN'T YOUR FAULT!

Forgive yourself. Please. For everyone.

I am still here in good old Dumford Mills. I am still playing the faithful spouse-in-waiting. I don't know if it's a role I want to play much longer.

Joanna

ON MONDAY MORNING, DAVID WAS stapling worksheets together when he saw Martin Staedelbauer enter the classroom. David went over to the chalkboard where Martin's and Martha Emerson's names were written in yellow chalk. David hovered an eraser over Martin's name.

"Martin! Do you have the permission form?"

Martin reached inside his backpack and rummaged around. After a minute he emptied the contents of his knapsack on the classroom floor. Papers scattered. An orange rolled against the wall.

"Martin, the suspense is killing me. Please tell me you have the form."

Martin waved a half sheet of white paper in the air.

"Eureka!" said David, erasing Martin's name with exaggerated flourishes. "One left. I can hear her voice in the hall. Our last applicant."

Martha entered the classroom.

"Good morning, Miss Emerson."

"Good morning, Mr. Woods."

"Miss Emerson, I'm sure you will have an easier time finding your permission form than Mr. Staedelbauer here." Martin was still on his hands and knees under a desk.

Martha stopped in front of David. She said, "Mr. Woods, my mother would like to talk to you."

Trouble. "Is she interested in volunteering?"

"My mom works. She can't volunteer. Anyway, she doesn't think we should go in the forest."

David felt the energy drain out of him. He erased Martha's name.

Robbie Dickenson said, "We can't go in the forest 'cause of Martha?"

David had only taught grade four for a short time, but he knew that nine-year-olds could read his body language like a book. He tried to maintain a professional front.

"Martha's mother has some questions about the permission form. I will talk to her. We'll get things worked out. The forest isn't going anywhere."

David had spoken to Nina Emerson a few times in the hallway and during parent-teacher interviews. There had been nothing problematic about their previous chats. Martha was a good student, and David had never had a reason to call her mother.

However, each day students took home a planner outlining classroom activities, and reminders about what to bring to school. Each page in the planner had a comments section where David could communicate back and forth with parents. The second time the class had planned to visit the conservation area, David had written in Martha's planner, *Remember to bring in your permission form for the stream!*

Nina Emerson had written back, *Again?*

TWENTY-NINE

TODAY THE KYOTO TRAIL HAD taken David to Kiyomizu-dera, a large Buddhist temple on a hill on the eastern side of Kyoto. On the street leading up to the temple were many small restaurants and shops that sold souvenirs. Outside one shop there was a large barrel of ice water filled with cucumbers impaled on wooden sticks. David bought one and munched on it as he walked up the hill.

The entrance to the temple consisted of a very wide, steep set of stairs. A Buddhist monk was waving a pot of incense on the steps.

At the top, David found a wide wooden platform that looked out over the city of Kyoto. An older white couple was standing at the railing.

The man told his wife, "You're supposed to make a wish. But, get this. To have your wish come true, you have to jump off this stage."

The woman said, "I'd prefer not to kill myself to have my wish fulfilled."

"It says here that hundreds of people have jumped off."

David looked over the edge. It was forty or fifty feet down to the bushes below. It wasn't certain death, but it would be difficult to come away without serious injury.

He thought about what Mitchell had said — how Joanna worried that David might kill himself. He had been depressed, that was certain. He had withdrawn socially. But despite possessing enough pills to kill a few dozen people, he had never considered ending his life. Whatever restitution David owed the world, he would pay in person.

Over the past year he had mastered the ability to perform tasks — whether it was chopping wood, hiking, or sketching — without thinking about anything else. He could go hours without thinking about his family or Dumford Mills or Joanna. Whether this mental isolation was good for his long-term emotional health didn't matter. It protected him now.

David joined the lineup of people under a small waterfall beside the temple. The water came down bamboo troughs in three streams. Tourists were sipping water from the streams using long ladles. When it was David's turn, he stood under the waterfall and watched the people beside him, looking for clues to the ritual. He wondered whether he should swallow the water or spit it out like they did at the Shinto shrine.

David's body language must have betrayed his uncertainty about the process, because a Japanese man stepped forward and explained the choices before them. The man pointed to the first stream of water and said, "That water is for long life." Pointing at the middle stream he said, "Good school. *Eto-ne*. For good grades." Pointing at the last he said, "Good love."

David considered the options and settled on "good love." He took a sip of the love water and gave the ladle to the man. The man smiled and nodded.

"Good choice."

ROGER DIXON WAS TYPING ON THE computer in his office. His glasses were halfway down his nose, and he seemed to be concentrating very hard. David sat in a chair on the other side of Roger's desk, squeezing a foam globe between his knees.

Roger stopped typing and took off his glasses. "Trouble?"

"Yes," said David. "With one of the parents."

"Let me guess," said Roger. "Nina Emerson or Tara Lin."

"Nina Emerson."

Roger said, "She's a lawyer. A tax attorney or something. I know her from parent council. She's a stickler for detail, but I haven't found her to be unreasonable. You should be able to smooth her over. Play nice. Let her have some control over the outings and you should be good."

"I'm nervous," said David.

"You should try to meet her in your classroom. If you try to catch her in the parking lot, she'll pretend to be in a big hurry and will probably blow you off. Better yet, there's a parent council meeting Wednesday. Ask to speak with her before the meeting."

"What if she torpedoes the whole thing?"

"Then you lick your wounds and come back with another plan. You try to go to the forest once a month instead of every day. Or you try again next year. David, teaching is a marathon. You've got thirty more years of this. There will be dozens of Nina Emersons. There will be parents way worse than Nina. And I don't know if you are aware of this — it's your first year — but you have a dream class. There are teachers in this school having mental breakdowns over the students in their classes. Count your blessings and move on if you have to."

Roger pointed at his computer. "Right now I am dealing with a situation where one of our students was left alone over the weekend while the parents went to a casino. Children's Services is involved. The police are involved. Over the course of a normal teaching career, this is what you get. I hope it works out with Mrs. Emerson, but this is just part of the deal. Welcome to teaching."

David stood up and put the foam globe back on a shelf. "I'm sorry," he said. "I shouldn't even be bothering you about this. You're right, it's nothing really."

"No, it's something, David. But this profession is a very long series of somethings. It's one battle in the war."

"Got it. Thanks."

Roger added, "Please don't stop coming in here. The teachers I see in this office are teachers who need permission to try something or need advice on how to start something new. Those teachers keep this school humming. The teachers who never come in here are the ones counting the days until their pension kicks in."

David said, "You're a good principal."

"When you meet Nina, wear a tie. Look professional."

David left the office feeling sheepish. Maybe he was just a farmer pretending to be a teacher.

THIRTY

ON THE GROUNDS OF THE Kiyomizu-dera temple, David found himself standing in another queue outside a brown and white building. David thought it was probably a museum of some kind, but he wasn't sure. It didn't matter. Wasn't this what Rochelle had encouraged him to do? Go with the flow, be open to whatever experiences presented themselves?

A Japanese man in brown robes was walking down the line, collecting coins from the tourists. David had no coins, so he gave the man a thousand-yen bill. The man bowed slightly and gave David a card. David expected some change, but the man continued down the line.

The front of the card was printed in Japanese. On the back it said:

You are entering the womb of the bodhi-sattva.
For security of person please hold to guard rope.
Upon spying of lighted stone rotate stone with wishful thinking.

David did not understand Japanese religion. He wasn't sure what the difference was between Buddhism and Shintoism. Temples were Buddhist and shrines were Shinto, but the two religions seemed to blend together in different places. Both seemed to combine grand ceremony with playful ritual. David did not know how all the stone-turning, water-sipping, bell-ringing, and wish-making fit together. However, he was prepared to grasp at any metaphysical straws and formulated a stone-turning wish ahead of time.

As people entered the building, they removed their shoes and placed them in plastic bags. David put his shoes in a bag and hoped that the odour was not noticeable to the people around him. An old

Japanese woman behind him was struggling to remove her shoes. David considered helping her but didn't want to lose contact with the people in front of him who were disappearing down a staircase.

He followed a group of schoolgirls down the stairs. As they descended it became darker, and the girls giggled nervously. David grabbed the rope on his right. At the bottom of the stairs the corridor made a turn to the left. As he moved forward, David was plunged into total darkness. The girls were farther ahead of him, and he could hear them screaming excitedly.

If David had considered more thoughtfully what entering a metaphorical womb would be like, he could have avoided this experience. He might not have gone with the flow. Fate will take you anywhere, his father had warned. Sometimes you got to decide not to let it.

However, having made the excessive donation, prepared his wish, removed his shoes, and followed Japanese teenagers down a stone staircase, he was now in a pitch-black underground tunnel. This was where fate had brought him. David was awake, breathing hard, and neck-deep in his nightmare.

He pressed himself against a stone wall. The cries of the girls had stopped. David could hear no one behind him. He stood shivering, listening for voices. The air smelled like wet soil. David grabbed the rope with both hands and crept tentatively forward.

He could have turned around, but, as in his dream, the thing he needed to find was in front of him. He dropped the bag with his shoes and grabbed at the rope, hand over hand. In the distance was a faint light. David let go of the rope and scrambled recklessly forward. Perhaps if he made it to the light, his nightmares would end.

When he reached the illuminated stone — the stone of wishful thinking — what David had prepared to say was "I hope Joanna Shayne will still marry me."

What he said — what he yelled — was "Anna!"

WHILE HE WAITED FOR NINA Emerson, David paced nervously around the classroom. He wore a shirt and tie with shiny new shoes.

94

He'd gotten an unnecessary haircut and felt the same anxiety he had experienced months earlier, waiting for his job interview.

The parent council meeting started at 7:30. It was 7:10 and David was beginning to fear (perhaps hope) that Nina would not show. At 7:20 he started realigning desks. At 7:22 Nina Emerson knocked on the door to Room 4. David spun around and hit his shin on one of the metal bars that connected students' desks to their chairs.

"Mr. Woods, sorry to frighten you," said Nina.

Nina Emerson was tall, with wavy brown hair and soft features. When David had seen her in the hallways, she had worn skirts and pantsuits. She had looked like a lawyer. Tonight she was in jeans and a white knitted sweater. She looked like a friendly mom.

They shook hands and Nina said, "So, Mr. Woods, about this permission form."

"Yes," said David. "As an educational resource, I believe the conservation area is a rich —"

She cut him off. "I'm not comfortable with you taking Martha wherever you want, whenever you want. I can't believe Roger is going along with this."

David had prepared a speech. He wasn't sure whether to continue it. "We have three different routes planned out. Let me show you a map." He lifted a folder off his desk and papers spilled out everywhere. David pawed around on the floor.

"Nice shoes," said Nina.

David stood up, the papers clenched in a messy spiral. He said, "The map was on top."

Nina looked at the clock. "It's November, David. It's cold. It's windy. There are no leaves on the trees. You've already finished the habitats unit."

David dumped the papers on his desk. He said, "We don't need the leaves. It's the forest itself. It's just being outside. It's seeing a bunch of crows."

David's hands were waving in the air. This was not the speech.

"Many other parents agree with me," said Nina. "I find it hard to believe that I'm the only one who did not sign the form."

David straightened up, the passion of his belief expanding his frame. "I've just found that the students are more engaged when we are in that environment. They have more questions. They want to learn more."

Nina said, "After the first trip, Martha came home with wet socks and a cut on her hand. She said Jesse's grandfather taught the class and you walked around taking pictures."

"Martha was very involved that day. She was right in there. She had wet socks because she ignored the boundaries and went in the deep section."

"Mr. Woods, most teachers need a few years to develop a good classroom routine."

"I've just found that the students, when they are active and moving and thinking, that their level of learning is, is —"

"I think, Mr. Woods, you've found something that you enjoy doing more than teaching. And yes, the students are very enthusiastic, because they have found something they enjoy doing more than learning."

A closing statement if there ever was one.

Nina said, "I'm late for the parent council meeting. If you'd like, we can continue this discussion at a later date."

David clenched his jaw.

Nina said, "You have a lot of potential."

As she turned away, David said, "They can't all be lawyers."

THIRTY-ONE

DAVID SAT ON THE GROUND outside the womb-shrine. His hair was wet, and he was crying. Just like a real birth.

I need help, thought David. *I need professional help.*

"*Sumimasen.*"

David looked up. A Japanese family stood around him. The family included the old woman who'd had difficulty removing her shoes. They looked at David like they were going to give him money.

David said, "I'm sorry. I don't know what's going on."

A younger woman said, "*Shu-su.*"

David hoped that they were inviting him home with them. "*Shu-su?*"

The woman held out a plastic bag. "*Shu-su.*" They had found David's shoes in the stone birth canal.

David rode the train back to Fushimi-Inari station and walked to Monterrey House in the rain. In the kitchen, Jock was cooking a Cajun stir-fry and playing dance music. There were people in the kitchen whom David had never met. He walked by them without speaking and trudged up the stairs to his attic room.

He sat at his desk and took out a piece of paper. At the top in pencil he wrote, *Dear Joanna.* An hour later there were no more words on the page. Underneath *Dear Joanna* David had sketched a picture of the pencil sharpener that was attached to the desk.

A floor below, David heard Tyler yell, "Tempura Night. Five minutes."

David knew that Guy or Rochelle would be banging on his door soon. He took his shaving kit and towel down to the second floor. Guy was brushing his hair in front of a mirror in the hallway. When he saw David's towel he said, "No time for that, mate. We're leaving."

David said, "I can't go. I'm too tired."

"Tough day in the hills?"

"Yes."

Guy reached into his pocket and pulled out a green barrel-shaped pill. He held it between his thumb and index finger in front of David's face.

"Need a pick-me-up?"

"Maybe," said David.

Guy put the pill in David's shirt pocket and patted him on the chest. "Join us later if you want."

David went down to the front hall and found his shoes. He took them into the bathroom and got undressed. He squeezed a tube of hotel shampoo into the foul-smelling shoes and turned on the tap that was halfway up the shower wall. David lay on the shower floor and put his feet up on the wall. He put the shoes on his chest and let the water run into them. He tilted his chin back, opened his mouth, and, from a foot above his head, dropped the green pill.

LYING IN BED, JOANNA ASKED, "Why did you say 'They can't all be lawyers'? What did you mean?"

"I don't know what I meant," said David. "'Go to hell' is what I meant."

Joanna was laughing. "You've got to talk to her again."

David pulled a pillow over his face. "I can't. It was awful. I had this great research paper on student achievement in the outdoors. I had the map. I had Martha's sketch of the stream. And I dropped everything all over the floor."

"You were presenting a case. You were presenting a case to a lawyer."

"Exactly. But she never listened to my argument." David threw up his hands. "It was 'Case dismissed!'"

"You have to talk to her again. You might need to apologize."

David groaned. "I can't talk to her again. It was like I was a teenager and she was the adult. I was out of my league. I can't relive that again. My year is screwed."

Joanna put her head on his chest.

David said, "If you want a picture that sums up the whole scene, it's me fumbling for papers on my hands and knees, like Martin

Staedelbauer looking for his permission form. And Nina is standing over me with her arms crossed saying, 'Nice shoes.' "

Joanna put her blonde ponytail in her mouth to keep from laughing, her body betraying her by convulsing against David's. David slapped her bottom.

When David fell silent, Joanna said, "I birthed my first cow today."

"What?"

"Becky and Tania were both working today, and the farmer said it looked a little complicated, so Don told me to get in the truck. We went out near Osgoode, and I birthed the cow."

"That's amazing."

"It was a riot. I had the chains on the front legs of the calf, and I was pulling, and Don just kept talking to the farmer. Occasionally he'd say, 'You're doin' fine.' I'm sweating and pulling and all of a sudden the cow gives a groan, and out slides the calf. I tried to catch it, but it just slid through my arms onto the ground. I didn't think it was breathing at first, but I cleared all the goop out of its nose, and it was good. It was fine. Don and the guy just kept talking the whole time. I was amped up, so I yelled, 'It's a girl!' "

"That's neat. That's great. What did Don say?"

"He said" — Joanna switched to a gravelly voice — "*They're all girls, Joey.*"

THIRTY-TWO

WHEN DAVID MOVED INTO MONTERREY House, he had wondered why the attic room was available. Why wouldn't the other tenants want a private room with a desk? Now that it was June, David knew why. In the morning, with the window open and a fan on, the temperature was tolerable. By the afternoon the combination of heat and humidity made the upper floor feel like a sauna. At night David slept in his underwear, and his white futon had become stained with grey Rorschach patterns of dried sweat.

He could have switched rooms when other tenants left the house. The second-floor rooms were cooler, but all four were shared rooms. Given David's proclivity for nightmares and the potential for emotional breakdowns, he didn't feel comfortable taking on a roommate.

The first floor of the house was the coolest, with a small air conditioner in the kitchen window. The two main-floor bedrooms in the converted living room were single rooms but were considered the worst rooms in the house due to the noise. The daily cacophony of English teachers began outside the washroom at seven each morning, and the Rising Son revellers returned just before midnight. Guy had recently moved from the main-floor bedroom beside the kitchen to a room with Rochelle on the second floor.

When Guy moved upstairs, David could have traded the overheated attic room for a cooler and louder first-floor bedroom. However, the hot, tortured sleep David experienced each night was penance for the easygoing days spent strolling and sketching. After he came home from the Rising Son, David felt guilty for enjoying himself. He felt guilty for not thinking about Joanna. He felt guilty for having run away. The nightly sweats helped cleanse his body of shame.

One night, David played cribbage with an Australian traveller named Dane. Dane occupied the other attic room. Dane taught English and worked more hours than the others. He didn't go out with the Rising Son crowd. They sat on the floor in Dane's room to play.

At one point, David said, "It *is* hot up here."

"Pick your poison," said Dane. "A hot room, or seven nights a week of Jock's bloody dance music."

DAVID KNEW HE HAD MADE an error by making the permission forms a big deal. He had pressured the students to bring in their forms, and then some of them had followed his lead by harping at their tardy classmates.

It was also a mistake to write the names of delinquent students on the chalkboard. David had been sure it was just a matter of time until all the forms were returned. He had never anticipated that a parent would balk at allowing a student to participate in activities that had been so successful.

Adding to David's distress, Martha Emerson was a good student. She did not participate in classroom discussions as much as she might have, but she was polite. She worked well with others and did the neatest work of all the students in the class. She was a nice kid, and her teacher had created conditions where she might be socially ostracized for keeping everyone trapped inside all year.

David needed advice but felt his options were limited. Roger Dixon was the staff member David trusted the most, but David thought he had gone to Roger too often lately. Rhonda Martin, who taught Grade Five, was easy to talk to, but she thought David was crazy for wanting to go outside all the time.

During lunch, the school secretary, Veronica Richardson, was making tea in the staff-room microwave.

When she saw David she said, "Now what are you going to do, Mr. Woods?"

David looked at her. "About what?"

"About taking your Scout troop into the wilderness."

"How do you know about that?" David wondered if there was a secret video of his exchange with Nina Emerson.

"Nina told us about her decision at the parent council meeting."

David groaned. "I don't get it. I don't understand why she doesn't want her daughter to take part."

"It's a power thing," said Ms. Richardson. "She does the same thing on parent council. She undermines good ideas just because they weren't hers."

"I'm worried that my students are going to blame Martha. Maybe I'll say I changed my mind, or that the school board wouldn't let us go or something."

Veronica said, "You should tell them the truth. Kids have lots of experience with parents being unreasonable. It's not Martha's fault that her mother is stubborn."

THIRTY-THREE

"HOLY FUCK, IT'S A FUCKING sauna in here."

Tyler had run up the attic stairs to David's room. David sat cross-legged on the floor with a map of the Kyoto Trail open in front of him.

"Jesus Christ, move downstairs. This is fucked."

David said, "It's supposed to cool down this week."

"Dude, listen, I can't do the Tanaka sisters anymore. I'm a terrible teacher, and it screws up my Sundays."

David looked at Tyler.

"It's two hours," said Tyler. "Two o'clock to four o'clock on Sunday afternoons at the Rising Son."

"I've never taught adults," said David.

"There's nothing to it," said Tyler. "They already know English. You just get them talking."

"Just talking?"

"Just talking. Kaori works at Nintendo and wants to go to conferences in America. I don't know why Den comes. It's seven thousand yen for two hours. Easy-peasy."

"Do you have textbooks?"

"Textbooks? That's not how it works here, brother. They bring notebooks, but I've never made them write anything. We talk about movie stars and pop singers for two hours."

"Tyler, to be honest, I don't even know if I want to teach while I'm here."

"I already told them you'd take over. They looked relieved. Sunday at two."

Tyler turned to walk out.

"Wait," said David.

Tyler kept going. "Dude, I can't stay up here. I've got ball-sweat dripping down my leg."

DAVID AND JOANNA WERE IN BED, with the electric heater turned up high. Joanna had the covers pulled over her head. David typed lesson plans into the laptop. A cat David had never seen before walked over the keyboard, and David's notes disappeared.

"This cat wiped out my lesson."

"What?" said Joanna, pushing the covers down.

"The cat stepped on the keyboard, and my file is gone."

"Everything is auto-saved. You sound panicky."

"I need to change all my units," said David. "Everything's off the rails because of one person. One personality."

"You have a nemesis," said Joanna. "You're so polite, you've probably never had a nemesis before."

"My brother was my nemesis for twenty years. Still is."

"You should have a meeting," said Joanna. "You should meet with Martha's mother and some other parents at the same time and explain your plans in more detail. That way would be safer."

"Roger said to give it a break until after Christmas."

"What did the kids say when you told them Martha's mom was killing the field trips?"

"I told them that we'll get out in the schoolyard as much as we can. I told them that we'll schedule formal field trips to the conservation area. I told them that we're all in this together. I said that I understood the Emersons' concerns."

"Mr. Emerson has concerns too?"

"I don't know. If he doesn't, he probably got overruled. Anyway, it was probably lucky for Martha that this week is so cold. The students were happy they didn't have to go outside."

"That's it then?"

"That's it. Though Amanda Dickenson is pretty angry. She's on parent council with Nina. She told me that Nina went on and on at the meeting about my inexperience and my crazy classroom activities."

"There might be some fireworks there. Amanda Dickenson can be abrasive."

"The whole family is pretty blunt. Robbie too. How do you know Amanda?"

"She got her dog spayed last week. She filled me in on everyone in town."

David repeatedly pressed the ESC key on the keyboard. "Amanda told me that to get Nina to relax, they should have a reverse intervention with her."

Joanna laughed. "What's a reverse intervention?"

"It's where you get all of Nina's friends and family together in a room, and you beg her to start taking drugs."

THIRTY-FOUR

DAVID MET KAORI AND DEN outside the Rising Son. The bar was closed on Sundays, but Kaori had a key. They sat at a booth with the two sisters facing David. David wore a short-sleeved dress shirt with a tie. He had bought a large pad of blank paper, which he placed in the middle of the table.

Kaori said, "Thank you for teaching us, Mr. David."

David smiled and nodded. After a pause, Den broke down giggling.

"*Yamete*," said Kaori to Den.

David asked, "What were you learning with Tyler?"

Kaori tilted her head to the side, "A-*no*, English conversation."

Right, thought David. *Just talking.*

David asked, "You are Tanaka-*san*'s nieces?"

"Yes," said Kaori, talking slowly. "Mister Tanaka is my uncle. Our father is another Mister Tanaka. They are brothers."

Den nodded and started giggling again.

"Why do you want to learn English conversation?" asked David.

Kaori said, "In September the conference for international gaming is in Los Angeles. I would like to go."

"Your English is very good," said David. "You will have no problem in America."

Kaori said, "My boss said I must improve my English to be going to the conference. This is my — how you say — personal objective."

"Good, good," said David. "Why do you want to learn English, Den?"

Den hunched in her seat, making herself look very small. She looked at Kaori. "She is my sister."

"You are here for support," said David encouragingly.

"Yes," said Den, grabbing Kaori's arm. "I love my sister."

David wondered how to begin the lesson. He looked around at

the Polaroid pictures of smiling faces tacked to the walls of the pub. Above the girls' heads there was a picture of Rochelle pretending to slap Guy.

David rubbed his hands over the blank pad on the table like a baker spreading flour. He began the only way he knew how.

"This session of the United Nations will now come to order!"

Dear Parents,

This Friday, November 13 at 7:00 p.m., I will be leading an "Owl Prowl" in the Condie Creek Conservation Area behind Emily Carr Public School. We suspect there is a Great Horned Owl living in our forest, and evening is a good time to find him/her. We will walk the Condie Creek trail for about 50-60 minutes, stopping at various points to play a recording of an owl call. Hopefully we can get an owl to call back. If your family would like to join us, meet us in the school parking lot. 7:00, sharp! All students must be accompanied by an adult. Hope to see you there. It will be a hoot!

Mr. Woods

THIRTY-FIVE

ON THE TABLE IN FRONT of Den and Kaori, the large pad of newsprint had become a collage of drawings, sentences, words, and maps.

After an hour it was apparent that the sisters' vocabularies were quite extensive. Their spelling was good and, grammatically, their written English was almost perfect. However, their confidence in speaking was low, and they lacked an understanding of common English colloquialisms. Den, especially, resorted to one-word answers, and David had to encourage her to explain herself more thoroughly. Tyler was right about the Sunday lessons. They would be mostly talking.

David flipped over a new sheet of newsprint. Across the middle he wrote, *When I go to _____, I will _____.* He flipped the pad around so the sisters could read it.

He said, "When I go to *Tokyo*, I will *eat sushi*. Now it is your turn."

Kaori said, "When I go to Los Angeles, I will visit Beverly Hills."

Den stared at the pad of paper. She spoke slowly, pointing a finger at the words. "When I go, I will eat ice cream."

"*Baka!*" said Kaori. She circled words on the page and berated her sister.

Den tried again. "When I go to Canada, I will eat ice cream."

Kaori rolled her eyes.

David said, "Good. When I go to *Nagasaki*, I will *go fishing.*"

Kaori said, "When I go to California, I will get a suntan."

Den said, "When I go to Canada, I will eat a fish."

Kaori punched her sister in the arm.

"*Nan-dai-o?*" said Den.

David looked at his new students. They did not constitute a class, and the scribbles on the page did not constitute a lesson, but in a meaningful way, David the Teacher was back.

ON THE FRIDAY EVENING OF the Owl Prowl, David and Joanna drove to Emily Carr in Joanna's hatchback.

"What exactly is this about?" asked Joanna.

"What do you mean?"

"Is this Owl Prowl thing your way of showing Nina Emerson that you can't be stopped?"

David said, "I mean, I hyped this stuff up for my students. The stream, the forest, the owl. I need to keep it going."

Joanna said, "You'll show Nina. You'll sneak all the kids into the forest at midnight. Nobody's gonna stop you."

"This is for the kids."

"This is about your pride."

David fiddled with his iPad. "You didn't have to come."

In the parking lot, a few families had already gathered. There were the Metzes, the Dickensons, the Youngs (including Grandpa George), the Findlays, and Chunhua with her mother. Holly Metz passed around cookies.

When everyone was standing in a big circle, George Young got a canvas bag out of his truck. The bag looked like it had a statue in it. George reached into the bag and pulled out a large stuffed bird. There were *oohs* and *ahs*.

George held up a stuffed great horned owl. He said, "My buddy hit this poor guy on the highway outside of Bracebridge. That would be thirty-five or forty years ago."

"It looks alive!" said Louis Metz. "It's looking at me."

The kids took turns petting the dead bird and poking at its glass eyes.

"A great horned owl can't do this," said George. He stood still, moving his eyes from side to side. "They can't move their eyes in their sockets. That's why they have such good neck muscles, for moving their head around."

One more car pulled in and Joanna whispered excitedly, "Is that her?"

"No," said David. "She drives a Mercedes."

David was pleased to see that it was the grade five teacher, Rhonda Martin, and her husband.

Rhonda said, "This is my first Owl Prowl."

"Mine too," said David. "I'm really glad you came."

"Well, you know, it was either this or the opera tonight."

"What? Really?"

"No, dear," said Rhonda. "Just *Wheel of Fortune*."

Ron Metz was holding the owl. It was mounted on a piece of driftwood. Ron said, "It's not as heavy as I thought it would be."

George said, "They've got hollow bones. For flight, you see. Lighter flight. Light flight at night."

The evening was cloudy but calm. It had been windier during the day, and David had worried they would not be able to hear an owl, or that no one would show up. The temperature was close to freezing, but at 7:15, twenty-one people were in the parking lot. David sensed that people might be getting cold standing around, so he suggested they head out to the forest. The kids led the way across the soccer field, and the adults followed behind, walking in twos.

Joanna walked beside Mrs. Wong. Mrs. Wong said, "You are too young to have a child in grade four."

Joanna said, "That's my boy there," pointing at David.

"Your husband?"

"Not yet," said Joanna.

"Oh, soon. You are a lucky woman."

"I am," said Joanna. "But he's lucky too. We're both lucky."

Up ahead, the students waited at the edge of the field where the path entered the forest. They waved flashlights around at the branches above.

Mrs. Wong said, "What are the children singing?"

Joanna said, "I don't know," and the two of them stopped to listen. Joanna laughed. "They are singing, 'Go in the woods, Mister Woods.'"

THIRTY-SIX

THE ENGLISH LESSON AT THE Rising Son was over, and Kaori went behind the bar and brought back three cans of Calpis, a sweet carbonated drink.

Kaori said, "Tyler said this drink is 'cow piss.' "

"Was Tyler a good teacher?" asked David.

The sisters looked at each other and tilted their heads from side to side.

"Yes," said Kaori.

"Yes," said Den.

"But he talked too fast," said Kaori. "I couldn't understand him."

"*So, so*," said Den. "No — *nan-dakke?*"

"No patience," said Kaori.

"*Hai*," said Den, nodding. "Yes."

David said, "It seems like your uncle gets annoyed at Tyler. Tyler upsets him."

"No," said Kaori. "My uncle likes Tyler very much. But Tyler moves everything." She motioned as if taking things off the wall.

"Tyler is funny," said Den. "I cannot understand him, but he is funny."

"I like when he is singing the songs," said Kaori.

"Me too," said David.

Kaori pointed at the classical guitar hanging behind the bar. "Tanaka-*san*, my uncle, played that guitar for us when we were children."

"Japanese songs?" said David.

"Yes, Japanese songs. And some American songs."

"*El-bees Pray-soo-lee*," said Den.

"Yes," said Kaori. "Elvis Presley."

"I've never heard Tanaka-*san* sing," said David.

"When we were small children," said Kaori, "my uncle would sing at night for us to go to sleep. He has a good voice."

"Is your father younger than Tanaka-*san*?" asked David. Mr. Tanaka looked too old to be their father.

"Yes. Our father is ten years younger. But he travelled with his business many days. Tanaka-*san* is like our second father."

"Does Tanaka-*san* have children?"

"No. Den and I are like his children," said Kaori. "And the teachers from the Monterrey House. They are also his children."

"Yes," said Den.

"And maybe this place is like his child," said David waving his hand at the bar. "Maybe that is why he called the restaurant the Rising Son. S-O-N, and not S-U-N."

Den grimaced.

Kaori tilted her head and looked at Den. "*Chotto chigao*," she said. "Different."

Kaori drew a Japanese symbol on the pad of paper.

旭日

She said, "This is the *kanji* for 'rising sun,' sometimes 'morning sun.' It is on the wall outside the restaurant, and on the advertisings. In the family we call this place 'Asahi,' which is 'Rising Sun,' or sometimes we just say 'Sun.'" She printed s-u-n on the paper.

"So the sign over the bar is a spelling mistake?" asked David.

"If you look closely, the 'o' was in the past a 'u.' One day my uncle changed it."

"Why?"

"The shop was not making money. Tanaka-*san* had a feeling that a change would help the luck."

"Did it work?"

Den and Kaori nodded at each other. "Oh yes. Everything changed."

IN THE QUIET OF THE November forest the Owl Prowlers of Dumford Mills stood in silence. David tapped on the iPad, and

Joanna held a portable speaker up to the night.

"*HOO-HOO-HOOOOOOOO. HOOOO, HOOOO,*" called the recording.

The group strained to listen, and David played the call again. Ron Metz told Anna to stop shuffling her feet. Dale Dickenson, Robbie's dad, pointed to the west. The group looked in that direction. There was a far-off noise, but not an owl.

"Just a dog barking," said Dale.

They followed the Condie Creek trail south along the stream for a hundred metres. Rhonda Martin told the kids to turn their flash-lights off, and David played the recording again. The dog could still be heard, but there was no response from an owl.

David said, "We'll try one more spot, down by the bridge. Every-one good?"

People nodded, but it was apparent that the cold was tempering their enthusiasm.

When they got to the bridge, everyone stood on it, but the sound of the water flowing below made it difficult to hear. The group crossed to the other side of the stream and huddled together. Some of the kids had their hands over their ears for warmth.

David said, "Last try. Cross your fingers."

The group looked around in expectation as David pressed *Play*. Joanna balanced the speaker on her head, with her fingers poking up like ear tufts.

"*HOO-HOO-HOOOOOOOO. HOOOO, HOOOO.*"

Silence.

"*HOO-HOO-HOOOOOOOO. HOOOO, HOOOO.*"

Silence.

A third time: "*HOO-HOO-HOOOOOOOO. HOOOO, HOOOO.*"

Nothing.

"Well," said David, "I know some people are getting cold. Maybe we can try another night."

"Let my grandpa try," said Jesse.

David looked at George. George said, "That machine sounded like a real great horned owl. I couldn't do any better than that."

"Do a screech," said Jesse.

Jesse's father, Terry, said, "Sure. Give it a shot, Dad."

George took off his Montreal Canadiens tuque and tilted his head back. There was a short pause, and then a haunting musical trill filled the air. It sounded like someone playing a flute under water.

"How did you do that?" said Anna.

George whispered, "That is the call of the screech owl. That's another common owl that lives around here."

George cupped his hands to his mouth and trilled again. The dog barked in the distance.

"There!"

Dale Dickenson pointed up at a tree. David saw it too. A small owl, only nine or ten inches tall, had flown in silently and landed on a branch twenty feet away. It was silhouetted against the grey sky. Those who could see it were whispering in hushed tones and pointing for those who could not. Joanna held on to David's arm, and he showed her where it was.

The screech owl looked around, seemingly oblivious to the whispered chatter below. It leaned forward a little bit, and David thought it was about to fly. But then a ghost-like warble sounded over the onlookers. Nobody moved or talked. The owl repeated its mournful call.

Joanna whispered in David's ear. "Oh my God. I have goosebumps."

David said, "This is pretty cool."

Joanna said, "I'm sorry for what I said in the car."

"What?"

"What I said in the car. Don't stop. I love you. I'm with you all the way."

When the group got back to the parking lot, Katie Findlay's mom, Candace, announced, "We should thank Mr. Woods for this enchanting evening."

Everyone applauded. David said, "And Mr. Young." They all clapped for George.

As the families piled into their cars, turning up heaters and radios, Mrs. Wong came over to David and said, "Thank you, Mr. Woods. Very enjoyable time."

David said, "Yes, maybe we can try again after Christmas."

"Yes," said Mrs. Wong. "I would like to join your club."

THIRTY-SEVEN

IN THE MONTERREY HOUSE KITCHEN, David poured boiling water into a teapot. He had started bringing green tea on his hikes instead of buying vending-machine coffee. Jock and Rochelle sat at the table, passing a *New York Times* crossword back and forth. David had given up the pretense of looking for work. Everyone knew he went walking each day, and Rochelle often asked to see his sketches.

Rochelle said, "Commander at the Alamo."

"Crockett," said Jock, "Davy Crockett."

"Six letters," said Rochelle.

"Davy," said Jock. "D-A-V-E-E-E. *Daveee*." Jock thought this was hilarious. He looked at David. "Makin' some tea, *Daveee*? Goin' for a hike, *Daveee*?"

David had always been "David," not often "Dave," certainly never "Davy." "Daves" were cool. In school, David had been too socially restrained to be cool. Whether due to his height or the amount of responsibility he was given on the farm growing up, by the time he was fifteen, everyone treated David like an adult. "David" was an adult's name. The Tanaka sisters and all the other Japanese people he had met pronounced his name "Day-beed." The Japanese language only used a certain number of sounds, and even in Japan his name sounded formal.

" 'Davy' is what my brother used to call me in high school. It was his way of pointing out that I was his little brother."

"Is he tall too?" asked Rochelle.

"He's five eleven," said David. "Not tall, but pretty tough. He used to beat on me pretty good."

"You, man?" Jock did not think this was possible.

"Until I was sixteen or so, yeah."

"You ever get him back? Teach him a lesson?"

David poured his green tea through a strainer into a thermos. "One time."

Rochelle said, "What happened?"

"I punched him in the chest. Broke a couple ribs."

"You were fighting?" said Rochelle.

"No. I just punched him."

"Why?"

"Something he said."

"What did he say?"

David tasted the tea with a spoon.

Jock said, "She's relentless, man."

David nodded in agreement. "My brother said, 'You gonna come play hockey or sit around with your girlfriend?'"

Rochelle said, "You punched him for that?"

"Yes."

"Oh, man," said Jock, "I'm not going to ask you nothin', man. It'd be like, 'Can you pass the salt?' and, *boom!*" Jock punched one hand into the other.

Rochelle said, "I don't believe you. I don't believe that for a second."

David blew on the hot tea. "Well, the girl was from the Philippines."

"So?"

David screwed the lid on his thermos and stuffed it in his knapsack.

"I think Kyle's actual words were 'Are you gonna come play hockey or sit around with your gook girlfriend?'"

"MAYBE I SHOULD START A club," said David.

It was Sunday morning, and David and Joanna were driving to a farm in David's pickup truck. Don Moreland had phoned Joanna and asked her to check out a horse that was having breathing problems. David was going for support.

"An Owl Prowl club?" asked Joanna.

"I don't know. We can't look for owls over and over. Some kind of nature club. That was a good group on Friday night. George Young has a lot of experience leading that kind of thing. I'll call him."

They pulled into a laneway that led to a house a long way off the road. A German shepherd ran alongside the car.

David said, "What if you can't diagnose the horse?"

"Don said to call him after church."

The farmer was in his seventies and walked with a stoop. David carried a blue plastic bin that said *Equine* on top. The farmer led them into a small barn that had a cracked cement floor and three stalls. There was a chestnut horse in the middle stall. It was sniffing and snorting and could not stand still. The farmer was clearly disturbed by the animal's pain.

David looked at Joanna nervously. "What do you think?"

"Hook his lead up to the rail."

The farmer clipped the horse's lead to the front of the stall. Joanna put her arm around the horse's neck and ran a hand down its throat.

David said, "There's green stuff coming out of its nose."

Joanna said, "Come around so you can hold his head."

Joanna got a flashlight out of the bin. David held the horse's head while it coughed and snorted. Joanna pulled at its lips and looked in the horse's nose and mouth.

The farmer said, "He's been coughing a lot lately, but nothing like this. He'll be twenty next month." The old man rubbed the top rail of the stall. "He's old, but I don't care what it costs."

Joanna told the farmer to get a bucket of water. She took a clear plastic tube out of the blue bin and smeared Vaseline over it.

"Loop the lead under the bottom board of the stall," said Joanna. "Pull his head down to the ground."

David pulled the horse's lead under a metal rail at the bottom of the stall. The horse shook its head and snorted. Its eyes were bulging and looking at the ceiling. Joanna took one end of the tube and started feeding it up the horse's nose. She put the other end of the tube against her cheek.

"What are you doing?" said David. "Should we wait for Don?"

"Feeling for breath. I'm making sure I'm not in the trachea."

Joanna took the end of the tube and attached it to a small hand pump. She put the pump in the bucket of water and pumped several times. A few seconds later, green sludge oozed out of the horse's nostrils. She pushed the tube in farther and pumped again. The process was repeated five or six times. When she was done there was a slimy pile of undigested food on the cement floor. The horse was shaking its head and breathing deeply.

Joanna told the farmer to remove all the hay in the stall. David helped the farmer sweep the floor clean while Joanna examined the horse's hooves.

The farmer said to David, "I thought you were the vet."

When they had cleaned the stall, David and the farmer watched Joanna repacking the box. Joanna's cheeks were red. The legs of her coveralls were stained where she had wiped her hands.

When she was done, Joanna took a deep breath. "Your horse has an abscessed tooth. Maybe two or three. It's probably painful for him to chew, so he's swallowing food without chewing very well. All that food is getting stuck in his throat. I flushed it out, but he shouldn't have anything to eat until we get that fixed. Just water. He'll need those teeth pulled before he can eat again. I can get a horse dentist here, but probably not until tomorrow morning."

The farmer said, "I thought he was dying."

Joanna said, "He was choking, but I think if you fix his teeth he'll be fine."

"Gosh, that's good news. Do you want to come up to the house?"

"No, thank you," said Joanna.

The farmer said, "My chequebook is in the house. What do I owe you?"

"Sir, I have no idea."

THIRTY-EIGHT

NONE OF THE RESIDENTS OF Monterrey House had ever heard
of the Kyoto Trail. Many of them had been to the Ginkaku-ji temple
and the Kiyomizu-dera temple, which were part of the route, but
no one seemed to have heard of the trail itself. David himself had
been on the Kyoto Trail a few times before he became aware that
there was an official path. If the old woman had not bought him
a map, David would have continued wandering randomly around
the perimeter of the city.

While hiking, David had trained his eyes to find the wooden
trail-markers that corresponded to numbers on his map. On the
eastern side of Kyoto, the trail went through neighbourhoods and
large tourist sites. As the trail curved north over the city it took
a more rural route, skirting rivers and passing through villages.
As the days grew warmer, it was pleasant to be on shady paths in
the mountains.

But despite the aid of trail-markers, David was not covering much
ground each day. It took time to navigate the train system to the
outskirts of the city. He would then retrace his path to the place he
had stopped the previous day. This meant that he covered a lot of
the same ground twice. Sometimes he missed guideposts and had
to find his way back to a previous marker. In the mountains the trail
might divide, with no signs indicating which was the Kyoto Trail.
At one point the trail followed a road down the side of a mountain
but required that hikers turn off the road through a gate. David
never imagined that he would need to unlatch a gate to get back
on the trail, and that missed turn left him lost for most of the day.
Sometimes there were detours to shrines or lookouts, and David
explored every diversion.

A dedicated hiker with knowledge of the route might have completed the main loop of the Kyoto Trail in five or six days. David had been hiking the trail for fifteen days and had completed half. His hikes were also cut short by a self-imposed curfew: he liked to be back in time for dinner at the Rising Son.

Most of the people David met on the trail were older men and couples. They strolled in a leisurely way with walking sticks and binoculars. Anyone he asked would try to help him interpret his map, regardless of their level of English. David carried some Canadian coins in his pocket to give to helpful strangers.

Occasionally there were school groups visiting shrines and temples along the trail. At Mount Hiei there was a cable car that ran up the side of the mountain. David rode in the cable car with a class of elementary students in blue school uniforms. One of the boys kept staring at David's knapsack, which had *University of Western Ontario* embroidered on it. Halfway up the hill the cable car stopped, and the boy asked, "Are you from Canada?"

"Yes," said David.

The boy said, "Are you a hockey player?"

Considering David's height and build, this was a reasonable speculation. He had not had a haircut in several months, and his wavy dark hair was now shoulder-length. He had what was known in Canada as "hockey hair."

David shook his head. "I play hockey for fun, but I am a teacher."

The boy said, "I been to Niagara Falls." Other students gathered around the boy talking to the giant Canadian.

"My home is near Niagara Falls," said David.

"*Kowai*," said the boy. "I was scared to see the big waterfalls. I was thinking about jumping."

"Don't jump," David said. "Never jump." It seemed like good advice for a teacher to give.

"No, just thinking. I — *nan-dakke* — I am imagining to jump. *Kowai*. Scary. I was scared."

"Don't jump," said David.

"No, no, no," said the boy. He pointed at David. "*You* don't jump."

He pointed at some of his classmates. "You don't jump, you don't jump, you don't jump."

This was also good advice.

"NASOGASTRIC INTUBATION," SAID JOANNA. "We did it in the equine course."

David was driving the car. He was impressed by what he had just witnessed. "You're a real vet," he said.

"It was more acute than colic would be."

"You are a full-blown veterinarian."

"It was choke for sure. And the horse was old, so it probably wasn't from eating too fast."

"Hershey would have bucked like a bugger if you shoved a tube up his nose."

"And it didn't look like it was getting great care, so I thought the teeth could be the underlying cause."

"I should have filmed it," said David.

"I didn't get a great look in his mouth, but the gums on the one side were ugly-looking."

"The old guy thought I was the vet."

"I only ever did that once so I was worried about getting in the trachea."

"It looked like pea soup coming out his nose. It smelled terrible."

"I didn't want to pump water into his lungs. Give him pneumonia or something."

"He gave us maple syrup. Isn't working in the country great?"

"When I put the tube to my nose, I could smell that I was in the esophagus."

"We should make pancakes."

"And then when the grass started to drain out, I knew I had it."

"Or French toast."

"Nasogastric intubation."

"My girlfriend is a vet," said David, drumming on the steering wheel.

"I'm a vet," said Joanna.

"Let's have French toast," said David.

"I'm going to call Don, and then let's get drunk."

THIRTY-NINE

SATURDAY NIGHT AT THE RISING Son was Taco Night. Taco
Night was usually very busy. The Mexican-Asian fusion was always
popular, and on this night Mr. Tanaka was serving shrimp tacos with
a teriyaki sauce.

Ta-ko in Japanese meant "octopus," so some people called Taco
Night "Octopus Night." *Ta-ko* was also Japanese slang for female
genitalia, so Tyler called Taco Night "Pussy Night."

David sat at the bar with Guy. Kaori was helping Tanaka-*san* serve
customers. She placed tiny bowls of shredded red pickles in front
of the young men.

Guy said, "Rochelle is getting antsy to go home."

David tried to pick up the oily pickles with his chopsticks. "Why?"

"To join the army."

"I thought she was avoiding the army."

"They turned down her application to be a pacifist."

"I like Rochelle," said David.

"I'm in love with her."

David raised an eyebrow. "What about your New Zealand girlfriend?"

"I've loved a lot of girls," said Guy, tipping the whole bowl of pickles into his mouth.

"You're pretty young," said David.

"You don't think I'm old enough to have loved a lot of girls? I've
been falling in love over and over since sixth grade."

"Maybe we just see things differently," said David.

"How many girls have you been in love with?"

"That's something Rochelle would ask."

"How many?"

"You may find this hard to believe." David swished beer around in his mouth.

"What?" said Guy. "One? Please don't say *one*."

"Well, I've never actually said that exact phrase to anyone."

"You've never told a Sheila that you love her?" Guy shook his head. "Jesus Christ, mate, you're twenty-six. No wonder your girlfriend left you."

"She knew."

"Knew what? That you're emotionally stunted?"

Rochelle came through the curtained entrance of the Rising Son. David groaned in anticipation of the conversation to follow.

"I love you," said Guy.

"Of course you do, baby," said Rochelle, kissing him on the cheek. She gave David a peck as well. "I've been thinking of tacos all day."

"I know," said David, looking at Guy. "I love Taco Night."

EACH TIME DAVID PUT WOOD in the stove, he liked to say, "That's good wood," imitating his father.

As Joanna loaded logs into the fire, David said, "Say it."

Joanna talked out the side of her mouth like Archie: "That's good wood."

They sat on the couch in their living room, watching the Buffalo Bills football game. Joanna put her wine glass on the floor and pulled a sleeping bag over them.

David said, "We can call it the Dumford Mills Outdoors Club. We can go fishing, snowshoeing, animal tracking, owling. And maybe next year I can get all the students' parents to sign on, and then I'll do the same stuff as part of school. I need to call George."

"Are you starting a club just for Chunhua's mother?" asked Joanna.

"She was very excited about the Owl Prowl. I don't even know her name."

"She told me her name was June. Or she said, 'You can call me June.' She's very cute. She looks like Chunhua."

"She looked like an Inuit woman in that parka," said David.

"She told me I'm lucky to have you."

"I need to call George," said David. "He was a Scout leader. He's led all kinds of hikes."

David's father cheered for the Buffalo Bills, so, growing up, David cheered for the Bills. Part of David's fun in watching the football games was imagining what his father would be yelling at the television. Today the Bills were losing badly. Archie would be yelling a lot.

David said, "If I start a club, it will help me organize outdoor activities for my class next year."

"What if Roger moves you to grade five next year? Then you'll have Martha Emerson in your class again."

"That won't happen. None of the teachers in the school want to develop new units for a different grade. I'm safe. Though, really, I'd give anything to have these same kids again. Except for Nina Emerson, the parents are great too."

"That's nice you can keep the same grade."

"It's nice that I have a job," said David. "I was talking to Mitchell, and no one we went to school with has a job. Some are supply teaching, but I'm probably the only person with a full-time teaching job."

Joanna said, "Who would have thought we'd end up in Dumford Mills? It's like Bedford Falls from *It's a Wonderful Life*."

David put his head under the sleeping bag and crawled on top of Joanna. He said, "And I'm Jimmy Stewart."

Joanna put her arms around David's neck. "Jimmy Stewart hates Bedford Falls. He wants to kill himself."

David kissed her. "He ends up just fine. He has an angel watching over him."

The woodstove filled the drafty house with a warmth that could only be appreciated when it was cold outside. Cats with various maladies washed themselves beside the fire, and the Buffalo Bills, full of so much promise at the beginning of the year, fumbled away their season.

"Oh, baby," said Joanna, "that's good wood."

FORTY

SITTING AT THE BAR, DAVID ordered another plate of tacos. Mr. Tanaka marvelled at how much David could eat.

Where there were no shops on the Kyoto Trail, David would hike without eating lunch. Given the number of calories needed to move his substantial mass up and down mountains, it was no wonder that he was famished by evening.

"Those are good tacos," said David.

"You love them," said Guy.

"It's the sauce," said David.

"You love tacos, but not women."

David said, "I bet we have the same emotions where women are concerned."

"You just don't like to tell women how you feel about them."

Rochelle was oddly quiet, listening to the exchange.

David swallowed the remains of a beer. He pushed the hockey hair out of his face. "I just think that when you say 'I love you,' that implies a commitment. A big commitment."

"Marriage?" said Guy.

"Yes."

"So the first time you say the words 'I love you,' that will be a marriage proposal?"

"I think so."

"You're either a hopeless romantic or a coward."

Rochelle broke her silence. "There's nothing brave about telling every girl you meet that you love them."

Guy recoiled at the retort. "Giving my heart to girls is the bravest thing I've ever done."

"And you're Mr. Goddamn Braveheart."

"Who are we talking about?" said Guy.

Rochelle gave Guy the finger and walked to the washroom at the back of the bar. Tyler came through the front curtain wearing a sombrero.

Guy asked David, "What just happened here?"

Tyler leaned in between the two and slapped their backs. "Happy Pussy Night, boys!"

JESSE YOUNG HELD HIS GRANDFATHER'S great horned owl at the front of the class.

"Everybody thinks these are ears, but they're just feathers. The ears are on the side of the head, like ours."

David said, "What is interesting about the placement of the ears, Jesse?"

"They're at different heights."

"And do you remember how that helps an owl?"

"It's for hunting."

"That's right," said David. "Try this. Everyone shut your eyes and look at the front of the classroom."

"How can we look at the front of the classroom with our eyes closed?" said Robbie.

"Just face the front of the room with your eyes closed."

David took a metre stick and tapped on the classroom door. "Open your eyes. Point to where the sound was coming from."

Everyone pointed at the door.

"How could you tell that with your eyes shut?"

"We heard it over there," said Anna.

David said, "Explain it using the concept of sound waves."

Anna said, "When you hit the door, it made a sound wave. The wave went across the room and went into my ears, and my eardrums vibrated."

"Which ear did the sound wave enter first?"

"My right one, 'cause it's just a little bit closer to the door."

"That's right," said David. "The sound wave reaches one ear a split second before it reaches the other. That's how we know the sound is over there. But if we are looking straight at something and it makes a noise, the sound waves hit both of our ears at the same time. If we have our eyes closed and something makes a noise right in front of us, the sound will hit our ears at the same time, no matter how high or low it is. With our eyes closed, it's difficult for us to pinpoint exactly how high something is if it makes a sound right in front of us.

"Now look at the owl. Let's say this great horned owl is in a tree looking down at a field. Maybe it's winter and there's a mouse scurrying around under the snow. The owl can hear the mouse, but in order to catch it, it needs to locate exactly where the mouse is, just by using its ears."

David drew a mouse on the blackboard. "Jesse, point your owl at this mouse. Now, because the owl's ears are on different sides of his head, he can figure out horizontally where the mouse is." David drew a horizontal line through the mouse.

"But because one of the owl's ears is higher than the other, he can also pinpoint vertically where the mouse is." David drew a vertical line through the mouse.

"Owls catch mice under snow and in the grass without ever seeing them. This *adaptation* of having one ear higher than the other helps them survive. Their brains can figure out, just by the teensy difference in time of sound waves hitting their ears, which place to dive into the snow to catch prey. Amazing. It helps them survive.

"Now, connections. Someone put up their hand and make a connection," said David. "Jenny."

Jenny Lin said, "We could just tip our head like this, and one ear would be higher. Then we could hear like owls hear." Many of the students tipped their heads sideways.

"I never thought of that," said David, "but I think you're right. Keep it going. More connections. Martin."

"If you make a weird noise at my dog, she turns her head like this." Martin turned his head inquisitively. "Maybe she's trying to see where the noise is coming from by making one ear higher than the other."

David said, "Martin, you might have just figured out an age-old mystery! Why do dogs tilt their head from side to side when you make a weird noise at them? Because they want to see where the noise is coming from. You're probably right. You figured it out."

"I have a question," said Robbie.

"Yes?" said David.

"Which ear on the owl is higher?"

The owl sat on David's desk for the next six weeks. It would teach the students and their teacher about food chains, camouflage, digestion, the difference between rods and cones, DDT, light dispersion, sound dispersion, the evolution of dinosaurs, and what a cloaca is.

FORTY-ONE

GUY HAD GIVEN UP HIS seat at the bar to Rochelle. He stood beside her with his hand on her shoulder. David used a pair of chopsticks to push around the remains of his teriyaki shrimp tacos. The atmosphere in the rest of the pub was boisterous.

Rochelle said, "I feel like the army service just hangs over me. I can't get a job or do anything in Israel until I put in two years, so maybe I should just do it."

"What's the hurry?" asked Guy.

"I feel like I need to get on with my life."

Guy said, "Look around this place. Everyone in here needs to get on with their lives. Japan is one big halfway house for *gaijin*. Japan is purgatory."

Rochelle said, "That's right. This is not a permanent situation, so why should I stay?"

Guy said, "Because this purgatory is pretty sweet. I mean, babe, look at the photos on the walls. These aren't the pictures of poor lost souls. These people may be wayward, but they are having the time of their lives. They're making friends, they're getting drunk, they're falling in love. Why wouldn't you want to keep that going?"

"Keep what going? Us?"

"You always say 'Embrace the moment,' 'Be open to experience.' Well, here you are."

Rochelle said, "When I leave, you'll get a new girlfriend, or you'll go home to your old girlfriend. What do you care?"

"I love you."

Rochelle crossed her arms on the bar and buried her head in them. Guy rubbed her back. He said to David, "Mate, I think she's really fallen for me. Chicks dig my accent."

FOR THE EMILY CARR CHRISTMAS pageant, David's class presented *How the Grinch Stole Christmas*. David played the Grinch. He wore green tights with gym shorts over them. Above the waist he had on a furry red coat, a Santa hat, and a white beard. Martha Emerson narrated the story, and the grade fours played the Whos of Whoville. Joanna sat in the audience with her parents.

"I've never seen this side of David," said Linda.

Joanna said, "Well, Mother, I can't say I've ever seen him in a green leotard either."

"That girl has excellent diction," said Doug.

"All I need is a reindeer,
The Grinch looked around
But since reindeer are scarce, there was none to be found.
Did that stop the old Grinch?
No! The Grinch simply said…"

David spoke. "If I can't find a reindeer, I'll make one instead!"

David the Grinch went behind the curtain and came back with Martin Staedelbauer's brown Labrador retriever, Muffin. The dog was wearing a pair of reindeer antlers and ran around excitedly. David attached Muffin's leash to the front of an aluminum toboggan. Martin scattered dog treats just out of the crowd's view. As Muffin strained to reach the treats, David jumped on the sled and pretended to whip the dog with a white scarf. The crowd roared in laughter. David took one foot off the toboggan, and Muffin strained toward Martin. David pushed the toboggan forward like a skateboard, waving at the audience. As he and Muffin disappeared from view, there was great applause.

"Oh my God," said Joanna. "That was the funniest thing ever."

Just then, Muffin ran back on the stage carrying the packet of dog treats in his mouth. The aluminum toboggan careered wildly behind him. The six-foot-four Grinch, looking like a fusion of Peter Pan and Santa Claus, chased the dog back out. As the sled swung toward David, he jumped on the back end. However, the physics of momentum favoured the dog, and the Labrador scampered back toward Martin who was clapping his hands at the side of the stage. David's feet flew out from under him, and he landed with a heavy thud. The crowd gasped. Muffin returned to sniff the body of the prostrate Grinch. A green arm rose from the wreckage and waved the white scarf in surrender.

This was the moment when Linda Shayne decided to give David her mother's sterling silver, Scottish, thistle-engraved wedding ring. Just in case.

FORTY-TWO

DAVID, ROCHELLE, AND GUY HAD moved from the bar to an empty booth. David sat across from the couple. At Guy's invitation, Kaori sat beside David. David's legs were sprawled diagonally under the table. The physical situation was complicated when Tyler sat beside Rochelle and invited his karate friend, Junichi, to sit beside Kaori. Now David's legs intersected with a number of limbs.

Tyler said, "Let's get down to it. You cannot leave, Rochelle."

Rochelle said, "I don't want to leave."

"We don't need another mountain of sadness walking around," said Tyler, gesturing toward David. "Guy needs you to be his mistress. David needs you to be his grief counsellor. Junichi needs you to lust after. Kaori... Kaori doesn't need you. She has Den. But, dude, I need you. I need you to sing harmony with me. I need you to walk me home at night."

David squirmed in the corner. Kaori smelled like baby powder.

"I'm not leaving tomorrow," said Rochelle.

"Good," said Tyler. He started serenading Rochelle with a Bob Seger song.

"We've got tonight..."

Rochelle said, "Your breath smells like fish."

"It's Taco Night, baby!" Tyler looked at the clock behind the bar. "Holy shit, it's almost ten. I need to get playing before Master-*san* kicks us out. Just promise me you won't enlist tonight. The day after you leave Kyoto, I'm out of here too."

Rochelle patted Tyler on the thigh. "You're sweet," she said.

Tyler leaped up. "How the fuck am I supposed to play guitar with a boner? I'm gonna poke a hole in the back of Tanaka's six-string." He strutted around with his pelvis sticking out.

"How can I leave here?" said Rochelle.

"You can't," said Guy.

"I will," said Rochelle. "We all will."

In the spirit of the conversation, Junichi said, "I don't want to be a salary man."

Guy said, "I don't want to be a jewellery salesman."

Junichi said, "I have no other way." He was as animated as David had ever seen him.

This would normally be the part of the conversation when Rochelle would offer touchy-feely advice, but she was silent. David nodded his condolences. Guy put his hands behind his head.

Kaori said, "*So, so.*"

At the bar, Tyler sat on a stool, tuning the guitar. He leaned into an imaginary microphone and said, "I'd like to dedicate this next song to my Kiwi Don Juan friend, Guy, and his lady friend, Rochelle. Guy's literally a hell of a guy. Except where I'm from, his name is pronounced *gi*, like a hockey player. He's a hell of a *gi*. Rochelle is an Israeli babe. Jewish, probably."

Tyler rambled on. Guy put his arm around Rochelle. Junichi pondered thirty years of wearing a suit and tie. David wondered if he should be pressed so tightly against one of his students.

Tyler sang:

"There is a house in Kyoto
They call the Rising Son
And it's been the ruin of many a poor boy
And God, I know I'm one."

AFTER THE GRADE FOURS LEFT the Christmas concert stage, they joined their parents in the audience. Joanna strained to see where Martha Emerson went. She wanted to see what Martha's parents looked like.

The grade fives took to the stage and sang "Do You Hear What I Hear," and the grade sixes followed with an enactment of 'Twas the

Night Before Christmas. Then the Emily Carr teachers sang "We Wish You a Merry Christmas."

After the concert, Joanna waited with her parents in the lobby. She caught pieces of many conversations commenting on David's performance.

Joanna's father said, "That really got me in the Christmas spirit. Let's ride the sleigh home and roast some chestnuts."

David came out through the gym doors, wearing his own clothes but still sporting the Santa hat.

Joanna said, "Are you all right? You went down hard."

"That's just the way we rehearsed it," said David. "I'm fine."

Martha Emerson came running through the gym doors into the lobby. "Mr. Woods, I still have the book." She waved *How the Grinch Stole Christmas* in the air.

Martha's parents followed behind.

David said, "Either bring it back Monday or put it in the classroom now."

Martha said, "I'll put it in the classroom."

Nina Emerson was wearing a form-fitting red dress with a black belt and black shoes. Her husband wore a brown smoking jacket with patches on the sleeves, and a pair of grey pants with sharp creases.

Nina said, "That was an award-winning performance, Mr. Woods."

"Thank you. Mr. and Mrs. Emerson, this is my girlfriend, Joanna, and her parents, Doug and Linda Shayne."

Nina nodded and smiled. "I'm Nina. This is my husband, Trevor."

Trevor shook everyone's hands.

David said to Trevor, "Those are nice glasses."

Trevor Emerson said, "Do you like them? I'm an optometrist, so I test out different frames. I thought these might be too retro for me."

"They look sharp," said David. "Joanna's a vet. She brings home different pets to test out."

Nina looked at her watch. "We can't all be lawyers."

Joanna said to Nina, "David is starting an outdoors club after Christmas. Perhaps you and your daughter might like to join. It will be for families. Good wholesome safe fun."

David opened his eyes wide at Joanna as a warning. He looked anxiously down the hallway for Martha.

"Perhaps we will join," said Nina.

"It might be very educational," said Joanna, full of mischief.

David took off his Santa hat and looked inside it.

Trevor said, "Will there be information sent home with Martha?"

David said, "Yes. We'll let you know about it somehow. It won't be a school-sanctioned club."

"I wouldn't expect the school to sanction non-curricular activities," said Nina.

"It will be parent-sanctioned," said Joanna.

Nina said, "But these club activities will take place outside school hours?"

"Yes," said David.

"When it's more appropriate?"

"Ah!" exclaimed David. "Martha, did you put the book back?"

Martha came down the hall. "Yes."

"Good," said David. "On the shelf?"

When the respective families were in their cars, Trevor Emerson and Doug Shayne both asked the same question: "What was that all about?"

FORTY-THREE

IT WAS SUNDAY AFTERNOON, AND the English lesson in the Rising Son was almost finished. David sat across from Den and Kaori at the same table he had occupied the night before. David was instructing the sisters to use different verb tenses.

David said, "Yesterday I drank tea. Today I am drinking coffee. Tomorrow I will drink water."

Kaori said, "Last year I learned Spanish. Today I am learning English. Next year I will learn French."

"Good," said David.

Den said, "Last week I made a bird. Today I am making a tree. The next day I will make a — *nan-dakke* — a snowflake."

Kaori stared at Den. "Snowflake?"

Den took a napkin and folded it a few times deliberately. "*Origami*," she said.

David said, "What if, for next week's lesson, we walked and talked."

Den said, "Walkie-talkie?"

"I have been hiking around Kyoto," said David. "In the mountains. Perhaps we could take the train to the mountains and walk around. It would give us something to talk about. It might be more interesting for you."

"I will ask my uncle," said Kaori, and she got up from the table.

David did not know why Kaori would need to ask Mr. Tanaka for permission. The sisters were in their early twenties.

While they waited for Kaori to return, Den said, "May I see your hands?"

David placed his hands on the table.

Den said "*Okii*. Big."

She turned his hands over and stared at the palms. "You will have long life."

"A good life?" asked David.

Den said something in Japanese. She tilted her head. "Uh, bumpy."

Kaori came back and said, "My uncle said we should go to Sawa-yama next Sunday. He will drive us. But maybe early. Ten o'clock."

David said, "He doesn't need to drive us. That's very nice, but we can take the train."

Kaori said, "It is fine. No problem. They need to go to Sawa-yama anyway."

"Outside English," said Den happily. "Outside education."

FOR CHRISTMAS DINNER, JOANNA BOUGHT a fresh turkey from the butcher shop in Dumford Mills and planned to cook it with a cranberry and pine nut stuffing.

Since Mitchell was unemployed and living with his parents in Kingston, David had invited him down for a couple of days. He had grown a beard since teachers' college. Mitchell sat at the kitchen table, drinking beer. He said, "It's like you guys are ten years older all of a sudden."

Joanna said, "Do we look ten years older?"

"No, Joanna, you look as young and perky as you ever did. What I mean is, you have jobs. You have a farm. You make things like cranberry-nut stuffing. Last year we were eating leftover pizza for breakfast. David and I had a Spice Girls poster hanging in the kitchen."

"Yeah, it's funny," said David.

"Nobody has teaching jobs," said Mitchell. "How did you get one?"

"Luck, I guess."

Joanna said, "He sent his application to the wrong place."

David said, "I got job listings sent to me from a website. *Educators-dot-com* or something. Anyway, I was supposed to apply through human resources at the school board, but I sent my resume to the school."

Mitchell said, "Everything just works out for you, doesn't it?"

"So far," said David.

Mitchell spun his empty beer bottle around on the table. He said, "I'm getting out of this country. I'm going to go to Korea or somewhere. Some Asian country where they hire white people."

Joanna said, "Isn't it dangerous there? Aren't the Koreans basically at war?"

Mitchell said, "They had the Olympics. It can't be too bad."

David said, "I wouldn't be able to eat the food over there."

"Just bring your own pork chops with you," said Mitchell.

"You're braver than I am," said David.

"It's not bravery," said Mitchell. "It's desperation. Desperation will make you do all sorts of things you never thought you would."

FORTY-FOUR

Dear David,

How are you doing? I do wish you would write or call. I don't want to bug you, but I don't want to be silent when you might need some support. I have decided to keep writing even if you don't write back.

The weather has been good for growing so far this year. Kyle has a new girlfriend, Megan, who is working at the fruit stand. Cherries are in season, and Kyle gets in asparagus and lettuce and such from Grover Farms.

Your Dad bought a racehorse! A standardbred named Far And Away. She's a six-year-old claimer, so we are not expecting any big payoffs. Perhaps she will replace Hershey when he's gone.

Gander the goose died last week. We miss his honking when anyone comes to visit.

Joanna is coming to spend a week with us the first week of July. You should call us then. She is a wonderful girl, and I hope you can make a new life together after September.

I made your dad go out for Japanese food the other night. I kind of liked it, but Archie had to stop at Burger King on the way home.

Please be safe. Send me another drawing to put on the fridge.

Love, Mom.

ON CHRISTMAS EVE, DAVID AND Mitchell walked through a field at the back of David and Joanna's farm. A neighbour who had been hunting on the property had told David there was an old well in the back forest that needed to be covered up.

Mitchell said, "Thanks for inviting me here."

"No problem," said David.

"Joanna's okay with it?"

"Of course," said David.

The ground was frozen solid, with a dusting of snow blowing through old furrows. Mitchell wished he had brought a hat and gloves.

"How are we supposed to find this well?" he asked.

"The guy said to follow the fence-line down to the woods and then look for an evergreen tree broken off at the top."

Near the forest there was a rusty sheet of tin rolled up beside a fence. David suggested they bring the metal to cover the hole. He unrolled the tin and jumped on it to flatten it out.

"I think it will be strong enough," he said.

Mitchell picked up one end of the tin and immediately dropped it. "I cut myself."

"Bad?"

Mitchell stared at his palm as blood dripped on the snow. "Shit. Sorry. I might need stitches."

David took off a boot and removed a grey wool sock. "I wear two pairs," he said. David tied the sock around Mitchell's hand, and the two headed back toward the house.

Mitchell said, "Can Joanna stitch it?"

David laughed. "She might be able to. She's been doing a lot of things I didn't know she could do." David told Mitchell about the choking horse.

"Are you guys going to get married?" Mitchell asked.

Joanna's mother had given David the engagement ring the previous week. Until then he had never considered a timeframe for proposing to Joanna.

He said, "We'll probably get a house first. Maybe in the summer. School has been so busy."

"Will I be a groomsman?" asked Mitchell.

David said, "There's my brother and Joanna's brother. Depends on the size of the wedding, I guess."

"Can I be best man?"

"There's no wedding yet," said David.

When they got back to the farmhouse, Joanna examined Mitchell's hand in the kitchen.

She said, "It's not even bleeding."

Mitchell said, "It was."

Joanna scoffed and said, "You guys need to go back out and cover up that well before one of the neighbour boys falls in."

"Shouldn't you put something on it?" asked Mitchell. "Pretend I'm a poodle or something."

After Joanna had treated the wound, Mitchell and David headed back outside.

Mitchell said, "You guys are adults now."

David said, "You're twenty-four."

"I'm a child. I'm a child with a Scooby-Doo Band-Aid on my boo-boo."

FORTY-FIVE

IN THE CRAMPED GAIJIN HOUSE kitchen, David made tea, and Jock and Rochelle worked on the *New York Times* crossword.

Jock said, "Davy, you have to come to the club this week."

"The Savannah?" said David.

"Yeah, man, come Saturday."

"Saturday is Taco Night," said Rochelle.

Jock said, "I'm thinking Saturday I'll make some Thai soup. We'll have Thai soup and go to the club."

"I don't usually go to dance clubs," said David.

"I've been working on something," said Jock. "You've got to see it. *Saturday.*"

Rochelle said, "Jock, why don't you ever come to the Rising Son?"

"I've done the Rising Son. I got twenty pictures on the wall there."

"It's so fun," said Rochelle.

"It was fun when I went there. But my friends, you know, they moved on."

"That's what makes it fun," said Rochelle. "There's always new people to meet, people from different countries."

Jock said, "I can't do the Rising Son again. Here I can cook and play my tunes, and the house streams through me."

"You go to the Savannah every night," said Rochelle. "Doesn't that get old?"

"No, see, that's it. At the Savannah I'm always working on stuff. New beats, new grooves. I put stuff out there, and the people, they get off. And if they get off, I get off. But the stuff that worked yesterday, it don't work tomorrow. Always changing. Always moving." Jock pretended he was shadowboxing. "Like a river."

Rochelle said, "Can I come to the Savannah too?"

"Anyone can come to the Savannah." Jock was out of his chair, throwing jabs at the air.

"Isn't it really expensive?"

Jock said, "I can get you in. What you spend after that is up to you." He ducked some imaginary punches.

Rochelle said, "It might be good to try something different."

Jock said, "Davy, you got to come. I got something for you." He pretended to throw a flurry of punches at David's midsection. "It will knock you out."

David could not fathom what Jock could have for him at a high-end Japanese nightclub, but he said, "Sure."

Jock danced around with his arms in the air. "The winner and still undefeated champion, James 'The Groove' Dobbs."

Rochelle said, "Your name is James?"

Jock said, "Yeah, Jock is just 'jockey.' You know, 'disc jockey.' At home I'm James."

"Oh my God," said Rochelle. "That's so funny. You're James."

Jock said, "Everyone in this house was someone different back home."

"Amen," said David.

CHRISTMAS DINNER WAS SET ON an old-fashioned white tablecloth with pictures of blue jays embroidered on it. David and Joanna laid out cutlery while Mitchell pulled books off a shelf in the living room.

"Why is Mitchell spending Christmas with us?" asked Joanna.

"Keep your voice down," said David. "You said it was okay."

"What I mean is, why isn't he spending Christmas with his parents?"

"His sister is going to Kingston tomorrow. They're doing Christmas tomorrow."

"This is our first Christmas in our own place," said Joanna.

David put his arms around Joanna. "Just you, me, and our adopted son."

Joanna said, "Can you please tell him to save some of the wine for supper?"

They sat down for Christmas dinner and David admired the

feast before them. Joanna said, "I feel like we should say grace or something."

Mitchell put down the bun he was eating and said, "For Thanksgiving, my family goes around the table and everyone says what they are thankful for."

Joanna smiled. "All right," she said. "Let's do that."

David said, "I am thankful for this amazing meal that Joanna has made. I am thankful for my first ever class at Emily Carr Public School. I am thankful for the people who have made us welcome in town. And I am thankful for a semi-white Christmas."

Joanna said, "Firstly, I am thankful to be here in the country with the love of my life, David Woods. His hard work and his optimistic spirit inspire me."

David regretted he hadn't said something about Joanna.

Mitchell said, "I now pronounce you man and wife."

Joanna ignored Mitchell. She continued, "I am thankful for my family and friends who are scattered around the country. I am thankful to Don Moreland for giving me a job and trusting in me to diagnose and treat animals. And I am thankful that our friend Mitchell can join us for our first Dumford Mills Christmas."

David squeezed Joanna's hand.

Mitchell nodded at Joanna and closed his eyes. "Dear Lord, thank you for the Boston Bruins and the Boston Red Sox and the New England Patriots. I am blessed to support such awesome teams. Thank you for my health and the vitamins and such. And thank you for delivering this orphan, this screw-up, to a nice manger when there was no room at the inn. God bless us all."

"Amen," said David.

"Did he just call our home a manger?" asked Joanna.

"Pass the stuffing," said David.

"Here you go, buddy," said Mitchell.

"Thank you, Jesus," said David.

FORTY·SIX

DAVID WAS THANKFUL FOR THE Kyoto Trail. If the Rising Son had given him a sense of place, it was the Kyoto Trail that had given him a sense of purpose. He had a place to go each day. He had things to see. He got exercise. He did something productive. His mother liked his sketches, so David began sending her the drawings without any notes — just a date and place where the sketches were made.

David had not written Joanna again. He had tried many times but could not make the words appear on the page. Thinking about Joanna made him think about Dumford Mills. Thinking about Dumford Mills made him think about Emily Carr Public School, and thoughts of Emily Carr took him right into Condie Creek. The fact that he could not picture Joanna in his mind without experiencing palpable anxiety was evidence that he probably needed therapy.

On Sunday, David would be going to Sawa-yama with the Tanaka sisters. Because the Sawa-yama area was part of his next stretch of the Kyoto Trail, he decided to skip that section and visit a portion of the Keihoku Trail.

The Keihoku course was a separate forty-kilometre trail that circled a rural area northwest of Kyoto. It was part of the Kyoto Trail, and David planned to hike the whole thing after finishing the main loop around Kyoto. It would take David ninety minutes each day to reach the Keihoku Trail by bus, but the long commute would extend his hiking experience. David was already worried about the day when he would complete the Kyoto Trail.

The Keihoku Trail turned out to be much more rural than even the north end of the main Kyoto Trail. There were fewer hikers, no shops or restaurants, and rarely even a vending machine. The trail snaked to shrines and statues and lookout points. On David's first day on the trail, his overwhelming emotion was loneliness.

On a hill overlooking a small village, David allowed himself to imagine that Joanna was sitting beside him. In this fantasy she was wearing the overalls she wore to visit farms. She had rubber boots on her feet, and her blonde hair fell loosely over her shoulders. She had her head on David's shoulder while David sketched a small stone statue of a child with a red bib. David told Joanna about Japan and the Kyoto Trail. He talked about Monterrey House and the Rising Son. Joanna rubbed David's arm.

"It wasn't your fault," she said. "Condie Creek wasn't your fault."

David looked out over the landscape of the ancient country. A solitary crow flew by. David knew that if he looked at the fantasy on his arm, Joanna would disappear. He focused his gaze on mountains in the distance.

He told his imagined girlfriend: "I killed Anna Metz."

THE FIRST OFFICIAL OUTING FOR the Dumford Mills Outdoors Club was scheduled for a Saturday in January. David had chosen ice-fishing as an activity that would appeal to both students and parents. He had put a short explanation of the club in the students' planners for them to take home.

Joanna and David sat in bed while Joanna set up a mailing list of interested families. The electric heater was on full blast.

Joanna said, "We only have eight emails so far."

David said, "Those eight emails could represent thirty people."

"Do you know anything about ice-fishing?"

"I've seen fishing huts on the Rideau River. I think if we head out to some huts and drill holes nearby, we'll have as good a chance to catch something as anyone."

Joanna said, "Can you even buy worms in the winter?"

"You use minnows," said David. "I'll get a bag of minnows from the sports store in Manotick."

"What if it's too warm?"

"The ice won't melt that fast. The risk is that it'll be too cold."

"Do you need fishing licences?"

"I don't know. I have one. Kids don't need them."

"Do you have a backup plan?"

"If we can't fish, then we go for a walk in the woods. We follow animal tracks. We keep it going."

"What is this 'it' you speak of?"

David looked at Joanna with wide eyes. "Mo-men-tum."

FORTY-SEVEN

ON THE NIGHT OF THE Savannah expedition, Jock made Thai soup. David helped chop celery and tomatoes and garlic. A smorgasbord of spices lined the counter — David counted about thirty ingredients in all. Guy and Rochelle sat at the kitchen table, egging on the cooks and drinking wine. The air conditioner in the kitchen window chugged non-stop. Jock had his urban beats thumping over the pulse of the air conditioner. In the main-floor bedrooms, two new tenants cursed their lodgings.

"This is for you, man," said Jock, dancing around David.

"It's like my birthday," said David. He had no idea what was going on.

At one point Tyler came through the kitchen wearing his Taco Night sombrero. "What the fuck are you doing making soup? It's like a thousand degrees outside."

"Celebrating, man," said Jock. "You should come."

Tyler said, "Dude, I'm not going back to that African gong show."

"It's a party," said Jock, pretending to limbo under an imaginary bar.

"It's some freaky jungle acid trip," said Tyler.

"It's a freaky jungle party. That's right." Jock kept dancing.

"Shake it!" yelled Rochelle.

Tyler said, "I can't believe you guys. This is fucking treason. Going to the Savannah on Pussy Night."

"Come out with us," said Rochelle.

"I'm too loyal, dude." Tyler made a final show of pretending to pee in the soup and headed out the door.

Guy said, "How weird is this night going to be?"

Jock said, "One step at a time, man. First we dine."

Jock ladled everyone a bowl of the soup. Guy made a motion to eat, but Jock told him to wait until the soup cooled a bit. "If you eat it when it's hot, you overwhelm the taste buds. Stir it around. Smell it."

Growing up on the farm, David had been raised on a diet of meat and potatoes. Ketchup and mustard had been the seasonings of choice. David had never tasted Thai soup, nor had he heard of many of the ingredients that went into it. However, when Jock motioned that they should eat, it was the beginning of the best meal David had ever had.

IN PREPARATION FOR THE ICE-FISHING outing, David had walked down to the picnic area where Condie Creek emptied into the Rideau River. There were no huts on the river, but someone had shovelled off a small rink for skating. David took that as evidence the ice was thick enough to walk on. To double-check, David made holes in the ice with a battery-powered drill. The bit on the drill was seven inches long and never hit water. There had been many people fishing here in the fall, so David felt this was the best place for the Dumford Mills Outdoors Club to try its luck.

The fishing store in Manotick would rent David a hand auger for ten dollars. Four dozen minnows would be twenty dollars. Maureen Armstrong's husband, Steve, was a Scout leader who took kids on fishing trips in the summer. He volunteered to bring several mini fishing rods. Dale Dickenson offered to cook hotdogs.

George Young had a curling bonspiel on the weekend and would be unable to attend. In David's mind, George was the foundation of the club. David was counting on him to offer advice, and to secretly tell him what kinds of fish people caught. He felt less confident in the success of this excursion without George backing him up.

In the week leading up to Fishing Saturday, the temperatures were consistently below zero. This helped alleviate David's concerns about ice safety.

Despite the details that needed to be worked out, David felt free from the administrative constraints of the school system. There were no permission forms. There was no curriculum to follow.

There was no need to take attendance. Families happily offered assistance. Even Joanna was eager to participate.

On the morning of the outing, David met Ron Metz at the river an hour before the families were due to arrive. It was sunny, and though the temperature was ten below zero, the wind had died down overnight. David felt comfortable in his winter jacket.

A four-inch layer of snow covered the ice on the river. The skating rink David had inspected before did not look like it was being maintained. Instead of shovelling off sections of the river, Ron and David decided to drill their fishing holes in the rink.

The first hole took them ten minutes to drill. After drilling another, they realized that if they put less pressure on the drill, it went faster. By the time the first families were arriving, Ron and David had six holes ready for the anglers.

Chunhua Wong and her mother, June, brought ladles and went around scooping the slush out of the holes.

David asked June, "How did you know to bring ladles?"

"YouTube," said June.

FORTY-EIGHT

AS THE SAFARI-BOUND REVELLERS WERE heading out the door of Monterrey House, a Finnish guy named Nartti was coming in. Nartti had moved into Tyler's room the week before. He was blond and had a slight build and soft features that made him look like he was sixteen.

In the hall, Guy said, "Nartti, want to go to a crazy nightclub?"

Nartti looked like he had just won the lottery. "Yeah!"

David, Guy, Rochelle, Jock, and Nartti took the train to the Pontocho district, which was famous for a narrow alley of clubs and bars along the Kamo River. David had walked the area in the daytime, but the nighttime transformation made the street unrecognizable to him. Dozens of red paper lanterns indicated places to eat and drink. There were neon signs pointing the way up staircases, and men handed out flyers for hostess bars. At one point they met two women in full geisha regalia, and Guy took pictures with his phone.

Without Jock leading them, David doubted they could have found the club. The only evidence of an African-themed disco was a white sandwich board on the street painted with tall green grass. A big cat's yellow eyes stared out of the grass. The club-goers descended a cement staircase and ducked through a black curtain. A doorman dressed as Tarzan greeted Jock in English.

When David walked by, the doorman bowed and said, "You should be Tarzan."

The cavernous club had a round dance floor surrounded by video screens. The video screens displayed animated jungle scenes with animals dancing about. The animals' red eyes pulsed with the beat of the music. Above the dance floor were three tiers of tables and couches that looked down on the action. Over the dance floor was a deejay booth that stuck out on a balcony. The ceiling was a tangle of green plastic vines, with an enormous blue snake weaving through the foliage. Guy, Rochelle, David, and Nartti sat on a gold couch. Jock disappeared.

Guy said, "There's no one here."

"It's only nine-thirty," said Rochelle.

"Last call at the Rising Son is ten."

This ain't the Rising Son, thought David.

"How do you get a drink here?" asked Guy.

They looked at the empty dance floor below. Jock returned with two Japanese girls wearing tight white dresses with black stripes. David supposed the girls were meant to be zebras. The girls placed two small black pots of green liquid on the table. The cauldrons had miniature ladles in them.

"More soup?" asked Rochelle.

"Aperitifs," said Jock.

The zebra girls gave them bowls painted like turtle shells. When they each had a shell filled with green alcohol, Jock said, "To a good night. *Kampai*."

David slurped at the sweet green liquid in his bowl. Nartti, the waif-like Finn who hadn't said anything all evening, leaned out over the rail above the dance floor and yelled "*Party!*" at the top of his lungs.

STEVE ARMSTRONG GATHERED THE KIDS around one of the holes in the ice rink and gave them a demonstration on how to use the fishing poles and what to do if they caught a fish. When the kids dispersed, David and Ron went around the rink putting minnows on the kids' hooks. The smell of burning charcoal from Dale Dickenson's portable grill filled the air. Joanna helped Holly Metz organize hotdogs and condiments.

While they stood around the barbecue, Steve Armstrong handed Joanna a Styrofoam cup with a dark brown liquid in it.

"Coffee?" asked Joanna.

"There's *some* coffee in it," said Steve.

Joanna took a sip and recoiled from the alcoholic strength. "Whoa," she said. "This will warm me up."

"Good turnout," said Dale, shuffling hotdogs around on the grill.

"I really hope someone catches a fish," said Holly.

"You can catch fish here in the summer," said Steve. "And they don't swim south."

Holly said, "Anna was so excited about this last night she couldn't sleep."

"I'm just happy Lyndsay isn't spending the whole day on the computer," said Steve.

Joanna wrapped a scarf around her neck. "Is it weird that my boyfriend is organizing social events in Dumford Mills? I mean, we've only lived here like six months."

"Is that all?" asked Steve. "It feels like longer."

"What's weird is that a teacher wants to spend time with students on a weekend," said Dale.

Holly hugged Joanna. "What's weird is that we never thought of doing this stuff ourselves before you guys showed up."

"It's all David," said Joanna.

"We just needed a social convenor," said Amanda Dickenson.

Joanna laughed. "David is not a social guy. I mean, he's friendly with people, but he's not a big conversationalist or anything."

"No, the weirdo teacher doesn't talk much," said Dale.

Holly scowled. "Dale! Joanna doesn't know your sense of humour."

Anna Metz ran up and asked for a hotdog. "It's not for me. I want to feed the fish."

Dale gave her a burned wiener he had tossed on the snow.

"Break it up," said Dale. "Like chum."

Holly and Joanna delivered hotdogs to the kids around the rink. At one point Jesse Young yelled that he had a fish, but it turned out his hook was caught on the edge of the ice. A few of the children tired of fishing and began playing soccer with a tennis ball. Steve lit a fire on a metal garbage can lid.

David and Ron had taken over an abandoned fishing hole. They leisurely bobbed their poles up and down in silence.

David surveyed the scene on the ice. He was pleased with the first official outing of the Dumford Mills Outdoors Club. True, no one had caught a fish, but the atmosphere was relaxed, and there was a lot of laughter. David was also happy that he was able to fish.

While David chatted with Ron about how to build an ice-fishing hut, he noticed a man in a T-shirt striding toward them from the opposite bank of the river. David motioned to Ron to look behind him. Ron glanced back and made a sucking sound.

"Do you know him?" asked David.

"Yup," said Ron, reeling in his line. "That fellow lives in the baby-blue cottage."

"He looks angry," said David.

"That's his regular expression."

FORTY-NINE

AT TEN O'CLOCK THE SAVANNAH Club started to fill up. By eleven o'clock the dance floor was packed with young Japanese partygoers pulsing to the thump of techno music.

From their gold couch, David, Rochelle, and Guy could see straight across the dance floor to Jock's DJ platform. Jock stood on the balcony overlooking the crowd. He was bare-chested and wore a gold crown and a grass skirt. He waved a bamboo sceptre over the people below, like an African dictator. He introduced songs by saying things like "Welcome to the jungle!" and "Never get out of the boat." The giant video screens played scenes from movies set in Africa and news footage of what looked like the Vietnam War. As the music pounded, Jock danced and strutted above his subjects.

Guy and Rochelle did not like the fluorescent cocktails, so David had drunk theirs. The volume of the music made talking impossible, and after a while Guy and Rochelle took to kissing. David leaned over the railing to give them some privacy. He could see Nartti's blond head bobbing in the mob below.

David thought of his father. He smiled, imagining his old man sitting beside him. Archie would have needed a beer and a pair of ear plugs. Of course, there was no possible set of circumstances that would have ended with Archie sitting in a Japanese techno-pop club. However, David would have thought the same about himself eighteen months before.

Jock pointed at David through the mist of dry ice that wafted up from the dance floor. David pointed back and downed another mouthful of phosphorescent green alcohol. He could feel the bass pulse in his chest. He bobbed his head to the urban beats while the

157

turtle shells piled up on the table. David was Marlow, following Jock's Kurtz into the heart of darkness.

Perhaps it was the quantity of alcoholic green soup that he had consumed, or perhaps it was the club's disconnect from his previous life-experience, but David felt oddly relaxed. The music was loud and the scene was surreal, but David was in a good place. He made long eye contact with a girl gyrating below him. He wondered how he might go about ordering more alcoholic soup.

David left his companions making out on the couch and wandered to the back of the upper level where he had seen bathrooms. He watched until someone came out to make sure which one was the men's room.

In the washroom was a line of urinals with poles in front of them. The poles enabled inebriated patrons to steady themselves while they urinated. David was thankful for the pee-pole, and for the video screen above the urinal that showed a black-and-white King Kong film. It reminded him of watching old movies at his grandparents' house.

As David lingered nostalgically at the trough, Rochelle burst into the washroom. She screamed wildly at David to come out. David zipped up and made a move toward the sinks. Rochelle intercepted him and pulled him out of the washroom. As they hustled back toward their seats, David could see that Jock was at the edge of his balcony making some sort of speech. It took a while for David to understand the words, as Jock's rhythmic cadence boomed over the music.

"…like a river, flowing ever downwards, deeper and deeper. But we are on this journey together. There is no going back now. We are pushed forward with our gaze locked on the future. Surrender to the current, my children. Give in to the force of nature. Flow with the tide of love until you are one with the ocean."

David and Rochelle were at the railing. From across the room, Jock had his arms stretched out toward them. The video screens filled with images of Japanese men dressed in suits of yellow feathers. The music pulsed louder until Jock was shouting.

"Get ready, my children! Get ready, Davy!"

The dance crowd morphed into several long lines.

"Davy, my man! My *gaijin* brother, this song is for you!"

Suddenly the music stopped, and the room went completely dark. The crowd cheered, and just as quickly the thunderous bass returned and lasers strobed the club. The dancers flapped and squatted in choreographed synchronicity. It took David several moments to realize what he was watching.

Rochelle screamed in his ear. "Do you know this? Do you have this in Canada?"

David did recognize the song. It was out of context certainly, and several times louder than he'd ever heard it before, but the music and movements retained enough familiarity.

David shouted back at Rochelle. "It's the fuckin' Chicken Dance."

AS THE ORGANIZER OF THE Dumford Mills Outdoors Club, David felt that it was his responsibility to confront the angry man in the short-sleeved shirt. However, Dale Dickenson stepped between David and the protester. Dale seemed pleased with the prospect of confrontation.

"You're all trespassing," said the man. "You're trespassing on my rink."

"You don't own the river, Lenny," said Dale.

The man tilted his head to the side, like a dog listening to a weird noise. "Huh? Did you shovel this off, Dale?"

"No, Lenny, but whoever did shovel it off did a pretty half-assed job. If the ice was any good, we'd be skating instead of fishing."

"You got the whole goddamn river to drill your holes in, and you drill 'em in the middle of my rink."

Some of the parents started rounding up kids.

Dale said, "It's minus ten, Lenny. What do you think is gonna happen to the water in these holes when we leave?"

Lenny said, "My boy is going to play goalie again next year. I take shots on him every night."

"Listen," said David, "when we're done, we'll scrape the ice for you. Maybe we could even flood it." David stuck out his hand. "I'm David Woods."

Lenny gave a reluctant handshake. "I know who you are. You're the guy at EC who wants to go camping with his teacher's pets."

Dale said, "This is the Dumford Mills Outdoors Club, Lenny. You want to sign up? The membership fee is your favourite amount. Free."

Lenny sneered at Dale. "I've spent my whole life outside. I don't need no one to organize me to go fishing. You powder puffs will be home playing video games when I'm out here shovelling tonight."

"Sir, we'll shovel," said David. "We'll flood it too."

"Lenny, I've got a pump," said Ron.

"You know," said Lenny, "if you knocked on my door and said, 'Excuse me, do you mind if we use your rink?' then maybe I'd feel more neighbourly about things."

"Can't picture it," said Dale.

"I think we're just about done here anyway," said David.

"That's my garbage can lid too," said Lenny.

David turned to look at the garbage can lid that was sitting on the snow at the other side of the rink. Steve Armstrong had started a fire in it, and now some of the children were warming their hands over the embers. Chunhua Wong was the only person still fishing.

As David watched her, the tip of Chunhua's rod bent toward the hole in the ice, and Chunhua struggled to maintain her grasp. June Wong ran over to Chunhua and started talking animatedly in Mandarin. June put her arms around her daughter. Amanda Dickenson yelled at the arguing men.

As everyone gathered around the mother and daughter, people shouted advice.

"Keep the rod up!"

"Let her run a bit!"

"Loosen your drag!"

Chunhua did all she could to hold on to the fishing pole. June waved off the men who tried to take control of the rod. A discussion ensued as to whether Lenny should get his chainsaw to make the hole bigger.

Lenny, the angry icemaker, offered the sagest advice: "Just wait, goddamn it."

For a while it seemed that Chunhua would be overmatched by the creature on the end of her line. But slowly, on her knees, she was able to reel the fish in, a few turns at a time. A long shadow crossed the opening in the ice. When it made a second pass, Lenny stuck his bare arm in the water and, grabbing the fish by the gills, hauled it out.

Members of the Dumford Mills Outdoors Club shrieked and clapped. Joanna hugged Chunhua. Lenny held up the fish.

"It's a muskie," said Dale.

"Pike," said Lenny.

"Must be fifteen pounds," said Dale.

"Closer to twenty," said Lenny.

"Look at those teeth," said Joanna.

The fish was laid on the ice, and Chunhua stretched out beside it for comparison. David picked up the pike in two hands and knelt on one knee. Chunhua pretended to kiss the fish. The other kids gathered for a group picture, and the parents stood behind them.

There was an awkward moment when Dale gathered everyone's cellphones to take pictures. Dale wanted to be in the picture, and he raised an eyebrow optimistically at Lenny. Lenny dismissed Dale with a wave of his hand and tromped back toward his cottage.

When the pictures were taken, David assumed the fish would be dropped back down the hole. However, a knife was produced, and June Wong proceeded to fillet the giant fish with calm efficiency. The kids watched in awe at June's knife-work.

"Where did you learn to clean fish like that?" asked David. "YouTube?"

"No," said June. "China."

FIFTY

MR. TANAKA'S FOUR-DOOR SEDAN WOVE through the mountains of Kitayama, northwest of Kyoto. In the passenger's seat, the top of his knees level with the dashboard, David studied the road intently, anticipating the bumps and curves. If he let his focus waver, the unexpected movements exacerbated his nausea.

That morning it had taken great concentration for David to walk down the stairs, undress himself, and lie on the floor of the shower. Four hours of dream-free sleep were insufficient penance for the revelry at the Savannah Club. The leg cramps and migraine were his body's way of making physical reparations for the emotional levity of the previous night.

Mr. Tanaka contributed to David's misery by being unusually chatty. At the Rising Son he cooked with his head down and acknowledged orders with a nod of his head. On this trip he peppered David with questions about Canada and farm life. He was also very interested in David's experiences hiking the Kyoto Trail. In the back seat, Kaori, Den, and Mrs. Tanaka listened to the men, offering up Japanese expressions of exaggerated interest.

"*Segoi!*"

"*Omochiroi!*"

"*Ehhhhhhh!*"

When David had suggested going for a walk as part of the sisters' English lesson, he had pictured them visiting a temple or museum. He felt that the experience would give the conversations with Kaori and Den an authenticity that was missing from their tabletop lessons. However, Den and Kaori were silent. In the confines of the car, the two students deferred to their uncle, whose intellectual curiosity and unpredictable braking were testing David's diminished powers of conversation.

"I might need a washroom soon," said David, looking for an out.

Mr. Tanaka said, "There is a tea house where we will park the car."

Fifteen minutes later they parked in front of a plain brown building that overlooked a valley on a curve of the mountain road. David stretched and breathed deeply. He had broken out in a sweat in the car, and now the cool mountain breeze made him shiver. In the washroom of the tea house, David splashed water on his face and steadied himself for the hike to follow. Once outside, he filled his backpack with water bottles from a vending machine.

The family stood at the side of the road, waiting for David. He was beginning to sense that this outing was no English lesson. Mr. Tanaka was bright and chatty, and the family had a sense of purpose about their day that David did not.

"Where are we going?" asked David.

"Outside education," said Den.

Kaori said, "My uncle was born in this area. Often we are visiting a kind of shrine. A *jizo*. My aunt and uncle go once in each season."

"What's a *jizo*?" said David.

Kaori searched for the words, but Mr. Tanaka waved them along. "*Ikimasho*," he said enthusiastically. "Let's go."

DAVID LAY ON THE FLOOR of the farmhouse living room in front of the woodstove. A lop-eared rabbit with a bandaged foot hopped on and off his stomach. Joanna came down the stairs wearing a blue blouse and makeup. This was not her usual Sunday morning attire. She sat on the couch and picked hairs off her pants.

Joanna said, "Don't answer this right away. Think about it."

"Okay," said David, lifting the ears of the rabbit.

"I was thinking that we should start going to church. All our neighbours go."

David said, "I'm meeting Ron at eleven o'clock. We're going to flood Mr. Ferguson's rink."

"I said 'think about it.' I mean not just this morning."

"I'll think about it."

"Everyone seems to go to the United Church in town."

David held out a piece of kindling for the rabbit to chew. "Whatever is closest," he said.

"We went to an Anglican Church growing up, but that's pretty close to United, I think."

"We went to Buffalo Bills games," said David.

"I'm going with Amanda Dickenson today, but I want you to think about it."

"I'll think about it."

Joanna took a lint roller out of her purse and started rolling her pants. "Why are you going to flood the rink?"

"Make amends."

"Make amends? Make amends for what?"

"The guy shovelled the rink off, and we had a little party on it. We'll just fix it up a bit."

Joanna stared at David. "Amanda says that Lenny Ferguson is a creep. He wasn't using that rink. He was just looking for a confrontation."

"We'll fix it up. Be neighbourly."

"I don't understand these people. These jerks who want to piss on you for trying to do good things. You're, like, the teacher of the year, and these losers are just running you down. I don't understand."

David said, "Mr. Ferguson is probably lonely in that cottage. He looks out his window and there are people out there, laughing it up on the rink he made. I understand why he might be ticked off."

"He said you wanted to take your teacher's pets camping. He made you sound like a pedophile."

"He was helpful when Chunhua caught the fish."

"I can't believe you're going to flood that rink. You're a more forgiving person than I am."

David rapped the rabbit on the head for nibbling his fingers. "You're right," he said. "Maybe I don't need to go to church."

FIFTY-ONE

THE KITAYAMA SECTION OF THE Kyoto Trail began with a steep climb through a pine forest. After fifteen minutes of walking up the slope, the path levelled out. David became concerned that for every step he took into the mountains, it would take another to carry his hangover-wracked body back out.

Usually when David drank he would get tired, and the pace of his consumption would fizzle out before it had any impact on his body. The night at the Savannah had been different. David had drunk the radioactive cocktails without considering their potential effect. After the Chicken Dance, another round of drinks was ordered, and David remembered downing them with Jock on the DJ platform above the dance floor. After that there was no continuity to David's memory. It was possible that the Chicken Dance had been played a second time. (It had been. David danced.) It was also possible that Nartti had passed David a can of beer from up in a tree. (Actually, Nartti had been on David's shoulders at the time.)

That morning it had taken Rochelle ten minutes to rouse David out of bed, and only a farmer's sense of duty had gotten him this far.

Out of respect for the English lesson, Mr. and Mrs. Tanaka were walking ahead of David and their nieces. With the elder Tanakas out of view, David did not conceal his physical distress, sighing deeply and bending over.

"Futsukayoi-desu," said Den.

Kaori asked, "Did you have a nice night with Guy and Rochelle?"

"At the Sa-ba-na?" asked Den.

"Do you know the Savannah?" asked David, squinting down the trail.

"It is famous in Kyoto," said Kaori. "Maybe the most popular club in Kyoto for young people."

"Tyler said you went there," said Den.

"Have you been?" asked David.

Kaori tilted her head as she often did when she wanted to answer something tactfully. Den, who was less tactful, started flapping her arms and clucking like a chicken.

Kaori punched Den on the shoulder. "*Yamete.*"

Den put her hands over her mouth and giggled.

"I'm sorry," said David, "I'm not feeling well. Will this be a long walk?"

Kaori said, "I think, from here, mostly downhill."

On the trail, Mr. and Mrs. Tanaka had stopped in front of a log cabin that would have looked at home in a Canadian forest. Mrs. Tanaka offered David a sandwich. David declined, but Mrs. Tanaka insisted. Against his better judgment, David choked down the white-bread sandwich with fishy-smelling mush in the middle.

They had walked forty-five minutes to this point, and the path ahead started a long decline. David swished water around his mouth and reluctantly picked up his backpack to follow the family. When they crossed a road, David despaired that they had not parked there in the first place.

After another twenty minutes of hiking, David started to plan his escape. If they continued any farther he would not have the physical capacity to return to the car. He contemplated a number of excuses for turning around. David had experienced a lot of growing pains during adolescence. He settled on back pain as the most plausible and least deceitful explanation for stopping.

David let his facial expression honestly express the agony he was experiencing and hustled ahead to offer the pretense for turning back. The family was waiting for him at a wooden marker on the trail.

"We are here," said Mr. Tanaka, pointing up a lightly used trail that left the main path.

"The shrine is there," said Kaori.

The path was so overgrown that David could not imagine there was a destination of any importance at the end, but he grudgingly followed the family up the track. After a minute, David bent over and the Tanakas disappeared ahead. His stomach churned, and his sense of balance left him. David considered whether he might still be drunk. He called out to Kaori. The forest came in and out of focus. David staggered forward, the taste of fish full in his mouth.

The Tanakas stood in a clearing facing David. They seemed to be welcoming him. In a space carved out of the hillside was a grey statue of a child wearing a bright red bib and a red knitted cap.

"I've seen this before," said David. His head swam.

Mr. Tanaka said, "This is Jizo."

"I've seen this before," said David, contorting his face.

"Yes," said Mr. Tanaka. "It is for a child."

Did they know? David stared at the statue. It was from the past or a dream, but he had seen this before.

Mr. Tanaka said, "It is for a child who died too young."

David slumped to one knee, looking up at the kind cook.

He said, "This is for Anna?"

"DO YOU BELIEVE IN GOD, David?"

Joanna piled firewood into David's arms from the stack beside their farmhouse.

David shrugged his shoulders. "There could be a god, I guess. I don't know."

Joanna said, "It doesn't matter. You didn't need to be religious to like this service. The reverend was amazing. Reverend Borbridge. He reminded me of Stuart McLean. He just told good stories.

"He told this one story about a doctor who had difficult patients — patients who were obstinate, or couldn't understand his instructions, or were hypochondriacs. And the doctor thought that he was a good doctor, but his patients were not letting him be successful because they were too dumb or had neuroses or bad personalities, or whatever.

"And then the doctor gets in a car crash, and he's not hurt, but the firefighters have to cut him out. They work hard, and they cut him out, and he's fine, but he thinks, 'They didn't care if I was rich or poor or dumb or smart or anything. They just worked hard, and it made no difference to them who I was.'

"So he has this epiphany. He thinks, 'There are lots of difficult people, lots of weird people, lots of people with emotional distress in the world. And they need health care just like everyone else. And maybe these people with difficulties need a better doctor than all the normal people.' And since he's a really good doctor, maybe this is the perfect situation for these people — to get him as their doctor. There's a reason that he gets the tough cases. Because that is the best outcome for these people. It's part of the plan."

David and Joanna had dropped one load of logs in the house and were back at the woodpile. Joanna was using her hands to talk instead of moving firewood. David leaned on the house.

"God's plan?" asked David.

"Sure. We were in church after all, but what a way to think about things. Sometimes I think I'm cursed when a family brings a pet in to the office to be put down. I feel sorry for myself that I'm going to have to carry around this sadness with me all day long.

"But what if I'm the best person in the world to understand and deal with this situation? I'm a good vet who can release their pet from pain and empathize with what they are going through. It sucks, but without me there, things would have been worse. I was meant to be there."

David could tell from the enthusiasm in Joanna's voice that he would probably be going to church too.

"The Findlays were there. George Young was there. It wasn't preachy. It was just good. Not too long either. But don't you love that sermon?"

David broke an icicle off the roof. "Do I need to dress up?"

Joanna said, "Sometimes I think about how we got together, and how we got jobs and ended up in Dumford Mills. It almost feels like it's just a plan that's unfolding. Do you ever think things happen for a reason?"

"I don't know," said David. "I think maybe things just happen."

FIFTY-TWO

DAVID COULD NOT UNDERSTAND WHAT he was seeing. He had expected that they were hiking to a Shinto shrine, but this was a family shrine for a child, a child "who had died too young." Of course this wasn't for Anna, but the way the family had looked at him, with kind eyes, it felt like they already knew his story. It felt like a door to the past was opening right there. David's response to the poignant scene was to throw up and pass out in the bushes.

Den poured water on David's forehead while the family went about the business of tidying up their shrine. Mrs. Tanaka snipped at plants that obscured the view of the *jizo* statue. Kaori raked the soil around the area with a straw broom. Mr. Tanaka lit incense and sat down to write in a leather-bound journal. Not much fuss was made over the Canadian teacher lying in his vomit.

When David regained his senses, Den was holding his hand, gazing down at him with a look of reassurance. The nausea was gone, and David was bathed in a cool sweat. He stared up at Den. She had always seemed like a silly schoolgirl, but in this situation it was David who was the child, and Den was the mother, patiently attending to her boy's illness. She pressed a water bottle to David's lips.

He raised himself to a sitting position and pulled his knees to his chest. Den rubbed his back. David looked at the *jizo* statue cut into the embankment. He had seen this figure before. It was the same statue he had sketched on the Keihoku Trail while the figment of Joanna rested against him. On a stone bench at the base of the statue were candies and trinkets. Mrs. Tanaka dusted the statue with a shaving brush.

Mr. Tanaka was sitting on the ground, writing in his brown book. When he noticed that David was conscious, he ripped a page out of his book, took off his glasses, and stood up. He approached David and, clapping his hands together, said, "Good. Come. Come meet Jizo."

David stood up. His legs were unsteady, but his senses were clear. The two men walked over to the red-bibbed statue. The stone sculpture was perhaps a metre high and looked like a child with the features of Buddha. The child was smiling and had his hands clasped together.

"This is Jizo," said Mr. Tanaka.

"Did you make this?" asked David.

"No, no. Jizo is a protector. He helps the children. He helps the children who have died."

David stared down at Mr. Tanaka. David had wanted to take his students outside. He wanted to spice up his English lesson. Somehow this suggestion had culminated in Mr. Tanaka taking them into the mountains and putting David, a self-confessed child-killer, in front of the Japanese patron saint of dead children. David could not shake the idea that Mr. Tanaka must somehow have knowledge of his past.

David said, "Why did you bring me here?"

"We come each season. Kaori said you are a good man, and I think so too."

David shook his head. "Who is this for?"

Mr. Tanaka smiled. "Shoichi. Little Shoichi. He was my son."

WHEN THE PICTURE OF CHUNHUA'S pike hit Facebook, interest in the Dumford Mills Outdoors Club soared. Initially, David had thought that he and Joanna would organize four or five outings a year by themselves. However, the larger enrolment seemed to necessitate more structure. If this was to be a true club, a democratic association, perhaps some organizational meetings should be held.

Ron and Holly Metz had a large heated shed that housed their farm machinery. In the corner was a social area with couches, chairs, and a kitchenette. They suggested their shed might make a good venue for a committee meeting.

Joanna sent an email to potential committee members, inviting them to meet on the first Saturday in February. In preparation, Holly and Joanna baked several dozen cookies, unsure how many people would come. Anna and Louis strung Christmas lights around the shed, proud that their farm would host Mr. Woods's club.

In the end the first official meeting of the Dumford Mills Outdoors Club was attended by David and Joanna, the Metzes, the Dickensons, the Armstrongs, George Young, and, to the group's surprise, June Wong and her husband, Gan. The group sat around a long coffee table in an eclectic combination of chairs. Dale Dickenson had brought a case of beer, and the first half hour was lost to social chatter. David was beginning to worry nothing of any substance would take place, when Amanda Dickenson yelled at everyone to be quiet.

There was no agenda, but Amanda had a pad of paper in her lap and took on the role of chairperson.

"So, the first two outings were a big success. We got a small owl and a big fish. What next, Mr. Woods?"

David shrugged. "I guess that's what we need to decide."

Maureen Armstrong said, "The owl walk was kind of educational, but the ice-fishing was more of a social outing. I don't know if we want to lean one way or the other."

George said, "I've belonged to the Perth Field Naturalists for thirty years. They have outings — a lot of birding hikes and such. It's mostly retired folks. This group seems more family-oriented."

Holly said, "It's for the kids, really, isn't it, David? I mean, this was really your way of getting your students out into nature."

"That's right," said Dale. "And if Nina Emerson wasn't such a prissy bitch, none of us would be here now."

Joanna choked on her beer. Anna was sitting in Holly's lap, and Holly clapped her hands over her daughter's ears. June and Gan Wong began speaking in Mandarin.

Amanda Dickenson called for order. She was sitting beside David and put a hand on his shoulder. She said, "We need to remember, this is really David's thing. We shouldn't hijack what he started. Do you want this to be an educational club, David? Or is it more for fun?"

David had his hands on his head. He said, "I think they can be the same thing. I mean, for the ice-fishing, we didn't sit the kids down and teach them anything. I think if you just take kids outside and put them in a new situation, or provide them with a challenge, they learn on their own. I think we just need to provide these experiences. With this group, we'll probably have fun no matter what we're doing."

"Well said," said George.

The group brainstormed possible outings, which included snow-shoeing, camping, bird-banding, and sheep-shearing.

"Let's do sheep-banding," said Anna.

Steve Armstrong said, "I haven't seen him in a while, but Ernie Graham up on Line 45 usually makes an NHL-sized rink on his property. He's immensely proud of it and would probably love having us out there."

Maureen said, "That's a good thought, but it's supposed to be really warm next week. Maybe Ernie will let us swim in his pond."

George said, "I help Lorne Pettigrew make maple syrup every spring. An afternoon at the sugar shack might be fun."

The Dumford Mills Outdoors Club Committee held its first vote. It was unanimous. Pending Mr. Pettigrew's approval, and cooperative weather, the next club outing would see the group making maple syrup.

FIFTY-THREE

"SHOICHI WAS MY SON, BUT he is dead."

"I'm sorry," said David.

"Dai-joubu desu," said Mr. Tanaka. "Long, long ago."

The monument for a child who died too young had nothing to do with David. It took some time for that fact to sink in, and as it did, David felt embarrassed for having appropriated the Tanakas' grief as his own. He felt ashamed for being so hungover on what must have been a spiritual day for the family.

Mrs. Tanaka opened a cloth bag and took out an orange and some plastic toys. She arranged them at the base of the statue. Then she reached into her bag and removed a handful of smooth black stones. She handed a stone to each person. On the ground in front of the *jizo* was a small pile of similar rocks. The family members took turns placing their stones on the pile. David looked at Mr. Tanaka for reassurance that he should do the same.

Mr. Tanaka said, "We Japanese believe that there is a river in the next world — the life after. The children need a help to cross the river. The stone is a help to build a kind of bridge. Jizo helps too."

He motioned to David to place his stone.

The children need help to cross the river.

David's teeth were clenched in a tight grimace. He set his stone carefully on the pile and thought, *Why are you doing this to me, God?*

DAVID AND JOANNA SAT IN the front pew of the Dumford Mills United Church. David thought Joanna had chosen a bold seat for newcomers. He was grateful for the legroom but was not very comfortable with the reverend making eye contact so frequently.

173

The sermon was called "The Purposeful Life." David felt like Reverend Borbridge was reading from a self-help book much of the time, but afterward, Joanna gushed.

"See, it's not all psalms and hymns. It was about real life."

"I liked the organ player," said David.

They followed some of the churchgoers down into the basement for coffee after. George Young was the first to engage with them.

"What are you doing here, David? You don't belong with us sinners."

"He has his vices," said Joanna.

"Our living arrangement, for one," said David.

Joanna said, "Mr. Young, today was the first day David has been in a church for something other than a wedding or funeral."

"Well, congratulations," said George. "Perhaps you'll take to it."

"I hope so," said Joanna. "My family attended church. It was a big part of our lives. I was an altar girl."

George said, "We were worried when our old reverend died. Reverend Taber performed every wedding and funeral in Dumford Mills for forty years. But Reverend Borbridge, he's a good man. He's held our flock together, and he connects better with the young people."

Reverend Borbridge, who had been talking to Candace Findlay, came over and put a hand on George's shoulder.

"Were your ears burning?" asked George.

The reverend beamed. "I trust you were forgiving of me. I have only known Mr. Young a short time, but I don't believe he is capable of an unkind word. Good to see you back again, Miss Shayne. And of course —"

"David."

"Yes," said Reverend Borbridge. "David Woods. Your reputation precedes you. Teacher, fisherman, early morning jogger, president of the outdoors club, and the Grinch Who Stole Christmas."

"That's my boyfriend," said Joanna.

David shrugged.

"Well," said the reverend, "it was good to see you here today. Our congregation is enriched by your attendance."

David said, "I don't know if…" and then thought better of completing the sentence.

The reverend waved his arm at the other people in the room. "The Lord brought everyone here today. Some came out of habit, some are true believers, and some were dragged by their spouses. But they were all brought here by the Lord for a reason. I believe it in my heart."

"No, it was good," said David.

Another couple stood off to the side, waiting politely to talk to the reverend.

Reverend Borbridge said, "The Lord leads us down many pathways. He opens doors for us. He gives us opportunities that we don't understand at the time are opportunities." The reverend moved to join the other couple. He nodded at David. "For now, just think of the church as another kind of club."

FIFTY-FOUR

KAORI AND DEN LED DAVID down the hillside where the path opened onto a small lake. The water was green. Several families sat under trees with blankets and picnic baskets. Mr. and Mrs. Tanaka had left to get the car. They would meet the others at the nearby road.

The sisters took off their socks and shoes and kicked water at each other along the beach. David sat on a rock and watched Den as she started to balance stones on top of each other. Kaori waded over to David's rock and sat down beside him.

"Were you part of this plan?" asked David.

Kaori looked at him. "Plan?"

"Why didn't you tell me where we were going?"

"This is the Kyoto Circuit Trail," said Kaori.

"I know," said David, "but you didn't tell me we were going to a memorial for your uncle's dead son."

"Mem-oh-ree-oh?" said Kaori.

"Up there," said David. "To meet Jizo. Jesus Christ."

Kaori shrugged. They sat in silence, watching Den build a figure out of stones. After a while, Kaori took David's hand and clasped it between her palms.

When Den was finished building, she yelled to them, "Ta da!"

Kaori said, "It is Canadian."

"It's an inuksuk," said David.

"Yes, Tyler taught us. He said it means 'We were here.'"

"It can mean a lot of things."

Den walked over and the girls started talking in Japanese. David heard Kaori use the word "memorial."

Den scrunched up her face at David. "No plan," she said. "We have no plan. Walking and talking. Outside education."

Den started twirling, kicking water at David and Kaori. "No plan," she said, dancing. "We are here. We are here."

JOANNA LOADED UP THE WOODSTOVE in the living room. The winter had been cold, but with not much snow. Ron Metz had ploughed their driveway four times, and only once was it really necessary. Most of their winter Sunday afternoons were spent in the living room, enjoying the warmth of the woodstove. David worked on his lesson plans while Joanna watched a movie. Today Joanna was watching *The Perfect Storm*, starring George Clooney.

"Don't you know how this ends?" asked David.

"I haven't seen this movie," said Joanna.

"But you know what's going to happen."

"My mom loves this movie."

"There's going to be a storm."

"There's going to be a storm, and I am going to drink my wine and watch George Clooney and Marky Mark ride it out. Do your lessons."

After an hour, David set aside his laptop and made himself a sandwich. He sat down at the end of the couch, and Joanna put her feet in his lap. David pulled a piece of gristly roast beef out of his mouth. George Clooney's boat bobbed up and down in the ocean.

"He needs help," said David.

Joanna had her hands clasped to her mouth.

"He needs help," repeated David. "From above."

Joanna paused the movie.

"Why didn't you say anything to Reverend Borbridge? You could have said, 'Nice to meet you' or 'I liked your sermon.' You just stood there."

"It was my first time."

"You weren't getting baptized or anything. Shake his hand. At least be friendly."

"I didn't want to commit to anything. Sundays are busy."

Joanna pulled her feet off David. "I know. You're a hard worker, and there's always stuff that needs to get done. But there's more to life than chopping wood and making lesson plans."

David said, "I know, but if I don't believe that stuff, then maybe a church isn't where I should spend my Sundays."

"Listen, David, church is nice people sitting around listening to a nice man tell us a good story. The reverend reminds us how we should be and how we should act. And when he's done, we drink a coffee with our neighbours. There's no downside. The church is the centre of our community."

The school is, thought David, but he didn't say it.

Joanna sipped at her wine. "You're really afraid to make this commitment."

"I think if you are going to a church, you're buying into something bigger, right? I mean, it's not just about the story and the coffee."

Joanna said, "This is just like your 'I love you' hang-up. If you do one thing, in your mind that means you need to commit to everything else. You can come to church with me without believing the wine is the blood of Christ."

David said, "You're not supposed to pick and choose what to believe."

Joanna snorted and put her ponytail in her mouth. She restarted the movie. The ship's crew tossed violently in the waves.

After a few minutes Joanna said, "And you might as well tell me you love me. I mean, who else are you going to marry?"

David turned his attention to the laptop while Mark Wahlberg was swallowed by an impossibly giant wave.

Joanna said, "Our relationship is just like this movie. We know how it's going to end."

FIFTY-FIVE

THE CAR RIDE BACK TO Kyoto was very quiet. Despite David's physical and emotional breakdown, Mr. Tanaka seemed pleased with the outing. He chuckled to himself and tapped on the steering wheel as he drove. In the back seat, Den and Kaori slept on either side of Mrs. Tanaka. David stared out the window, too tired to sleep or think. Things went by.

In Kyoto, Mr. Tanaka dropped Kaori and Den at their apartment. However, instead of taking David home, he drove to the Rising Son. David thanked the Tanakas and said he would walk home, but Mr. Tanaka shook his head. He motioned for David to come up the stairs.

David said, "I'm sorry. I'm very tired."

Tanaka-*san* said, "Atsuko will make a soup. Have a soup."

David reluctantly climbed the stairs and entered the small apartment. Mrs. Tanaka led David into the room with *tatami* mats on the floor — the room that served as their bedroom, living room, and entertainment area. Mr. Tanaka turned the television on to the Yomiuri Giants baseball game and went about tidying the room. David watched the game but longed to be back at Monterrey House, where he could take his pills and sweat out his guilt in private.

Mrs. Tanaka brought them tea and disappeared back to the kitchen. An Alcatraz-themed clock on the wall indicated that it was seven-thirty. Mr. Tanaka talked about the players on the Giants' baseball team while David fantasized about collapsing into the perspiration-stained futon of his sweltering attic bedroom.

When the soup was ready, they sat cross-legged around a square table on the floor. David did not think he was hungry, but he readily finished off the soup as well as the small bowls of pickles and ginger noodles that accompanied the meal. When the dishes were cleared, David thanked the Tanakas and stood to leave.

Mr. Tanaka said, "*Mada, mada.* Not yet. Please."

If David had had just a little less respect for the family or had been just a little less polite, he would have excused himself and bolted. In the face of so much undeserved kindness, he sat back down and waited. There was no indication from the Tanakas about why he should stay. No dessert was served. There was no discussion about the day. They watched the Yomiuri Giants and the Hanshin Tigers battle for top position in the Central League.

Mr. Tanaka described how the Giants' uniforms were designed in the same manner as the New York Giants baseball team, which was now based in San Francisco. That was the last thing David remembered hearing.

RHONDA MARTIN, EMILY CARR'S GRADE five teacher, carried a stack of photocopies down the hall. Coming the other way was David Woods with his fourth-grade class. The students were loud and were wearing jackets and snow pants.

"And where are you off to?" asked Rhonda.

"Out to work on our fractions," said David. He had several ropes over his shoulder.

Robbie Dickenson walked straight into Mrs. Martin, bouncing off her without apology. Mrs. Martin continued to her classroom where her grade fives were engaged in silent reading. Rhonda quietly shut the blinds so her students would not have a view of the grade four class. Only Louis Metz complained.

Rhonda's students were reading a survival story called *Jack Knife*. She wrote a list of questions on the blackboard for the students who had finished reading. While the class was silent, Rhonda wandered to the back of the classroom and peered out through the blinds.

Mr. Woods' class was divided into small groups. Each group had a rope tied to a tree and was using the rope to mark out a circle in the snow around the tree. Once the circle was completed, the students started piling up snow in a line between the tree and the edge of the circle. One group cut pieces out of the crust on the snow and used them to mark its line. Mrs. Martin was surprised at how all the lines from the trees came out at the same angle. She realized, however, that the lines in the snow all followed the shadows of the trees. Her interpretation was that the class was making sundials.

Louis Metz asked her what she was looking at, and Mrs. Martin admonished him to work on the questions.

To Rhonda, David Woods was a lot like her son, Jamie, who worked for a renovation company. Both men were hard workers, conscientious about their jobs. They kept their social interactions simple. Neither had any obvious vices. Indeed, Rhonda had developed a soft spot for the first-year teacher.

However, as she watched David's class through a crack in the blinds, Rhonda chewed her cheek. The students were making snowballs and were using the balls to make lines across their circles. She saw Robbie Dickenson tackle Jesse Young to the ground. David scooped Robbie up like he was a doll and carried him to the centre of one of the circles. Robbie stood in the centre, and the rest of the class gathered around him. David began motioning instructions, and students began switching positions with the person in the middle of the circle. It wasn't clear to Rhonda what was happening in this activity, but for some reason, watching the outdoor math lesson, taught by a hard-working young man who reminded Rhonda of her son, made her feel resentful.

FIFTY-SIX

DAVID AWOKE IN THE DARKNESS of the Tanaka's multi-purpose room. The blue glow from the Alcatraz clock gave the room a dreamlike quality.

As he sat up, David could see the outline of Mrs. Tanaka on a futon. She snored softly in the corner. Under the Mount Fuji curtain that separated the room from the kitchen, David could see a shadow moving about. He stood up slowly and ducked under the curtain to enter the kitchen. Mr. Tanaka was washing dishes. There were candles lit at the small kitchen table. David sat in one of the two chairs.

"Did I wake you?" asked Mr. Tanaka.

"No," said David, rubbing his eyes.

"Atsuko enjoyed watching you sleep," said Mr. Tanaka, drying his hands. He poured a cup of tea for David and sat in the other chair.

Mr. Tanaka was wearing a robe and a pair of thick reading glasses. There was a newspaper on the table, which Mr. Tanaka folded and set aside. David sipped his tea and the candles flickered. Mr. Tanaka stared at David in silence.

As David was about to excuse himself, Mr. Tanaka said, "My son was Shoichi."

David looked at his tea.

"He was five years old when he died."

"I'm so sorry," said David.

"He came home from school one day with a fever."

"You don't need to tell me about this," said David.

"Yes. His head was hot. He would not eat. We went to the doctor, and he gave us the medicine. It was the nighttime."

Mr. Tanaka was no longer looking at David. He was looking over David's shoulder into the memory of his son's death.

"I gave Shoichi the medicine, and I put him in his bed, in the room where the boxes are now. He was crying and calling for us. His throat was very sore."

David looked over at the room beside the kitchen where cases of bottles were stacked to the ceiling.

"Atsuko said he should sleep with us, but I said, 'Let the medicine work. Our doctor is a good doctor. Let the medicine work.'"

David pictured the boy trapped behind the wall of boxes.

"Shoichi was a brave boy. He did not cry often. He called for his mother, but I said, 'Let the medicine work.'"

Mrs. Tanaka called out from the next room. David jolted at her voice. Mr. Tanaka did not respond.

"Soon, Shoichi stopped crying. I looked in his room and he was sleeping. He had a Yomiuri Giants shirt. It said 'Nagashima' on it. He was lying on his belly, and I could see the number three on his back."

Mr. Tanaka held a hand out to his side and looked at David. "In the morning I went into that room. I was going to feel his head for the fever, but I couldn't roll him over."

Atsuko Tanaka entered the kitchen. She grasped her husband's outstretched hand.

Mr. Tanaka said, "I couldn't roll him over because his arms were stiff. His arms were stiff because he was dead."

The candles flickered and Japanese shadows danced.

"Shoichi had the allergy to penicillin. I gave him the medicine, and he died."

WHEN THE DAY CAME FOR the outdoors club visit to the sugar bush, the temperatures were too cold for sap to run. A warm front was forecast to pass through on Thursday night, so the outing was rescheduled for the Friday of March Break. David worried that many families would be travelling south during the spring holiday, but in the end the maple syrup event brought out twenty-eight people.

Lorne Pettigrew's wife, Ginny, welcomed the crew at the farmhouse and led the group back across a field to the sugar shack.

There were three hundred and fifty maple trees tapped in the Pettigrews' sugar bush. George helped Lorne with boiling during the big runs. Thin blue tubes connected the trees to larger black pipelines that ran the length of the forest, and the sap from the trees ran downhill to a stainless-steel tank in a swale at the edge of the forest. A gas-powered pump was used to propel the sap from the tank up to the sugar shack for boiling.

Lorne toured the families through the woods, explaining the process of maple syrup production. The tour ended at the sugar shack, a corrugated tin building that housed the evaporator. In the sugar shack, George explained how the water was boiled off to produce the sweet syrup. He stuffed wood into a long black stove under the evaporator pans, and the sap rolled in a foamy boil. The sweet smell of warm maple syrup filled the air. As George answered questions from the families, Lorne came into the shack and announced that they had a problem.

"The pump is broken," said Lorne. "We've got no way to get the sap from the storage tank to the evaporator."

"We can't make syrup," said George, "unless we can get the sap up here. What should we do?"

"I've got some buckets in the shed," said Lorne. "Maybe these folks could help us out."

It was David's idea to pretend that the pump was broken. The ruse gave a sense of urgency to the moment, and the children were excited to be involved in the solution.

David and Holly watched as George led the kids down a muddy trail to the storage tank. Robbie Dickenson was the first to come running back up the path, sap sloshing out of his bucket and onto his pants.

"The sap is sweet," said Robbie.

"Tastes like water to me," said David.

"Mr. Woods, you got to boil it. It's sweeter after you boil it," said Robbie.

There was another sap tank outside the sugar shack that connected to the evaporator inside. Lorne put a crate on the ground for students to stand on while they dumped their buckets into the bin. Amanda Dickenson took pictures as the sap brigade delivered their loads.

Holly said, "The kids just keep going."

David said, "Dale is trying to find some snow. When the kids are done, Lorne is going to make some taffy. That will be a good way to end."

Woodsmoke from the sugar shack chimney wafted lazily through the trees. In the distance a pileated woodpecker called. David shifted position so the noonday sun was on his face. He listened to the laughter of the children in the forest.

"I hear Joanna has you going to church," said Holly.

David smiled. "This is church."

FIFTY-SEVEN

DAVID SLID OPEN THE DOOR to the Monterrey House. The Monday-morning teachers were getting ready for work. Guy poked his head around the kitchen corner to see who it was.

He laughed at David. "Holy Christ, mate, you look like shit."

"I need a shower," said David.

"You need a car wash," said Guy. "Did you walk back from Kitayama?"

"No. I spent the night at the Tanakas."

"You slept with Kaori!"

"No. What? No, I stayed with Mr. and Mrs. Tanaka. They made me dinner and I fell asleep."

"I would, if I were you," said Guy.

"Sleep with Kaori?"

"She's a cutie-pie."

"Uh, no. I have to go lie down in the shower."

Guy waved a note at David. "Your mate Mitchell phoned last night. Freaking two a.m. Doesn't he understand time zones?"

"He should. He lived here."

"I told him to phone back this morning. Before you go on your walkabout."

It was eight o'clock. David thought it was unlikely Mitchell would remember to call or would figure out the time difference correctly. However, as he was drying off in the bathroom after his shower, the pink phone in the stairwell rang. David wrapped a towel around his waist and poked his head out the door. David never answered the phone. It was never for him, and he was afraid that one day it might be Joanna.

Dane the Australian called down the hall. "David, it's your travel agent."

David went through the kitchen to the phone on the staircase. Rochelle and Guy whistled at the shirtless Canadian with the hockey-player build.

Mitchell said, "What time is it there? It sounds like a party."

"No, it's morning. Hi, Mitchell."

"Hey, buddy. Where have you been? I've phoned every six hours for, like, two days."

"What's up?"

"If you were partying, that's good. Don't feel ashamed."

"I was out of town," said David.

"Do you have a pen?" asked Mitchell.

There was a Hello Kitty notepad and pen tied to the phone.

"Go ahead," said David.

"This is a phone number. You have to call it."

"Whose number is it?"

"The Ministry of Community Safety and Correctional Services."

David scribbled on the pad. "Okay."

Mitchell said, "Look, it doesn't matter to me if you're coming back or not, but they're trying to find out from your parents, and they don't know anything, so…"

"Yeah," said David.

"It's only two months away."

"Yeah."

"It might help you," said Mitchell. "It might help a lot of people to hear you testify."

DAVID HAD SEEN JOANNA'S CAR pull into the Pettigrews' laneway. Now she was walking through the field from the farmhouse to the sugar shack. David had not expected her to come to the maple syrup gathering.

Since Don Moreland had entrusted her to go on veterinary outcalls, Joanna had left a lot of self-doubt behind. David could see the change in her confidence just by the way she walked. Joanna would still second-guess her diagnoses of farm animals, but more often than not her instincts as a veterinarian were good.

As she approached, Joanna looked around to see if any students were watching and then gave David a kiss. She asked, "Did I miss the tour? Was it good?"

David said, "We just finished the tour part. George was entertaining. Lorne was good too, but he doesn't talk very loudly. People at the back couldn't hear him. I thought you weren't coming."

"I'm on my way back to the clinic. I lanced a boil on a cow down the road."

"Just in time for taffy," said David.

The kids were gathered around a picnic table. Lorne put a plywood sheet on the table, and Dale Dickenson dumped a bucket of slushy snow on it. Lorne had a pot of syrup boiling on a propane barbecue. When the syrup had a frothy yellow foam on top, Lorne brought the pot over to the picnic table. He poured some of the hot syrup on the snow and the liquid stiffened into a thick taffy. He showed the kids how to twirl the taffy on popsicle sticks until they had a ball of sweet maple candy.

Anna said, "This is our reward for carrying sap."

Martin said, "Mr. Woods should give us taffy for doing homework."

"Is there enough for adults?" asked Martin's mother.

"There's enough for two or three more clubs," said Lorne.

Amanda came out of the crowd with a ball of brown taffy rolled around a stick. She offered Joanna a bite, but Joanna said she would get her own.

"Well isn't this fun," said Amanda. "Sun and sap and friggin' maple taffy."

"You almost need sunscreen," said Joanna.

"Dale gets sunburns all the time in the winter," said Amanda, biting off a big chunk of candy.

"That looks so good," said Joanna.

Amanda scrunched up her face. "Is it supposed to be salty?"

"Maybe it's saltwater taffy," said David.

Amanda stared at her husband, who was leaning on the sugar shack, chewing his own candy. She frowned. "Dale, where did you get the snow?"

Dale pulled his cap down over his eyes.

Amanda said, "Beside the road?"

"I couldn't find snow anywhere else."

"That's disgusting, Dale. What else could be in this snow? You take that bucket and bring back some —"

Amanda was interrupted by screams. Several adults moved quickly toward the picnic table. David and Joanna ran to the table but could not see what was happening.

Steve Armstrong said, "Maureen, I'll get the truck," and ran toward the house.

Holly said, "Oh, God," and moved away from the table.

As David leaned in, he saw Lyndsay Armstrong lying on the table, crying. Her arm was stretched out on the plywood board, and her mother was piling snow on it.

Lorne Pettigrew had his hands on his head. He said, "I was pouring syrup and she just stuck her hand underneath."

George put his coat over Lyndsay. Everyone looked anxiously toward Steve Armstrong running for his truck. After an agonizing few minutes the pickup bounced over the frozen field toward the group. Steve pulled up, and David lifted Lyndsay into the back seat. Maureen and Amanda climbed in, and Steve pulled away.

The remaining parents looked at each other anxiously. Some busied themselves tidying the area around the sugar shack.

Lorne said to David, "There were lots of kids watching me pour the syrup, and suddenly she just stuck her arm out. She had a coat on, but her hand was bare."

"It was an accident," said David.

Lorne said, "That lady got snow on it fast, but that kid's hand must be burned pretty good."

Anna Metz said, "That was so gross."

"Yeah," said her brother, still eating his taffy. "Her skin was falling off."

FIFTY-EIGHT

AFTER TALKING TO MITCHELL, DAVID was filled with a sense of dread. Just hearing the name of the Ministry of Community Safety and Correctional Services made his cheeks hot.

With no food of his own in the house, David dressed and bought a package of *onigiri* rice cakes at a 7-Eleven. He continued walking to the Fushimi Inari shrine, where he bathed himself in incense smoke. He looked hopefully for the old woman who had introduced him to the rituals of Shintoism.

When the courtyard began to fill with a busload of school children, David escaped up the mountain through the tunnel of orange *torii*. He started up with a quick pace, but an hour later the weight of the previous days' events pulled him back down the hill. By the time he returned to Monterrey House, it was all he could do to haul his body up to the attic. It was late afternoon, and David slept for the next fourteen hours.

David had come to judge the quality of his sleep by the amount of sweat that soaked his futon each morning. Dry bedding was evidence of a restless night, during which images flashed and thoughts raced. A thoroughly soaked mattress usually indicated a deeper sleep, a sleep in which nightmares were played out to completion. To awake drenched in perspiration made David feel that something had been accomplished in the night — like he had completed some laborious task. The sweat was also an indication that his body had rid itself of emotional toxins.

The next morning the futon was a moist confessional mess. Lying in the salty dampness, David found it difficult to process the last couple of days in proper chronological order. There had been delicious Thai soup, and a Chicken Dance in a jungle-themed nightclub.

There had been a hungover hike in the mountains. He had passed out in the bushes as the Tanakas tended to a childlike statue with a red bib. He had listened to Tanaka-*san* tell of the death of his child in the flickering candlelight of the apartment above the Rising Son. And somewhere in that timeline, Den had twirled in the water laughing, "We are here. We are here."

Despite the number of scenes that needed to be replayed, David felt the pull of the Kyoto Trail. He had no idea what time it was, but he had the sense that he was late for work. He had a quick, too-jovial breakfast with Jock, who shadowboxed around the kitchen, reminding David of his un-teacherly behaviour at the Savannah Club.

After breakfast, David took a clean set of clothes into the bathroom. In the shower he turned on the water and assumed his preferred position in the stall, his back on the floor, his feet on the wall, and the shower stool upside down on his belly, with his hands clasped to it as if it were a steering wheel. The Keihoku section of the Kyoto Trail would take a week to finish. He also needed to properly hike the Sawa-yama section that had been partially covered during the outdoor English lesson. The rest of the main Kyoto Trail might take another three or four days to finish, or perhaps more, with David's propensity for backtracking and getting off-course.

Despite his current physical position in the shower stall, David was no longer a lost astronaut in a leaky Asian rocket. He was a man going somewhere.

IN THE KITCHEN OF THE farmhouse, David ate a sandwich while Joanna walked around murmuring expressions of sympathy into her cellphone. When she ended the call, Joanna made a whistling sound. "It's not good."

David continued chewing.

Joanna said, "Lyndsay has pretty bad second-degree burns on the back of her hand. The doctor said that there will probably be some scarring. They'll wait to see if it needs plastic surgery."

"That's kind of what we figured," said David, rubbing mustard off his pants.

"That's only half of it. Maureen says Robbie pushed Lyndsay's hand under the syrup."

"What? On purpose?"

"Lyndsay thinks it was intentional. Her mother is quite upset."

David said, "No way. Robbie is a bull in a china shop. He's oblivious to other people, but he's not mean. He was probably pushing his way in so that he could get the taffy."

"Maureen said that Robbie should be suspended."

David looked at a squirrel that sat on the windowsill. "You can't suspend kids for things they do on March Break."

"You should talk to Maureen."

"We just need to let a few days go by."

Joanna said, "I'm surprised that you're not more concerned. This is not good for the outdoors club."

"It was nobody's fault. Mr. Pettigrew feels terrible."

"Whether it was on purpose or not, you should get Robbie to apologize."

David said, "It was an accident, and everyone is upset, but we should just let things settle a bit."

Joanna scrolled through her phone. She said, "When that crazy cottager accused you of messing up his skating rink, you apologized up and down. We didn't do anything to that crappy ice, and you went out of your way to smooth things over. Over nothing." Joanna put her phone down and stood in front of David. "This is different. You need to visit Lyndsay. You need to talk to Maureen, and you need to talk to the Dickensons and get Robbie to apologize. Whether you like it or not, you're the kids' teacher. You're the president of the club, and you have some responsibility in this."

David finished a glass of milk and wiped at his lips. He would indeed visit Lyndsay Armstrong. He would also talk to her mother. He would not need to talk to the Dickensons, because at that moment Robbie Dickenson was on the Armstrongs' front porch apologizing to Lyndsay about bumping her hand. There were a lot of things Joanna was saying that David agreed with. Some of the things he did not. But with Joanna staring at him, her blue eyes imploring some response, David fell back on words his father used to explain just about everything.

"Shit happens."

FIFTY-NINE

WHEN DAVID WAS LEAVING THE Monterrey House, Tyler's friend Junichi was putting on shoes in the hallway. Junichi had spent the night in Tyler's room and was going home. Junichi and David walked to Tambabashi Station together. The Kyoto Trail pamphlet suggested that for the section David intended to hike, he should take a bus from the north end of Kyoto. The bus stops in Kyoto did not utilize as much English as the train stations, and David was concerned that he would not be able to find his way back to the area where he had hiked with the Tanakas. Junichi used a pad of paper to try to explain to David which bus to get on, and where he should get off.

As Junichi sketched out a rough map, David asked, "Would you like to go with me?" This was an invitation born of spontaneity, and it surprised David even as he said it.

Junichi looked at his watch and said, "Maybe. I have a karate lesson at seven."

David said, "I want to be at the Rising Son at seven-thirty."

"*Dai-joubu*," said Junichi. "Let's go."

They took two trains and a bus to reach the Kiyotaki bus stop, which marked the meeting point of the western section of the Kyoto Trail and the northern section. David had been hiking the trail counter-clockwise around Kyoto, but today's hike would require two hours of clockwise hiking on the northern section to reach the Sawano-Ike Pond, where Den had built the inuksuk.

When they reached a stone footbridge crossing a river, David paused at the shore and took off his shoes. He tapped sand out of them and shook out his socks. David's preferred method of crossing the bridge would have been at a full run.

"It's funny that you and Tyler are friends," said David.

Junichi nodded.

David said, "He is loud and rude, and you are quiet and polite."

"He has become a good friend."

"Is Tyler good at karate?"

Junichi laughed. "No. He is terrible. But he is — *ano* — fresh."

"Fresh?"

Junichi said, "Not Japanese."

"He swears a lot."

"Yes, yes," said Junichi enthusiastically. "He is rude and loud, but also pure."

David put on his backpack and mentally prepared for the river crossing.

Junichi said, "With Tyler, there is nothing hidden. He is all there. Very honest. I'm sorry, I can't explain."

"I think I understand," said David.

"Our sensei calls Tyler his 'Canadian *Shukuteki*.'"

"Shoo-koo-tay-kee?"

Junichi took out a cellphone and typed with his thumbs. "Neh-meh-see-su. Do you understand?"

"*Wakata*," said David, using one of the few Japanese phrases he had learned. "Nemesis."

REVEREND BORBRIDGE SMILED DOWN AT the congregation. Once again, David Woods and his girlfriend, Joanna Shayne, sat in the front pew of the church. These attractive newcomers with their community connections and growing social status would make excellent additions to the flock.

Joanna was hooked, the reverend could see that. Some of the Sunday regulars were enthralled with the pastor's folksy storytelling and would line up to thank him over post-sermon coffee. Joanna was always in the queue.

David was a different kettle of fish. There was a suspicion behind his eyes and a restlessness during the sermons that led Reverend Borbridge to doubt whether his attendance would be ongoing.

The reverend always wrote his sermons with one parishioner in mind. The chosen parishioner would change from week to week, but this process helped the reverend focus his thoughts. When Reverend Borbridge heard about the girl being burned at Lorne Pettigrew's sugar shack, he wrote the week's sermon with Lorne in mind.

"Let us consider Isaiah, chapter forty-three, verses eighteen and nineteen, where the Lord says, 'Remember not the former things, nor consider the things of old. Behold, I am doing a new thing; now it springs forth, do you not perceive it? I will make a way in the wilderness and rivers in the desert.'

"I hear many people, old and young alike, expressing regret for things in the past. They say, 'If I could only go back in time, if I could only climb into a time machine, a DeLorean perhaps, and dial myself back to a point in time, I would do things differently. I would choose a different path. I would take back something I said, or perhaps I would find the courage to say words that I kept bottled up inside.'

"Myself, I wish that I could go back to my high school graduation, to that rainy Friday night in Kingston twenty-five years ago. If I could just go back to that moment in time when the deejay played 'Forever Young' by Alphaville, and Tania Mulligan was standing against the gym wall, under the exit sign, wearing the cutest blue dress with puffy frills. Lord, if you could transport me back to Kingston Collegiate and Vocational Institute, I would do it. I would summon the courage to ask Tania to dance. Because — what if she said *yes*?"

The reverend dropped to his knees. "Oh sweet heaven!"

The congregation laughed.

The reverend added, "Sorry Jill," waving to his wife. "I'm just making a point for the sermon."

When the crowd settled down, he continued. "Listen, we all carry these regrets. We wish that we could set an old wrong right, or go back and do something that we had left undone. It might be something that happened yesterday, but it might be something that happened fifty or sixty years ago. These regrets are so poignant, so heartbreaking, that we cannot let them go. Just as the undanced song with Tania Mulligan haunts me all these years later, so we all bear the weight of remorse and misgivings.

"If we could just go back in time. If the Lord would only allow us to replay a scene in our past, then we could move forward in life with a clear conscience, with an absence of doubt. If we could only go back…"

Reverend Borbridge paused for effect.

"But, folks, perhaps we have been given this gift. Perhaps the Lord *has* allowed us to go back in time. And perhaps today is the day to which we have returned. Today is the day when we can tell a loved one how much they mean to us. Today is the day when we can leave an unkind word unsaid. Today is the day when we can make the change that will set us on a course for a better future. Today is the day when I will do that thing that will make me look back and say, 'That is when it all started.'

"Today is the day when we can say, as the Lord emboldens us, 'Behold, I am doing a new thing. I am making a way in the wilderness and a river in the desert.' "

Joanna squeezed David's arm in appreciation of the minister's words. David readjusted his position.

Reverend Borbridge smiled. "Remember not the former things. Let them go. They are a burden upon our souls. For now is the moment from which all good things can transpire. Today is the only locus from which we can effect action. And regardless of whether today is a replay of a previous Sunday or a brand new one, it is a gift from God. It is precious. Take advantage of the opportunity it presents."

The rapt silence led the reverend to believe that his words were having their intended effect.

"Make a way in your personal wilderness. Make a river in your personal desert. Let us pray."

SIXTY

DAVID AND JUNICHI SAT ON the shore of the Sawano-Ike Pond, beside the inuksuk that Den had built two days earlier. David was happy to see that the stone figure was still standing. There was no wind, and the still water reflected the trees around the perimeter.

We were here.

Junichi pulled two giant cans of beer out of a plastic bag. He gave one to David and said, "I have never been here. It is nice."

David said, "I was here Sunday, but we came from the other way."

Junichi said, "You have been to more places around Kyoto than I have been in my whole life. You are lucky."

"I just have the time to explore."

"Why don't you have a job? Don't you need money?"

"It's a long story." David opened his beer. "I do need money, but my school in Canada is still paying me."

"I don't understand."

David threw a stick into the water and immediately regretted disturbing the calm surface.

He said, "The school is paying me for a year, hoping I will get better."

"You are sick?"

"No," said David, pointing at his head. "*Baka.*" *Baka* meant "crazy" in Japanese.

Junichi said, "In my thinking, you are the least-*baka* person in the Monterrey House."

David looked at Junichi and said, "Thank you for saying that. But, buddy, I'm a mess. I have no home. I have no job. I have no girlfriend. I screwed up, and now I'm nowhere."

A crow flew over the lake.

"That is why I love the Monterrey House," said Junichi. "Everyone is — how you say? — *in between*."

"Lost," said David, taking his sketchbook out of his backpack.

Junichi said, "Yes, like me. We are all young and not knowing about the future. But when we are together in the house, no one is sad. We are laughing."

David said, "I like the Rising Son. Monterrey House is too small."

"The Rising Son is the same. Many lost young people enjoying themselves. Maybe in the future days we will look at these times and say that they were the best."

David drank his beer and started sketching the inuksuk.

Junichi continued, "Maybe this is not in between. Maybe this is the middle. *Ne, Day-beed, ne?*"

"I don't know what this is," said David.

"My father wants me to start a life with a company. I am trying not to be a salary man as long as possible."

David said, "Tonight is Kare Raisu Night."

Junichi lay back on the grass with his palms stretched toward the sky. "I want to explain to my father that the Monterrey House is real life."

David sketched an outline of the lake. He wasn't sure how to sketch the reflections on the surface of the lake, so he added waves that were not there.

Junichi said, "I am such a lost Japanese guy, David, that a *gaijin* house feels like my home."

A dragonfly alighted on the stick that David had thrown into the lake. It used its front legs to clean its eyes.

David showed Junichi his sketch of the inuksuk. He said, "We are here. We are here."

DAVID HELD UP HIS HANDS to the class and said, "This session of the United Nations will now come to order."

It was unnecessary to call for order, since after a week-long March Break, most of the students were in a sleep-deprived fog.

Five students had not even arrived at school yet.

At the beginning of the year, David had started a Monday routine of asking students if anyone had done anything interesting over the weekend. The responses tended to emphasize the economic inequality among students, so David resorted to asking if anyone had *learned* anything interesting since the previous Friday. There was no way for the class to discuss their personal histories without revealing which families were well-off, but David felt more comfortable framing the conversation around learning experiences.

"It's been ten days since we were here together," said David. "What did you learn out in the world?"

Martha Emerson said, "I learned that Florida and Ontario are in the same time zone. I thought in Florida we would need to change our clocks."

"That's right. Both places are Eastern Standard Time. Yes, Anna?"

Anna said, "I learned that maple syrup boils at one hundred and four degrees Celsius, and syrup for taffy boils at one hundred and twelve degrees Celsius."

David looked at Lyndsay Armstrong, who was rolling her eyes at Anna. David said, "It's up to you, Lyndsay, but would you like to talk about the sugar bush?"

Lyndsay said, "I told mostly everyone already. I was waiting to taste the taffy, and stupid Robbie pushed my hand under boiling syrup and I got burned."

"It was an accident," said David.

"And my hand felt like it was still burning two days later. I'm not supposed to show anyone underneath the bandages in case it gets infected."

"That's probably a good idea," said David.

"Plus, I'm having nightmares."

Thankfully, Robbie was one of the absent students and was not there to absorb Lyndsay's vindictiveness.

Ainsley Wallsworth said, "I still don't understand who gets to go on these field trips." Ainsley's parents were recently divorced, and a judge had given Ainsley's father custody of their three children, even though he was unemployed. Ainsley did not have the best hygiene, and her lunches were usually made up of pudding cups and chips. David speculated that her father was unaware of the existence of the outdoors club.

David explained, "These are not school field trips. These are events run by the Dumford Mills Outdoors Club. Last week the club visited a sugar bush to see how maple syrup is made. I went and so did Lyndsay's family."

Ainsley said, "How do you decide which students get to go?"

Carrie Connelly said, "My mom said it's a clique."

David looked quizzically at Carrie. "No. Listen. Anyone can join. I put information in your planner and on the class website. You can join too, Ainsley. Any student can come as long as they are accompanied by an adult."

Lyndsay said, "You can take my place, Ainsley. I have to go to the doctor, like, twice a week until May."

Lyndsay sounded like her mother, Maureen.

Martin put the class back on track when he said, "I went to Ripley's Aquarium, and I learned that there's fish that sleep with only half their brains. Half their brain sleeps, then the other half sleeps." Martin tipped his head from side to side.

When the students were going out for morning recess, David pulled Carrie aside and asked, "Why does your mom say that the outdoors club is a clique?"

Carrie didn't say anything for a moment and then confessed, "She says you have your favourite students, and you want to do extra stuff with them."

David said, "You're one of my favourite students."

Carrie said, "Plus it's mostly townies."

"Townies" was the term used by families in the new subdivision to refer to people who lived in the actual town of Dumford Mills. The term also was used to distinguish between new residents and those families who were native to the Dumford Mills area. Amanda Dickenson called the residents of the Conservation Meadows subdivision "Connies," or sometimes just "Cons."

David told Carrie, "Anyone can join the club. Chunhua and her family have joined." The Wongs lived in Conservation Meadows. Carrie shrugged. "I dunno. Talk to my mom."

SIXTY-ONE

WHEN DAVID GOT TO THE Rising Son, he found Tyler, Rochelle, Guy, and Nartti sitting in a booth. As David approached, Nartti chanted, "Chicken! Chicken!" which was what David had yelled at the Savannah Club to entice Jock to play the Chicken Dance a second time.

David pulled up a stool and stared enviously at the plates of curry his housemates were enjoying.

Tyler said, "Holy shit, dude. I haven't seen you in three days and, correct me if I'm wrong, but in the past seventy-two hours you invented some kind of fucked-up Colonel Sanders dance, puked on the grave of the Tanakas' dead son, and started banging Kaori."

"False," said David.

"Where there's smoke, there's fire," said Tyler. "Fill me in, brother."

David said, "Today I hiked with Junichi."

"No, no," said Tyler. "Details, dude. I don't want to hear about the trees and shit."

David said, "There are some details I don't quite remember."

Rochelle said, "He didn't sleep with Kaori."

"No," said David. "I fell asleep watching a baseball game with Mrs. Tanaka."

Tyler and Guy speculated about how David might have seduced Master-*san*'s wife.

"That's disgusting," said Rochelle.

Tyler said, "You're misled, babe. This churchgoing farm boy is really a hard-drinking, disco-dancing womanizer. He's some kind of chicken-Hulk hybrid. Get him going and suddenly he's turning yellow, flapping his arms, and banging anything that moves."

David tried to make eye contact with Mr. Tanaka so that he could get some curry.

"Good times, mate," said Guy, slapping David on the thigh.

David sifted through the memories of the past seventy-two hours and picked out the most salient fact.

"Master-*san* had a son."

Tyler said, "Yeah, dude, that's why it's called the Rising Son. Master-*san* told me he cooks in memory of his kid."

Guy said, "I originally thought it was a Jesus reference. Or maybe just bad English. Lots of signs don't make sense here."

"I know," said Tyler. "At the dojo there's a sign that says *Be your own karate*. I mean, what the fuck?"

"Dedicating the restaurant to the memory of his son is a beautiful thing," said Rochelle.

"How'd his son die?" asked Guy.

Rochelle said, "I think he had cancer." David did not correct her.

Mr. Tanaka waved at David to acknowledge that his food was coming.

Rochelle said, "Master-*san* cooks with love. He puts everything into his food."

Guy said, "I don't even use the names of the days of the week anymore. I just think, 'Today is curried rice. Tomorrow is tempura.'"

Tyler said, "Anyway, David, dude, back to Saturday. You skipped Pussy Night to go to the Savannah Club. That's bullshit, but whatever. What happened?"

Before he could speak, Mr. Tanaka placed a plate of curry in front of him.

Tyler said, "I'm sorry, Master-*san*, but you know what else is bullshit? That David gets twice as much food on his plate as I do."

Mr. Tanaka said, "Tyler-*san*, David pays twice."

David asked, "Is this pork?"

"No!" said Nartti, banging his fist on the table, startling everyone. "Chicken! Chicken!"

204

THE SECOND OFFICIAL MEETING OF the Dumford Mills Outdoors Club was again held in the Metzes' cavernous farm shed. There was a level of tension in the room, as Maureen Armstrong had publicly declared her suspicion that Robbie Dickenson had intentionally pushed her daughter's hand under the hot syrup.

The Dickensons brought beer, but so far they were the only ones drinking it.

Amanda Dickenson shouted over the din, "All right, sit down. As David says, this session of the United Nations will now come to order. Dale, read us the minutes from the last meeting.".

As there were no minutes, Dale looked around and then pretended to read off his palm. "It was hereby unanimously decided that the club would go to Mr. Pettigrew's sugar bush on March nineteenth and engage in activities of a, um, sweet nature."

Amanda said, "Yeah, let's deal with that first."

Holly said to Maureen, "I heard that Lyndsay's hand is healing well."

"I guess so," said Maureen. "It doesn't look like she will need a skin graft, but there will be scarring."

George said, "Lorne was really busted up."

Maureen said, "He came by the house this week with some flowers. He cried, apologizing to Lyndsay. I mean, he's a nice man, but he shouldn't have been pouring boiling syrup with all those kids crowded around."

Amanda shook her head in disagreement. "Old Man Pettigrew has no experience working with kids. He was just doing what he always does. It was our fault for not controlling the kids."

Dale said, "Well, it was our kid that caused it. He screwed up, and he apologized."

Holly said, "We should be more safety-conscious in the future. Let's make sure we learn from this."

Amanda said, "Other than the taffy incident, would we agree that the outing was a success?"

People nodded.

"Seriously? A success?" said Maureen. "My daughter wakes up screaming every night."

Steve made a motion with his hands for Maureen to calm down.

"No, Steve. Lyndsay is scarred, physically and emotionally. There needs to be accountability."

Joanna looked uneasily at David.

"What do you want, Maureen?" asked Amanda. "Do you want us to spank Robbie? Do you want us to pour boiling syrup on his hand?"

Maureen burst into tears. Holly put her arms around her.

Dale mouthed to his wife: *Apologize.* Amanda shook her head.

Maureen said, "I cry every time I change the bandages."

"It was an accident," said Amanda. "Accidents happen."

Dale offered beers to people, and a few were accepted.

Candace said, "I don't mean to be callous, but the reason we say that parents must accompany children is so that the club does not have to take on liability. Every child has a guardian present, and that's ultimately where the accountability lies."

Maureen blew her nose. "So it's our fault. That's what you're saying?"

"I'm in the insurance business," said Candace. "It's my job to analyze the cause of accidents, and I will tell you, every accident has a thousand little causes that lead up to it. There's rarely a single reason why something happened."

Maureen said, "Well, I did accompany my child, and that didn't help, did it?"

Steve said, "Lyndsay is a strong girl. She'll get over this."

"Will I?" asked Maureen.

George stood up. "Can I say something?"

David was about to twist the cap off a beer, but he stopped.

George said, "I was never a teacher, but I was a Scout leader for thirty years, and we planned a lot of events. We talked a lot about safety too, but I remember that the number one thing we wanted for our Scouts was a challenge. We wanted to make them uncomfortable, to stretch their limits in some way, whether we were kayaking or climbing or building an igloo. All those activities came with risks, and sometimes kids got hurt, but that was part of it. You can't always manage risk, and sometimes I believe you need to encourage it. That's how you build young men and women.

"When David suggested that we pretend the pump was broken, I applauded that. You saw how the kids responded to the challenge. I heard all the parents saying that their kids had never worked so hard in their lives. There was hard work and boiling sap and hot fires and, yes, risk. And the kids are better for having experienced it."

David turned his bottle cap with an audible hiss.

"I'm sorry," said George. "I'm old, and sometimes we geezers rant."

"I generally agree with that sentiment," said Candace, "but there is prudence for us to consider a little risk management."

Maureen stared red-eyed into the corner, dissatisfied that no one would be convicted of hand-burning.

Holly said, "I think it's important to evaluate our outings so that we can replicate the good stuff and try to reduce future issues. Where do we go from here?"

Up to this point, David had been silent. He could feel the eyes of the group turn toward him. He was choosing his words carefully when June Wong spoke up.

"I am here to help Mr. Woods. We should be helping Mr. Woods."

SIXTY-TWO

AT THE RISING SON, GUY and Rochelle recounted David's antics at the Savannah Club. David ploughed through his plate of curry, vaguely remembering some details, disputing others. Nartti kept clucking like a chicken.

Guy said, "You had four bowls of those cocktails all by yourself. I can't believe you got up the next morning."

David asked, "Did I pay for them?"

Rochelle said, "You threw, like, forty-thousand yen on the table, but our waitress said it was free. Maybe Jock paid."

Guy said, "You had a stuffed giraffe between your legs, and you were tossing ten-thousand-yen bills in the air."

"I found money in my jeans."

"I undressed you," said Rochelle. "I put the money in your pants."

"Dude," said Tyler, "it's like she paid to undress you. If you remember anything, please tell me you remember that."

David said, "I remember the first Chicken Dance. I remember going up to the DJ platform."

Rochelle said, "The Savannah Club was so fun, David. I loved seeing you laugh. I loved seeing you dance."

"It was hard getting you home," said Guy.

David cringed as Guy described how he and Jock had wrestled David onto trains and through alleys.

What David wanted to say was: "I had fun. I needed that. Thank you." What he said was: "I'm sorry."

David had a hard time understanding his companions' concern for him. Why this collection of random people was interested in his exploits, or why they would expend energy looking after an emotionally disturbed drunk was baffling. He had come to Japan with the intention of remaining anonymous, but, with no effort on his part, a monosyllabic basket case had somehow acquired friends.

Rochelle said, "That was the weirdest, funnest night. I wish you'd been there, Tyler. It doesn't seem like it was real."

"Listen, dude, I'm like the Jock of the Rising Son. People are counting on me. If I don't play guitar for last call, all these poor chumps are gonna go home with nothing but a full belly."

"There's a girl," said Nartti.

Tyler said, "I got karate and I got the Rising Son. I like to load up with *ki* during the day and pump out classic rock at night. If I go to —"

"What did you say?" asked Rochelle. "There's a girl?"

"Dani," said Nartti.

"The Dutch girl?"

"What the fuck, Nartti?" said Tyler.

Guy screwed up his face. "The blonde chick from Apple House?"

Tyler said, "You fucking Finnish fuck. I spent two hours today learning Beatles songs! Because you said you liked the Beatles."

"She talks less than David," said Guy.

"She's so shy," said Rochelle. "Oh, that's wonderful."

"There she is," said Nartti, pointing to the booth in the corner.

"Where?" asked Guy.

Tyler said, "Nartti, when we get out of here I am going to kick the shit out of you."

"She's quite pretty," said Rochelle. "Guy and I were talking to her and a couple of other Apple House girls here last week."

Guy said, "Those Apple chicks will tempt you every time."

"Apple chicks rock!" said Nartti loudly.

Tyler elbowed Nartti in the ribs. "Would you fucking keep it down. I've never even talked to her."

"She might be the one," said Guy. "She might be your special dude."

David was happy that the conversation had veered away from his drunken exploits. He looked at a Polaroid photograph on the wall of Rochelle hugging Den. He wondered if his behaviour during the outdoor English lesson would change his relationship with his two students. Could they respect a *sensei* who had been so embarrassing?

He remembered Den holding his head in the bushes. Despite the racked condition of his body at the time, David remembered the scene warmly. It felt good to have someone rub his neck. It felt good to be mothered. His lack of physical contact with other human beings probably contributed to his psychological issues. The last time he had his head in a girl's lap was in Dumford Mills, watching movies in the farmhouse with Joanna.

These connections between Japan and home were so tenuous. The sights and smells and people of Japan bore so little relationship to their counterparts at home. If it weren't for the sweaty darkness of David's attic bedroom, where his mind would force itself to confront images of Joanna and Emily Carr students, it would have been possible to let the fragile connections simply fade away. Perhaps this was why Jock said that *gaijin* either stayed in Japan for a few months or never left.

Junichi entered the Rising Son and put his hand on David's shoulder.

"What is new tonight?" he asked.

Guy said, "Tyler's sweet on a girl."

"Dani?" Junichi asked.

Tyler shook his head. "Listen, when we get out on the street, I'm cracking some heads open."

Nartti stared at Tyler with a wide grin. Tyler pointed a finger at Nartti's chest. "I'm starting with you, you Scandinavian prick."

Nartii patted Tyler's arm. "Let's go," he said. "I will be your karate."

THE MEETING OF THE DUMFORD Mills Outdoors Club regained some direction after June Wong admonished the other members to support David.

David said, "Some of the teachers at Emily Carr have taken classes to Valley Ridge Farm near Osgoode. They have an apiary. I was thinking we could go there."

"What's an apiary?" asked Dale Dickenson.

"Where you keep bees, dumdum," said Amanda.

Ron said, "Isn't that a little risky, with bees flying around everywhere? Shouldn't we choose something a little safer, especially after what happened to Lyndsay?" He looked at Maureen, hoping she would see him as an ally.

"They have special beekeeping veils to put on," said David. "We just have to wear long shirts and pants."

"Bees can sting through clothing," said Maureen. It was clear from her tone that she would have difficulty supporting any excursion.

George said, "I don't mind driving out there to see what's what. Retirement allows me a lot of freedom that way."

"That's a good idea," said Ron. "Maybe David and George and I can check the place out. See how legitimate it looks, how many people they can take. Our membership keeps rising."

Joanna said, "We have seventeen families on our email list, and some of those families are pretty big. If everyone showed up, we might overrun the place."

Holly said, "We should probably get people to RSVP."

"We need some kind of registration form," said Candace. "Then we would know for sure who is in the club. If we really want to be proactive, families could sign a waiver absolving the club from liability."

There was an awkward silence as people waited to see if Maureen reacted to the idea of the group protecting themselves from blame.

"No one is going to sue anyone," said Dale, popping a cap off a bottle of beer. "This ain't America."

"I don't know," said Candace. "It wouldn't be a bad idea to cover our butts right from the start."

Dale said, "Isn't this getting more complicated than it needs to be? Christ, we're just going out on a Saturday morning for a couple of hours. Do we really need waivers and registration forms and spreadsheets? I know I sound like Lenny Ferguson, but is going outside really so difficult?"

Candace said, "Well that's the difference between having a club and just going somewhere with your friends."

"Maybe I shouldn't be on this committee," said Dale.

Amanda said, "Honeybunch, you're friggin' sitting on a stool drinking beer, making snarky comments. That's what you do all day anyway."

David had never been on a committee before. He was appreciative that people were willing to help organize events, but he wished the meetings could maintain cohesion. He looked at Joanna for help.

Joanna said, "There's going to be some risk in taking kids outdoors, but that's where all of the benefit is, right, David?"

"Mmm-hmmm," said David. "Outside."

"We need to organize events for families who wouldn't go out and do these things on their own," Joanna continued. "As a committee, I think our job is to take care of the organizational details so that families can just show up and enjoy themselves."

"That's right, kiddo," said George. "And we can all take a piece of this pie. I mean, David here seems to have a good feel for the kinds of activities that would be enjoyable for kids and their parents. Joanna knows her way around computers. Candace wants to see that everyone is safe, or at least knows the risks. Holly likes to bake. I think we just need to divide up responsibilities along those lines. We don't all need to worry about everything."

Amanda said, "For an old fart, you got some useful ideas rolling around in that brain."

"Compliment accepted," said George.

So the committee members of the Dumford Mills Outdoors Club accepted different roles. David, George, and Ron would handle trip planning. Joanna would send out communications. Holly Metz and June Wong would organize food. Amanda was in charge of meetings and would take minutes. Candace would look after safety and legal considerations.

The Armstrongs refrained from taking roles, as Maureen expressed doubt about their ongoing participation in the club.

Dale and Gan were given the role of "members at large."

"That's appropriate," said Dale, "because we have large members."

Holly whispered in June's ear. June, whose face had turned red after drinking a bottle of beer, giggled and placed her hands on her cheeks.

"No," she laughed. "That is false."

SIXTY-THREE

FOR HIS CLOSING-TIME SET AT the Rising Son, Tyler played three songs, ending with the Beatles' "With a Little Help from My Friends." Nartti stood on his seat, adding outrageously off-key harmonies. During the song, Rochelle whispered to David that he should watch the number of times Tyler glanced into the corner toward Dani, the demure Dutch girl.

"He's not very subtle," said Rochelle.

"That's true in general."

As the tenants of Monterrey House were walking home, Nartti bounced around, karate-chopping at moths that flitted under streetlights.

Tyler said, "Nartti, you probably fight as good as you sing."

Rochelle asked, "How did Nartti know that you had a thing for Dani?"

"Dude's my roommate," said Tyler. "I talk to him. I don't know if he understands English, but we shoot the shit."

"You need to find a way to talk to Dani," said Rochelle.

"I can talk to her," said Guy. "I'll set you up, mate."

"No way," said Tyler. "I don't want you and your juiced-up fucking Kiwi sex-drive coming within ten miles of her. No offence, Rochelle."

"I can ask her if you'd like," said Rochelle.

Tyler said, "No, babe. I'll think of something."

Guy ducked into a variety store to buy a toothbrush. Rochelle and Tyler sat on a bench. Nartti swung from a tree along the street. David and Junichi chatted about the possibility of hiking the Keihoku Trail together.

Tyler said, "Dani started coming to the Rising Son a few weeks ago. She smiles at me when I'm playing guitar."

Rochelle hugged Tyler's arm. "You're in love."

Nartti was now hanging upside down by his knees in the tree. He had his hands over his eyes like goggles. He said, "She likes David Bowie."

Tyler let out a stream of profanity and made Nartti repeat what he had said.

"She likes David Bowie."

Tyler said, "Dude, what the fuck? How do you even know that?"

"Texting," said Nartti, dangling precariously.

Tyler grabbed Nartti by the arms and pulled him out of the tree. The two fell into some bushes, and Tyler emerged with Nartti's cellphone in his hands.

"She does like Bowie."

"Maybe you could use that information to your advantage," said Rochelle. "*Mr. Guitar-player.*"

Tyler pulled Nartti out of the bushes and said, "I don't know whether to thank you or pound on you."

Nartti put his arms around Tyler and, straining, picked him up.

"You're my big brother," said Nartti.

"Every day in Japan is the same," said Tyler as he was carried down the street. "Mixed emotions."

DAVID STOOD OUTSIDE THE METZES' steel shed. The meeting had broken up, and he had taken the first opportunity to escape.

Joanna followed him out and took David's hand in hers. "Afraid of Maureen?"

"Lyndsay's healing good. She should just let it go."

Joanna said, "I hope the Armstrongs don't quit now. If they do, I'm afraid Maureen will always hold a grudge."

"Against who? Us for organizing a trip to a sugar bush? Mr. Pettigrew for making taffy? Robbie for reaching for candy?"

"She wants a pound of flesh from someone."

Anna came around the corner pulling a picnic basket on wheels. "Mr. Woods, wanna see?"

Joanna and David peered down as Anna lifted a flap on the basket.

Two yellow chicks hopped out and scurried for the long grass. Anna covered one with the front of her dress while Joanna chased the other down. David pushed other yellow heads back into the basket.

"It's okay if they escape," said Anna. "They're printed on me. They printed on me, and now they follow me around."

"How many are there?" asked Joanna.

"I think there's eleven, but they're hard to count when they're awake. We had thirteen, but the cat got one, and Uncle Johnny stepped on one."

Anna put the chicks back in the basket and sorted through them. She pulled one out and held it up for Joanna. "This one has an eye that won't open. Can you take him home and fix it?"

Joanna pulled the eyelid open. "It's infected. I can give you some drops to put in."

"Okay," said Anna. "It'll just be another chore. I have to change their water and shavings every day. And you might not know this, but you have to wipe their butts. It's true. Baby chicks need their butts wiped."

Joanna laughed and hugged Anna. She said, "Sweetie, if I have a daughter, I hope she's like you."

"That's nice," said Anna, "but I'll tell you, being a mom is hard."

SIXTY-FOUR

ON THE WAY HOME, THE Monterrey group stopped at Karaoke Box, where customers rented rooms by the hour to drink beer and sing karaoke. David and Tyler sat on a couch behind the others. They drank Sapporo, listening to Rochelle sing "My Way."

Tyler said, "It's too bad you weren't here a few months ago."

David said, "What do you mean?"

Tyler said, "Monterrey House used to be fun."

"It seems pretty lively."

Tyler said, "When I moved in, everyone hung out together. We ate together. It was a party."

"It would be nice to have a living room," said David.

Tyler said, "There were two brothers from Australia, Mark and Andy. They played guitar. After dinner we'd drink and sing. Those guys could play anything."

"Nice."

"My dad plays guitar, so I knew some chords, but I never sang before or anything. But Andy gave me a guitar he found in the trash. Dude, we jammed every night. Everyone from the High Five House would come over. There were girls everywhere. It was a scene."

David grunted his empathy.

"I fucking loved those guys," said Tyler.

Guy was now singing "Born to Be Wild" with his collar turned up.

"And one morning," said Tyler, "Kim comes in with these workmen. We're fucking sitting in the living room, and Kim says we need to clean the room out so they can start building a wall. Like, what the fuck? It was a total shit show. Girls were crying. Mark threw all the workers' tools out in the alley. The cops came."

"Really?"

Tyler was now standing, looking down at David.

"Yeah, dude, like, three days later our living room is fucking gone. Mark and Andy are gone. People are, like, walking in wondering where the party is. Sorry, dudes, the party's over. The music's died."

"That's tough," said David.

Tyler was shaking his head. "That motherfucking landlord, that greedy piece of shit, you know what he did? He stole joy. We had a fucking great thing going. We were like a family. And that cocksucking slumlord maggot blew it all up. What for? Two hundred thousand yen a month? I would have fucking paid him that much to leave it alone. Fuck. One day there was joy. There was joy, and then the next day it was all fucking gone." Tyler slumped back on the couch.

David watched Guy serenading Rochelle with a big red microphone.

Tyler said, "And you know what Mark told me? Andy didn't find the guitar in the garbage. He fucking bought the guitar. The dude had known me, like, three weeks, and he bought me a fucking guitar.

"I was going home too. I was planning to get the fuck out of here. But then one night I'm at the Rising Son. I'm drunk, and I take Master-*san*'s guitar off the wall. Thing's in tune, and I start playing 'Brown-Eyed Girl.' Everyone starts singing. It kind of felt like I was back in the living room, you know?"

"Sure," said David.

"I had to make a decision. Do I go home, or do I try to keep it going? I thought, Maybe I can keep it going. Maybe I can be Andy and Mark for someone else, you know?"

"Yeah."

"I'm learning all kinds of shit in karate. We all have power in us. We can all be superheroes. It's not all about kicking ass."

"You're a superhero," said David, meaning it.

Tyler said, "Ah, I just wanted to hold on to this thing. You know when you've got something fucking good happening, and you just want to keep it going?"

"I do," said David.

DAVID AND JOANNA JOLTED UPRIGHT in their bed. Cats scrambled for safety. In the darkness of the bedroom, an alarm was ringing.

"It's the laptop," said David.

Joanna opened the computer. "I think it's the video chat." She pushed a button and the screen glowed to life. A wobbly image of a bowl of rice appeared. The camera angle swung around, and a bearded face beamed at them.

"I just ate eel!"

Joanna gave the laptop to David and put a pillow over her head.

"Where are you going, Jo-Jo?"

David squinted into the screen. "Hi, Mitchell."

Mitchell yelled, "I'm eating eel, buddy."

David said, "What time is it?"

"Dinnertime," said Mitchell. "Did I wake you? I thought you'd be up."

"I guess I'm up," said David. "Where are you?"

Mitchell said, "My students are taking me out to dinner. I ate eel. Here, this is Mika. Say hello to David. This is Kumiko. And this is Suzu."

David waved at the Japanese girls.

Mitchell said, "When are you guys coming to visit? It's wild here. Tokyo is amazing."

"I don't know."

"You're looking pretty ragged. Are your students wearing you out?"

"I'm in bed," said David.

"You should teach here. This is my whole class. Three university girls. I'm a *sensei*."

David stared at his bearded friend.

"And look at the size of the beer cans. It tastes just like Canadian beer. It's awesome. You need to visit me. Soon, though, because I applied to law school for the fall."

"Really?" said David.

"Yeah, teaching is a grind, man. Not here, but, you know, in a regular school."

Joanna groaned to let David know the conversation was keeping her awake.

David said, "It looks like you're doing well."

Mitchell now had his camera pointed at one of the Japanese girls.

Mitchell said, "Ladies, this is my best friend. You can't tell, but he's a big man. He's a stand-up guy. I would follow him anywhere. And he's got a great girlfriend. Show them Joanna. Where's Joanna?"

David did not adjust the computer.

Mitchell said, "I'm going to be the best man at their wedding. Joanna is a really pretty girl."

"Good to hear from you, Mitchell," said David.

Mitchell reappeared on the screen. "Yeah, no, things are good. I'm a *sensei*. I'm eating eel. It's all pretty sweet. You gotta visit."

"Might be tough," said David.

Mitchell said, "When will you ever get the chance to come to Japan? I can show you around. You wouldn't want to live here, but for a wicked vacation, Tokyo is a crazy scene."

"We'll talk about it," said David.

"Come. It will blow your peach-growing mind."

"Okay," said David. "Goodnight, Mitchell."

"*Sayonara*, buddy."

David watched the screen as Mitchell's students took turns saying "Bye-bye" in singsong voices. David turned off the computer, but the screen continued to glow green in the darkness.

From beneath the covers Joanna said, "Mitchell's going to be your best man?"

"I don't know," said David.

"I don't care if he is," said Joanna, "just as long as he doesn't make a speech."

SIXTY-FIVE

DAVID SKIPPED KATSU-UDON NIGHT AT the Rising Son to prepare himself for the phone call he needed to make. The phone in the house did not allow for outgoing long-distance calls, but David had seen a green international phone at Fushimi Station. His plan was to wait until dark and take an unhurried walk to the station. By then, the time difference between Kyoto and Ontario would be appropriate.

As David waited for the sun to set, he fretted that the phone call would be the beginning of the end. September loomed over the summer like a Kyoto mountain. Each day the mountain got closer. By the end of August he would have to climb the mountain. It was not something David wanted to think about. Just walking to Fushimi Station would require all the courage he could summon.

David had completed the main loop of the Kyoto Circuit Trail that afternoon. It ended unceremoniously at a train station. The final section included a dense bamboo forest, a restaurant that served fish-head soup, and a shrine dedicated to the Japanese founder of hairdressing.

The Keihoku Trail would be next and, with an extended commute from the south end of Tokyo, would take David nine or ten days to complete. Though if Junichi were able to accompany him and interpret signage, the journey would be quicker. Considering the anxiety this phone call was causing, a week wandering remote mountain forests would be therapeutic. David remembered some words from a high school English class: *The woods are lovely, dark and deep.*

At dusk, David grabbed his Hello Kitty paper with the phone number on it and headed out the front door. The evening was windy and warm. In the alley down from the Monterrey House, children were playing with flashlights. David walked between them, and they stopped playing to shine their beams in his face. The angle of the light on David's face, combined with the sheer size of the man, scared one of the girls and she called out for her mother.

David zigzagged his way to the station, passing neighbours conversing in doorways. At Fushimi Station he found the international pay phone he had passed dozens of times before. He inserted a phone card with a picture of the Kiyomizu-dera temple on it. This would be the only phone call David would make to Canada.

After David entered the string of numbers there was a long pause, and he resisted the urge to hang up. Eventually a recorded voice offered several options, and David entered the extension Mitchell had given him.

A woman answered.

David said, "Hi, is this Yvette?"

"Yes."

"This is David Woods."

"Oh, David, thank you for calling. You're a hard man to reach."

"I'm sorry."

"No, it's good you called. We just have a few things we need to discuss with you. Have you done any reading about how this whole process works?"

"No," said David.

"Well," said Yvette, "let me start by explaining what an inquest is."

ERNEST GRAHAM TIED UP HIS boots and asked his spaniel, Simon, if he wanted to go for a walk. The spaniel shook his head in excitement and went to the back door. Ernest's wife, Margaret, sat in a rocking chair by the woodstove, working on a crossword puzzle.

Ernest said, "I'm going to check the fields."

"You should wear your rubbers."

"I'll be fine."

"It's muddy back there."

"How do you know?" asked Ernest.

222

"It's April," said Margaret.

"Do you want to come?"

"Nope."

The Grahams' farm went back from the road in a long narrow strip. The farm had been passed down through the family beginning with Ernest's grandfather. Ernest and his brother, Rich, had divided the property in two, and Rich had built a new house on his half. Many of their neighbours were also Grahams, an assortment of cousins and relatives by marriage. The stream flowing through the back forest was called Graham Creek.

Due to the rolling nature of the property, different fields could be planted at different times. The slopes dried first in the spring, but the lowest areas might not be free of standing water until mid-May. Because of the negligible amount of snow received the past winter, Ernest expected he might be able to start planting the first crops the following week.

Simon scampered ahead, darting from one clump of dirt to the next. Yesterday the dog had caught a mole, and that success fuelled the excitement of today's hunt.

In the fall, Ernest had watched helplessly as Simon danced around a porcupine. Even after the porcupine caught Simon square in the face with its tail, Simon still tried to find a weakness in its defences. By the time Ernest made it to the dog, the spaniel had taken another blow to his muzzle and, somehow, one to his backside.

Most of the property was in the condition Ernest expected, except for the field farthest back. There was much more water flooding into it from the bordering swamp than he had ever seen. This field always flooded in the spring, but given the lack of snow cover, such large ponding was unexpected.

Despite the unreliable nature of the field, this part of the property was Ernest's favourite. If Mother Nature cooperated, wet weather in the fall allowed Ernest to make an outdoor rink in the winter. Family would gather from around the county, and Ernest played host to a cohort of young relatives. Some of Ernest's best winter memories were of his family gathering for evening skates. In the Grahams' living room there was a framed photograph taken from the hill where Ernest was standing now. In the photo, kids played hockey on the rink, while adults sat on ATVs and watched from the sidelines. Each October, when the crops were in, Ernest hoped for rain. Well-timed precipitation would allow the chance for that Christmas scene to be recreated with another generation of Grahams.

Simon was wading around the edges of the flooded area. Ernest whistled and yelled for the dog to start heading back.

"Go any deeper and you'll sleep in the barn tonight."

SIXTY-SIX

YVETTE, THE CASE MANAGER FROM the Ministry of Community Safety and Correctional Services, asked David if he had a pen. David scanned the train station but did not see any potential for finding a writing implement.

"No," he said.

Yvette, not knowing that David was standing in his shorts in the corner of a Japanese train station, waited for him to indicate he was ready to take notes.

When the silence stretched out, David said, "Sorry, I don't have anything."

Yvette said, "Well, I'll just give you a general overview of how this works. First of all, this is not a trial. No one is accused of anything, and no one will be found guilty or liable. The coroner will oversee the proceedings, and a lawyer will ask questions on his behalf."

David slumped against the wall beside the phone. He wished he had borrowed someone's cellphone and called from the sticky darkness of his bedroom.

"The questions are designed to create a clear picture of what happened, and to determine the chain of events that led to the fatality."

David moaned.

"I know it will be difficult, but the inquest is just a process to uncover factual information. A five-person jury will listen to the facts of the case. They will rule on how the child died and make recommendations to the coroner to prevent similar incidents.

"The inquest is scheduled to begin on September 14. However, there are several witnesses scheduled to testify before you, so the date of your summons is September 15. Your testimony is central to the facts of the case, and we anticipate that you will be on the witness stand for approximately two hours."

David's eyes were closed. The receiver of the phone was pressed against his forehead, but he could still make out most of what the woman was saying.

"When you are called to testify, the counsel for the coroner will ask you questions. They are typically open-ended questions, which will allow you to give your account of the incident as you remember it. Counsel for the Metz family may ask questions, as well as counsels for the school board and the conservation authority. It is not a bad idea for you to seek representation as well so that a lawyer can guide you through the process. Your lawyer may also be able to suggest to the coroner the best way to frame the questions directed at you.

"Mr. Woods, do you understand?"

"I guess so," said David.

"This is not an adversarial process," said Yvette. "By law, neither the jury nor the coroner can assign blame."

I wish they would, thought David.

"We also need you to provide a witness statement before the proceedings. This is your opportunity to provide an account of the facts surrounding the incident. This statement can form the basis of your testimony in the courtroom. I have a package of information that details the information I've shared with you here and includes the official court summons. What's the best email address to send the information to?"

"I don't have email right now."

Yvette said, "I can print it and mail it to your home."

David thought about giving Yvette his parents' address, but then gave her the address of his post office box in Kyoto.

Yvette said, "Mr. Woods, we didn't realize you were in Japan. Are you travelling, or have you moved there?"

"Kind of both," said David.

Yvette hummed, trying to make sense of the statement. "Mr. Woods, is it your intention to return to Canada to testify?"

ANNA METZ STOOD IN FRONT of David's desk. The bell to end the school day had rung five minutes earlier.

"Anna," said David, "I want to talk to you for a minute."

"Am I in trouble?" said Anna.

"No," said David, "but I heard you talking earlier, and I would prefer if you would not tell the other students that I am going to your house for dinner tonight."

"You've been to my house three times," said Anna.

"I know," said David, "but let's not advertise it."

"Do you think they're jealous?" Anna leaned forward and started doing push-ups on the edge of the desk.

"The other students may not know that I am friends with your parents."

Anna said, "If they want to spend more time with you, they should join the O-C."

"O-C?" asked David.

"Outdoors Club."

"Yes, but —"

"Not everyone's going to get burned."

"No," said David. "But tonight is just neighbours getting together. It's not —"

Anna's hands slipped off the edge of the desk. She fell to the floor and popped up just as quickly. "Phew," she said. "Close one."

David said, "Do you understand what I'm saying?"

"Yes," said Anna. "When you come to my house, that will just be a secret between you and me."

"Kind of," said David. "But I don't want the other students to think that you and I keep secrets."

"So our secrets should be secret."

"Let's talk about this with your parents."

The gym teacher, Jeff Kressler, stuck his head into the classroom. "Is this a good time?" he asked.

"Yes," said David. "Perfect time. Excuse us, Miss Metz."

Anna skipped toward the classroom door. Before she left, she turned back to David and put her finger over her lips.

Jeff Kressler was tall and sinewy, and wore shorts throughout the year. He seemed to enjoy his job.

He said, "How's the environmental club going?"

"Good," said David. "We might visit an apiary in May."

"I don't know what that is," said Jeff, "but it sounds like fun."

"Honeybees," said David.

"Sure. Listen, Dave, I want to build an obstacle course. I'll do it on school property if I have to, but what might be better would be along the path beside the creek. We could have chin-up bars and balance beams, rope swings, maybe those tire things on the ground that football players use. What do you think?"

"Sounds good," said David.

"Maybe I can get grant money from somewhere. Wouldn't that be good?"

"Yes," said David.

Jeff said, "What about the conservation authority? Would they care?"

"Can't hurt to ask," said David.

"What about leaving school property to run the course?"

David told Jeff about his discussions with Roger Dixon, and how the permission form debacle had played out.

Jeff said, "My wife teaches grade one in Kemptville. They have a field beside the school that is owned by the town, but the kids all use it during recess. I doubt anyone gets field trip forms for that. There must be some arrangement that could be made."

"That's interesting," said David, nodding.

"Dave, your schoolyard lessons have got me thinking. I'm in a bit of a rut here and I need a project I can get excited about. This obstacle course might be just the thing."

"I understand," said David.

"Are you on board?"

"Maybe," said David.

"*Maybe?* Of all the teachers here, I thought you'd jump at this."

David bounced his fingertips together. "I don't know if I want to get into it again with Roger over property boundaries and risk-management stuff."

"I get it," said Jeff. "You got burned. But, man, you can't be gun-shy. Dave, you and me are young. The staff here is going to turn over soon, and if we play our cards right we can run this place for the next twenty years. Roger's a good guy, and we should take advantage while the iron is hot."

David wasn't sure what "running the place" would entail, but he would be happy to have another teacher advocating for outdoor activities. "Keep me posted," he said.

Jeff said, "We'll have to jump through some hoops, but hey, you can't do an obstacle course without jumping through hoops. Right, Dave? Right?"

SIXTY-SEVEN

DAVID SKIPPED A SECOND CONSECUTIVE night at the Rising
Son. The phone call with the Ministry had opened up a stressful new
artery between Canada and Japan, between the past and the present — between the halves of his brain that he tried to keep separate.
Considering the events of the previous weekend, lying low for a few
nights was probably a good recuperative strategy.

David also wanted to prepare a proper English lesson for Kaori
and Den for the next afternoon. He would not be able to make up
for his shameful behaviour in one day, but he wanted to make a
start.

The sisters had obviously received a comprehensive English
education over the course of their schooling. Practising grammar
patterns and verb tenses at this point in their lives was not going to
be helpful for them. They needed to put their language skills to use
in some meaningful way. Perhaps walking could still play a part.

David put a big pad of paper on the floor of his attic room. In
purple marker he wrote phrases like "have a debate," "write a mission
statement," "act out a play." He had not settled on an approach, but
the words seemed to point a better way forward.

David was asleep when his bedroom door opened. David squinted
into the crack of light streaming in from the stairway.

"Dude, you up?"

"Tyler?"

"Did I interrupt your night terrors?"

"What time is it?"

"Closing time."

Tyler threw a blue envelope onto David's futon. David picked it up.
Tyler said, "It's from Kaori. It smells like potpourri."

David examined the envelope sealed with stickers of cartoon puppies.

Tyler said, "Maybe rub it around your room," and left David in the darkness.

David turned on the light, afraid of what the letter would say. After his performance in Sawa-yama, David worried that the sisters might not want to continue the English lessons. If this were a termination letter, it would derail the rehabilitation of David the Teacher.

David picked at the puppy stickers until the contents spilled on his chest.

There was no note, only seven one-thousand-yen bills. For some reason the Tanaka sisters felt it necessary to pay him for staggering around in the mountains north of Kyoto.

DAVID LOOKED OUT A WINDOW for Ron's truck. George and Ron were picking him up to visit Valley Ridge Farm, where the Dumford Mills Outdoors Club might learn about bees. Joanna was dressed in coveralls, preparing to go on a farm call.

Joanna said, "I would have thought you'd plan your visit for tomorrow so you could get out of going to church."

David said, "I did, but George wants to go to church."

"Good," said Joanna. "I reserved us a pew. *Pew for two.*" Joanna giggled at her joke.

David said, "Why do we have to sit up front?"

"Are you intimidated by Reverend Borbridge?"

"No. Isn't the front row reserved for old people?"

"David, I sit there so you can stretch out your legs. And be closer to God."

When Ron arrived, George Young was in the passenger seat of the SUV. David climbed into the back.

George said, "Welcome to our first subcommittee meeting."

Ron said, "I motion that we get coffee first. All in favour?"

"Aye," said David.

In the drive-through, George said, "Remember the Owl Prowl?"

David said, "If you hadn't called that owl in, there wouldn't be an outdoors club."

"I wouldn't say that," said George.

"I would," said David. "Until you lured in the screech owl, that night was a bust. Everyone was freezing. If we hadn't seen that little guy, no one would've come back."

George said, "It was good timing."

Ron looked at David in the rear-view mirror. "Did you really want to create a club, or did it just happen?"

"I don't know," said David. "All I know is that back in October I told my students we were going to look for an owl in the forest, and when I couldn't get permission for that, I thought we could try after school sometime. When that went well, people were asking me what was next."

"You just got carried along," said Ron.

"It all worked out," said David.

George said, "There wasn't this much planning for the Owl Prowl, was there? You said, 'I'm going to look for owls. Join me if you want.'"

Ron said, "Now it's subcommittees and waivers and mailing lists."

"It's a measure of the club's popularity," said George.

Ron paid the girl at the drive-through window. "It's a sign of the times," he said.

George took the coffees from Ron and handed one to David. He said, "When I was a Scout leader, we would take kids winter-camping in Gatineau Park. We'd leave on a Friday afternoon and come back Sunday. When we got into the bush, no one knew where we were. There was no way to contact us. If something had gone wrong, we would have just had to hike back out." George leaned back to look at David. "Different era."

Ron said, "Parenting is different now. I don't know if we're more responsible than our parents were or if we're just suffocating our kids."

George said, "Louis is a bit of an explorer, isn't he?"

Ron said, "Yeah, we give him a little more rope than Anna, that's for sure. Holly and I might have a double standard in that regard."

David said, "My brother used to ride his horse around our farm. He'd tie a rope to the saddle horn, and he'd pull me on my bike. I was probably nine or ten."

"And you weren't wearing helmets," said George.

"No." David laughed.

"That could be our next activity," said Ron. "We'll pull the kids behind horses. We'll race them."

"There'd be a lot of paperwork for that," said George.

A cellphone rang. George pulled the phone out of the console and tapped on the screen. He said, "Mr. Metz's answering service."

Ron and David could hear Holly's voice talking excitedly. George murmured expressions of understanding.

When he hung up, Ron said, "What's the crisis?"

"Nothing to worry about," said George. "The Emerson family has joined our club."

SIXTY-EIGHT

FOR THE SUNDAY AFTERNOON ENGLISH lesson, David had bought two copies of the *Japan Times*. It seemed to be the most common English-language newspaper in Japan, and on the weekend included an Opinion section. David felt that the articles in that section might provoke conversation.

When David entered the Rising Son, Kaori and Den were seated in the first booth, arms at their sides, cups of tea in front of them. David placed the newspapers on the seat and put the large pad of paper on the table. He turned the pad over. On the back, in large block letters, he had written *I'M SORRY*.

"I don't want last weekend to be how you think of me."

"You should have stayed in bed," said Kaori. "You were sick."

"I thought we were just going for a walk. If I'd known where we were going on Sunday, I never would have gone to the Savannah Club."

"No problem," said Den, pointing at her sister. "She was drunk last night."

Kaori glared at Den.

"I really want to be your teacher. I want to be your *sensei*."

"So teach us," said Den, shrugging.

David had the sisters read an article about a scandal in the Japanese government which involved a male politician's female secretary writing most of his emails for him. Some of the emails contained classified information and discussions about national security issues. Both girls were aware of the scandal.

During their discussion, Kaori showed sympathy for the secretary, noting that her own boss was an alcoholic. Many people in her office covered up his behaviour. For Kaori, the secretary's actions were just a sign of loyalty. However, Den thought it was "super, super crazy" that the secretary was advising government officials on matters of national defence. It was the first time David had seen Den disagree with her sister.

During the conversation, David motioned for them to get up, and they continued talking in the park across the street. Den sat on the same dragon David had ridden into the ground during his breakdown a month earlier.

The discussion was animated and more authentic than most of the forced conversations of previous lessons. David occasionally corrected their grammar, and suggested better vocabulary choices, but did not try to stop the flow of the conversation.

Back in the Rising Son, David had the sisters write letters to the editor. He was happy with this lesson and wondered how they might use the neighbourhood around the pub for future lessons.

When Kaori handed him another blue envelope, David said, "No, no. The money you gave me yesterday will be for this week."

Den was playfully trying to put the money in David's pocket when Mr. Tanaka entered the bar. He spoke to the sisters in Japanese, and they hurriedly gathered up their backpacks. Den handed the envelope to her uncle and the girls made a hasty escape.

Mr. Tanaka gestured for David to sit back down. "Have a tea?"

David shook his head. Mr. Tanaka tapped the compensation envelope on the edge of the table.

David said, "I'm sorry about last week."

"*Zen-zen*," said Mr. Tanaka. "Not at all."

There was an awkward silence that David hoped would be broken with an explanation of why Tanaka-*san* wanted him to stay. The master seemed absorbed in studying the creases of the envelope.

Rochelle appeared in the curtained doorway.

David's heart began to pound. Another ride on the dragon was not out of the question.

Rochelle sat beside him and put one of his large hands between both of hers.

"It's okay," she said.

Tanaka-*san* put the envelope down and clasped his hands in front of his chin.

"Who is Anna?"

TWO STAGECOACH WAGONS FRAMED THE entrance to Valley Ridge Farm, and freshly painted white fences lined the lane down from the highway. Scarecrows and neatly stacked hay bales gave the farm the feel of a rural tourist attraction. Ron parked his truck in a gravel lot surrounded by several farm buildings.

A woman in a wide-brimmed hat emerged from the main farmhouse and greeted the men. She said that her name was Marlena, but they should call her Marley. Marley led them down a hedge-lined path to a sunny clearing where the hives were kept. There were about forty stacks of boxes painted in different colours.

"They all know which box is theirs," explained Marley.

"How many bees are there?" asked Ron.

"All together? Maybe a million now. Two million by the middle of summer."

George whistled.

Ron said, "I don't see any bees."

"It's sunny today, but still too cold for the girls to fly. A lot of trees are flowering, so they'll be out when it gets warmer this afternoon."

David said, "Would you bring our group down here?"

Marley said, "We'll give you a little slide show in the barn, and then we'll get the veils on and come down here. I'll open up a hive and show everyone what's going on inside. Then we'll go up to the shop to taste the honey, and people can buy some if they'd like."

Ron said, "Do people get stung?"

"No," said Marley.

"We can just stand in the middle of a million bees?"

"Yes."

When Ron raised an eyebrow, Marley said, "Listen, it'll be more dangerous for you guys just to drive here. During the tour we'll give you hats with veils and a pair of gloves. We'll get everyone to tuck pants into socks and that type of thing, but it's mostly for show. Just to make folks feel safe."

"I get stung by bees around my farm all the time," said Ron.

"That's wasps," said Marley. "Honeybees don't want to sting nobody."

Ron stared at the hives. David wondered why Ron seemed so skeptical about the bee tour.

"I hear that a lot of people find beekeeping therapeutic," said George.

"Sure is," said Marley. "There's something reassuring about watching bees work their asses off."

David asked about the cost.

"It's two hundred bucks for a two-hour tour. You can bring as many folks as you want, but we only have twenty-five sets of veils. If you bring more than twenty-five, then some people can go without, or some can stay behind if they're too chicken."

David looked at Ron and George for consensus.

George said, "Sounds good to me."

"I guess," said Ron with a lack of conviction.

David said, "I think we should do it."

Marley said to Ron, "We keep EpiPens around, if you're worried."

"It's just that we had an incident at our last outing," Ron said. "A girl got burned. It was an accident, but I'd rather that nothing happens this time around."

"I'm not guaranteeing that no one will get stung," Marley said, "but in the grand scheme of things, there're better things to worry about."

"I just want to minimize the risk," said Ron.

Marley turned away. "Life's a risk."

SIXTY-NINE

TANAKA-SAN'S QUESTION SENT A COLD spasm through David's body. Rochelle tightened her grip on his hand. Mr. Tanaka nodded silent encouragement.

After a long pause, David's first words came out as a croak, forced between clenched teeth.

"Anna was a student."

With the pressure of Mr. Tanaka's stare compelling further detail, he added, "She was a student in my class."

In this way, David told his story. It was delivered in short sentences, punctuated with sighs and deep breaths. He spoke as if trapped under a slab of cement.

When he finished speaking, the front of Rochelle's blouse was wet with tears. Mr. Tanaka smiled kindly.

Rochelle pulled David's hand to her mouth and kissed it. "It wasn't your fault."

"I understand why people say that," said David.

NONE OF ERNEST GRAHAM'S CHILDREN had any interest in taking over the family farm. Ernest's wife, Margaret, often encouraged Ernest to sell the property to his brother so they could move to Ottawa. Margaret dreamed of buying a condominium downtown so she could spend her golden years going to plays and eating in restaurants that had tablecloths. Ernest's stomach turned to knots each time Margaret suggested this. Ernest wasn't keen on farming much longer, but he would be happy retiring on the farm. Living out his days grouse-hunting with his dog would suit him fine.

When Margaret began reading him a real estate listing describing a condominium overlooking the Rideau Canal, it sent Ernest looking for his hat. Simon the spaniel sensed the possibility of an outing and pressed his nose to the seam of the door.

"Goin' to check the fields," said Ernest.

"They're still there," said Margaret.

Out the back door, Simon hit the ground running. Ernest didn't meet up with him again until the third field back, where Simon was digging into a groundhog hole.

"If we lived in the city, what would we do at Christmas?" Ernest asked Simon. "Drive out for dinner at Rich's place, and go home three hours later?"

Simon tilted his head at his owner's rhetorical questions. He was often privy to Ernest's anxieties and happily absorbed the words that Ernest was afraid to share with his wife.

"Where would our kids stay? Not in our house. Probably Donny would get the house. Probably turn it into a goddamn meth lab."

Simon had absorbed a lot of words by the time the two made it to the back field. Ernest looked over the depression below.

"For Christ's sake, there's more water than before."

SEVENTY

"IT WAS AN ACCIDENT," SAID Rochelle. "If anyone is to blame, it's the farmer."

Mr. Tanaka poured them *kocha* in ornate porcelain cups.

Rochelle said, "There was nothing you could do."

David pulled his hand out of Rochelle's grasp. Rochelle looked at Mr. Tanaka, wondering what else could be articulated.

Rochelle said, "We always thought you were saying 'Joanna.' Sometimes in your sleep you call out. But it's 'Anna,' isn't it?"

"I have nightmares," said David.

"No wonder." After a silence Rochelle added, "You should talk to a therapist. The more you can talk about what happened, the better."

"Maybe."

"You should talk to your girlfriend. I think you should talk to your family."

David said, "There's nothing to say."

Rochelle said, "But you still love Joanna?"

Tears welled up in David's eyes.

"Call her," said Rochelle, rubbing his arm.

"I can't."

"Why?"

Mr. Tanaka reached across the table and grabbed Rochelle's wrist.

"Because David must die."

BEFORE THE CLUB'S VISIT TO Valley Ridge Farm, David tried to contact parents of students living in the Conservation Meadows subdivision. He wanted the outdoors club to be as inclusive as possible, and it bothered him that Carrie Connelly had said the club was for townies.

Joanna had gone over the list of families on the mailing list, and it was true that only three of the eighteen families — the Wongs, the Brocks, and now the Emersons — were from the new development. David did not know where he and Joanna fit in the divide.

The Conservation Meadows families tended to be fairly wealthy, and the subdivision was more culturally diverse than the greater Dumford Mills area. Indeed, the Wongs were the only non-white family to participate in the outdoors club's events. Jenny Lin's mother said that Jenny was too busy with dance on weekends to join the club. Jing-Shen's father told David that Jing-Shen would rather play video games than go outside.

One day after school, David was on parking duty, keeping students on the sidewalk and guiding cars to empty spots, when he spotted Carrie Connelly's mother, Laura, weaving her bike through a crowd of departing students. David waved at her.

"Mrs. Connelly," he called.

Laura Connelly took off her bike helmet and sunglasses. She shook her head and pushed the hair out of her eyes. She was athletic like her daughter, and David mused that an outdoors club should be right up their alley.

"I had the wind behind me coming here, but it will be hard for Carrie going back." She peered around David at Carrie, who was standing with a group of girls.

David said, "The Dumford Mills Outdoors Club is visiting a farm that keeps honeybees this weekend. I thought your family might be interested in joining us."

Laura said, "I know. It sounds like fun. Weekends are just so busy. We will get out one day."

Carrie ran up to her mother. "Jenny wants to show me a video. I'll be right back."

David and Laura chatted about the weather, but when the conversation reached a lull, David said, "Carrie mentioned that the composition of the outdoors club may not be for everyone."

Laura laughed. "You can't say anything around kids, can you?"

"I just want everyone to feel comfortable joining our activities."

"We would be comfortable. Really. It's just that our Saturdays fill up so quickly."

David raised an eyebrow. "So we might see you at an event?"

"Yes. It's inevitable."

"Great," said David.

While they waited for Carrie to return, Laura said, "You have to understand that most of the people in Dumford Mills did not want Conservation Meadows built. People resented that so many houses went in and changed the character of their town. If I lived here before, I would feel the same way."

"They might not be happy with the houses," said David, "but I don't think they have any problem with the people."

Laura smirked. "When I'm talking to people from town, 'townies' as we say, the conversation inevitably steers to some local topic I know nothing about. They start talking about someone I don't know, or something that happened twenty years ago. I don't know if it's purposeful or unconscious, but it's real. I know how minorities must feel."

"I haven't experienced that," said David.

"You're on a farm. You talk their language. They don't see you as a con. That's what they call us. 'Cons.' "

"Yeah."

"Amanda Dickenson says it the most, but at least she's honest. She calls us cons to our faces. She knows there is a split in this town, and she's open about it. It's the people who whisper and make little inside jokes who make us feel like outsiders."

"Maybe the outdoors club can bring people together," said David optimistically.

"We will come out some day. It's not that big a deal for us. For some people, though, if you start up a club with the Dickensons and the Metzes and the Findlays, it just looks like a townie frat club."

Carrie Connelly returned and put on her bicycle helmet.

Laura said, "When town council approved the subdivision, it saved this town. It saved Emily Carr."

David said, "That's a lot to think about."

"It has nothing to do with you. You are the best thing that's happened to this school."

SEVENTY-ONE

"WHAT DO YOU MEAN THAT David has to die?"

The look on Rochelle's face made David think she was unsure whether the declaration was metaphorical.

"I had to die," said Mr. Tanaka.

"I don't understand."

Mr. Tanaka told Rochelle about his son.

"I gave him the bad medicine, and he died."

Rochelle tried to process the stories she had just heard.

Mr. Tanaka poured himself more tea. "After Shoichi died, Atsuko and I went to Toyama Prefecture, my hometown. My father was a baker, and he said, 'Help me bake. Help me in the shop.' I sent Atsuko home, and I helped my father. But I was not really there. I was gone. Like a ghost."

David nodded.

Mr. Tanaka said, "You cannot go on living, knowing what has happened. You cannot enjoy food. You cannot watch a baseball game. You cannot accept words from others. This is the punishment that our minds have decided for us."

Rochelle said, "There must be something that can help."

Mr. Tanaka said, "There is nothing that can be done. Nothing to say. To make a peace with the world, we give up everything. When our life is gone too, then there is a fairness."

Rochelle said, "But you and Atsuko are still together. You are living again."

"Yes," said Mr. Tanaka. "I came back to life. I am happy, *ne?*"

"How?" asked Rochelle. She thought it was important to ask for David's sake.

"In Toyama Prefecture, there is the Imizu Jinja shrine. It is beside the Takaoka Castle Park. I was going there after working in my father's shop. I was walking and sometimes watching the weddings. One day I met a priest, a Shinto priest. He was sitting at an outside table, and he waved to me to come. I went to him, and he said, 'Sit with me. Play some *shogi*.' *Shogi* is like a Japanese chess.

"So each day I am playing some *shogi* with the priest. I told him about Shoichi, but he did not say anything. And then one day I am crying. I am saying to him, 'What can I do?'

"He said to me, 'Serve Shoichi. Live in service of your son.'

"These were good words for me. After that I am returning to my shop and to Atsuko. Shoichi liked the shop. He helped me cook, giving me pots and also stirring food. He very much enjoyed turning on the gas, watching the fire. So now I am cooking foods that Shoichi and I would make."

"You made tacos with your son?" asked Rochelle.

"Yes. We went to Japanese Disneyland, and Shoichi ate a taco. I said, 'It is too spicy for you,' but Shoichi ate the taco and said it was good. He liked them, and so now I make tacos. Shoichi would like that."

Mr. Tanaka smiled at David. "The priest had good words for me, *ne?* 'Serve Shoichi.' Maybe I have good words for you."

David looked up from the tea he had been studying. Bygone patrons of the Rising Son smiled down from their Polaroid prisons.

Mr. Tanaka said, "Serve Anna."

THE MORNING OF THE BEE tour was sunny and warm. David and Joanna stood in the grassy parking lot, directing families to the red barn where the slide show would take place. Robbie Dickenson and Katie Findlay sat on stools at the barn entrance collecting money.

Joanna said, "If everyone comes who RSVP'd, we'll have thirty-four people."

David said, "That means nine people will have to go to the bees without protection."

When the Metzes arrived, Anna was dressed in a black-and-yellow bee costume. Styrofoam balls danced on top of pipe-cleaner antennae on her head.

Anna said, "I've got a stinger that's really a sword." She waggled her bottom at David. A grey plastic blade flopped around behind her.

"You have to be careful not to sting anyone," David said. "If you're a real honeybee, you'll die."

Anna turned her attention to stinging her brother.

Joanna said, "Here's a Mercedes. It's the Emersons."

The black sedan parked at the end of the row, and Martha Emerson popped out, followed by her mother. Nina was wearing jeans, a white sweater with a black vest, and cowboy boots.

She beamed at Joanna and David. "What a day. My flowers at home are in full bloom. The bees love them. Thank you for organizing this. Pollinators are so important."

David said, "It's a nice day."

"And I read so much about how bees are in trouble. It's a shame."

Joanna said, "Everyone is meeting in the barn."

Nina said, "Look at this place. This is just wonderful. You guys are wonderful."

When Nina walked to the barn, Joanna asked, "Was that genuine?"

David shrugged. "I'm happy Martha is here."

A few minutes later, Marley, the bee-lady, waved at David to indicate she was going to start.

Joanna said, "You go. I'll stay here a bit longer in case anyone shows up late."

David gathered students who were running around in the parking area. Anna ran by David and shook her sword-stinger at him.

"Don't," said David. "You'll die."

SEVENTY-TWO

THE TOWN OF KEIHOKU WAS officially part of Kyoto, but David had to take a ninety-minute bus ride to reach it. The bus wove through mountains and passed landscaped rows of pine and cedar trees. The last stop on the line left David in front of a white wooden inn.

The town consisted of a narrow strip of houses and shops framed by steep mountains on either side. Like most rural towns in Japan, it looked like the buildings had slid down the mountains over the centuries and settled into living estuaries. The trees on the hillsides formed a patchwork of light and dark colour. The colour of the trees depended on when the area had last been logged; the older the trees, the darker the shade of green.

The start of the Keihoku Trail was tucked behind an abandoned schoolhouse. David's map had several footnotes, one of which advised that the chain across the trail could be opened, but that hikers should "replace the chain for the respect of others." David stepped over the chain and began the second leg of his hiking journey.

The hard-packed trail led down a slope to the edge of a river. Giant cedar trees formed wooden walls along the river, stretching up hills on either side. The roots of the trees jutted out into the trail like gnarled hands, grabbing at the soil.

Where the trail met impassable rock walls, it crossed the river on simple wooden bridges. Because access to the forty-kilometre trail was limited, David would have to cross these same bridges several times in order to complete the circuit in stages. The constant traversing of water made David feel that the gods were testing his resolve. On one nervous river-crossing, David raised a middle finger to the sky.

At a turn in the trail, the roots of one large cedar tree melded into a rock face. At the base of the tree was a cave that disappeared into murky darkness. David peered into the cave and shuddered at the thought of entering the crevice.

Later, the trail emerged at the base of a small waterfall. A stream poured down the side of the mountain and splashed on flat rocks below. A small stone monument engraved with *kanji* characters commemorated the waterfall. David sat on a rock near the falls and started sketching the oblong marker. He poured himself tea from his thermos and wondered what the Japanese writing meant.

Mr. Tanaka's description of walking through life like a ghost seemed apt. The sketches he sent to his mother were the only contribution he made to any relationship that remained in Canada. For most everyone else in his past, he was dissolving. Soon, even Joanna would have little to hold on to.

Since stepping over the chain, David had not seen any other people. This section of the Keihoku Trail was never particularly busy on weekdays, and the heavy August heat dissuaded hikers from setting out in the middle of the day.

When David finished his sketch, he took off his clothes and found a position among the slippery rocks where he could stand under the waterfall. The day was hot, and the cold water came as a shock. He sucked in shivering breaths, the rivulets of water careening off him and disappearing down rock crevices into the Yamadadani river.

Standing under the mountain stream, framed in granite and cedar, David stared at the sky, sobbing. "I'm sorry. I'm so sorry."

THE HONEYBEE PRESENTATION IN THE barn stretched to an hour, as parents peppered Marley with questions about life in the hive. Members of the Dumford Mills Outdoors Club sat on hay bales, and restless kids pulled at the straw. When Marley finally cut off the discussion, the crowd was herded into a coatroom where they were handed straw hats with mesh veils. Marley showed them how to tie the veils securely around their necks. Each person was given a pair of tan leather gloves with long cuffs that covered their arms.

Outside, everyone gave Marley their phones to take pictures of the group.

Holly asked Marley, "Don't you get a veil?"

"Nah, why start now?"

At the hives, Marley lifted the lid off a stack of white boxes. She used a metal tool to pry apart slats of wood the bees had glued together. The visitors let out hushed gasps as Marley used her bare hands to lift out a frame. There were hundreds of bees covering the frame's surface.

"Why don't they sting you?" asked Robbie.

"Honeybees are programmed to do a certain job," said Marley. "If you move slow and easy, they just keep doing the job as best they can. If it was raining or I dropped them or something, then they might get fussy."

"The bees keep making honey even when you take them out of their home?"

Marley said, "You learn a lot working with bees. I've learned that you should do the job that needs to be done, and don't pay much attention to what's going on around you."

When the session at the hives was over, Marley asked everyone to put the veils and gloves back in the coatroom. Anyone who wanted to buy or taste honey was invited to meet in the shop across from the barn.

As David and Joanna were walking out of the barn, Nina Emerson put her arm through David's and said, "Let's have a chat."

David looked back as Nina led him away. Joanna's mouth was wide open.

Nina led David to a children's play structure beside the farmhouse. She sat on a swing, her cowboy boots dragging in the tall grass. David hoped that she would not ask him to push her.

Nina said, "I know you hate me for not signing the permission form."

"That's not true."

"It probably is, but it doesn't matter. Martha really enjoys your lessons. Even when you teach inside."

David said, "I just thought, you know, the conservation area is right beside the school."

"I think that's a problem today. Teachers don't know how to structure their unit plans."

David looked at rows of corn stretching into the distance.

Nina said, "They don't follow a textbook. They just pick stuff off the Internet. Anything goes."

"What does that have to do with taking students into a forest?"

"At this age, the education system should be focused on establishing intellectual discipline. We graduate high school students who don't know their times tables."

David didn't want to argue with the lawyer.

"I think, during your first year, it was prudent of me to anchor you in the classroom. I think it was best for you, best for Martha, and best for all of the other students."

"I don't hold it against you," said David.

"In a school setting, going outside for the sake of going outside is not proper justification."

"Don't know," said David. He looked toward the barn for some excuse to extricate himself from the conversation.

"As you learn what works and what doesn't, you can start to incorporate the outdoors in ways that make sense. But to ask me, as a parent, to agree to let a first-year teacher take my daughter into the woods every day, in all kinds of weather, David, that was a stretch."

David leaned his arm on the cold metal slide. Families were emerging from the honey shop.

"Someday you'll thank me," said Nina. "I'm probably the reason this amazing club exists."

David could see Joanna looking toward them. He said to Nina, "I should go help clean up."

Nina swung her legs freely under the swing. "Aren't you going to push me?"

SEVENTY-THREE

MONDAY AT THE RISING SON was Okonomiyaki Night. *Okonomiyaki* was a Japanese pancake filled with cabbage, onions, and seafood. Mr. Tanaka topped the dish with mayonnaise and a sweet brown sauce. Of all of Mr. Tanaka's offerings, this was the dish that David liked the most. The sweet topping would have made it a children's favourite, and probably explained its place in the weekly dinner rotation.

David used chopsticks to push strands of shredded cabbage around the perimeter of his plate. At the table with him were Junichi, Guy, and Rochelle.

Rochelle said to David, "I told Guy about Anna. I told him the whole story."

David nodded.

"What a crazy tale," said Guy. "No wonder you're on a walkabout."

Rochelle said, "When I heard you and Master-*san* tell your stories, I realized that my problems are nothing. They are dirt under my fingernails."

David reached for a piece of onion he'd dropped on the floor.

"It makes you look at that Rising Son sign differently," said Guy.

Rochelle said, "That's the thing. We just don't know everyone's stories. Most of the time we just scratch the surface with each other."

"Sometimes I get deeper," said Guy.

Rochelle said, "It was a bit of a trap, but, David, I'm happy that you trusted us. Do you feel relieved at all? Was it good to open up?"

David thought about how to answer. He looked at Rochelle and held his hand over the middle of the table. The hand was trembling noticeably.

"Are you okay?" asked Rochelle.

David said, "I'm scared that Junichi is going to ask me what we are talking about."

"I'm sorry," said Rochelle. "I shouldn't talk so freely."

They all looked at Junichi to acknowledge the awkwardness of the conversation. Junichi shrugged his shoulders. David clinked his beer bottle against his Japanese friend's glass.

Guy said, "David, the way I see it, you need to finish up your hiking and go back to your girlfriend. That's the only place to start. Either that or find a teaching gig here and start getting it on with Kaori."

Rochelle said, "Is there any advice you can offer that isn't sexual?"

Guy said, "Babe, my advice to any mate who is trying to get his life together is — number one — get yourself a girl and go from there. Or if he's already got a girl, then start worshipping her. Start there."

Rochelle said, "Are you implying that you worship me?"

"Every night, if I can," said Guy, burying his face in Rochelle's neck.

Junichi was also in love with Rochelle. It pained him to hear Guy speak so openly of his relationship with Rochelle. To distract himself from their courtship, Junichi asked David about the Keihoku Trail.

David said, "The problem with Keihoku is that there is only one place to access the trail by bus. Unless I take a taxi, I'll have to start at the same point every day. It's a circle, so I can go the opposite direction too. But it's forty kilometres around the whole thing. Even to go halfway and come back, that makes for a forty-kilometre day. I won't be able to make it."

"*Wakarimasen*," said Junichi. "I don't understand."

David drew a circle with his finger on the table. He wished he had his big pad of paper to explain the dilemma.

After more explanation, Junichi said, "You should be camping."

"Where?" said David.

"Just sleep on the path," said Junichi. "I have a camping mat. I will come. We can sleep on the path."

Guy interrupted. "Junichi's a good guy, but he's not the one to be taking camping in the mountains. Take Kaori."

"Kaori and I have hiked," said David.

Guy said, "I know you've been kicked around, but, David, the gods have been messing with you. You're a victim of randomness. You need to get back on your horse. Start with your girlfriend or a new girlfriend. Start with love."

"Thanks for the advice," said David. *But could anyone love a ghost?* he thought.

FOR HIS ONE HUNDREDTH SERMON at Dumford Mills, Reverend Borbridge spoke about the need for good manners. He knew it was not his strongest sermon, and it sounded preachy, even for a man of the cloth.

David Woods stared at the base of the reverend's lectern, going over the next day's lessons in his head.

After the service, Joanna said to David, "I asked the reverend to talk to us after coffee."

"Why?"

"For some guidance."

"About what?"

"The ways of the world," said Joanna.

George Young approached the couple in the church lobby. "Can we squeeze in one more club outing before the summer?" he asked.

Joanna excused herself.

David said, "Sure. Something easy. Like a hike or a hayride or something. And then take a break until the fall."

"I could lead an edible plant hike."

"Really?" said David. "Could we cook what we found? Joanna would love that."

"To keep the kids interested, we could build a fire and prepare a meal."

"Sounds good," said David. "Maybe we wouldn't even need a committee meeting."

"Perfect," said George.

When most of the congregation had cleared out, Joanna and David met Reverend Borbridge in the Sunday School room in the church basement. They sat on the floor around a table the children used for crafts.

The reverend clasped a chunk of clay between his hands and said, "Let us play."

"Ha ha," said David.

Joanna said, "Reverend, I haven't said anything to David about this, but I was hoping that I could talk to you about the outdoors club."

"You should call me John."

"Oh, sorry. Sure. John. Well, John, I have been bothered by something someone told David."

The reverend pulled the clay into a long strip.

Joanna said, "A parent of one of David's students told him that because he started the outdoors club with the Metzes, the Dickensons, and the Findlays, he was alienating people who live in Conservation Meadows. This person described our group as a 'townie frat club.'"

"I live in Conservation Meadows," said the reverend. "Across from the park."

Joanna said, "Those families this parent mentioned are good people. They welcomed us to Dumford Mills with open arms. They volunteer. They go to this church. And they've come together to organize events for kids and for the community. I mean, how can anyone find fault with that? Do residents of Conservation Meadows really feel like outsiders in this town?"

The reverend said, "If this person feels this way, then it is real for them."

Joanna said, "I just don't understand how something so pure in intention, run by good people, could be seen in a negative way."

Reverend Borbridge said, "Conservation Meadows is essentially a bedroom community. Most people in my neighbourhood commute to Ottawa every day. They buy groceries on the way home from work. They invite each other over for barbecues. In some ways, they do isolate themselves from Dumford Mills proper.

"But on the other hand, in town, you have families who have grown up together, who have histories together, who know everything about each other. In social situations it's inevitable that people will gravitate to those with whom they feel most comfortable."

Joanna said, "I can see how someone might feel a little awkward joining a club where they don't know anyone, but to run it down, to say that it's a 'frat club' for townies, I just don't get it."

The reverend said, "It would be a mistake to interpret this person's words without knowing their experience."

"There's another parent who thinks that David is a bad teacher for wanting to teach lessons outside. And there was a guy who suggested David was a pedophile for organizing weekend events with kids."

The reverend said, "There once was a man who walked among us who did nothing but speak of love and forgiveness. And they crucified him."

David was leaning back on his elbows, his legs stretched out in front of him.

The reverend said, "I don't mean to imply that David is on the same level as Jesus, just that, despite all of our good intentions, there will always be those in the world who will interpret our words and actions in a negative light. It's unavoidable."

"So I shouldn't worry about these people?" said Joanna.

"First seek to understand, then to be understood."

Joanna nodded.

The reverend said, "I believe in the Word of God. I believe that it is my duty to spread knowledge of the glory of my Maker to those around me. I try to open my heart to the Lord and let him guide my sermons. And yet, to some in the congregation, their main concern seems to be the quality of coffee in our urn."

Joanna laughed. "So you get it? You're trying to do good work, and even as a man of the cloth, you get criticized."

"More than you will ever know. However, if you were hoping today that I could help you understand other people's thoughts and motivations, you'll probably be disappointed."

"No," said Joanna. "I just — I love your sermons, and you seem to have more insight into human nature than most people."

"I appreciate that. But regarding the outdoors club, I would just keep going the way you are. Do your best. Involve as many people as you can and don't worry too much about how the world reacts."

Joanna said, "That's what Marley, the beekeeper, said. She said we should be like honeybees. Work hard and ignore what's going on around you."

"We can learn a lot from beekeepers," said the reverend.

"Amen," said David.

SEVENTY-FOUR

AT THE KITCHEN TABLE OF Monterrey House, Junichi and David studied a map of the Keihoku Trail. Jock added spices to tandoori chicken, annoyed that the map was taking up most of his workspace.

David pointed with a pencil. "If we can hike twenty kilometres the first day, then we can camp along here somewhere."

Jock said, "Aren't there bears and shit up there?"

"Yes," said Junichi. "Sometimes there are attacks."

"Really?" said David. It had never occurred to him that there was any danger along the trail.

"You couldn't pay me to sleep in the mountains," said Jock.

"Aren't you the king of the jungle?"

"I am," said Jock, moving to an imagined beat. "I'm king of the urban jungle. I tame the masses. Every night I take a bunch of animals and train 'em. I get those wild kids all lined up, moving in rhythm. It's a skill. I'm a conductor. I'm a lion tamer."

"Please protect us from the mountain bears," said Junichi.

"That's a whole different environment," said Jock. "Davy, man, he's as big as a bear. The animals need protectin' from him. He might roll over in the night and squish you. Ju-man, you got, like, some karate move to protect you from that?"

David was grateful that Junichi was helping him complete the Keihoku Trail. However, he was concerned that if they hiked twenty kilometres each day, he would not have an opportunity to stop at each shrine and waterfall. He would not have time to sketch or explore side trails. Even though he would have hiked the entire circuit, if some elements of the trail remained unexplored, in David's mind the journey would be incomplete.

Jock pulled a piece of chicken out of a thick brown sauce and separated it with his fingers. He said, "You guys can have some chicken if you wash up the dishes."

David looked at Junichi for agreement and said, "Please. Thank you."

Junichi folded up the map and Jock placed steaming bowls of rice and chicken in front of them.

Junichi said, "I will miss the smell of the Monterrey House."

Jock said, "You going somewhere, Ju-man? 'Cause I'm not. I'll be stinkin' up this joint for a couple more years at least."

"Maybe I will be joining a company," said Junichi.

"Oh, boo hoo," said Jock. "You can't visit your friends if you have a job?"

Junichi said, "I am afraid that things might be changing soon."

Jock said, "There's only one thing that stays the same, and that's that things is always changing. I've been here three years, and I probably met a hundred people in this kitchen. Everybody's passing through. They're all going somewhere else."

David ploughed through the chicken. Each day in Japan expanded the dietary repertoire of a boy raised on steak and potatoes.

Jock said, "What about you, Davy? When you're done all this walking, what are you going to do? Join a company too?"

The question made David tense up. "I don't know. I don't want to think about it."

Jock said, "Man, everyone in this house frets about what they're going to do next. You know what I'm doing next? I'm going to enjoy this chicken. Then I'm going to enjoy my bike ride downtown, then I'm going to enjoy playing music, then I'm going to enjoy my sleep. It ain't complicated."

David said, "In September I need to —"

"Forget September, man! Just eat your chicken." Jock shook his head. "Are you even tasting it?"

AS ERNEST GRAHAM DROVE HIS ATV over the ridge down to the swale in the back field, he kept checking to make sure Simon was not running between the four-wheeler and the trailer. On the trailer behind him was the dented aluminum canoe that he and Margaret used to take camping. There was a time when the canoe would have held the two of them as well as their three kids and a dog or two.

In a moment of nostalgia, Ernest had optimistically asked Margaret if she would like to go for a paddle with him through the swamp to explore the source of the flooding.

"What for? It's beavers."

"Well, I know it's beavers," said Ernest. "But we've had beavers back there for fifty years, and they've never flooded the fields."

"Take Donny," said Margaret.

"I don't want a pothead in my canoe."

"He's looking for things to do. Ask him."

Ernest looked out the window. "You used to love to go for a paddle."

Margaret turned on the television. "I used to love a lot of things."

When Ernest talked to his brother, Rich, about the potential for his nephew, Donny, to help him with the canoe, Rich suggested that Donny might be motivated by a little compensation.

Now, as Donny followed Ernest on his own ATV, Ernest seethed at the idea that he was paying a family member to help with a chore on the farm. He imagined that the day would end with the canoe upended, or Simon caught under the wheels of Donny's ATV.

When they unloaded the canoe, Ernest said, "Your end's the bow. The bow's the front."

Donny pushed hair out of his face. "Uncle Ernie, I paddled the Magnetawan River from one end to the other."

As they shoved out from the edge of the flooded field, the dog sat in the middle of the canoe, Ernest steering from the stern. They entered the swampy forest of silver maples. Donny grabbed at tree trunks and branches, pulling the boat forward.

"Dad has hip waders," said Donny. "We could have walked back here."

"I wouldn't be paying you twenty dollars to walk with me."

"I don't want any money. That was just Dad fooling with you."

They paddled and pulled their way until they emerged into the main beaver pond.

When Ernest was a kid, he and his cousins had caught bass in the pond. Upstream there had been trout. The trout were harder to catch, but Ernest's father had preferred the taste of them. In the summer, when the trout were holed up in deeper pools, Ernest would coax them out of their hiding places with worms. In the fall, when the trout were spawning, Ernest would catch a basket of crickets and let the hooked insects drift on the surface. One trout had been worth five bass in his father's eyes.

At the west end of the pond was a long beaver dam that had been there since Ernest was a teenager. The dam had cemented itself with silt over the years, and now grass and saplings grew out of it. At the east end, where Graham Creek escaped the pond, there was a smaller dam that was responsible for holding most of the water back.

The smaller dam had been there for years, but its effectiveness had been undermined by the flow of the current tunnelling into the north bank. The beavers had always been stymied by the water escaping through the underground cave.

On examination, Ernest and Donny found that a large beech tree on the bank had succumbed to erosion. As it had fallen, its roots had lifted the embankment, revealing the secret waterway. The beavers had simply extended the dam to the base of the tree's upended roots. In the process, they raised the level of the pond to new heights.

As they floated by the dam, Simon looked like he was preparing to jump from the canoe, so Ernest grabbed the dog's collar.

Donny said, "You know what I think, Uncle Ernie?"

"No, I don't."

"I think you're screwed. You can't get a backhoe in here to take out the dam. I mean, you could try trapping the beavers, but between here and Durnsville there are probably a hundred more beavers on the creek. New ones will just move in."

"I'm not paying you to talk."

"You're only losing a few acres. My advice is don't worry about it. Think about the rink."

Indeed, leaving the field flooded was an option Ernest had considered. However, if Margaret ever thought that Ernest was no longer able to cope with the day-to-day issues of farm management, she would quickly relocate them to Ottawa. A perennially flooded field would indicate to Margaret that Ernest had given up on farming and it was time to move on.

Donny said, "You're probably only grossing five hundred an acre in corn. If you leave the beavers alone, you might be giving up fifteen hundred bucks, but you'll save yourself a major headache, and by Christmas we can make us an Olympic-sized rink."

The words coming out of Donny's mouth exceeded Ernest's expectations of what a stoned university dropout should be saying. All he could muster in response was "Shut up, Donny."

SEVENTY-FIVE

BECAUSE OF THE WAY DAVID hiked, exploring side trails and stopping to sketch statues and stone monuments, completing the Keihoku Trail in two days was not feasible. David convinced Junichi to camp for two nights so they could complete the circuit over three days. In this way, David would feel that the entire loop was finished in a satisfactory manner. This was how it had to be.

During the first day of hiking they passed the waterfall where David had showered the previous week. On one of several detours they walked up a ridge that had been clear-cut. Gathered on the ridge were a group of four young men preparing to hang-glide.

David and Junichi sat on their backpacks to watch. Junichi said, "I was not expecting this."

One of the men seemed to be in charge of the group, and he helped a man with a rainbow-coloured glider get ready. After a few minutes the man with the coloured glider took a few steps down the side of the hill and was soon flying in a slow arc over the valley.

"They are brave," said Junichi.

"Risky," said David, nervously watching the second man get ready.

Junichi said, "They are jumping off a mountain. The risk is the enjoyment, *ne*, David?"

The second man, with a yellow hang-glider, ran off the edge. As he did, he yelled, "*Banzai*."

Junichi asked David if he was familiar with the expression.

David said, "Sometimes in English we say *banzai*, but I don't know what it means in Japanese. My friend Mitchell says *banzai* when he is excited about something."

"*Banzai* means 'ten thousand years.' Usually 'ten thousand years of living.'"

"Is it a prayer?"

"No," said Junichi. "It is a hope for the future."

"Isn't that a prayer?"

Junichi said, "There are different meanings at different times."

"What did that man mean?"

Junichi typed in his phone for a translation.

"He meant 'Yay.'"

Now there were only two men left, and the man in charge hooked them both into a red glider.

Junichi said, "The man in front is the teacher. The man behind, I think this is his first time."

As they started running down the hill, the man in the rear stumbled at the brink. The man at the front kept pumping his feet, and the glider lifted off the edge of the hill.

Junichi said, "The student was nervous."

"I shut my eyes," said David.

They watched the gliders circle lazily over fields below.

Junichi said, "You were right to take three days on the trail. If we were in a hurry, we never would have seen this. It is good, don't you think?"

"Yeah," said David. "I am meant to see it all."

IN THE SECOND-FLOOR BEDROOM OF their farmhouse, David typed lesson plans while Joanna brushed an orange cat.

David said, "Why didn't you tell me we were going to meet with the reverend?"

"Your pride gets in the way."

"He didn't have much advice anyway. He basically said, 'Don't worry about it.'"

"Why didn't you talk? I mean, you were the one who said there was a problem with the Conservation Meadows families being left out."

"There's not much to say," said David. "I'm trying to get all of the students to come out."

The orange cat rolled over on its back, swatting at the brush.

Joanna said, "Reverend Borbridge is a smart guy. I thought if anyone could help us understand the makeup of the Dumford Mills community, it would be him."

"I'd just as soon talk to George."

"Doesn't it disturb you that some people think you're running a clique?"

"I've been telling more families to sign up. I talked to Laura Connelly."

Joanna said, "I can't get past this idea that there are people in the world who can find fault with taking kids fishing or learning about bees."

David closed the lid on the laptop. "It's not the fishing that's the issue."

"I know. But what is?"

"I don't know. People are strange. You can't make everyone happy."

"That sounds like an excuse not to think too much about a problem."

"I'm just repeating what the reverend told us," said David.

Joanna pulled at a clump of hair on the orange cat's belly, and the cat bit her on the hand. She pushed it off the bed and turned off the bedside lamp.

"You know what's going to resolve this problem?" said David. "Kids. The kids will all make friends with each other, and that will bring their parents together. It's inevitable."

Joanna said, "It makes me crazy thinking about this stuff."

David said, "You can't control what people think."

"David," said Joanna, "what I love about you is that when you get a good idea, you just do it. You build something or plan something, and you put your head down and get it done. I mean, that's your thing."

David slid the computer under the bed. He pulled the covers up to his chest.

Joanna said, "And you know what else I love about you? That you can just fall asleep. I lie awake replaying my day over and over, and you can just roll over and start snoring. Do you even dream?"

"Maybe. If I have dreams, I don't remember them."

"You don't dream about me?"

"I don't remember dreams," said David.

"Maybe if I go off to a veterinary conference somewhere, you'll have visions of me dancing in your head."

David pretended to snore.

"Maybe," said Joanna, "it will take my absence for you to realize what you've got."

SEVENTY-SIX

ON THEIR FIRST NIGHT ON the trail, David and Junichi camped in a plantation of pine trees. Junichi had brought the camping equipment, including a metal can with a red jelly-like substance inside. When he put a match to the can, a pale pink flame glowed in the fading light. Junichi heated a can of noodles over the flame, and they split the contents in two cups.

Junichi said, "I don't think we should build a fire. This is company land."

"Are we trespassing?"

"It is better if we are not seen."

By the time they had split another can of noodles, darkness had enveloped them. They watched the pink flame dance around in the can.

Junichi asked, "Are you still *baka*? Still crazy?"

"Most of the time I feel normal. When I am talking to you now or when I am at the Rising Son, I feel fine."

"But..." said Junichi.

"But," said David, "my mind is in two halves." David motioned like he was cutting something with his hand. He said, "My Japanese brain works pretty good. My Canadian brain is broken."

Junichi lit the tip of a stick from the flaming can. He waved the glowing end around, tracing circles of light in the darkness.

David said, "I don't know if Rochelle or Guy told you, but I watched one of my students die. I watched her die, and I feel like it was my fault."

Junichi extinguished his stick in the dirt. The two men said nothing for several minutes.

Junichi said, "Maybe you should stay in Japan."

David nodded. "I think Japan is helping me. I think nature is helping me."

"*Wakata*," said Junichi. "Do you know *shinrin-yoku?*"

"No," said David.

"In Japan, some people feel that being in the forest is like taking medicine. It helps many things."

"I hope so," said David. "What I like about nature is that it doesn't care about anything. We could be eaten by a bear tonight, and nature would not care."

"*So, desu-ne*," said Junichi.

"And that's what I need," said David, shadows from the can flickering on his face. "In nature there is no right and wrong. There is no judgment. I need a place where even death does not matter."

"But I am here," said Junichi, relighting his stick. "And so, this is a problem."

"It's not a problem," said David.

"I am here, and tonight, death matters."

"I am glad you are here," said David.

"I am afraid of bears," said Junichi.

ERNEST GRAHAM SAT ON HIS front porch with a bucket full of water and a scrub brush. He had the contents of his golf bag spread over the deck and was cleaning his irons with soapy water. He didn't golf often, but a couple of times each year he went out with Nate and Bill, two friends he'd known since high school. Nate had invited him to golf that morning, and Ernest was happy to get out of the house.

Margaret leaned out the front door and said, "Rita tells me you're not finished planting."

Ernest shared farm equipment with his brother, and the families were aware of each other's seasonal progress.

"Everything's in. It's just the back field that's still flooded."

Margaret said, "Your whole life is spent worrying about water. Too much water. Not enough water."

"It's only a few acres," said Ernest.

"A few acres is the difference between having a nice vacation or not. You said we could go to Nashville."

Ernest poured the soapy water into the flowerbed.

"We'll go to Nashville," he said.

"If it's beavers back there, shouldn't you be out shooting them instead of golfing?"

"We're only doing nine holes. I'll be back after lunch."

At the golf course, Ernest made a long putt on the last hole. The lucky stroke meant that Bill would be buying lunch.

Ernest bought a pitcher of beer in the clubhouse, and the three men drank while they waited for their sandwiches.

Nate said, "If you guys would retire, we could do this all summer."

Bill said, "Why would I want to go through this hell every day?"

"Hit down on the ball," said Nate. "You scoop all your irons."

Bill said, "I've got two years left at the mill and then you can take my money all summer long."

"What about you, Ernie?" asked Nate. "Are you close to hanging up the overalls?"

Ernest said, "I ain't never retiring. If I did, you'd never see me."

"We're not good enough for you?" said Nate.

"Margaret has it in her head that we're going to move to Ottawa. If it ever looks to her like I'm tired of working, she'll have us in some goddamn assisted-living facility."

"Some people dream of retiring to a farm," said Bill.

"I dream of retiring on the farm," said Ernest. "I just don't want to run it forever. Too many headaches."

"Seems pretty easy to me," said Nate. "Most of the farmers I know spend all day watching the Weather Network."

"It never rains when you need it," said Ernest. "Stuff is always breaking. I got a goddamn colony of beavers flooding out my property."

"I could get you a job at the mill," said Bill. "A couple days there and you'd get a whole new appreciation for sunshine and wildlife."

The waitress served their sandwiches, and Ernest portioned out the remains of the pitcher.

"Beavers is like rats," said Nate. "Rats with degrees in engineering."

"We've always had them," said Ernest. "It's just that this generation has fixed things differently."

Nate said, "There's things called 'beaver bafflers.' It's like a tube you rig up in their dam. You can basically set the water level to whatever you want."

"I got to drain things out somehow," said Ernest.

After lunch, when the men were packing their clubs into the trunks of their cars, Bill came over to Ernest and said, "If you want someone to help with your beaver problem, I might know a guy."

"A trapper?"

Bill said, "He can probably do that too, but he might have an alternative."

"I don't have time to put in a beaver-confusing contraption like Nate was talking about."

"The guy I'm thinking about is a little more down-and-dirty than that."

"What do you mean?" said Ernest.

Bill made a ball with his hands then separated them quickly.

"Boom!"

SEVENTY-SEVEN

DURING THE NIGHT, DAVID HAD rolled off his blue camping pad, and his body was covered in pine needles. When he woke, he stood up to brush himself off. Junichi was awake and boiling water over the tin of flammable jelly.

"I didn't dream," said David.

"You were snoring," said Junichi.

"I usually have bad dreams," said David.

"You should sleep outside every night."

They ate a breakfast of rice balls and instant coffee before setting off down the trail. When they emerged from the pine forest, David was surprised to see how close to a town they had camped.

Junichi had purchased a trail guide that was much more detailed than David's wrinkled English map. Junichi led the way through the small village and down a road alongside a mountain. There was a grassy ditch between the road and the mountain, and David could see frogs half-submerged in the shallow water.

Junichi said, "This is typhoon season in Japan. Sometimes these small rivers become big rivers."

After twenty minutes they came to a parking lot at the base of a hill. Several signs marked the beginning of a trail into the woods.

Junichi said, "This is the way to the Joshoji temple. This is our path too."

Within the grounds of the temple, David sat down to sketch a stone Buddha while Junichi read the Keihoku Trail guide.

"This statue is four hundred years old," Junichi said.

"Are you a Buddhist?"

"More Shinto."

"Do you believe in God?"

"No. Just kinds of spirits."

"Ghosts?" said David.

"*Chigao*. If you go to a shrine, that is a home for a *kami*. Like a special energy. Not a ghost."

David squinted at the *kanji* characters at the base of the statue.

Junichi said, "In Japan, if there is a special place, Shinto people believe that a *kami* lives there. There are *kami* at shrines but also at wild places like a mountain or a river."

"I've been to fifty shrines," said David.

"That's good," said Junichi. "They will help you." Junichi typed into his phone for a translation. "For purification."

David said, "Every time I go to a shrine or temple, I sip the water. I do the smoke thing."

"Shinto is a good religion for you," said Junichi. "It is like nature."

David looked up from sketching.

Junichi waved his hands in the air. "No judgment."

DAVID'S CLASS BOARDED THE BUS to go to the Condie Creek Conservation Area. They were scheduled for a two-hour pond program and would be back at Emily Carr by lunch. David sat beside Holly Metz in the seat behind the bus driver.

"We could have walked to the nature centre," said David.

"A bus ride is exciting for the kids," said Holly.

"We could have walked."

At the conservation area the students were met by a nature interpreter named Zoe. Zoe took them into a log cabin where the students sat in a circle on the floor. Zoe talked about animals they would be catching in the pond. She used rubber animals to demonstrate the life cycle of a dragonfly.

"Can anybody guess how many eyes a dragonfly has?" asked Zoe.

Anna said, "About sixty thousand."

"Nope," said Zoe. "Five."

Anna said, "Each big eye is compound, and that's like having thirty thousand eyes in one eye."

"That's right," said Zoe. "And they have three eyes on top of their heads called ocelli."

Anna said, "Those don't see very well, but if you count them, maybe it's sixty thousand and three."

David said, "We have an aquarium of aquatic invertebrates in our classroom. We've covered a lot of this stuff before."

"Hmmm," said Zoe.

At the pond, students worked in groups to catch animals and place them in white buckets.

David said to Holly, "This is costing the school four hundred dollars."

"Okay, sourpuss."

"We could have done this all year for free."

"This is exactly what you want students to do. Relax."

"It's good," said David. "That's what's so frustrating."

On the bus ride back to the school, David timed the trip. "Seven minutes," he announced.

Holly said, "I'm sorry I wasn't better company."

As David led the students down the hallway to the classroom, Jeff Kressler was coming the other way. David grabbed him by the arm.

"I'm on board," said David. "Let's run this place."

SEVENTY-EIGHT

BEHIND THE JOSHOJI TEMPLE, THE Keihoku Trail continued up a ridge through a cedar forest. At a junction there was a circle of benches. Five different trails led out from the circle.

Junichi said, "The map shows that all of these paths lead to the river. It doesn't matter which one we take. What way, captain?"

David wanted to say "All of them," and indeed, if he were solo, that is probably how the hike would have gone — a long series of circles and backtracking.

"It doesn't matter," said David.

"Pick one," said Junichi. "I am a Shinto man. I won't judge."

"The longest one," said David.

Along the river they came to a village. They stopped at a small shrine where David continued his journey of purification, rinsing his mouth with water and wafting incense smoke over his head. They ate cheese sandwiches under the bright orange *torii* marking the entrance to the shrine.

Junichi said, "We will have to hike over this mountain, and then it is four or five kilometres to our second camping place."

David said, "Thank you for taking me up here."

Junichi said, "It is you who is taking me."

"Tomorrow I will have finished all of the Kyoto Trail."

"Amazing," said Junichi.

"Scary," said David.

From the village they followed a logging road that zigzagged up a hill.

"We are going up Kuroo-yama," said Junichi.

A trail left the road and hugged the side of the mountain. A hand-written note was tacked to a tree along the trail.

Junichi said, "The person who left the message says that the way ahead becomes dangerous."

As the trail continued, there were areas where water had eroded the path. They clung to shrubs and tree roots to traverse the gaps. As Junichi was stepping over one crevice, his backpack became stuck on a branch, and he cursed in Japanese. When David looked back, Junichi gave him a thumbs-up.

The trail improved, and they came to another intersection.

Junichi said, "We have to go straight, but the other trail lets you see the top of the mountain."

David motioned up the summit.

They followed the switchback. David was impressed by Junichi's stamina.

At the top of the hill was a small clearing with a signpost in the middle. Junichi explained that the arrows pointed to other mountaintops. David peered between pine trees, trying to identify a peak in the distance.

"I feel like everything is supposed to mean something," said David.

Junichi said, "It is a good view."

"The hang-gliders, the shrines, *jizo* statues. I feel like someone is showing me these things for a reason."

"God?"

"I don't know. I don't understand any of it."

"It is like the inuksuk, David. We are just here."

Suddenly Junichi started talking rapidly in Japanese. David turned and saw Junichi running toward a bench in the clearing. Junichi leaned into some shrubs. David rushed over and found Junichi putting his water bottle up to a man's mouth. The man was elderly, and most of the water ran down his chin.

The man spoke in a voice that sounded like a child's.

Junichi said, "He is glad we came. He took a rest but could not get back up."

"How did he get here?" said David.

Junichi talked to the man in Japanese.

"Walking," said Junichi.

SIMON THE SPANIEL BARKED AT Ernest as Bill Allen's pickup truck bounced up the laneway to the Graham farm. Ernest grabbed the dog by the collar as the truck parked beside them.

Ernest was nervous about meeting the dynamite man. It felt like he was arranging a murder. However, Ernest's sense of desperation when he thought about the possibility of losing the farm made such measures necessary. If he could deal with the beavers and get seeds in the ground, it would feel like a normal season again, and Ernest would buy himself another year of farm life.

Ernest recognized the TNT expert as one of the icemakers at the curling rink. He was dressed in blue coveralls, and his hands were calloused and grease-stained. Bill introduced him as Lenny.

Lenny said, "Let's go look at the problem."

Ernest said, "Should I get the canoe?"

"Nah. All dams are attached to land somewhere."

They hiked to the back field, Simon running ahead with Lenny. When they reached the flooded depression, they followed the edge of the water into the forest.

Bill asked Ernest, "Shouldn't you be leading us?"

"It's going to get thick back here, but he's going the right way," said Ernest.

The land rose and fell, and soon the men were faced with a tangle of shrubby willow trees and dogwoods. Lenny pushed his way through the branches. Bill and Ernest followed, their boots filling with water in the puddles between grassy hillocks.

The bushes gave way to open water, and Lenny skirted the perimeter of the pond until they were standing on the dam.

Lenny said, "Not wide, but she's high."

"Can you do it?" said Bill.

"Easy," said Lenny. "We'll need your boat to get out to the lodge."

"You'll blow the lodge too?" asked Bill.

"Yup," said Lenny. "Beavers is nocturnal, so we'll do it the morning. We'll put a quarter stick in the lodge and take care of that first. Then a full stick should do the dam."

Ernest worried that Lenny's use of the word "we" meant he would need to be present for the crime.

"What if someone hears it?" said Bill.

Lenny spat in the water. "They'll say, 'I wonder what that was.'"

Ernest considered that he might be blowing up the best Christmas rink he would ever have. He was about to tell Lenny he would need time to think about the beaver-removal plan.

Lenny said, "We'll do it Tuesday morning. Four hundred cash. Two hundred for the explosives, and two hundred for my time."

When they were hiking out, Ernest said to Bill, "You have to come on Tuesday."

"No way," said Bill, laughing. "I'll be at the mill working on my alibi."

SEVENTY-NINE

THE OLD JAPANESE MAN AT the top of Kuroo-yama was named Hisao. Junichi said, "He is from Keihokudaiichi. It is a village to the west."

"Is he injured?"

"I don't think so. But he can't stand up."

Junichi studied his map. David estimated that Hisao could not weigh more than ninety pounds.

"I'll carry him," said David.

Junichi said, "We could bring him to the shrine."

David said, "The trail wasn't safe."

"We could take him to his home in Keihokudaiichi, but that is six kilometres."

"Yeah, let's do that. *Ikimasho*," said David, using one of the Japanese phrases he had learned. "Let's go."

David cradled the man in his arms, and Junichi took David's backpack. Hisao started speaking excitedly.

Junichi said, "He said he has become like a baby."

David started down the trail, but Hisao's body blocked David's view of his feet. Afraid of tripping, he stopped. They switched positions, and David carried Hisao on his back, his arms under Hisao's legs, and Hisao's arms around his neck. The man continued talking in a high-pitched voice.

Junichi said, "He is proud now that he has become a boy."

After thirty minutes of walking they came to a bench made of logs. David lay Hisao on the bench, and they all drank water.

Junichi said, "He left his home at the sun's rising. He walked to the top and had no more energy."

David said, "I still don't understand how he got up there."

Hisao had his hands behind his head and was babbling cheerfully to Junichi. Hisao lifted a leg slowly in the air.

Junichi said, "One foot, then another."

When they had rested, Junichi lifted Hisao onto David's back, and they continued down the trail. Junichi led the way, counting his footsteps to estimate the distance travelled. They turned down a gravel trail and emerged on a logging road. David felt anxiety at leaving the Keihoku Trail behind, wondering if fate was testing his determination to complete the circle.

As they walked, Hisao talked in David's ear, and Junichi translated.

Hisao was eighty-two years old. He had lived his whole life in Keihokudaiichi. His wife was dead, but he had four children and six grandchildren. As a young man he had worked as a logger, and later in life as a carpenter.

At a fork in the road, Hisao pointed to a wooden sign.

Junichi said, "He made that sign."

They stopped along the dirt road and David sat Hisao up against a tree.

Junichi said, "He apologizes for the trouble."

"No problem," said David, giving Hisao the okay sign.

Junichi said, "He thanks you for the extra days."

"What extra days?"

"The extra days of living. We are saving his life."

The humidity of the Japanese summer, mixed with the cooler mountain air, meant that everything in the hills had a dewy sheen on it. David's shirt was soaked in sweat, and drips of perspiration hung off the whiskers around his chin. He drank half a bottle of water and poured the rest on his head.

He turned to Junichi, pointing a finger at him. "If you think this means something, it doesn't."

Junichi shook his head. "I don't understand."

"This doesn't make anything even."

"I don't understand."

David pulled the bottom of his shirt over his face. Hisao said something in Japanese.

Junichi said, "He says you would be a good logging man."

WHEN DAVID GOT HOME FROM work, Joanna met him at the front porch. She was bubbling with excitement. David took a fly swatter off a nail on the wall and tapped Joanna's behind.

"Spit it out."

"Holly called."

"New casserole recipe?"

"No."

"Dog needs fixing?"

"No. Just listen."

David swatted at a cat running by.

Joanna said, "Don't say anything right away."

"About what?"

"Listen."

"I will not say another word. I will not talk until —"

"Stop!"

There was a lawn chair leaning against the house, and David unfolded it and sat down.

Joanna said, "Holly called. There's a house for sale on Glasgow Line. It's nineteen acres. Five acres of bush."

David nodded.

"The house was built in 1849. It has some updates. There's a barn with four stalls."

David tipped the chair back against the wall.

"It has a stream."

David rolled his finger around, indicating Joanna should keep going.

"It's $340,000."

David grunted.

Joanna said, "I'm getting almost full-time hours at the clinic. I think if you're going to be at Emily Carr for a while, then maybe we can talk to the bank. Maybe —"

"And it has a woodstove."

"Yes, it does."

"And a cold cellar."

"Wait."

"Ron sent me the listing at work. It looks pretty good."

Joanna straddled David on the chair.

"I've been excited all day."

"We can drive out tonight," said David. "We can drive out right now."

Joanna said, "Are you with me? Because this is big. This is really big."

"You could get a horse."

"We'll have to. And chickens. Look at my arms."

"Bumpy."

"I love you," said Joanna.

"Let's go see that house," said David.

EIGHTY

JUNICHI TRIED CARRYING HISAO FOR a few hundred metres, but he couldn't keep the old man from sliding down his back. David gave Junichi the backpacks and they returned to their original roles.

The logging road emerged from the forest at a paved road.

David said, "Let's stop a car."

Hisao talked in David's ear and pointed down the road.

Junichi said, "He says he lives in that house."

At the house, Junichi slid the front door open, and Hisao yelled, "*Tadaima!*"

A woman of about fifty ran to them in the hall. She led them into a living room, and David put Hisao on a futon. Hisao was smiling and talking quickly.

Junichi said, "This is his daughter. She is Hidemi."

The daughter bowed deeply to David and Junichi. She grasped David's hands and talked to him in Japanese. She motioned for the men to sit down, and she left the room.

On the wall was a picture of a man, presumably Hisao, harnessed to the top of a tree. David imagined Hisao talking to himself alone in the forest.

Hidemi returned to the room with a tray of tea. They sat on the floor around a wooden table. The daughter told them that Hisao had made the table. Hidemi made several phone calls while Junichi and David sipped their tea. Hisao kept talking. For a man unable to walk, he seemed to have a lot of energy for conversation.

A young man came into the room and gave Junichi and David high-fives. He had a bag full of Kirin beer with him. Drinks were poured, and several more family members arrived to join the celebration. Everyone had been out looking for Hisao.

Junichi said, "They cannot believe he was on the mountain."

"Me neither," said David.

Junichi said, "They say that each morning he leaves the house and says, 'I am going up the mountain. I am going to see Kuroo-*san*.' But he only walks down the road to a bench and has a cigarette."

A delivery man showed up with an enormous tray of food. David was given a bowl of miso soup and a cardboard box with curried rice in it. Many toasts were made. Hidemi used pillows to prop Hisao up against the wall. Even Hisao started drinking beer.

At one point, one of Hisao's granddaughters got up on her knees and made a short speech.

Junichi said, "Hisao says that he walked up the mountain as an old man, but coming down he was like a young man. He was feeling that your legs were his young legs."

David said, "Tell him that he wasn't too heavy."

Junichi said, "He says he is much lighter these days because of the cancer."

DAVID AND JOANNA STOOD IN the back of David's pickup truck, looking at the $340,000 farm.

David said, "It has apple trees."

Joanna said, "I can pick apples for my horse." She put her hands to her face. "I'm flushed. I'm shaking."

David said, "I don't think anyone lives here. Grass isn't cut."

They walked up the laneway to the house. The curtains were closed, but through cracks they could make out furniture and paint colours.

"I think the $340,000 is for the land," said David.

"The house was built before Canada was a country. It's going to need some work."

"Needs a new roof. New siding."

"It has a shed. That could be your woodshed."

"It needs new windows."

Joanna said, "David, don't tell me what you see. Tell me how you feel."

A barn swallow flitted into a nest on the side of the chimney.

David said, "I feel like I should call Archie."

"To ask his advice?"

"Maybe he can loan us a down payment."

Joanna hugged David and then hugged a corner of the house. They walked around the property, talking about possibilities.

Joanna climbed up on a stack of cedar rails. She said, "It's all unfolding perfectly."

"God's plan?"

Joanna jumped on David's back. She said, "You sent your resume to the wrong place and we ended up in Dumford Mills. Don Moreland needed an employee at a large-animal practice. Holly took a backroad out of town and saw this house. It's fate."

David said, "If things had turned out differently you might think that was great too."

Joanna squeezed her legs around David.

"It's fate."

David fell into the long grass and pulled Joanna on top of him.

"Fate is just whatever happens."

EIGHTY-ONE

DURING THE PARTY CELEBRATING HISAO'S return it started raining. With some persuasion, Hisao's daughter convinced David and Junichi to spend the night. It wasn't clear to David which family members lived in the house, but after dark, he and Junichi were shown to a bedroom with *tatami* mats on the floor. They unrolled their sleeping bags and used folded clothing as pillows.

David said, "We won't be able to complete the trail, will we?"

Junichi said, "I would camp another night, but I have an evaluation at the dojo. You may continue."

David said, "No. I'll go back to Kyoto with you. We'll finish the trail together."

In the morning, different family members arrived for breakfast. Hidemi served miso soup with toast, while Hisao demonstrated how he could take a few steps on his own.

Junichi said, "He says that he would have had peace dying on the mountain, but now that he has more time, he is making plans."

David said, "Tell him that I will always remember taking him down the mountain."

Junichi translated. "He says that if you keep that memory, then you will always carry him."

Hisao spoke to his daughter, and Hidemi left the room. She came back carrying two wooden walking sticks with Japanese writing engraved on them. The daughter gave one to David and one to Junichi.

Junichi said, "He hopes we will climb many more mountains."

"What do the words mean?"

"Mine says '石橋を叩いて渡る.' 'Hit a bridge before you cross it.' And yours says '石の上にも三年.' 'Three years sitting on a rock.' " Junichi talked to Hisao and Hidemi about how to explain the proverb. "It is not comfortable sitting on a rock, but the rock will become warmer."

"Okay..." said David.

"Everything gets better," said Junichi.

After some discussion it was decided that Hisao's grandson would drive David and Junichi back to Kyoto. Junichi exchanged email addresses with Hidemi, and many kind words were spoken. Hisao offered to carry David to the car.

David sat sideways in the back seat of the grandson's hatchback. At a stop sign the grandson turned around and took a picture of David with his phone.

Junichi said, "This is a great memory for us, *ne*, David?"

"It is," said David, running his fingers along the ridges of his walking stick. "But we have to finish that trail."

AS MAY DISSOLVED INTO JUNE, the students of Emily Carr Public School became more boisterous. The warm days teased the students with hints of a summer that was still a month away. The end of the school year was a busy time, with field trips, track meets, and year-end silliness like pyjama days. Roger Dixon saw an uptick in the number of students sent to the office for general impertinence. Even the staff room buzzed with the anticipation of summer holidays.

David addressed his class. "Take ten minutes to read chapter four in *Lead Dog*. Then work with your reading buddies to answer the who-what-where-when-why questions."

The best classroom management advice David had ever received was from a professor at teachers' college who said, "Whatever you tell your students to do, you do exactly the same thing." So David sat at his desk and read chapter four of *Lead Dog*.

Jing-Shen approached David's desk and said, "Martha is my reading buddy, but since she's not here should I do the questions on my own, or join another group?"

David said, "Your choice."

"On my own."

David nodded.

Nina Emerson had called David the week before and told him that the Emersons were going to Paris for "eight glorious days." Nina had described the itinerary in great detail, oblivious to David's lack of interest. He was regaled with descriptions of boutique hotels, art museums, and clothing that she and Martha would be wearing.

"Springtime in Paris!"

Nina had asked, "Will there be any homework for Martha during her absence?"

What David said was: "Martha will be able to catch up when she gets back. Enjoy your trip."

What he wanted to say was: "Make Martha sit indoors for five hours conjugating French verbs. That's the best way for her to experience France."

David looked out the window at Jeff Kressler organizing soccer drills in the field. Thoughts of Paris gave way to thoughts of summer and, potentially, a new home.

Anna said, "Can't we read outside?"

David put his finger to his lips and shook his head.

Anna put her hands out to the sides, palms up, and mouthed *Why not?*

This was the moment when it clicked in David's head that the only student who did not have a signed permission form allowing the class to enter the conservation area *at any time during the school year* was at the Louvre, wearing a brand new black-and-white dress with musical notes on it.

EIGHTY-TWO

MID-AFTERNOON AT MONTERREY HOUSE WAS usually a quiet time when most residents were either working or napping. When Hisao's grandson dropped him off, David was surprised to find several housemates gathered in the kitchen.

Rochelle sat at the table wiping her eyes. Guy talked on a cellphone.

David whispered to Jock, "What's going on?"

"Guy's father died."

David tiptoed between Dane and Nartti and went up to his room. He dumped his backpack in the corner and cleared off a respectful place on the desk for his new walking stick.

He came back down, and Tyler handed him a cup with wine in it.

Guy got off the phone. He said, "I fly out tomorrow morning."

When no one spoke, Guy added, "I guess I'm a jeweller now."

Rochelle ran her hands through her hair.

Tyler said, "Jock, dude, you got any music that's not dance shit?"

Jock fiddled with his laptop and Neil Young filled the kitchen. Under the cover of music, conversations started up. David went over to Rochelle, who was sitting in the corner. Guy was busy texting.

Rochelle said, "I'm not going with him."

"No?"

"I can't. His girlfriend will be there."

"Hmm."

"This is it."

When he couldn't think of anything else to say, David told Rochelle about carrying Hisao down the mountain.

Rochelle said, "You're a hero."

"No," said David.

Guy looked up from his phone and said, "You two would make a good couple."

Rochelle closed her eyes. "Don't say that."

Guy put his phone in his pocket. "You don't like me to joke, and you don't like me to tell the truth. The truth is I love you, and I would happily live forever in this tiny house in this foreign country just to be with you."

David picked at a blister on his hand.

Guy said, "But you probably don't want to hear that either."

Tyler handed Guy a beer and said, "Do you want all these people here? I can tell everyone to fuck off if you want."

"No, mate," said Guy. "I'm going up to pack, and then I want to go out with my friends. I want to go to the Rising Son."

GRAHAM CREEK EMPTIED INTO CONDIE Creek just downstream from the bridge where David had caught crayfish in the fall. If David's class crossed the bridge and walked north a hundred metres, there was an area of hemlock trees where students could read, bounded by both streams. The weather forecast called for clear skies.

Roger Dixon said, "You've got proper supervision?"

David said, "There's myself and three parents. Actually, two parents and a grandparent."

"I have all of the permission forms?"

"They're in the folder. I included a map of where we will be."

Of all the decisions Principal Dixon had made over the year, this one seemed innocuous. Kids reading in the woods. The only thing he could remember saying to David was "Take a first aid kit and a cellphone."

When David sent out the email looking for volunteers, George Young had responded with one word: "Absolutely."

Amanda Dickenson had called to ask if she should wear her hip waders again. David had told her to wear walking shoes and, if she wanted, bring her own book.

June Wong would later testify, "Being a teacher is not easy. If I can help Mr. Woods, I will help. And the children, they should be outside. So when Mr. Woods says, 'Will you help?' I say, 'Of course.'"

EIGHTY-THREE

IT WAS TEMPURA NIGHT AT the Rising Son. The gang from Monterrey House came through the Golden Gate Bridge curtain in single file. Mr. Tanaka was excited to see Jock make his first appearance at the pub in over a year and immediately commemorated the occasion by taking a Polaroid photograph.

Jock sat down at the bar. He said, "Master-*san*, I'm the only black man on your walls who never played baseball."

"Yes," said Mr. Tanaka, "I make you famous."

Jock said, "You should take down Barry Bonds. Man, if I juiced like that cheater I could have hit seven hundred home runs too."

"Yes," said Mr. Tanaka, pointing at the photographs of baseball pictures behind the bar. "It should be Willie McCovey, Juan Marichal, and Jock."

David sat at a booth with Guy, Rochelle, and Junichi. Tyler divided his attention between tables.

Guy said, "Listen, David, the woman who owns the Blossom Academy is named Michiko. She's a great lady, easy to work for. She asked me if I knew anyone who could take over my classes, and I mentioned you."

David squinted at Guy.

"I told her that you have a Working Holiday Visa, that you're a teacher, and that you're a good bloke."

Rochelle said, "You should do it. If you're staying, you should do it."

Guy said, "It's twenty hours a week. All adults, mostly corporate clients. We have a couple classrooms at the academy, but mostly I travel around town to companies. I go to Murata, a big electronics company. I go to Nintendo in the building where Kaori works."

David said, "It's tempting."

Guy said, "You can think about it, but I'm leaving tomorrow."

"I'll think about it."

Mr. Tanaka served dishes of tempura with cold soba noodles. Junichi poured beer.

Guy snapped apart his wooden chopsticks. He said, "This is my last Rising Son meal."

Rochelle poked at her noodles. "I can't eat."

Guy said, "We knew this was coming. I mean, not that my dad would die, but we knew this would have to end. You started planning your return weeks ago."

Rochelle said, "I know. But now it's here. There's no more pretending."

Guy said, "This week is going to be killer for me. Let me pretend for one more night."

Junichi despaired at the thought that Rochelle might also be going home. He wished he could replay the last twenty-four hours, when he and David had been celebrated for their bravery. He couldn't wait to tell his own father that he had saved a man — that he and a *gaijin* had rescued a man off a mountain top. Would a salary man do that?

Mr. Tanaka motioned at the group to pose for a picture.

Guy said, "Cheese."

Mr. Tanaka said, "No cheese. Just smiling."

Considering the number of different emotions lurking below the surface, coaxing four smiles out of the diners was a considerable feat.

Guy said, "Master-*san*, please take two." When the second photo was snapped, Guy hugged each of them.

David leaned in to Guy and said, "Thank you for everything."

"For what?"

"I don't know. For letting me eat with you guys."

Guy looked David in the eye. He said, "If you need a new start, this could be it. Take the Blossom Academy gig. You can make decent money and still have time to enjoy the mountains. You've got some pretty good friends here."

"It's tempting."

Den reached around David to clear some glasses off the table.

Guy said to Den, "Don't you want David to stay in Japan?"

She looked at Guy like it was a silly question. "Of course," she said. "We are here."

JOANNA GOT OFF THE PHONE and started dancing around the kitchen. She said, "My parents can lend us ten thousand. And we have four thousand in the joint account. Do you have any money in your account?"

David said, "Not much. Maybe a thousand. Hey, the Emersons went to Paris. Martha too."

Joanna said, "I have two thousand. That's seventeen."

"The Emersons are in France."

"Twenty-seven thousand would be enough for a down payment, but if we want to avoid paying mortgage insurance, we'll need more."

"I'll call Dad. Martha's gone to France. I have a week. A week of freedom."

"Should we go to your bank or mine?" asked Joanna.

"We've got the joint account at yours," said David. "We're going to the stream tomorrow."

"But the car loan is at your bank."

"I don't like my bank. George is coming. So is Amanda and Mrs. Wong."

"Do you think your parents would lend us money?"

"I don't know. We're just going to sit and read."

"Can you call them after dinner?"

"Yes. We're reading a story about a wolf, so I think that makes sense, to be outside."

"Isn't this exciting?"

"It's all good."

"What if the bank turns us down?"

"We'll rob it."

"They won't turn us down. We're professionals. Employed professionals."

"I might try recording birds again," said David. "There are birds everywhere."

"I don't like begging from our parents, but this is such an opportunity."

"There's a bird building a nest on the bell."

"I want to take that bell with us."

"We'll bring the nest too."

"What if there are other offers? What if someone outbids us?"

"We won't teach their kids. We won't neuter their cats."

Joanna said, "I need to calm down. I'm getting ahead of myself."

They went outside and watched the robin adjusting strands of grass in the nest above the dinner bell.

Joanna said, "I wonder if she's as excited about her new home as I am about mine."

David said, "Once her nest is finished, she'll start thinking about eggs."

"That's how we roll," said Joanna. "That's how we roll."

EIGHTY-FOUR

"LAST CALL!" YELLED TYLER.

"No!" said Rochelle. "It's still early."

"I know, babe, but Master-*san* is shutting it down early tonight so that he can watch the fires. I'll get the guitar."

Rochelle looked at Guy. "What is he talking about?"

Jock pulled up a chair. "The *Daimonji* festival is on tonight. They light these big-ass fires up in the mountains. It's worth checking out."

Junichi nodded agreement.

"It's too early," said Rochelle. "I don't want to leave."

Guy leaned back in his chair and tapped his finger on a Polaroid photo of him and Rochelle on the wall.

"We'll always be here."

Tyler stood on a booth at the back of the pub with Mr. Tanaka's classical guitar. The Dutch girl, Dani, sat with some other girls from Apple House in the opposite booth. Tyler nodded at her.

"Excuse me," he said. "Everyone." He waited for silence. "Tonight we are celebrating our friendship with a guy. Not just any guy. *The* guy. Guy." Tyler pointed at Guy. "He's an amazing teacher. He's a great dude. He's an attentive lover, right, Rochelle? And he's a loyal son. And life has just dealt him a bullshit hand. So we have to say *sayonara*, but we still have the fires tonight, and we can still text and shit. So, a toast to my Kiwi buddy. To Guy. May our footsteps meet again."

The patrons of the Rising Son raised their glasses. Tyler started playing guitar and singing.

"Oh, I love this song," said Rochelle. "It's 'Changes.' Isn't this song perfect?"

"Yes, it is," said Guy. "But he's only singing it so he can get laid."

THE DAY DAWNED SUNNY AND warm. The robin on the bell packed mud into the crevices of her nest. Joanna packed sandwiches into lunch bags.

David said, "We'll probably eat at the stream, so don't give me anything I need to microwave."

Joanna said, "I made your favourite. Beef on a kaiser with extra-old cheddar."

"Thank you."

David left for work first. He kissed her. He would remember that. He wouldn't remember if he had said anything.

Emily Carr Public School kept two first aid kits in backpacks for classes going on field trips. Before leaving for the stream, David sent Anna to the office to pick up one of the kits. George Young was signing in at the office while Anna waited for Ms. Richardson to help her.

"It's a beautiful day," said George.

Anna said, "It's just reading this morning. Mr. Woods said that maybe Thursday we can pick some flowers for art class."

"I might come Thursday too," said George.

"Martha's gone until next week sometime. I hope we go to the forest every day."

"That would be fun."

"I don't *want* Martha to not be here," said Anna, "but she isn't, so let's go. That's what I think."

"That's probably what Mr. Woods is thinking too," said George.

In the classroom, David addressed his students. "Hold one finger in the air if you have your backpack. Hold two fingers in the air if you have your copy of *Lead Dog* in your backpack. Hold three fingers in the air if you have your lunch in your backpack."

David scanned the room. "Your daybooks should not be in your backpacks. Leave them on your desks."

Chunhua said, "What about other books?"

"Don't take anything to the stream that you don't need." David arranged his own backpack. "Now remember, this is school. This is an opportunity to do schoolwork in a setting that kind of matches the setting in our story. I know a great spot where two streams meet, where we can sit and read chapters five and six. We'll discuss the who-what-where-when-why questions in the forest, and then we'll eat lunch and come back to do our written summaries.

"This is not a science walk. We're not catching anything. We're not picking anything. We're doing language arts. If this is successful today, maybe we can go into the forest tomorrow. It depends on today. If today is a good day, if you are focused, and respectful of the adults joining us, then hopefully we can repeat the experience. It's up to you. Do you understand?"

Students nodded.

Amanda Dickenson said, "Do you understand, kids? Don't blow it."

EIGHTY-FIVE

MR. TANAKA LOCKED THE DOORS to the Rising Son. Every year since his son had died, he and Atsuko had gone to the *Daimonji* festival to watch the fires being lit. It felt different this year, going with his nieces and such a large group of *gaijin*. As they walked to the station, Mr. Tanaka tried to explain the meaning of the fires to Guy.

"Today is the last day of *Obon*."

"I know," said Guy. "Many of my students were absent this week."

"Yes, many Japanese people are returning to their hometown. But we also believe that our, *nan-dakke*, our past generations —"

"Ancestors?"

"Yes. Our ancestors are with us for three days."

"Do you feel like your son is here?" said Guy.

"I don't know if his spirit is here, but during these days Atsuko and I are thinking of Shoichi."

Guy said, "It doesn't seem to me like my father is really gone. It doesn't seem real."

"The fires that you will see are the way that we say goodbye to our ancestors until next year."

"Thank you," said Guy. "I will think of my father."

"It is appropriate," said Mr. Tanaka.

At the train station, Rochelle organized people to pose for pictures around a bench. During one group shot, David had Den and Kaori sitting on his knees. For another they lined up in order of height, with David at one end of the line and Mrs. Tanaka at the other.

The train was very crowded going downtown. When they spilled out of the station they found the street along the Kamo River filled with hundreds of people. The air contained a medley of scents, with vendors selling *yakitori*, fish cakes, and fried tofu. At Jock's urging,

David bought a skewer of *dango*, dumplings coated in a sweet sauce.

They sat on the bank of the river, and Mrs. Tanaka spread a blanket on the grass. Mr. Tanaka poured them glasses of wine in plastic cups. Jock passed around a plastic container of *takoyaki*, which looked to David like chicken balls but was later revealed to be octopus.

Mr. Tanaka checked his watch and instructed the group to face east. After a few minutes the first glow of firelight appeared in the distance. Other fires started up, and they combined to create a symbol on the side of a mountain:

Having hiked in those mountains, and knowing how far away they were, David found it hard to believe the scale of what he was seeing.

When Rochelle expressed doubt about the size of the display, Junichi conferred with Mr. Tanaka.

"One hundred and fifty metres," said Junichi.

"What's a hundred and fifty metres?" asked Rochelle.

"The height of that symbol. And perhaps eighty large fires."

Rochelle murmured her amazement.

Mr. Tanaka told them there would be four more series of fires lit in the mountains around Kyoto, but these would be difficult to see from their location. Someone suggested that one of the bridges crossing the Kamo River might make a good vantage point from which to glimpse the other blazes.

When David volunteered to stay with the blanket, Mr. Tanaka felt disappointed. Considering the tragic story David had told him, Mr. Tanaka thought David might have more interest in viewing a ceremony dedicated to departed souls.

A few minutes after the others left, Kaori returned and dropped a bag full of beer in David's lap.

She said, "For my teacher."

"Thank you," said David.

"Thank you," said Kaori, and as she was stepping over him, she leaned down and gave him a kiss.

ERNEST PICKED UP SIMON AND placed him in the middle of the canoe.

Lenny Ferguson turned around and said, "Don't bring the dog."

"If I don't put him in the boat he'll swim after us."

Lenny scoffed, and Simon scampered over the dynamite man's canvas knapsack to greet him.

Ernest had tried to summon the courage to tell Lenny to forget the whole project. His pot-smoking nephew was right. He wasn't losing much land to the beavers, and they were providing him with a guaranteed Christmas rink.

The only thing that made him go forward was the sense that he had lost control of his land. If he left the field flooded, Margaret would conclude that he was no longer interested in farming and would cover the dinner table with brochures of condominiums featuring exercise rooms and on-call nurses. For Ernest, the fear of city living outweighed the fear of detonating explosives with a shady character.

They manoeuvred the boat through the flooded forest, emerging on the beaver pond. Ernest steered the canoe toward the lodge, but Lenny told him to go to the dam.

"I thought we were going to blow up the lodge first," said Ernest.

"We will," said Lenny. "I got a twenty-minute fuse on the dam stick and a ten-minute fuse on the lodge stick."

Ernest gave Lenny a confused look.

"Relax, man," said Lenny. "I'll light the dam fuse first. Then we'll have ten minutes to light the lodge fuse, and ten minutes to find a good seat for the show."

Ernest was too nervous to follow the dynamite man's logic, but at Lenny's instruction he guided the canoe to the dam. Lenny reached into his knapsack and removed a red baton. It looked more like a movie prop than a destructive device. Lenny jammed the dynamite stick in his back pocket and put a lighter behind his ear.

As Lenny climbed out of the canoe onto the dam, Simon scrambled out as well. Lenny yelled at the dog and grabbed it by the scruff of the neck. He threw Simon back into the boat, like a trapper working a line.

Simon yelped, and Lenny said, "I ain't saving you twice, mutt, so you better stay put."

Lenny climbed over the dam to the downstream side and stood astride a large log. Ernest held his trembling dog. They watched the top of Lenny's balding head as he stared into the wall of sticks and mud. When he was satisfied he had found a position that would inflict the most damage, Lenny twisted the stick of dynamite into the crevice.

"All right," said Lenny, "start timing." He lit the fuse.

EIGHTY-SIX

KAORI'S KISS WAS QUICK, AND David considered whether it could have been just a friendly gesture. She had never been affectionate before. Though given his state of mind, David thought it was possible he had been oblivious to previous advances. Regardless of Kaori's intent, he was happy for the beer and watched the *kanji* symbol for "large" burning on the side of Mount Higashi.

David had finished the first beer when Guy and Rochelle came to say that they were leaving. Guy made a crude comment about his plans for the rest of the night.

After David's second beer, Mr. and Mrs. Tanaka returned and gathered up their bags. They told David to keep the blanket.

After three more beers David began to think his friends had left him on the bank of the Kamo River. The fires still burned on the hillside, but only half the crowd remained to watch.

David shut his eyes. If Junichi had been able to hike another day, David would have been spending the night in a forest beneath Kurooyama. It would be another week before Junichi could complete the Keihoku Trail with him. In the interim, David considered hiking into the mountains around Kyoto to try to find the sites of these massive fires.

When he awoke, Kaori was sitting beside him, a hand on his belly.

David said, "Where's Den?"

"Gone," said Kaori.

David leaned up on his elbows. "Did everyone leave?"

Kaori nodded.

The second kiss was no friendly gesture. It was deep and warm, and David offered little resistance.

Kaori opened a beer and took little sips. She said, "My boss is permitting me to go to Los Angeles for the international gaming conference."

"That's great," said David.

"Maybe you do not need to be my teacher anymore." Kaori chewed her lip while David pondered what that meant.

They finished the beer together, and Kaori was over him again. The interlude was interrupted by clapping. David opened his eyes to find Nartti standing beside the blanket.

"Yay. Kissing," said Nartti.

Nartti sat down on the blanket and started eating a bag of chips. Kaori giggled and rolled off David.

When Nartti showed no intention of leaving, Kaori began picking up cans and food containers. David folded up the blanket, and the three of them walked to the train station together.

On the way to the train, Nartti bought a pack of cards and entertained David and Kaori with magic tricks. Once they reached Fushimi Station, Kaori walked with David and Nartti on the route to Monterrey House. Nartti made kissing noises and tried to make David and Kaori hold hands. When they reached Monterrey House, Nartti asked, "More kissing?" and swung from the awning above the front door.

There was no way David was going to invite Kaori up to his sweat-stained futon in the attic bedroom, home to antidepressants and nightmares. He gave Kaori an awkward little wave, and she imitated him in return. When she didn't move, David backed through the sliding door, leaving Nartti and Kaori in the alleyway.

David brushed his teeth and went through the empty kitchen up to his bedroom. Being drunk as well as totally exhausted from the previous days' events, he decided to skip the sleeping pills. He stripped down to his underwear and spread out the sleeping bag Junichi had lent him for camping. He felt guilty about fouling his friend's bedroll with his sweat, but the futon seemed more inviting covered with the sleeping bag.

He had just closed his eyes when there was a tap on his door. David tensed up in expectation that Kaori might walk in, but Nartti stuck his head through the crack.

In a singsong voice he said, "Your girlfriend, she wants to talk."

David put on a T-shirt and track pants. His first physical contact with Kaori, as brief as it had been, had felt good. Over the past year he had felt very few twinges of physical desire. Despite Guy's encouragement, he had not felt any attraction to Kaori until the moment she pressed herself against him.

At the bottom of the stairs David stopped and thought about what he would say. He could bring up the taboo nature of a student-teacher relationship, or perhaps talk about his reluctance to break Tanaka-*san*'s trust. He finally decided that his best strategy would be to tell Kaori that he would call her in the morning. There was no sense risking a conversation that might get loud or emotional.

Walking down the hallway, he ran his hand through his hair, exaggerating his fatigue. He squinted through half-closed eyes, pretending he'd already been asleep.

When David saw her, he stopped quickly, and the damaged half of his brain sloshed though porous membranes into the healthy half. As his body directed most of its blood supply to vital organs, David braced himself against the wall to keep from falling. There was a ringing in his ears, and a sudden detachment from the situation. He tried to speak, but because he had stopped breathing, nothing came out.

She said, "David," and it was all he could do to croak a reply.

"Joanna."

WHEN THE CONDIE CREEK TRAIL was constructed, the planners envisioned a path going from the nature centre in the conservation area, alongside Condie Creek, all the way to the Rideau River. However, the nature centre was on the west side of Condie Creek, and Graham Creek and Trout Creek emptied into Condie Creek from the west. In order to keep the trail on the west bank, two bridges would have been required to cross the tributaries. To save money, the planners had opted to build one bridge spanning Condie Creek so the trail could continue unimpeded to the Rideau River on the east bank.

The fourth-grade class from Emily Carr Public School stopped on the bridge before crossing over to the west side of Condie Creek. George Young passed around licorice sticks, and David made another speech about academic expectations.

Carrie Connelly said, "Are we walking all the way to the nature centre?"

"No," said David. "When we cross the bridge, instead of following the path, we're going to turn right."

"Bushwhacking," said Robbie Dickenson.

"We don't have to go far. Where the two streams meet there are some evergreen trees. When we get there, I'd like everyone to find their own tree and sit under it for twenty minutes of silent reading. I'll time you."

"What if we get lost?" said Carrie.

"It's right over there," said David, pointing down the stream. "I know where we're going."

Carrie said, "I mean, what if one of us gets lost. What if the twenty minutes is over and I can't find anyone."

"We will all be right there. We'll all be in the same place."

"I just don't want to get lost."

"Don't worry," said David. "We're not going to lose anyone."

EIGHTY-SEVEN

DAVID'S BRAIN, WHICH HAD DONE such a good job of emotionally insulating him from events of the past, was now short-circuiting on many levels. Adding to the cosmic disorientation, not only was Joanna standing in his Kyoto boarding house, but his brother, Kyle, stood behind her in the open doorway, hands in his pockets.

Joanna said, "We're staying at a place called the High Five House."

"I know where that is," said David, grabbing on to the first fact that floated by.

"We're in Kyoto for two nights, and then we're going."

"Where?"

"Home, David."

David stood paralyzed in the hallway. His brother looked out at the alley.

Joanna said, "You have to come to me. Do you understand?"

When David said nothing, Joanna said, "I've come ten thousand kilometres." Her voice was shaking. "If there is anything left of us that you want to save, you have to come to me."

She turned to leave, and Kyle stepped out of her way.

David put his hands on his head. Carrying Hisao down the mountain had been easier than speaking or moving at this moment.

"Hey," said Kyle, waving his hand as if to catch David's attention. "Hey, bro, if you're not going to run after her, maybe you could invite me in or say 'hello' or something."

David said, "Does she know where she's going?"

"Her phone's got GPS."

David stared over Kyle into the darkness. When Kyle started walking toward him, David said, "You have to take off your shoes."

"Whatever," said Kyle, and he pushed past David into the kitchen.

WHEN THE DYNAMITE MAN TOLD Ernest to start timing, Ernest panicked. He didn't have a watch, and he couldn't remember if it was ten minutes or twenty minutes until the dam exploded. As Lenny climbed into the canoe, Ernest started paddling hard.

Lenny said, "Christ, buddy, take it easy."

"Sorry."

"We got lots of time," said Lenny, "unless we tip."

When they reached the beaver lodge, Lenny took a trowel and dug a cavity in the mud. He placed the second stick of dynamite in the hole and lit the fuse.

They paddled into the trees and turned the canoe so they could watch the explosions. Ernest held Simon between his knees.

Lenny lit a cigarette and said, "One problem just makes more problems."

Ernest had no idea how long they had until the blasts started. He prepared to cover Simon if debris rained down on them.

Lenny said, "It's best to pinch off problems at the source." He pursed his lips and blew smoke out in a thin stream. "My ex-wife has a cat that's pissing all over the house. Now she got newspapers on all the floors. She got air fresheners everywhere." Lenny turned and looked at Ernest. "That ain't a solution. The solution is to remove the problem."

Ernest's gaze flipped back and forth between the dam and the lodge.

Lenny said, "Buddy, you made a good decision. You took control."

Simon could sense his owner's anxiety and looked at Ernest for reassurance.

Lenny said, "In about two minutes your problems are gonna go away."

EIGHTY-EIGHT

DAVID FOLLOWED KYLE INTO THE kitchen, and Kyle opened the fridge.

"You got any beer?" he said.

"No," said David.

"Really? You smell like a brewery."

When Kyle started opening cupboards, David said, "I've got some rye."

David rummaged around under the sink. He emerged with a black bottle. He poured rye into a tin cup and handed it to Kyle. They sat at the kitchen table. Kyle looked around.

"Your place isn't too oriental."

David said, "What are you doing here?"

"Dad made me come. I'm supposed to look after Jo. I thought maybe when we got here you'd take over. No luck, eh?"

"I wasn't expecting her."

"How many more countries do you need to hide in?"

Rochelle came down the stairs wearing a bathrobe.

Kyle tipped an imaginary hat and said, "Ma'am."

Rochelle knew immediately who she was looking at.

David said, "This is my brother. This is Kyle"

Rochelle sat down at the table. She looked back and forth between the Woods brothers. She said, "You boys are cut from the same cloth. I mean, really, Kyle, you are a smaller version of David."

"In every way," said Kyle.

"David told us all about you," said Rochelle.

Kyle raised his cup to David.

Rochelle said, "He said you made life difficult for him."

Kyle started pulling off his shoes. "Who is this chick?"

"Rochelle," said Rochelle, extending a hand.

Kyle looked like he might kiss it, but gave it a weak shake.

"David says you were rough on him growing up."

"Well that's bullshit," said Kyle.

"You were hard on him."

"I did what I had to."

"That doesn't sound like the kind of relationship most brothers have."

"You must not know too many brothers."

"I have three." Rochelle got up and retrieved the bottle of rye from the counter. "They wrestled and fought, sure, but they stood up for each other. They loved each other."

Twenty-four hours of travel had left Kyle exhausted and honest. He said, "If you want to know, I'm very fond of my kid brother."

Rochelle poured some rye into a teacup and topped up Kyle's mug. David took the act to mean that this painful conversation would continue. Rochelle was still emotionally raw from the news of the day and quite willing to redirect her fear and sadness into confrontation. Kyle and Rochelle clinked their cups together.

Rochelle said, "Let's call you what you are. You're a bully."

Kyle laughed. "I may have given him a thousand wedgies, but I had a harder time growing up than he ever did."

Rochelle wheezed through the alcohol burning her throat. "Tell, tell."

"You probably know what he's like," said Kyle. "Polite. Hard-working. Fucking ethical."

"I see," said Rochelle. "That must have been hard to take."

"Well, Mom and Dad liked him better than me. That was hard to take."

David wondered if Joanna was lost in the grid of Kyoto streets. Life had changed a lot in the last ten minutes.

"Parents love all their children," said Rochelle.

Kyle said, "He was better at school, better at sports."

"He made you feel inferior."

"Well, Dad had a nickname for Davy here." Kyle pointed his finger like a gun at David. *The Good One.*

Kyle gulped his rye. He asked Rochelle, "Are you his girlfriend or his shrink?"

"Just a friend."

David said, "I was always the little brother. That was never in question."

"Well, sorry, bro, but I had to ride you. If I didn't make your life shitty, you'd have stayed on the farm and I would be nowhere."

"I don't think that's true," said David.

"The farm is all I've got," said Kyle. "You, little brother, can do anything."

"It was insecurity," said Rochelle. "You saw David as a threat."

"He had good grades and trophies, and everybody loved him."

"That's an exaggeration," said David.

Kyle emptied his cup. "We had a hundred-and-thirty-acre farm to run, and Dad suggested I go to fucking electrician school."

DAVID FOUND A CENTRAL POSITION in an area of hemlock trees. He told the students, "You can sit anywhere, but you have to be able to see me. If you sit beside one of the streams, you can't go near the water."

Robbie said, "Can we cross the beaver dam?"

"No," said David.

"There's a path," said Robbie.

The beaver dam crossing Graham Creek was old and was not holding back any water. It was only fifteen feet across and had plants growing out of it. There was a path that led down the bank, crossed the dam, and led up the opposite shore. This allowed more adventurous hikers to stay on the west side of Condie Creek instead of following the main trail on the other bank.

The students peered down at the dam.

Katie Findlay said, "Can we read on the other side? It's the same as this side."

The students pleaded their case. David looked at his parent volunteers.

Amanda said, "It would be fun to say we crossed a beaver dam."

"Let me test it," said David, and he climbed down to the dam. He stood in the middle and jumped up and down. He climbed up the far bank and surveyed the area. Indeed, it did look similar to the other side.

"Okay," said David, and the students cheered.

George and Amanda helped students down the bank. After they picked their way across the dam, David hoisted the kids up the other side, where June Wong stood with them. When everyone had crossed, David stood in an open area and instructed the students to find a reading spot within sight of him. David sat down on a log to read *Lead Dog*. George Young pulled out a notebook and began sketching a twisted cedar tree.

The students took a few minutes to settle in. Once they did, the residents of the forest resumed their activities. A downy woodpecker tapped tentatively on a dead beech tree. A mallard quacked farther down Condie Creek. David admonished Anna not to read out loud. George smiled at David and pointed at a chickadee that was flitting above their heads.

The first explosion was far enough away that no one jumped. But the students stopped reading, and the adults gathered together.

"That was a gunshot," said Amanda.

"That was bigger than a gunshot," said David.

George said, "I can't think of anything that would be back there."

"Like what?" said Amanda.

"Like a quarry. Or an artillery range."

"It doesn't matter what it was," said David. "We need to go."

David called the students together and told them that they would cross the dam in the same manner as before.

The second explosion was louder and added urgency to the crossing.

"Are those bombs?" said Martin.

"No," said David.

"What are they?"

"Hurry up," said David.

EIGHTY-NINE

KYLE POURED MORE RYE FOR himself and Rochelle.

He said, "I should have come to Japan earlier. This chick has got me saying things I should have said years ago."

Rochelle said to Kyle, "You were worried that David would get the farm."

"The fucking guy would be out chopping wood in the dark. I couldn't compete with that."

"Dad always said the farm would be split fifty-fifty," said David.

"That never works," said Kyle. "Farming is a business, and you can only have one CEO."

"Well you're it now," said David.

"For now," said Kyle. "I'm sure the reason Dad sent me here was to bring back the prodigal son."

Rochelle said, "Your father sent you here to bring David home?"

"And to look after Joanna. Plus there's the inquest, so…"

"Joanna's here? His girlfriend is here?"

Kyle chewed on a piece of ice. "At the High Five House."

"Why isn't she here?"

"Too proud to beg," said Kyle.

David put his chin to his chest. He gripped the edge of the table.

Rochelle looked at David. "You should go to her."

"He's been fucked up for a year," said Kyle. "I don't know if he told you, but this kid died, and now his brain's fried."

Rochelle put a hand on David's. "You should go to her."

"He's a basket case," said Kyle. "A chick flies across the ocean to throw herself at him, and he can't even say hello."

Rochelle said, "I know about the student. It's a tragedy. That would affect anyone."

"I know," said Kyle. "But no one blames him. Most people think he's a hero."

MARTHA EMERSON WAS IN FRANCE. Jenny Lin was at the dentist. Twenty-two students needed to cross the dam. David counted them as he lifted bodies up the bank.

Sixteen. Seventeen.

Chunhua.

Eighteen.

Water filled David's shoes.

"It's sinking!" yelled Katie.

The dam seemed to be sinking because the water was rising.

David turned around, and the four remaining students were knee-deep in rushing water. David grabbed Martin and Katie, who were closest to him. He tossed them up the embankment like dolls.

Nineteen.

Twenty.

Anna and Carrie clung to branches sticking out of the dissolving dam. George Young hugged the root of a tree on the far bank.

There was no time to process what was happening. Graham Creek had turned into a river, but for David, all that mattered was a number.

David edged toward Carrie as the gushing water threatened to push him off the shelf. She reached out to him, and David grabbed her arm and pulled her across the top of the current. With Carrie over his shoulder, he turned back toward the shore, feeling for footholds in the flow. David was now waist-deep in water. When he reached the bank, Amanda Dickenson grabbed Carrie's wrist and dragged her screaming up the bank.

Twenty-one.

When David turned around, he saw an image that would flash repeatedly in his futon dreams.

Only Anna's feet were above water, kicking wildly. The strap of her yellow backpack was twisted around a branch in the dam, and though it kept her from washing away, the tightly wound knot held Anna's body submerged.

David inched back into the current. The water kept rising, and he doubted he could reach her before he was swept away. When he was within a few feet of Anna, he prepared to lunge at her. George looked down from the bank, his eyes telling David, *I can't help you.*

David placed a foot against a web of branches that threatened to collapse under his weight. He intended to leap toward Anna and grab her leg or her backpack. They would both be swept downstream, but he would have her.

As David pushed against the branches, they buckled. David fell forward, reaching for a foothold. Somewhere under roiling water he stepped on the branch that had snagged the strap of Anna's backpack. The branch broke, and Anna, the precocious daughter of Ron and Holly Metz, joined the torrent of water racing toward the Rideau River.

NINETY

"THE GIRL'S PARENTS DON'T BLAME him," said Kyle.

"Her name is Anna," said David.

"No one holds anything against you except you."

"How can you know how David feels?" Rochelle pulled the top of her bathrobe tight.

Kyle said, "He feels sorry for himself."

"You need to stop," said David.

"He's given up on everybody."

"That's not fair," said Rochelle.

"The first time in his life something goes wrong, all he feels is pity for himself."

"You should go," said Rochelle.

"No," said Kyle. "Somebody needs to say this shit. He's always been the golden boy."

"That's sour grapes," said Rochelle.

Guy stood at the bottom of the stairs, assessing the scene.

Kyle said, "He's always been a man. He's always been the strong one. Well it's easy to be a man when everyone loves you, when everything goes your way."

Guy stepped forward. "C'mon, mate, ease up."

Kyle looked at David. "Sure, you got a shitty break, but if you are the man everyone thinks you are, then fucking stand up. Fucking testify. *Be David fucking Woods.*"

When the glasses in the cupboards started tinkling, everyone looked toward the noise. Then they looked at each other. The house rocked with a strong side-to-side motion.

Guy grabbed Rochelle and ran for the front door. Kyle stumbled after David, and the four of them pushed through the hallway and into the alley. People shouted from bedrooms.

"Go to the road," yelled Guy.

The ground continued to shake. Kyle looked back to his younger brother for direction, but David had disappeared into the night.

WHEN THE BRANCH HOLDING ANNA broke free, David threw himself into the current. Where Graham Creek joined Condie Creek, David slammed into the far bank. A log struck him in the temple, and blood flowed freely. He pulled himself along the shore until he could propel himself back into the main flow.

The water carried David as easily as it did the poplar logs that once buttressed beaver dams. He could swivel his head and look for shapes and colours in the current, but control of his body was surrendered to the brown tide.

At a bend in the stream he spotted the yellow of Anna's backpack and his heart leaped in hope. The bag was still tangled in a branch, but Anna had slipped free of it.

At one point David's feet touched bottom, and fighting the instinct to save himself he used the opportunity to propel his body forward. This would be the compulsion in David's nightmare. Push ahead. Keep going. Even though what is ahead is unthinkable.

David whispered, "Help me, God."

NINETY-ONE

DAVID RACED DOWN AN ALLEYWAY, leaping over bicycles and pushing by families and garbage cans. The ground had stopped moving and sirens rang out around the city. When he reached Kuradori Avenue, smoke poured out the window of an office building. People were shouting. Children cried.

David followed the sidewalk until it was blocked by fallen vending machines. He swerved into the street. Traffic was stopped by debris in the road, and David wove between stalled cars.

It was two-thirty in the morning in Kyoto, and David Woods ran frantically through the aftermath of a powerful earthquake. It was a different time and a different place, but David was back in Condie Creek.

AT A BEND THE STREAM widened, and the force of the current slowed. David stood up in chest-deep water. His body was numb from the cold, and he stumbled to find footing. His feet sank in the mud as he shook his head to clear the water from his eyes.

David saw the man standing at the side of the stream, Anna draped over his arms. Water ran out of her nose and mouth. David yelled at the man to do something, but the man just stared at the body in his arms.

Do mouth-to-mouth!

Anna's skin was grey and her eyes were rolled back in her head.

Put her in a recovery position!

Anna's dress was torn, and the man fumbled to pull the fabric over exposed skin.

Forget about the dress! Get her to a hospital!

In this way, David continued to berate the man.

But, of course, David is the man. And this is the way he remembers the scene, in the third person. He cannot remember picking up Anna. He cannot remember how she felt so heavy, filled with water. He cannot remember looking into her face and knowing that she was gone.

However, he remembers the man. The man who stood on the bank of Condie Creek doing nothing.

NINETY-TWO

RUNNING THROUGH THE STREETS OF Kyoto, David saw fires and collapsed buildings. There was a road with asphalt lifted in the middle. With so much damage, people must have died. When you saw something like that on television, people were dead.

At an intersection, David hesitated, thinking he had taken the wrong road. He raced down the middle of the street. There was the 7-Eleven store, but was it the right one?

He saw a sweater on the ground. *Could that be Joanna's sweater?*

Although David felt the same panic as he had at Condie Creek, there was a significant difference. He was able to move his limbs. He could control where his body went. The freedom of movement meant that his strength, his stamina, his long stride could make a difference.

As he ran, he pictured what he would do when he found Joanna. If she were trapped under rubble, he would tell someone to go for help. He and the volunteers would carefully lift the pieces of cement off her body until they could pull her out safely. If she wasn't breathing, David would start CPR. Twenty-five chest compressions followed by two breaths.

At the bottom of the hill there was a wide set of steps leading up to a grey stone building. Young people sat on the steps talking on cellphones.

He bounded up the steps in his stocking feet, three at a time.

The front door of the dormitory was open, and David ducked through the entrance. He pulled open a glass doorway that led into a long hallway. There were no lights except for the red glow of an exit sign at the far end. David grabbed the handle of the first bedroom door he came to. It was locked, and he pounded on the door. "Joanna!"

When no one responded, he worked his way down the corridor, turning doorknobs and calling frantically.

At some point David's mind took measures to protect him from the possibility of what he might find. He imagined hang-gliders floating over Keihoku Valley. He saw the warm orange glow of many *torii* leading up the side of a mountain.

While David's thoughts veered from image to image, his body continued the torturous course down the corridor, feeling for doorknobs in the darkness.

He stopped suddenly, trying to determine if the image before him was real or imagined.

Joanna stood under the exit sign, her body intact and upright. David looked for signs of breathing and whether her lungs might be full of fluid.

"David," she said.

It was more difficult to keep going now that Joanna was in front of him. He took the remaining steps heavily, like he was wading through water. He kept his eyes fixed on her in case she might drift away. When he was right before her, he placed his hands on her face. She was warm and dry and full of life-breath.

"I've got you," he said.

"I'm okay."

"I'll get help."

"I'm fine, David."

He buried his face in her hair.

"I love you," he sobbed.

"I know," she said.

NINETY-THREE

THE MAGNITUDE 6.8 EARTHQUAKE KILLED twenty-six people and caused damage to roads and buildings across the Kansai region of Japan. NHK News reported that it was the nine hundred and seventy-sixth earthquake greater than magnitude 4.0 to hit Japan that year. Residents of Kyoto were warned that aftershocks could be expected.

Like all Japanese people, Takahiro Matsuoka had grown up with an understanding that the earth could shift at any moment, and everything he knew would disappear. Because of this risk, even large earthquakes were greeted with a sense of relief that things were not worse.

Takahiro had lived through the Miyagi earthquake of 1978. Many houses around his university had been destroyed. Classes had been cancelled for a week, and Takahiro and his schoolmates had helped clean up damage in the area. This was the first time since 1978 that Takahiro had felt fear during a quake.

This morning, because work was cancelled, and because the earthquake was not the Big One, Takahiro was making omelettes for his family. His wife listened to news reports on the radio, and his daughter cleaned out a cupboard of broken teacups. Usually a late sleeper, his son, Junichi, was dressed and sat at the kitchen table texting. Although there had been casualties in the city, the Matsuoka household hummed with a mood comparable to a North American snow day.

Takahiro served breakfast in bowls usually reserved for special occasions. His family chided him for adding ginger to every recipe.

Takahiro said, "If you do not like the eggs, Ginkgo and I will finish them." Ginkgo was their cat.

When the meal was done, Junichi cleared the dishes and sat across from his father. He placed a laptop computer on the table and opened the website of a Japanese newspaper. Without talking, he turned the computer so his father could see it.

His father read the story about a local man (Junichi himself) and a Canadian teacher who had carried an elderly Keihoku man six kilometres through the mountains to safety. Takahiro was expressionless as he read, and Junichi was worried that his father might berate him for hiking in the mountains instead of looking for a job.

Takahiro tapped on the screen of the computer. "How can we print copies of this?"

Junichi said, "I will go to the store and buy this newspaper."

"My father will want one. And get one for your mother's family."

Junichi said, "My Canadian friend is going home in two days."

"We could put copies in our New Year's cards."

"Can I use the car tomorrow?"

Junichi drove the car occasionally, but only for errands that served the family. He would pick up groceries for dinner or take his grandmother to appointments.

He said, "My friend needs to go back to Keihoku."

Takahiro said, "Can he take the bus?"

"It is difficult and would take too long. He only has tomorrow."

When Takahiro was awoken by the earthquake, he had run toward his children's bedrooms. In the darkness of the shaking apartment, in a half-conscious state, he could not remember how old they were. He had expected to find scared teenagers. Instead a young man and woman had met him in the hallway and led him out of the building.

Takahiro said, "Probably my office will be closed again tomorrow. If not, I can take the train."

"Thank you," said Junichi.

Takahiro pushed the laptop back toward his son. "One day I may need you to carry me."

~

DAVID STOOD OVER A LARGE boulder on Kuroo-yama. He was talking animatedly.

320

"This is where Hisao was. We were up here for five minutes before Junichi saw him. We didn't hear him. I was standing here, looking this way. We never saw him. He had on a grey shirt. It was like he was camouflaged."

Joanna said, "You are getting better."

"Yes," said David. "Why?"

"David, for a year there hasn't been anything you've wanted to tell me. You might answer my questions, but you never told me anything. I got one letter."

"In these mountains I talked to you. Up here I told you everything."

"That didn't help me in Dumford Mills."

"I'm sorry," said David.

"No," said Joanna. "Just keep talking."

David told Joanna about carrying Hisao down the mountain. He talked about the inhabitants of Monterrey House. He told her about the Chicken Dance and getting drunk and visiting the *jizo* statue in the mountains. He told her about the Tanakas and the death of their son.

Joanna said, "I worried that you were fading away."

"I was," said David. He placed Joanna's hand against his face, proving to her that he was real.

JUNICHI KNOCKED ON THE DOOR. Hisao's daughter, Hidemi, answered. Junichi bowed to her and asked about Hisao's health.

She invited him in, and Junichi said, "Excuse me, please. This is my father. This is Takahiro Matsuoka."

THE LAST FEW KILOMETRES OF the Keihoku Trail went through an evergreen forest. The main point of interest along the way was the ruins of an old castle embedded in a hillside. Joanna sat on a stone, hugging her backpack.

David said, "These walls were built in 1579."

Joanna said, "I can't believe I'm here with you. I can't believe you're talking."

"I didn't want to leave Japan without finishing the trail."

"This is surreal. I mean, it's good. I just didn't know what I would find."

"What do you mean?"

"I don't know. I worried about you. I imagined a lot of stuff."

"Mitchell said you thought I was suicidal."

"You were depressed. You were taking a lot of pills. You stopped interacting with people. I thought you were going to turn into an addict or a hermit or worse."

David said, "I'm not too bad during the day. Nighttime is still hard."

"Just by the way you walk, I can tell you're getting better."

"Walking has helped. People have helped. I've seen a lot of things in Kyoto."

Joanna sipped from a water bottle.

David ran his hand over the stone wall. He said, "I feel like all this stuff is all supposed to mean something."

"What stuff?"

"I don't know. This wall. Everything."

"I don't know what you're trying to say."

"I've seen so many things. I've been to dozens of shrines and temples. I've seen statues dedicated to dead children. Two nights ago I watched a giant fire on the side of a mountain. It was supposed to have something to do with people who passed away."

"It's normal to look for meaning in the things we see."

"I know, but it's like I'm being shown things. I just can't make sense of any of it. Maybe I'm too dumb."

"Who do you think is showing you these things? God?"

David leaned against the four-hundred-year-old wall. He said, "It doesn't feel random."

Joanna said, "After what happened at Condie Creek, don't you think that life is full of randomness?"

"An old lady showed me the start of the Kyoto Trail."

"That doesn't seem like evidence of divine guidance."

"I feel like I was put on this path."

Joanna drew a circle in the dirt with a stick. She said, "I don't believe God is guiding our lives."

"I thought that's exactly what you believed."

"Maybe I did. But I don't want to believe in a God who kills off nine-year-old girls."

THE TRAIL FINISHED AT THE town of Shuzan. David and Joanna sat on a bench and waited for Junichi to pick them up. A teenaged girl walked by, staring at the couple.

David said, "They don't see as many foreigners in rural areas."

Joanna waved at the girl, and she turned away. Joanna held David's hand and they sat in silence.

Joanna said, "Were you going to come home?"

"Yes," said David.

"Really?"

"Yes. The inquest is another trail I need to complete."

NINETY-FOUR

ON DAVID'S LAST MORNING AT Monterrey House, Jock woke up early and made scones. Rochelle, David, and Jock sat at the kitchen table.

Jock said, "Davy, this ain't much of a going-away party."

"It's good," said David.

Rochelle said, "Guy told me to give you a big kiss on the lips when you leave. From him. I won't tell you what else he said."

"Shelley," said Jock, "I don't think you've seen the last of that boy."

"Really? Why do you say that?"

"Experience."

Rochelle typed on her cellphone. "Tyler didn't come home last night. He sent me a long email for you, David. I'll forward it to Joanna."

Jock said, "Tyler's gone Dutch. He's wearing wooden shoes now, boy."

"I bet he moves to Apple House," said Rochelle. "It has a big common room. He can play guitar."

Jock said, "Soon it'll just be me and Nartti."

"Why do you stay here?" said Rochelle.

"C'mon, Shelley, this is my home. Living in the Monterrey House is like living on the bank of a river. People flow by. I like tapping into that current. I move with the world's tides."

"Your food was great," said David.

Jock slapped David on the back. He said, "I tapped into Davy here, and now we're riding a wave, man. A freaky Chicken Dance wave."

Rochelle said, "I will never forget that night at the Savannah Club."

Jock said, "Soon that wave is gonna crash, and then I'll catch some new wave." He posed like Usain Bolt. "You don't need to worry about Jock. I surf above the crowd, baby."

Rochelle asked David, "Was Japan everything you expected?"

David laughed. He didn't offer a response.

Rochelle said, "What surprised you the most about your time here?"

David bit into a scone. "That you guys talked to me."

KYLE AND JOANNA STOOD IN the hallway, waiting for David to say his goodbyes.

Rochelle handed Joanna a black leather book with pheasants on it. "This is the house guestbook. You guys need to sign it."

"I was only here an hour," said Kyle. "I yelled at my brother and then the house started shaking."

"That's karma," said Rochelle. "You need to be nice to David."

"The gods are usually on his side."

Joanna and Kyle made notes in the book. David went last.

While David was thinking about what to write, Joanna said to Jock, "Thank you for looking after him."

Jock said, "Ain't nothing but inmates in this asylum."

"*O Canada*," sang Nartti, opening an umbrella.

David closed the guestbook. He told Rochelle, "Say goodbye to Kaori and Den for me. Thank Tanaka-*san* for everything. Tell them I'll write."

When David bent down to hug Rochelle, she whispered in his ear, "Your brother is right. Be David Woods."

As the three Canadians dragged suitcases to Fushimi Station, Joanna asked David, "What did you write in the book?"

"Nothing," said David. "I drew an inuksuk."

NINETY-FIVE

THE WEEK BEFORE THE INQUEST, Joanna stayed with David at his parents' farm. She urged David to practise his testimony, but David was happy to spend the days picking fruit with the Mexicans.

One night he showed his mother his sketchbook. Lillian made David tell her where he was when he drew each picture. He could describe the scenes accurately, though the names of places often escaped him.

"You got better," Lillian said.

David said, "I've still got a long way to go. But I have cut back on the medication."

Lillian said, "I meant that you got better as an artist."

"THE PICKERS LIKE YOU," SAID Archie.

David lifted a crate of apples onto a wagon that Archie had harnessed to Hershey, his old workhorse.

"You should pay them more," said David.

"It's a balance."

Archie loosened the nose strap of Hershey's harness and pulled the bit out of the horse's mouth. David threw his father an apple to feed to the gelding.

Archie said, "You could take over the contract negotiations if you'd like."

David said, "Joanna and I are going to try again."

"Try again here."

"Her boss knows a vet near Barrie who's looking to hire someone."

"You're going where the wind blows you?"

"I can't go back to Dumford Mills."

"I know, but you're just going to leave your life up to fate again?"

"Yes," said David. "We all do."

NINETY-SIX

THE DAY BEFORE DAVID WAS scheduled to testify at the inquest, Mitchell picked him up for the six-hour drive to Ottawa. Joanna drove separately with her parents.

Mitchell said, "You look great, buddy. You lost some weight."

"No steak and potatoes for four months," said David.

"Couldn't you find a McDonald's?"

"I ate well," said David.

In Toronto they got stuck in a traffic jam. Mitchell played a David Bowie CD and tapped on the steering wheel.

"I only went to Kyoto once," he said. "It seemed pretty laid-back."

"Yeah," said David.

"Did you make any friends?"

"Yeah."

"Any Japanese friends?"

"Yeah."

Mitchell sang along to "Heroes." David appreciated that his friend was satisfied with one-word answers.

At a truck stop in Kingston, Mitchell and David picked at a plate of French fries.

David said, "Thank you, Mitchell."

"No problem, buddy," said Mitchell. "I miss road trips."

"Thank you for giving me Japan."

"I know, right? Isn't it great?"

"Yeah," said David. "You saved me."

~

DRIVING NORTH ON HIGHWAY 416 to Ottawa, David told Mitchell

to take the exit that would lead to Dumford Mills. Mitchell worried that David might be taking him to Condie Creek, but instead they followed the roads to the farmhouse that David and Joanna had rented. Mitchell parked along the road, but David told him to go up the driveway.

At the house, David knocked on the door and peered through windows. When no one answered, David pulled a key from his pocket and started to unlock the door.

"Whoa, buddy," said Mitchell. "You don't live here anymore."

David pushed the door open and said, "Hello?"

When no one answered, David entered the house, and Mitchell reluctantly followed.

"What are you doing?" said Mitchell. "What if there's a dog?"

David wiped his feet and went to the kitchen. He opened the door to the basement and pulled on a string that illuminated the stairs. David was at the bottom before Mitchell had decided whether to follow.

"What if someone comes home?" said Mitchell. When David did not answer, Mitchell went down a few steps and looked for his friend. A light flicked on in another room.

"Bring down a chair," called David.

"No," said Mitchell. "Why?"

"Come here," said David.

Mitchell held the railing carefully, afraid that he might trip in his nervousness.

The illuminated room was a workshop. Tools hung from nails above a workbench. David was standing on an upturned bucket, feeling around above a furnace duct.

David said, "I'll lift you."

"We shouldn't be here," said Mitchell. "This is nuts. What are we stealing?"

David knelt behind Mitchell and grabbed him around the waist. As David hoisted him up, Mitchell grabbed at a beam for support.

David said, "Do you see a piece of wire hanging down? I tied it up there somewhere."

Mitchell squinted into the darkness above the metal duct. "An electrical wire? No."

"It's a piece of copper wire," said David.

"No," said Mitchell. "Wait, yes. I see it."

"Pull it down."

Mitchell twisted at the wire until it came free. David lowered Mitchell to the floor, and Mitchell looked at the brown metal strand in his hand. The wire was looped through a sterling silver ring engraved with thistles.

David slipped it off the wire.

"Is it yours?" said Mitchell.

"It was Joanna's grandmother's."

"It's nice. Can we go now?"

David pressed the ring into Mitchell's palm and folded his friend's fingers closed.

"Hey, no," said Mitchell. "You keep the loot."

David kept his hands closed around Mitchell's. "It's a wedding ring, Mitchell. I think the best man is supposed to hold on to it."

NINETY-SEVEN

IN OTTAWA, DAVID AND MITCHELL checked into a downtown hotel on Lyon Street. Joanna and her parents occupied the adjacent room. For dinner they ate at an Italian restaurant called Tosca.

Doug Shayne asked David, "Are you ready for tomorrow?"

David said, "They kind of let me know what the questions would be."

"Are you ready for those questions?"

"All I can do is tell what happened."

Linda Shayne said, "We support you, David."

The unspoken implication was that David's family did not support him. They were not coming.

David said, "I told my family not to come. I just want to get this over with. I don't want any drama."

Linda said, "Oh goodness. Maybe we shouldn't be here."

"No," said David. "You're good. You guys are great."

Linda said, "I pray for you and Joanna every day. The whole thing was just a terrible accident. You did your best, and I think everyone knows that."

David grunted.

Doug said, "I get the feeling that's not what you want to hear."

"I'd prefer to hear someone tell me that I screwed up."

"Oh, but why?" said Linda.

David stuck a fork into a piece of bread. "So I don't have to keep doing it myself."

IN THE MORNING, MITCHELL AND David drove to the courthouse. Joanna and her parents followed behind. In front of the courthouse there was a small crowd, and David recognized some of the people.

When Mitchell parked in a garage under the courthouse, Doug and Linda's vehicle was nowhere to be seen. David and Mitchell took an elevator up to the third floor where David would testify.

In the courtroom, David sat in the front row, just like at church. The chairs behind him filled up with people. David did not turn around to see who was there.

On schedule, the jury was brought in and the coroner sat in the judge's chair. Joanna slid in beside David.

"Where were you?" whispered David.

"Sorry. I stopped to talk."

A woman motioned for David to come forward, and he was led to the witness box. David saw the Metz family and looked away.

A court officer approached David and said, "Do you solemnly affirm that the evidence that you will give at this inquest into the death of Anna Metz will be the truth, the whole truth, and nothing but the truth?"

"Yes," said David.

The lawyer for the coroner wore a dark jacket and a skirt. She pursed her lips before asking each question. She led David chronologically through the school year, touching on the initial field trips and the circumstances surrounding the permission forms. As David responded to her questions, she pushed him to provide more information than he was volunteering.

As they worked their way through the day of June 1, David talked faster. By the time he got to the account of the dam crossing, David was breathing hard.

David said, "After I got Carrie, Anna was the last one."

"What was Anna's physical condition at that time?"

"She was underwater. She was stuck on a branch."

"But you couldn't reach her?"

"The water kept rising. I couldn't even tell where the dam was anymore."

"But you tried to reach Anna."

"I got pretty close."

The woman motioned with her hand. "As close as I am to you?"

"Closer," said David.

"This close?" the lawyer asked, taking a step forward.

"Closer."

"So you could almost touch her."

David looked at the Metz family.

"I tried. I'm sorry, Holly. I'm sorry, Ron. I'm sorry, Louis."

DURING THE ADJOURNMENT THE CORONER told David to make sure he directed his testimony to the attorney.

"You are free to say whatever you want to people outside the courtroom."

Joanna gave David a package of tissues. "It will soon be over."

People in the courtroom chatted among themselves, avoiding eye contact with David.

Joanna said, "When you're done on the stand, do you want to stay for the rest of it?"

David shook his head.

The coroner instructed everyone to be seated.

The attorney with the pursed lips asked, "When Anna was being swept away from the dam, was she struggling? Did she attempt to swim?"

"I don't think so," said David. "I don't know."

"What did you see?"

"I saw her feet in the air."

"What did you do?"

"I tried to swim after her, but the current was strong. It just carried me."

"Between the time you saw her body floating away and the time that you found her, did you have any visual contact with Anna?"

"No," said David. "I saw her backpack."

"How much time passed until you were able to find her?"

"I don't know," said David.

"More than ten minutes?"

"Probably."

"More than twenty minutes?"

"It might have been half an hour."

"How do you know?"

"I found her in a section where the creek widens. It's a couple of kilometres from where we were reading."

"What condition was Anna's body in when you found her?"

"I don't remember."

"What position was the body in? Was her head above water?"

"I don't remember." David didn't know if he should describe seeing himself in the third person.

"Did you perform CPR? Did you try to administer first aid?"

"No," said David.

"Do you think that you were physically capable of performing first aid at the time?"

"I don't know," said David.

"Officer Lancaster testified that you were in shock and hypothermic when he found you."

"Yeah. I don't know."

The coroner swirled his finger at the lawyer to indicate that she should move the questioning along.

"How long did you carry Anna until you met Officer Lancaster?"

"I don't know."

"Do you remember where you met Officer Lancaster?"

"No," said David, looking up at the coroner. "I have dreams. I have trouble remembering what was real."

The lawyer asked, "Do you remember if Officer Lancaster performed CPR?"

"He did," said David. "He did chest compressions."

"For how long do you think?"

"I don't know."

"Did Anna show any sign of movement or breathing?"

"No."

"Do you remember Officer Lancaster saying anything?"

"No."

"Do you remember saying anything to Officer Lancaster?"

"No."

"Officer Lancaster testified that you kept repeating something over and over."

David shook his head.

"Do you remember what that was?"

David knew what he said in his dreams.

"Maybe."

"What do you think you said?"

David tried to avoid eye contact with the attorney and spotted his brother standing at the back of the courtroom.

"Do you remember, David?"

"Maybe," said David.

"Tell us what you think you said."

David sighed and looked back at the lawyer.

"Twenty-two."

WHEN THE CORONER'S LAWYER FINISHED, a lawyer for the conservation authority asked David about emails related to the use of the conservation area. David had given the Ministry of Community Safety and Correctional Services a written description of what had happened. The coroner had based his questions on David's submission. David did not know what the other lawyers would ask.

"Did the superintendent communicate to you that you could take your class off the marked trails?"

"No," said David.

"At the Condie Creek Nature Centre there is a sign asking visitors to stay on the trails. Have you ever seen that sign?"

"No."

The next lawyer to interrogate David introduced herself to the courtroom as Sandra. She represented the Metz family.

"Mr. Woods, what kind of student was Anna?"

David looked from the lawyer to Ron and Holly Metz. Tears started to stream down his face. He said, "She was a good student." After a pause, David added, "Helpful."

The coroner said, "I know this is hard, but if you can expand on your answers, it will help the jury get a picture of the whole set of circumstances."

David closed his eyes and tried to remember what being a teacher in Room 4 was like. He imagined Anna coming through the classroom door in the morning.

"She was smart. She was happy. She came to school happy. She made my classroom a better place."

The lawyer asked, "Did she get along with the other students?"

David said, "She had a lot of friends. But she could be independent. She was a leader."

"On the day in question, what was Anna's behaviour like?"

David said, "She was excited. Any time we were going outside she got excited."

"Was Anna in good health? Was she physically strong enough to hike to Condie Creek?"

"I think so," said David.

"When you crossed the beaver dam the first time, did Anna struggle at all? With the physical demands of crossing?"

"I don't think so," said David. "The adults were helping the students."

"Were the parents of the students aware that their children might cross a beaver dam as part of their school day?"

This was a different kind of question.

"We were going to the forest to read," said David.

"Yes, but were parents made aware of the risks you would take as part of this excursion?"

"No."

Keep going, thought David.

"The decision to cross the dam was your own?"

"Yes." *It was a terrible decision.*

"And when you heard the explosions, you made the decision to return to school."

"Yes," said David. *I put everyone in danger.*

"You told the children to cross back over the dam?"

"Yes." *I was responsible.*

"Did you have any previous experience leading children outdoors?"

"Some." *I really didn't know what I was doing.*

"Were any children hurt during previous —"

"Stop!" Holly Metz was yelling at her lawyer. "Stop. Please. Just ask the questions we talked about."

The coroner called for a fifteen-minute recess, and the courtroom buzzed with conversation.

Joanna talked with David in the witness box. "That bitch. Are you okay? Do you want to walk around?"

"No," said David.

Joanna rubbed David's big hands. "You're not on trial."

"I made some mistakes."

"Just tell what happened."

When the court reconvened, the Metzes' lawyer asked, "When your class made the initial crossing of the beaver dam, do you remember having any interactions with Anna? Did you speak with her?"

"Yes," said David.

The lawyer opened her hands, encouraging further response.

David said, "When we were reading, I heard Anna talking so I walked over to where she was sitting. I told her to start reading, and she said she was. I told her to read silently." David took a breath. "She said she was reading to a tree."

"Did she say anything else?"

"No."

There was a pause and David said, "Except on the dam. Anna and Carrie were screaming at me to help them."

The lawyer probed for more details of Anna's last minutes. When David retreated to one-word answers she said, "That's all."

The final interrogation was led by a lawyer for the school board.

One of his questions was: "Did you have any reason to believe that on a sunny day in June thirty thousand cubic metres of water might suddenly rush down Graham Creek?"

NINETY-EIGHT

AFTER DAVID FINISHED ON THE stand, Joanna and David drove back to the hotel. Mitchell went with Joanna's parents to a restaurant.

In the hotel room, David sprawled on the bed. Joanna looked out the window at the Ottawa River.

Joanna said, "You were good. You described what happened, and that's what this was about. The Metzes' lawyer was totally out of line. But it's over."

A hot-air balloon floated in the sky over the Gatineau Hills.

Joanna said, "Did you see everyone in front of the courthouse?"

"Yes," said David. "I saw the…" He mumbled something, his voice trailing off.

Joanna stared at David. "What did you just say?"

"Nothing," said David.

Joanna stood over David. "What did you say?"

"Nothing."

"I heard you."

David shut his eyes.

"Look at me, David."

David opened his eyes.

"I heard you. You said *protesters*."

David turned away from Joanna. She pulled him back over.

"David, you saw them. I know you did. The Dickensons, the Findlays. The Wongs were there. The Youngs. Rhonda Martin. Jeff Kressler. All your students. You saw them."

Joanna straddled David, her arms pinning his above his head.

"Stop it," he said.

"No, David. You saw them. Reverend Borbridge was there. Ms. Richardson. George Young. The Armstrongs."

"No."

"You saw them. You saw the banner. The students made a banner."

"No," said David.

"Tell me what it said, David. You saw it."

"No."

"What did it say, David?"

David shook his head.

"We're not going back down the hole, David. Tell me what it said. You saw it."

David said nothing.

Joanna slapped him hard across the face, and David cried out. "Yes."

"You saw it."

"Yes."

"What did it say?"

"I couldn't —"

"The students made it. Tell me what the banner said."

"I can't."

"It was four feet high, David."

"I can't."

"Say it."

"..."

"Fucking say it, David."

In the mountains north of Kyoto, in the village of Keihokudaiichi, surrounded by his family, Hisao Yamada took his last breath.

David pulled Joanna down on him and pressed his lips to her ear. *"Go in the woods, Mr. Woods."*

EPILOGUE

ERNEST GRAHAM WOKE BEFORE IT was light. He was nervous and drove to the Tim Horton's in Kemptville, just for something to do. In the coffee shop he picked at a muffin and watched his coffee grow cold. His knee bounced up and down under the table.

After an hour he drove back to the motel and took a long shower. When he was getting dressed, Margaret said, "Why are you putting on your suit? It's not a funeral."

"We didn't go to the funeral," said Ernest. "I'm just showing respect."

"I'm going to wear the clothes I've got on," said Margaret.

"Wear whatever you goddamn want," said Ernest.

They drove to Emily Carr Public School in silence. In the parking lot, students greeted them, and a boy handed Margaret a folded sheet of paper with Anna Metz's picture on it. A girl in a bright yellow dress led Ernest and Margaret across the soccer field. At the edge of the forest a boy stood behind a table with pitchers of water on it. He offered the Grahams a drink, but they declined. Behind the boy the path entered the forest, and a line of candles in jars marked the trail.

The girl said, "Just follow the path. You can hear everyone down there."

"Thank you," said Ernest.

Where the path met the Condie Creek trail, Roger Dixon welcomed them. "Thank you for coming," he said, not letting on that he knew who they were. "We'll get started in a few minutes."

Strung along the path were perhaps fifty people. Rhonda Martin chastised some children who were hitting each other with sticks. George Young made the sound of a screech owl for his grandson, Jesse.

Ernest walked over to the stream bank and watched sunlight glint off the ripples. In the calmer water he could see stones on the creek bottom. The water might have been a foot deep. He imagined the amount of water needed to push David and Anna two kilometres down the course. The thought made Ernest shudder, and he looked at the sky to dilute the scene in his mind.

Joanna joined Ernest at the stream. "It's good you came, Mr. Graham."

"David invited me," said Ernest. "But you probably know that."

They stood silently.

Ernest said, "I never thought about where the water would go."

Joanna nodded.

Ernest said, "I heard a rumour they were going to sue me."

"They're not that kind of people," said Joanna.

"I wish they would," said Ernest, looking at Joanna. "Mr. Ferguson and me, we should have gone to jail."

"Today is about moving forward," said Joanna.

The sound of a guitar playing indicated that the ceremony was about to begin. They turned to join the others.

"We moved to Ottawa," said Ernest, "but in my head I spend part of every day right here."

REVEREND BORBRIDGE STOOD WITH HIS back to the stream. He wore a plaid shirt and jeans. He had considered wearing his clerical collar, but in this setting it did not seem appropriate. He motioned to the people at the fringes that they should gather closer.

He said, "Thank you, everyone, for coming today. Such a beautiful setting. Nature is bursting in all her springtime glory. I tell everyone, if you want evidence of God, if you want proof of a benevolent Creator, take a walk in a forest. Astounding.

"I am honoured today to give a blessing on behalf of the Metz family. Ron, Holly, Louis, it is a privilege to be part of this day."

The reverend surveyed the crowd.

"Friends, time separates us from events, but grief has a way of keeping some episodes close to the heart. Memory can be both a comfort and a burden. We stand here today with warm memories of Anna, but we are also saddened by her premature departure from this world.

"The Lord created heaven and earth and set the universe in motion. The interaction between matter and energy would have played out to the end of time, following the laws of physics.

"But the Lord created man, and in His wisdom He gave men and women the freedom to choose their actions. With the gift of free will we could go left or right. We could love or hate. We could pursue life's ambitions as we saw fit.

"And so, with millions and billions of imperfect agents interacting with the world and with each other, it is inevitable that some outcomes will be calamitous. The billiard balls on our table will roll and ricochet in ways no one could foresee. It is not that we act with malice. It is simply that we are blind to the countless consequences our actions will have on each other. Take solace in the knowledge that God is aware of our shortcomings and will forgive us as we must forgive each other."

Ernest felt those words were directed at him.

The reverend continued, "But the forces that contribute to randomness — some would call it chaos — those same forces also contribute to creation and community, to works of art, and to people falling in love. We cannot judge. We must accept the consequences of forces beyond our control. So be it. Or as we say every day in the church, Amen.

"Eternal Creator, bless this trail and safely guide the hikers who find adventure and solace along its path. Inspire those who enter this forest to learn, and reveal to them the greatness of Your glory through the magnificence of nature. Let the students experience the hardships of the seasons so that they may appreciate water on their sun-parched lips and warmth on their frost-nipped toes.

"In this forest that Anna loved so much, may the birds sing, may the fish swim, and may the water run clear and cold. Amen."

342

WALTER GRAF, A SPOKESMAN FOR the conservation authority, was next to address the crowd.

"The Condie Creek Conservation Authority is honoured to dedicate this plaque in memory of Anna Metz, and to rename this pathway the Anna Metz Memorial Trail."

People clapped, and Walter removed the red satin blanket that was draped over a waist-high monument.

"Let me read the inscription," said Walter. "This trail is dedicated to the memory of Anna Metz, a girl who loved the forest. She read to the trees and talked to the animals."

HOLLY STOOD WITH RON AND Louis in front of the crowd.

Holly spoke. "Thank you for coming today. We are Anna's family.

"Today is the first time we have been down here in almost two years. In my head I remembered this as a dark place, but, as you can see, it is anything but.

"There has been a lot of talk — at the school board and in the newspaper — about whether children should go into forests. Whether they should be allowed to wade in streams. Whether kids should be crossing beaver dams.

"I just want to say that my children have spirits that are too big for a classroom. What happened down here was an accident. No one should be using my daughter's death as justification for cancelling canoe trips or downhill skiing programs.

"I'm sorry. I just had to say that.

"When David came to us with the idea of this monument, I must admit, I hated the idea. It didn't make sense to me that we would commemorate the site of a tragedy. I think I was quite blunt with him at the time.

"But in the fall, Ron and I were doing some landscaping, and I asked the landscaper where he thought we should plant some flowers. He told me, 'Plant them in the ugliest part of your yard.'

"I asked him why, and he said, 'These flowers are beautiful. If you put them with other flowers, you won't notice them. If you put them in the worst place in your yard, it will improve how you feel about your whole property.'"

Holly put her hand on Louis's head.

"This is the worst place in my life. Today we are making it a little better."

DAVID HUGGED THE METZES AND THEN took his turn beside the memorial. He ran his fingers over raised letters on the plaque. People were silent as he looked from face to face in the crowd.

David said, "This stream really is lovely." He started to choke up and paused. He said, "My name is David Woods. I was Anna's teacher." He took another deep breath.

"I wish that Reverend Borbridge had talked about heaven. That's a place I really hope exists.

"Like everyone else, it's hard for me to make sense of Anna's death. She was a great student — a great kid. When she died, I didn't know what to do. I was sad and confused.

"But I went to Japan, and when I was there I told a man about Anna and what had happened. This man had lost a son many years ago. This man — Mr. Tanaka — he told me I should serve Anna. I didn't know what he meant at the time, and maybe I still don't.

"For a long time I tried not to think about Anna. I found it hard. But that was a mistake. Anna was a shining light. She brightened the world. She was funny and smart, and she was —"

A blue jay cawed. David looked up from his notes.

"Why would you want to keep someone like that out of your heart?"

He continued. "As I was telling some of you, I have a new job. West of here. In Simcoe County. I design and help build hiking trails. I think Anna would like that. I think Anna would love walking in those forests.

"Anna loved this trail and this forest, and I am thankful that Mr. Graf supported the idea of naming the trail in Anna's memory."

David moved to stand where he could see the front of the stone monument. He said, "There is a picture on the front of this marker. It's a picture of Jizo. He's kind of like a saint in the Buddhist religion. He helps look after children who have died. I don't know if that's true or not, but that's what it is.

"Some Japanese people believe that children who have died need help crossing a river. Before you got here today, Holly and Ron and Louis and Joanna and I, we waded around in the water. We collected some stones. They are nice stones. They're smooth. Holly and Joanna have them in bags. If you'd like, before you go, you can take a stone and place it at the bottom of the monument here."

Behind David, Condie Creek gurgled softly as it followed its destiny down to the Rideau River.

"It might help Anna. I don't know."

ACKNOWLEDGEMENTS

There are several people who facilitated the events that allow me to add "novelist" to my obituary.

Susan Fish is a Waterloo, Ontario, writer and editor who read *Outside* first and told me flat out that it merited publication. That felt good. She was also instrumental in getting me to tighten up my writing style.

Thank you to my friends Margo Delaine, Tim Stone, Susanne Ruder, and my sister, Erin Carter, who read early drafts of the novel. Voluntarily! All were encouraging.

Thank you to Vlad Cristache and Melissa Swann, two of the hardworking staff at New Star Books.

Thank you to Audrey McClellan for being such a thorough editor and being willing to discuss the most excruciating grammatical minutiae.

Thank you to Rolf Maurer at New Star for taking a chance on me. I only get to be a first-time novelist once, and Rolf has made the experience a smooth ride.

And thank you to my wife, Kelly, who allowed me to take time off work to sit in a chair all day long for months at a time. Her tears reading the book were the best evidence I had that *Outside* was worthy of being in the world.